THE LAST HIGH GROUND

Also by Robin A. White

The Flight from Winter's Shadow

Angle of Attack

The Sword of Orion

THE LAST HIGH GROUND

ROBIN A. WHITE

CROWN PUBLISHERS, INC.

NEW YORK

Published by Crown Publishers, Inc., 201 East 50th Street, New York, New York 10022. Member of the Crown Publishing Group.

Random House, Inc. New York, Toronto, London, Sydney, Auckland

CROWN is a trademark of Crown Publishers, Inc.

Manufactured in United States of America

Design by Mercedes Everett

Library of Congress Cataloging-in-Publication Data

White, Robin A.
    The last high ground / by Robin A. White.—1st ed.
      1. Airlines—United States—Fiction.   2. Organized crime—Japan—
    Fiction.   3. Conspiracies—Fiction.   I. Title.
    PS3573.H47476L37   1994
    813'.54—dc20   94-25534
                                                                            CIP

ISBN 0-517-59694-6

10 9 8 7 6 5 4 3 2 1

First Edition

This book is dedicated to the men and women who make the "B" in Boeing stand for *best*.

PREFACE

IN AVIATION, IT'S CALLED THE DEATH SPIRAL.

An airplane, no matter how well it's built or balanced, will enter a bank, a turn, if no hand is at the controls to stop it. Left uncorrected, the bank will steepen, tighter and tighter. The nose drops to compensate for the loss of lift. The plummeting ship, out of control and utterly doomed, exceeds its maximum structural speed and rips itself apart. The investigators peering into the smoking crater will call it pilot error.

As it is with an unguided airplane, so it is with an unguided economy.

At the end of World War II, America dominated the world's aerospace market. But today, aerospace, the last jewel in our technological crown, the single largest source of export income, is under attack. The Big Three in commercial aviation—Lockheed, McDonnell Douglas, and Boeing—have been reduced to one and a half: a struggling Boeing and a dying McDonnell. Why?

It's tempting to blame foreigners. From Europe comes Airbus Industrie, an aerospace consortium created with government funds and run with little concern for profit. And Asia is the land of supermodern factories, ultralow costs, and the uneven playing field. Japanese airlines require a high percentage of Japanese-made parts in every Boeing they buy, or else.

But the Japanese aren't supermen, and European governments must ante up billions every year to keep the doors at Airbus open. It isn't foreigners who are responsible for putting American aerospace at risk. We have ourselves to blame for it.

America has fallen under the snake-oil spell of the free traders, who spread the gospel of the unguided market. If something can be made more cheaply overseas, then so much the better. If a job can be performed more efficiently someplace else, then send it there. Never mind the costs of crime or ignorance, or the price we pay as a nation when our workers cannot afford to buy the products they build.

Millions of jobs vanish when we try to compete against Korean steelmakers, Indian computer programmers, or Asian aircraft makers on the basis of the bottom line alone. Our *ability* to compete is damaged when the skills necessary to advance into the next century, and to assure our prosperity in it, get developed elsewhere. With each industry lost, the process accelerates.

The death spiral.

Without smart, self-interested guidance, our technical dominance has receded like an eroding spit of dry land before a storm tide of foreign competition. Automobiles. Consumer electronics. Robots. Advanced materials. Supercomputers. Microchips. Software. Today, this storm is crashing against the very last technology—and market—that remains in America's grasp: aerospace.

It is America's last high ground.

A country's wealth is measured not by what its citizens can buy, but rather, what its citizens can make.

—Friedrich List, German economist, 1837

It's not up to government to figure out whether the U.S. should lead the world in computer chips or potato chips. Let the free market decide. If our guys can't hack it, tough.

—Richard Darman, the White House, 1987

The Last High Ground

PROLOGUE

A full October moon sailed through a torn curtain of cloud. Wet brown leaves lay plastered on the ground. The gentle summer breezes were gone, driven off by wind so cold and dank it might have been piped up from a cave at the bottom of the Inland Sea.

The Mercedes roadster purred up the hospital driveway, a fat fish nosing its way upstream. The buckled pavement showed signs of recent repair. Hiroshima was nearly four hundred miles away from the epicenter of the recent earthquake known as the Little Big One, yet its power could still be seen. Shintaro Ishii flicked on the high beams. He was glad to have ridden out the tremor here and not up in Tokyo where the damage had been more severe.

Except for a flashing blue light at the emergency entrance, the Medical Institute at Hiroshima University was nearly deserted. The lights of the city burned a dull orange against the bottoms of the clouds. A few students hurried home under umbrellas. The low, insistent beat of American rap music floated across the campus from a late party.

The 560SL's lights swept across two parked cars: a 600-series Mercedes sedan and his father's gold-trimmed Cadillac. The sedan belonged to Kazuo Ibuki, his father's lawyer. That was not good news. This was the death watch for old Susumu, a feast for scavengers, and Kazuo Ibuki was a man with sharp teeth and long claws. He could strip warm flesh straight to the bone.

Shintaro pulled up to a two-story stone building and stopped. There were no windows, just a double door illuminated by flanking ornamental lanterns. He shut the engine down. His hand shook as he lit another cigarette. When had he last seen his father? Three years. Shintaro took a long drag, then let out the smoke slowly.

Shintaro Ishii, only son to the head of Japan's second-greatest crime syndicate, the Inagawakai, stepped out into the wet night. Everything about him spoke of the new Japan, the Japan risen from the ashes. The Japan that could survive even the collapse of the Bubble Economy.

Shintaro's business degree was from the best university. His clothes were custom-made in London. His legs were long, his body lean and tall. The mist beaded properly on a Burberry trenchcoat. The symbols were all very proper. The money that had bought them, that was a very different matter.

He stepped up to the front door of the clinic. A brass plaque mounted on the wall read HEALTH PHYSICS INSTITUTE: GIFT OF THE HIBAKUSHA FOUNDATION. He pressed the buzzer.

Hibakusha. Literally, the children of fire. His father's favorite charity. They were the surviving victims of the atomic bombings on Hiroshima and Nagasaki, plus a few unlucky fishermen who steered their boat under a South Pacific mushroom cloud. Mutations. Radiation sickness and cancers of all types had been the bombs' legacy. Susumu Ishii had always been a major benefactor. Now, here he was. Dying. Perhaps he had known.

The door opened. A middle-aged doctor in rumpled hospital whites stood in the golden light streaming from inside. His eyes darted to the smoldering Marlboro.

"Sorry." Shintaro tossed it back into the darkness. It flared red, arcing like a dying meteor as it fell to the earth. He stepped inside. The smells of autumn dissolved under an assault of disinfectant, ozone, and hot electronics.

The doctor bowed his head ever so slightly. "I'm sorry to have disturbed your evening, but it's urgent. Your father's guardian insisted you be called."

Guardian? Did he mean that ape who protected him, Yoshi? Or did he mean Ibuki? Old Kazuo was more like a demon perched on his father's shoulder. "How is he, *oisha-san*? Is he asleep?"

"Sleep? He's had too many visitors. He was just admitted this afternoon, and it's been a parade. One after the next. He was—"

"At the country club. I know," said Shintaro. "This is his golf day. I don't suppose it was his heart?"

"His heart is stronger than mine. No. It's cancer."

"We always tried to stop him from smoking. Will he need to go to a specialist?"

"No." The doctor looked down at the carpet, then up. "Your father has come to the best place. A move would only weaken him now. We are the best-equipped facility."

Shintaro looked at the stacks of electronics, the computers, the unknowable complexities of the clinic. "Well, you ought to be. He bought it all."

"Susumu Ishii has always been generous. But many others have benefited from his gifts. There are three hundred thousand hibakusha in our data files, you know."

Shintaro checked his watch. The gold Rolex flashed under the cold glare of the fluorescents. "Can I see him?"

"Go." The doctor nodded at a room at the end of the corridor. "See him. Ask about the pain. We can still do something for it."

"Thank you, Doctor." Shintaro walked up to the door at the end of the short corridor and peered in through the small window.

Kazuo Ibuki was arguing, his spindly arms animated as though he were chasing a cloud of flies. He had been the Ishii family lawyer for two decades, as well as manager of the Foundation's affairs. Ibuki was small and bony, with thin black hair drawn over the scalp in a style called "moonlight through bamboo." A battered attaché sat at his feet like an obedient dog. Shintaro remembered when he was small enough to hide behind that same leather bag. Ishii and Ibuki. He thought of them as one person. One the brains, the other the muscle. He saw the figure on the bed. His dying father. What would happen to the brain when the body departed? A third person in the far corner of the room caught his attention.

The hulking presence was his father's personal guard. Yoshi was a fireplug in a tight suit. His hair was shaved close to the scalp, his skull battered, dented as a back-alley Dumpster. A prominent old scar slashed down from one ear, plunging below his jawline. He caught sight of Shintaro. His eyes blinked in recognition. Then, like a battle tank's turret, his head slowly swiveled toward the man who was speaking.

Shintaro saw his father's fist rise and shake. The lawyer took a step back. Look at old Kazuo, he thought. The vulture is too early to dinner. The carrion is still alive.

At sixty-five, he should have been at the very height of his power. But Susumu Ishii was like a shrunken, desiccated insect caught in a web of tubes and wires, guarded by the squat shapes of heart/lung machinery and blood-gas analyzers. Only his face seemed the same. It was rigidly fixed, the line of his jaw tense, eyes staring straight up at the ceiling. Shintaro took a deep breath and opened the door. His father's voice came out, surprisingly strong.

". . . my final word. That's how it must be. Do you defy me now?"

"There may not be another chance like this. How can we waste it on someone with no experience?" Ibuki replied. "He is a *wakazo*."

Shintaro cleared his throat. The lawyer spun. A quick flash of surprise gave way to an oiled smile. Ibuki bowed his head. "Shintaro." Sweat glistened from his bald spot.

His father spoke. "It's about time you came, you little fart. Out whoring or just pulling your own noodle tonight? I'd say you smell like a pimp, except a pimp works for his money. Get in here."

Shintaro walked to the bed. Ibuki watched. Yoshi stared straight through him. "Hello, Father." Soft beeps kept time with his father's heart. "I came when they called." The eyes, he thought. Look at them! When had he ever seen his father look frightened? "The doctor wants to know about the pain. How are you feeling?"

"Like any man about to die. I am deeply disappointed." He snorted. "Pain. What a joke. What do you know about pain? I gave you everything so that you would never have to feel any. Tell me, lawyer! Is this not so?"

Ibuki knew enough to remain silent.

"Yeah. A big allowance. House of your own. New car every year. Women. And how did you repay me? You pretended I was dead. How long has it been, shrimp?"

"Last year?"

"Some businessman. Can't even count. *Three years*. Plenty of time to forget your father and what he was. An honest businessman, my son. So where's his business?"

Shintaro's neck reddened.

"I gave you too much." Then, an evil smile slowly came to the dying man's lips. "What time is it, runt?"

"After midnight." Shintaro positioned a chair at a safe distance from the bed and sat down. Ibuki walked over and placed his hand on his shoulder. The lawyer squeezed once, again. A crab's pinch.

"Your father has had many visitors," said Ibuki.

"I made them rich," his father said with a slight growl. "I could crush them like beetles!" It was the tone of voice that had once sent foot soldiers of the Inagawakai on their midnight missions. A car wreck. A fire. A knife flashing in moonlight. A woman and a camera. "Now they dare to defy me."

Ibuki spoke. "No one defies, *sensei*. They see the world from their own perspectives."

"Liar! Fuck all of you. Get out. Do you hear me? *Out!*"

Yoshi stared straight ahead. Ibuki bowed his head. Nobody moved. The lion could still roar, but not bite.

The lawyer finally spoke, his words embedded in the same sing-song tone that had lulled half the prosecutors in Japan to sleep at one time or another. "Shintaro, it is the end of one day, but the beginning of another. We must decide how to protect everything your father has built up over his long and fruitful life. Naturally, as your father's only legitimate heir, you must be included in this discussion."

"Naturally."

Ibuki continued, "Times are difficult in Japan. Money is not like it used to be. Even the great companies are sweating. We were the richest country on earth. What happened? We forgot who we are, what makes us special. Look how hard we have worked. Now, all that work is supposed to mean nothing. Or worse. A crime."

Shintaro nodded. "Times are hard," he said.

"They will get much harder. The government wants to point fingers. There will be investigations. Prosecutions. A storm is coming, Shintaro. It threatens all of us here in this room. We must act boldly, but wisely, for the sake of our future."

"Of course," said Shintaro. The future. What could he be talking about except the inheritance? "You said my father has had visitors. Who were they?"

"They all want my money, just like you," his father growled.

"They came to watch a thief die, but not before they took their little piece home."

"An official from the LDP," Ibuki explained, meaning the Liberal Democratic Party, "a division president from Yomiuri Heavy Industries, and a gentleman from the NPA."

NPA was the National Police Agency. "The police?" said Shintaro. Wasn't it a little late to arrest his father?

"Not in an official capacity. They all came to pay their respects, and to discuss possibilities," said the lawyer.

"Come to collect," said the dying man. "Tell me, Son. You went to Tokyo University. You have your business degree. So you decide. Do I give my money to them, or should I burn it? Which?" He cackled, but the laugh dissolved into a racking cough that sent the heart monitors wild. Ibuki placed a tube to his master's mouth, and the old man sipped clear, cool water.

"What exactly did they want?" Shintaro asked directly.

"There is a considerable sum of money," Ibuki answered. "Where it came from no longer matters. Where it may go, what it might accomplish, these are the central issues. A new strategy is called for."

Shintaro couldn't help sticking a small needle into Ibuki's tough hide. "The Foundation has always been able to absorb whatever my father has given it."

The lawyer didn't so much as flinch. "This is far more. Far more."

It would be impolite to ask the precise number. But Shintaro dearly wished to know.

"You must understand," said the spidery old lawyer, "today, your father's fortune can buy almost anything. Tomorrow, after the investigations, the reports, the prosecutions, his money will be tainted. Worthless. Even, I am sorry to say, a liability. The men who came to respect your father know this. They wished to suggest a solution. One that I support."

Shintaro watched his father's chest rise slowly, his breath rattling out between clenched lips. Where did it add up? "What do you want my father to do? Buy another golf course? All of Hawaii? What is it this time?"

"Shintaro, your father does you a very great honor," Ibuki went on. "But it is also a very great challenge. He wants you to be in charge of his memory."

In charge? Shintaro didn't like the ring of that. "Of what?"

"Come here, squirt." His father's voice held only a shadow of its old command. Shintaro got to his feet and leaned over the bed. Susumu's breath was coming in labored gasps now. The dying man winced, then spoke.

"It's funny," his father said at last. "Bunch of thieves running the banks, the government, everyplace. They call me a criminal? Just a different business, that's it. Now, not even different. We are all Japanese, aren't we? Used to mean something. Can't give that away." Speaking drained him more and more. "But that's all ancient history." Susumu stopped, his mouth working, his jaw clenching as though he were chewing the word and swallowing it. "Yes. History. Come close, *ebi*. I want to tell you something. Here. Take my hand."

Shintaro took the old man's fingers. They were cold as winter rain.

The eyes turned to look squarely at Shintaro. His father squeezed his hand. "I will be respected. I will give to Japan what it needed so badly once, but did not have." The words sounded plain, nearly normal. "I wish to die in peace, Son. But you must help. You must do this one thing. You have lived in my shadow. Now you must find your own place in the world. I will help you, but the way is hard."

"What can I do, Father?"

The dying crime boss turned to Ibuki. "Bring the papers."

"Hai." The lawyer cracked open the battered briefcase. He extracted a folder, then a small wooden block with a short spindle of a handle attached. Ibuki brought them to the bed, along with an inkpad.

Susumu let go of his son's hand, took the block, pressed it into the inkpad, then onto the paper. Ibuki shifted the sheets, and the old man stamped again. A third time.

Susumu Ishii, don of the Inagawakai, looked up at his son, eyes tearing. "My money," he said, "my mistakes. I give them both to you. All of them. I have not forgotten. Do not forget me, *ebi*. Do not forget. My memory, my life. They belong to you now."

All? Shintaro paused. All? He took the papers and scanned them.

Shintaro Ishii was now the president and chief executive officer of the Hibakusha Foundation.

"Shintaro, *gambare*," his father whispered. "Do as Ibuki tells you. He is your father now." The heart monitor beeped, then went silent. It beeped again.

The son turned back to the lawyer. He'd expected a tidy, nicely wrapped present. Not this. "What does it mean?"

"Shintaro," Ibuki began, "I have guided the investment policy of the Foundation for twenty years. When the bubble economy burst, it thrived. When the Little Big One shook the Nikkei into dust, we made money. Trust me to steer you as I steered your father. Trust me."

Shintaro just shook his head. It was all coming too fast. Why was Ibuki nattering on about investments? The cardiac monitor beeped.

"By this time tomorrow," said Ibuki, "the Foundation will receive a rather large sum of money. Never mind where it is coming from. It will be deposited in the Manufacturers Credit Bank of Tokyo, an institution with which we have had long and profitable dealings."

"How much?"

"In dollars . . ." Ibuki flipped open a small notepad, then looked at Shintaro. "One billion, nine hundred thousand at yesterday's closing exchange rate."

"One . . . billion?" Shintaro steadied himself. He felt nauseated by the sheer weight of the number. He'd wanted his allowance to continue. A mortgage forgotten. Perhaps a few investments, the clean ones. But this?

Yoshi was standing next to him now. It gave him strength. Only then did he realize there were no more sounds from his father's heart machine.

The old lawyer gazed at the dead Ishii, then turned to the one he could still control. "They say the flutter of a butterfly wing on Fuji makes the rain fall in New York." Ibuki patted his shoulder. "Think of this money as a very large butterfly." He took the papers back from Shintaro's shaking hand. "It has begun to stir. Tomorrow it will fly."

ONE

OCTOBER 1995

"Here it comes."

The waypoint annunciator chimed and the letters *GJT* scrolled across the cockpit's center navigation screen. Thirty-five thousand feet below the belly of the westbound jet, the VOR beacon at Grand Junction, Colorado, poked its dunce-cap cone through drifts of last year's snow. It was the last Tuesday of October, and the first big storm of the year was whistling down out of Canada.

The captain turned to his right. "Run the numbers," he told the first officer.

Flight 262, a brand-new Boeing 7X7, was two hours out of Chicago. It was running nearly full: three hundred passengers and eleven cabin attendants. They were still six hundred miles from Los Angeles. The captain checked the time on his old Hamilton. He let the gold-braided sleeve fall back over his tanned wrist. He didn't need the ship's triple-redundant computers to know they were running very late.

The weather was lousy over the western United States, backing up all California-bound traffic. Battlements of cloud thrust high into the Colorado sky, reaching up through the flight levels, their tops shredded and roiled by wind. It was not a good sign.

"The head wind's kicked up some," said the copilot as the navigation computer flashed its answer with four-decimal accuracy. "Fifteen more knots on the nose." He looked over the tops of his glasses at the captain. "I think we're still gaining on L.A."

The captain smiled, but it wasn't much of a joke. He knew there would be hell to pay in Los Angeles. The newest ship in the fleet, a Boeing 7X7 fresh from the Everett paint shops, superbly equipped and commanded by a veteran crew, would arrive an hour late to their gate at LAX. The repositioning schedule would be shot. Connecting flights would be missed, baggage lost, and nasty letters sent to the home office. A black mark would be entered against both their names. All because of the wind.

"What do you want to do?" asked the first officer.

"Retire." The captain checked the big center screen on the all-glass panel. The CRZ symbol was displayed on the Engine Indication and Crew Alerting (EICAS) display. Two round dials dominated it: the Exhaust Pressure Ratio (EPR) readouts measured the health and happiness of his two big engines. The captain could see they were safely below EPR limits. There was a lot more thrust out there in those sweet Pratt and Whitneys. "Let's see if we can win some time back," he said.

The captain smoothly advanced both of the big black power levers to the next setting, confident that the automated systems would keep his engines from overthrusting. The EPR arrows went from green to yellow as they approached their upper limits.

Both PW4000 turbofans stabilized at the higher power setting, still below maximum values, though not by as much as before. Not that there was a shred of danger. The central flight computer, called the Octopus by the pilots, monitored everything. It would politely refuse any human command it deemed excessively risky.

"Picking up a little speed," said the copilot.

The 4000-series engines were enormous, each one as wide as a Boeing 737's *cabin*. There were only two of them on the 7X7, a ship nearly as big as the venerable four-engined 747. But for all their size, their newness, their pushing of the engine-maker's art, the turbofans responded like Swiss watches under a blizzard of calculations and commands issued by the Octopus.

"Point eight," said the copilot. Eighty percent of the speed of sound, and it still felt as if they were crawling.

Down below, ninety-mile-an-hour gusts smashed headlong into the high peaks, whipping the air into waves and whirlpools of invisible violence. The cockpit rose, then fell, then lurched crabwise as Flight 262 nibbled at the edge of the jetstream storm. A thin, arcing lenticular cloud appeared off their right wing. A rapier of vapor and tortured air. Bad news indeed.

The captain wasn't one to hesitate. "Denver Center, United 262 heavy. We need to deviate south for weather."

"Roger, United. Deviate at your discretion. Proceed direct Bryce Canyon when able."

"Direct Bryce when able, United 262." The captain banked the airliner away from the strange cloud.

He leaned over and pressed his temple against the cold side window. The reassuring rumble of the Pratt and Whitneys buzzed directly against his skull. There was no way to see them from the cockpit. Only the instruments registered their health. *Damn wind,* he thought as the mountains crawled under the 7X7's nose.

The long, graceful wings began to rock and flex. The captain sat up straight. His face became wrinkled and his jaw tensed as he scanned the flat-panel screens with their reassuring lights and symbols. Everything was as it should be. Perfect. He'd been strangely silent the entire flight. Sometimes, for no apparent reason at all, he would reach out and touch some control, some switch, as though unsure of what his eyes told him. He did it once again, poking the radar display painting the sky out ahead, tapping his finger against the cool glass. He seemed to be trying to remember something just beyond recall.

"Something wrong?"

He glanced up at the first officer. "Call Center. See if anybody's complaining out ahead."

The copilot nodded. "Denver Center, United 262 with a request." As he waited for the reply, he gazed out at the gray landscape, thinking of his car parked in LAX long term. It had a weak battery. Would it start?

"Denver Center, United 262," he repeated. The silence on the frequency was unbroken. The right wing suddenly shook, then began to rise. The autopilot-disconnnect chime sounded.

"I have the airplane." The captain placed his hands on the yoke and firmly leveled them once more. His fingers stroked the cool metal, as though he were trying to crack the combination of a safe. It felt so solid, so secure; so perfectly predictable. Yet he knew that no one lived beyond the reach of fate. There were no special places, no sanctuaries from misfortune. A ship identical to this one had fallen out of the sky and no one yet knew why. The long-haul JAL flight had been scattered over a hundred square miles of North Pacific water. They were still using sonar to hunt for the pieces.

"Denver Center, how do you hear United 262?"

The captain had tried to put the wreck out of his mind. But like a tongue finding a cracked tooth, he couldn't. All the technical harmonies annihilated; masterful skills overcome by chaos and death. And nobody knew why.

"Go ahead, 262, I was on the landline," came the reply at last.

"How's the ride out ahead? Any complaints?"

"Be advised that SIGMET Charlie Five is current, calling for occasional severe turbulence below one eight thousand, mountain-wave action, and low-level wind shear. I haven't heard any problems at three five zero. Stand by and I'll check for you."

The cabin door popped open and the senior cabin attendant came in with fresh coffee. She closed the door by leaning back on it. "How's it going, guys?" she asked. Her smiled seemed strained, nervous.

A ship, just like this one . . . The captain looked back. "Fat, dumb, and happy," he said.

"And slow," the first officer added. "Any squawks?"

"The same one we had going into Chicago." The attendant handed both cups to the copilot. "The coffee urn in first class is still leaking. Oh, and there's an SOB who swears the engines are moving around too much." SOB was airline speak for "soul on board," a passenger. "He says the engines are going to fall off. Is the air going to get rough?"

"Probably," said the copilot with a chuckle. "We have some weather out ahead. I hope you don't have anybody waiting at LAX. We'll be running a little—" The radio suddenly came back to life.

"United 262, Denver Center."

The copilot set the steaming cups down into their carefully engineered nooks. "Two Six Two, go."

"You're right on the edge of my sector, and all the bad stuff is to the north and west. I only have one report for you. A 737 reported moderate plus turbulence at three three thousand in the vicinity of

Mormon Mesa. He's in the climb to three five now, talking to Salt Lake, so I don't know if his ride improved any. You can ask when I switch you. My radar shows the weather moving a little ahead of schedule. Will you need to deviate?"

"Stand by." The copilot looked over at the captain. Mormon Mesa was directly on their route of flight. *Moderate* could mean a pretty bad ride; the next rung in the ladder of violence was *severe*. But a 737 was a small ship. The wide-body drivers called them guppies. A bad bounce or two for them might be nothing much at all for the bigger Boeing. On the other hand, passengers hated turbulence. They expected the plane to fall apart at the first gust. "What do you think?"

"Let's keep best forward speed unless we really start getting knocked around."

The copilot nodded. "No thanks, Denver. We'll continue direct Bryce Canyon at three five thousand. United 262."

"Roger. Contact Salt Lake now on one three three point six. They may have additional reports for you out ahead on your route. So long."

"Good day," said the copilot as he punched up the next frequency.

The nose took a sudden dip, then a sideways lurch as though a gloved fist had playfully pushed it aside.

"Here it comes." The captain switched the FASTEN SEAT BELTS lights on, hit the cabin chime four times, and turned to the stewardess. "Better make sure everybody's buckled in," he told her as he nodded out ahead. "Turbulence."

Lawson Wheelwright eased outside, closed the door, and stood beneath the torn awning. Rain had started falling over Washington, D.C., while he ate his dinner at the shelter. He watched for signs of the two men. A short bulldog of a man and a tall Latino with a ponytail. After his months on the run, he knew what a homeless man looked like, how he walked, and how he smelled. These two were from another world entirely. And that meant trouble. Were they after him, or was he letting fear rule his thinking?

Overhead, the white neon sign buzzed GOD'S LOVE, the name of the E Street shelter. A cold drop spattered on his forehead and ran down his cheek. Wheelwright sniffed the air. The stink rising from the dirty men inside was masked by the sweet odor of the kerosene heater. *Kerosene.* The smell of jet fuel reminded him of his former life. His lost life, now.

Wheelwright was just under six feet, though he looked shorter all stooped and hunched inside a long, heavy overcoat. A greasy wool watch cap was pulled almost down to his eyes. He'd been called young-looking before. Now, at forty-seven, he looked sixty. Five months in the open, running, had aged him a decade. His face was dark, tanned by the sun and layered with grime. Each day another piece of his old life had fallen away. He had no skin left, only a kind of leathery hide.

Bit by bit, everything was pared down to bone, gristle, and a small cloth sack he'd sewn into the lining of his coat. He stepped out into the rain and began to walk.

Cold water seeped into his boots as he hurried south on Fourth Street. He was heading for his hidey-hole. He stopped and turned. No sign of the short one with his too-neat crew cut. No sign of the tall one with the greasy ponytail.

He'd never had to move with the alert awareness of a wild animal. As a quality-control inspector at Boeing's Propulsion Engineering Group, a part of the 7X7 Division at Renton, Washington, his life had been orderly and meticulous. Five months later, that was all gone.

He reached down into a pocket. There, beyond a carefully stitched seam, padded by filthy rags, he felt the small sack. People had died because of what he had in there. He knew it. He had played a part in their deaths. That was what ate at him, what he thought about when he put the reeking neck of a wine bottle to his mouth. He'd let it happen.

He walked south toward Stanton Park. He was already shivering. As he crossed D Street, Wheelwright stopped and turned again. The street was empty. Rain sizzled against the overhead wires.

He came to the curb at Massachusetts Avenue. The park on the far side was his destination. His sanctuary. He crossed into darkness and sank into the park, a man clutching a plank of half-sunken timber, bobbing on a wild and dangerous sea.

The ride got rougher. "I've got it." The captain pulled both power levers back out of the first detent. The ATS symbol went out on the EICAS screen, marking the disengaging of the Boeing's autothrottle system. Turbulence meant slow speeds. You could do some real damage to the structure otherwise. But slow speed meant they'd be even later to the gate, and you could do some real damage to your career that way. Which was worse? It was a toss-up.

The sky was full of invisible holes. The wings shook and the nose wagged back and forth, not gently, but sharp-edged and nasty. He resisted fighting the sudden darts and falls.

You weren't supposed to be able to bend this new Boeing. The Octopus kept it from flying too slow or too low or too fast when the air was rough. It was all programmed. The system was idiotproof. To the engineers that meant *pilotproof.* But the airplane that could not be pulled apart by the pilot's two hands had yet to be invented. The Octopus be damned.

"Rough as a cob," said the copilot. "Might be a better deal above four zero. Smoother, anyway."

The captain considered it. "The prog charts called for more head wind up there. But if it smooths out, we can flog her some more. Might cancel out. Might come out a plus." He weighed and decided. "Let's give it a try." He nodded for his first officer to put in the request.

Salt Lake Center came back with a terse, "Approved. Report reaching four three zero."

"Here we go," said the captain as he toggled the EICAS mode selector out of CRZ and into CLMB. He relaxed his hands around the big throttle levers and ran them forward to the second-to-last detent. The EPR gauges began to stir. He thought of those huge Pratts, suspended from the wings by delicate-seeming braces and pins. Well designed, but so were the mounts that had proved fatal back on the 747. The fuse pins broke and . . .

The cabin call light illuminated, and the first officer picked up the handset. "Flight deck."

"That guy, you know, the one who's worried about the engines? He's going bonkers back here," said the stewardess. "Can you talk with him? He's scaring everybody. Me, too."

"Tell him to let you know when they stop moving," the copilot replied. "Then we'll *really* have a problem. How's the coffee machine?"

"I wedged a cup under it."

"Way to go."

As the altimeter arrow flickered up through thirty-eight thousand feet, the ride became eerily smooth. Glassy.

"Well, how about that?" the copilot said with a relieved laugh. "Higher's the better deal after all. All this time."

"You can't win for losing." But the captain was pleased. Smooth air meant he could fly faster, and faster was just the ticket. "I'm going to hang on to a bunch of speed. See if we can win back a couple of minutes." He turned to his copilot again. "Go back and give that guy the personal touch. Maybe he won't write the company about how we're dangerous and inconsiderate."

The altimeter passed through thirty-nine thousand feet.

"The personal touch, coming right up." The copilot unbuckled, stood up, and made his way back through the six-abreast seating of first class.

The cabin was steady as a rock. The copilot's smile was genuine. All's well that ends well. But he could smell the dripping coffee as well as the sloshing chemicals from the toilets. And something else. A dark, animal scent that blew in from the ten-abreast economy cabin like a pheromone fog. He straightened his tie and walked on, feeling the passengers' eyes fix on him as he came. He put on a smile. See? I'm here. If my ass gets to L.A., so will yours. No problems. Just a few little bounces.

At last he came to an emergency exit directly next to the gaping nacelle of the right engine. The tiny porthole in the middle of the panel had a clear view out to the leading edge of the wing, and the great engine itself.

The Pratt *was* moving. But it was supposed to. Boeing made

them that way. Safest airplanes in the world, minus one incident. Okay. Not an incident. JAL was a crash. Nobody built their jets bombproof. Some Arab group took credit for it before the pieces had sunk. But the structure? He wished that was all he had to worry about. Did he have a job next year? Would he ever move to the left seat? Would his car start at LAX? These were bigger worries by far.

He had no trouble identifying the scared passenger. He could see the fear in the middle-aged man squirming in the window seat. "I hear you're a little concerned about our airplane holding together."

"I . . . I've never seen an engine move so much," the man said. "I mean, never." The airliner shivered, faintly, then a bit stronger, then the motion died down. "It's better now."

"We're above the turbulence." The copilot leaned over and watched the turbofan swing slightly from its mounting strut. "I know it looks terrible. You'd be surprised just how much give they have built into them. They're designed to move around. It's a safety feature. And you know, even if one fell off, we'd just fly away on the other. It's all designed in."

"I'm an engineer. I know. But . . . ." The man stopped and cocked his head to one side. "What's that?"

A shiver coursed through the jet, through the floor and right up into the copilot's legs. Then a slewing, sideways motion, as though the plane were trying to turn without banking. A skid? The pilot could do that by stomping on a rudder pedal. The strange, uncoordinated motion deepened. What the hell was the captain doing up there? His inner ear was screaming that something somewhere was very, very wrong.

Suddenly, the 7X7 snapped into a steep bank, its right wing pointed straight up into the sky. There was an instant of stunned silence. Then the world fell away. A tray flew by his ear and crashed against the opposite cabin wall. A scream was drowned by the thunder of overhead rack doors spilling open, bags flying.

The first officer struggled to his feet. A tremendous roar filled his ears, the sound of an engine spooling up. The lights flickered once, again, then went out. Suddenly, a new light, hot and yellow as sunlight, flooded the cabin. It wasn't coming from the sunlit portholes across the aisle. It was coming from the right wing. The copilot scrambled over the passenger and pressed his face against the Plexiglas. *Jesus!*

The number-two engine was no longer hanging in its mount. It was *above* the right wing, propelled by its own thrust like a tethered skyrocket, trailing a comet's tail of pure fire.

As he watched, ninety thousand pounds of runaway thrust sent the engine arcing up and over the wing, pulling a hundred different cables and tubes with it as it went.

A fuel tank was breached in a flash of igniting kerosene. In an eyeblink, the long, elegant wing was chopped off to a fiery stub. The airliner rolled. The unmistakable cracks and groans of structural breakup filled the copilot's ears. No. This cannot happen.

The image of the empty gate at Los Angles flashed through his brain as they tumbled, the first angry explosions wracking the doomed ship's fuselage, falling, falling. All notions of up and down were lost as the building g forces alternately pinned him to the deck and threw him against the legs of the passenger. A blast of frigid air swept through the cabin, although the copilot could no longer tell whether it was fire or ice. His hat flew off. The empty gate; the people waiting . . . his car parked in LAX long term . . . falling, faster and faster.

It was a blustery Tuesday afternoon. A typical autumn day. Typical, except that the worst airline accident in American history had just taken place.

Wheelwright reached overhead and threaded in the fifteen-watt bulb he'd stolen from the shelter. It was just like Washington to leave the power on in an abandoned pump room. It offended his sense of order.

The bulb blinked on, off, then burned steadily. Its weak yellow glow illuminated a chamber eight feet wide by ten deep. A charred area on the floor showed where others had found a warm, safe spot. He couldn't afford the luxury of a fire. Not now. Roots had intruded through the stone perimeter. A steady drip came from the cracked ceiling. On one wall, hanging high and dry, was a duffel bag. Wheelwright made his way to it.

His hand closed on a small pad of paper. He slipped a pencil stub out of his overcoat, opened the pad of paper, and carefully began to write.

JAL 6-22-95 I know why our A/C went down . . . He stopped and looked up.

In the dark distance of the nighttime capital, sirens began to wail.

The phone rang just as MacHenry was bringing in another armload of wood. I hope it's Princeton, he thought as he dropped the white birch and kicked the door closed. A cold wind followed him into the snug old farmhouse. His wet boots tracked in a few sodden leaves. The phone rang again.

Dressed in his down jacket, wool shirt, and neatly pressed khaki pants, Brian J. MacHenry looked like a gentleman farmer. But the military cut of his iron gray hair, his pale blue eyes, and the precise way he walked, the way he held his arms, all these told a different story. MacHenry was a veteran of a quarter century spent on airline flight decks, of four years as a safety specialist for the Federal Aviation Administration. At fifty-six, he was well into his third career as a freelance airline–accident investigator: a hired gun to the legal profession. He caught the phone on the fourth ring. "MacHenry."

The voice on the other end jumped straight to the attack. "Roger Case here. It's Tuesday night. Where are those conclusions you promised us on the Arrow Air crash?"

"I've been working on them, sir."

Arrow Air had been a military charter airline before one of their DC-8s crashed under mysterious circumstances back in 1985. Two hundred and fifty soldiers of the 101st Airborne, plus eight aircrew, died on that cold night at Gander, Newfoundland. Was it wing ice or a terrorist bomb?

"I'm so very pleased to hear it. But I asked a question. Where are the final results?" Case was a senior partner at the prestigious Washington firm of Case, Rudge, McDivitt et al. His specialty was aviation litigation.

"I'm afraid I have some bad news. It's Professor DeMarco up in Princeton. He's not returning my calls. His office says he's out of the country."

"He's *what?*" DeMarco was one of the best forensic chemists around. A superstar in the expert-witness world of bombs and airline sabotage. "Listen. This case has dragged on since 1985. *Ten years,* MacHenry. We're coming down to the wire here. Everything's in place except for your *expert* conclusions. We go to preliminaries next week. I want to close on this fast. I have something new coming up. Something that could turn big. DeMarço's on vacation? Fuck him. We'll go without his analysis. You know that airliner was bombed, don't you?"

"Probably. But we need the lab studies, and DeMarco's office won't release them with him out of the country."

"Where's he hiding?"

MacHenry knew there was only one place where the leading expert in the chemistry of sabotaged airliners might be. "If I had to guess, I'd say he's in Tokyo working on the JAL loss." It was like tickling the nose of a snorting bull with a red flag. Case was an ex-Marine from the Pacific war, and he was inclined neither to forgive nor forget.

"God damn!" Case roared. "He walks a week before my court date? What the hell? I have two hundred military families waiting *ten years* to hear whether their sons and husbands were killed in an accident or in the line of duty. You know what a difference that makes? The insurance companies say it was an act of war. No coverage. The feds say it was an accident. The charter outfit's responsible. So no dough until their insurance pays off. They're screwed nude and this asshole plays footsie with the Japanese one fucking week before my court date?"

"I can't write up my conclusion without his analysis."

"Then I hired the wrong man." Case was breathing heavily into the phone as though he'd just run a sprint. "Forget DeMarco. You have his original stuff? The eyewitness accounts? The chemical-trace studies? The Canadian board of inquiry report?"

"Yessir."

"Go with them. Write it up. I'll paper over the gaps somehow."

"I'll try to put together what I can before the weekend."

"No. Too late," said Case. "I'll drive out and pick it up tonight. I want to talk with you about something else anyway. Something much bigger. About nine?"

"It's raining." The driveway down to the county road would be slick.

"So? You have a roof? You allergic to rain? What?"

"Nine o'clock will be fine, Mr. Case. I'll try my best."

"Don't try, MacHenry. Just do it." With that he hung up.

"Yes, sir." *Just do it.* MacHenry hung up and retrieved the wood that lay scattered inside the front door. He fed a couple of logs into the stove and opened the damper. The birch crackled and spit. The smell of hot iron rose to fill the farmhouse parlor. He checked his watch. Nearly six. MacNeil-Lehrer would be on in a moment. He could catch the headline news and then go back and finish the report.

He left the parlor and switched on the small set in the kitchen. The counters were spotless. The dishes were all stacked behind the glass-fronted doors on the cabinets. Towels neatly folded; wooden floor scrubbed to a shine. But it was empty. The hum of the TV set seemed to echo from the plaster walls. How long had Julia been away? He glanced up at the calendar as the screen came to life. *Five days.* It felt like five months.

Dr. Julia Hines, research meteorologist and specialist in the mathematical modeling of weather, had had the good sense to attend the annual global-warming conference in Kona, Hawaii. It was sure a lot nicer there than in Round Hill, Virginia. MacHenry turned up the TV volume.

". . . latest. The tragic fire that claimed the lives of fifteen homeless men has been declared under control by district fire officials. The God's Love shelter was run by . . ." MacHenry changed the channel and caught the tail end of the familiar MacNeil-Lehrer theme music.

"Tonight, following a campaign update, we take a look at rough weather at Boeing." The scene cut to a group of Boeing workers picking up paychecks, then to long lines at a Seattle unemployment office. "Can the world's number-one builder of jets survive its tumble on Wall Street? Finally, we'll close with a newsmaker interview with Shintaro Ishii, the CEO of the Nippon Aerospace Consortium. Ishii will discuss the planned merger between the Japanese and Boeing, and his visit to Washington for the controversial dedication of the *Enola Gay* . . ."

MacHenry stopped listening. He hadn't cared when foreigners bought Manhattan real estate. He barely noted the purchase of those fancy California golf courses. It wasn't as if they were going to take them home, was it?

But Boeing was different. He'd spent a lifetime flying the big gleaming ships wrought in Seattle. Boeing was, for MacHenry, a hard crystal nugget of what was right about America. Everything else was falling apart. But not Boeing.

When the world was building airliners with propellers, Boeing bet the entire company on the 707 and won. When airlines feared there would never be enough passengers to justify buying wide-body jumbo jets, Boeing bet the company on the 747 and won again. Even when the Saudi deal for fifty new jets collapsed—along with the kingdom that ordered them—Boeing survived. The Chinese wouldn't buy an airplane without the name *Boeing* on it. But times had clearly changed. Without a cash transfusion from the Japanese, Boeing might have to close its doors. How had that happened?

MacHenry reached to switch off the set. Suddenly, before he'd touched the power button, the lights dimmed once, then blinked off as the electricity died.

MacHenry listened to the wind pick at the old house's bones. Rain spattered against the glass. He walked over to a cabinet to fetch a candle. How long would the charge on his laptop computer last? MacHenry got the candle lit.

His shadow danced along the kitchen walls as he walked to the window and pulled aside the insulating drape. It was dark down in the valley, all the way to the West Virginia border. The village was blacked out, too. As he watched, the yellow flicker of candlelight appeared in first one window, then more, until the entire village was measled with them.

In two months it would be 1996. A new year, a presidential

election year, for all that meant anymore. Four more and the magic year of 2000 would roll into view; a year synonymous with a golden, modern future. He thought about the news. About the way everything seemed to be running downhill. National Guardsmen were on permanent patrol in the nation's capital. It was only a matter of time before other cities reached the same level of exhaustion, of desperation. Julia in Hawaii as he sat here in the dark. The year 2000. All those bright visions. Where had all that promise gone?

MacHenry shivered and let the curtain fall closed.

TWO

It was nearly nine o'clock, but the accumulated smog of a day's cigarette smoke still hung in the air. Shig Onishi, the youngest investigator working the Economic Crimes Section of the National Police Agency (NPA), sat in the stream coming from his little desktop purifier. It was better than nothing.

In an office landscape filled with rows of desks, his was the only one without an ashtray. A poster was mounted by the watercooler, showing a busy young man with a telephone pressed to each ear. The caption read, *Mild Sevens give me the energy I need to succeed!* Shig interpreted the ad's presence to mean the government had invested again in offshore tobacco; now it was everyone's patriotic duty to smoke. Shig refused. It was hard to see it as anything but another sign that Onishi's career had taken a very bad turn.

Economic Crimes occupied an entire floor of a new Kabuto-cho office building. The steel tower was specially braced for earthquakes and had ridden out the Little Big One with no damage. They'd been very fortunate to leave their old, postwar stonepile near Hibaya Park, where they were still clearing the rubble.

Kabuto-cho meant "helmet town," a reference to an ancient warrior king who had buried a golden helmet on the shores of Tokyo Bay to commemorate a victory. The shrine was still there. But the harried stockbrokers, investment bankers, and traders who swarmed Kabuto-cho's narrow streets worshiped at new shrines bearing the holy symbols of the D mark, the dollar, and the yen. Kabuto-cho was Tokyo's financial district. A symbol of the New Japan, as well as a battleground where more fortunes had been lost in the last three years than were made in all the years since the Great Pacific War.

The young accountant neatened the papers on his new desk. He opened the drawer and pulled out a little folding knife. It was painted white with a red sun rising on a wind-whipped flag. A Japanese Self-Defense Forces knife, studded with screwdrivers, a clever little adjustable wrench, a metal saw, even a toothpick. His father had given it to him on his acceptance to the NPA.

Shig was tall and gangly. He lived off fast food: colas, bags of peanut balls flavored with fish, and the special pork-cutlet noodles served at a particular stall at the nearby train station. His bones seemed undecided about how they might fit and work together. He might be a basketball player, except for his thick glasses. A Yomiuri Giants ballcap sat on top of his in-box, a leather-trimmed baseball jacket was draped across the shoulders of his wooden chair. A framed photograph of his graduation ceremony from Waseda was the only other personal item in sight. A Waseda man was supposed to be guaranteed a good position in the world, especially a graduate of its accounting department. Where had he gone wrong?

Shig Onishi was in trouble. His new desk was just one away from the windows. Without so much as getting up from his chair, he could look across the bright lights bobbing on Tokyo Bay. In America, a desk near the window was a prize. Here, it meant that Onishi was but one step away from joining the *madogiwa-zoku:* the tribe of the window sitters. Failures who were given a desk, no telephone, and no work. How could this happen to a Waseda man?

He swiveled away from the cold glass. By not fitting in, he thought. By not listening to the unspoken words. By taking his job too seriously.

It was very quiet now. You could nearly hear the decorative ferns curl and shift in the warm breezes cascading down from the ceiling vents. A hundred tiny cooling fans hummed from idling computers. They were old NEC models, far less capable than ones available from America. But they were Japanese and that counted for more. Shig let the freshened air spill by his face.

One row away from the window. It was a message, of course. A warning delivered by the section chief. The entire floor knew what it meant, from the lowliest clerk to the OLs, the office ladies, who served tea from rolling carts and knew to serve him last. Onishi stared at the pile of papers and floppy disks. The Rondon Doyukai case. He eyed the papers warily, as though they might suddenly burst into flame.

Rondon Doyukai versus Nomura Securities. It was a simple matter of extortion. Gangsters borrowed money to buy shares in Nomura. Not as an investment, but in order to be eligible to attend the stockholders' general meeting. The thugs threatened to break up the meeting unless they received a fee. The sums were not enormous: 250 million yen borrowed to buy stock, 850 million yen to keep them away from the meeting. A clean, tidy profit that would be used to replace money siphoned off from illegal activities such as gambling, drugs, and prostitution. Good yen would cover bad.

Usually, nobody complained. It was far cheaper to pay the hush money and go on with business. Peace and tranquillity were worth a lot in Japan. But this time the hush money was too much for Nomura. The big securities company had lost heavily when the Little Big One had sent the Nikkei tumbling like a pile of unbraced masonry. The 850-million-yen fee was more than they were willing to spend for peace and tranquillity. They did what a normal company in America or Europe might do straightaway: they called the police.

The section chief had assigned the case to Shig personally. Ozawa's chop was all the countersign he needed to dive into the case with both feet. Be diligent! Follow the money trail! Bring the criminals to account! These were his guiding words.

Shig was a details man. It was his gift. He went about laying out the case like an electrical engineer maps a computer circuit. He'd found out the names of the *sokaiya* gangsters. That was easy. They were registered with the NPA as industrial lobbyists. He'd found out their source of money: one of Tokyo's largest, and most troubled, banks. But then it turned odd.

The Manufacturers Credit Bank of Tokyo had a huge, teetering cliff of overinflated real estate hanging over it. It was one step away from collapse. Where, he wondered, could a poor bank come up with so much money to lend out to gangsters? He found that out, too. Huge drafts of overseas funds had washed through the bank's accounts. A tidal wave of money.

If he'd stopped there, his desk would still be safely near the center of the office floor. But he'd asked another question: Who would deposit so much money in a failing bank?

Sometimes Shig believed that everything in Japan was connected to everything else, and everyone. Pluck a string here and the whole country resonates. Who was behind this particular extortion operation? Shig plucked the string. Who was behind Rondon Doyukai versus Nomura Securities? Such a simple question. Where had the money come from? It required more digging. More computer time. Some help from other investigators. He made the request to his section chief on Monday morning. By Tuesday, his papers had all been moved, his telephone reprogrammed. Tonight, his future seemed as black as an elevator shaft.

He got up and walked to the window. Fifteen floors down, the busy financial-district traffic choked the narrow streets. He could see the lush green rooftop driving ranges on some of the lower buildings, lit up and busy even at this hour.

What was the point of an Economic Crimes Section not permitted to go to the source of the stink? Why catch a few flies and leave the rot behind? He stared at the play of lights far below. The commuter rush was slowing, the jammed streets gradually becoming passable.

His telephone buzzed. A light flashed on his desk. Instinct took over. He ran to catch it before it had a chance to buzz again. *"Moshi moshi!"*

"I want to speak with you, Onishi." It was Ozawa. The big boss. The line clicked dead. There was no reason for the gods to expect a discussion.

Shig gathered up the Rondon Doyukai papers. He slipped the DSDF knife into his pocket. It felt cold and heavy. But it gave him courage. Maybe if the worst happened, he could use it to disassemble the plate-glass window, hop onto the tiny sill, and jump. He made straight for the closed door across the room. He raised a fist to knock, but the door opened.

"Get in here."

The big boss was a tiny man with straggly gray hair, a wide, wrinkled face, and glasses pushed to the tip of a nose so small it barely offered them a perch. He had the expression of a man chased down a street by a pack of dogs: frantic, exhausted, and indignant. Plush pink slippers poked from beneath a gray steel desk. Books lined every wall. There was an open bottle of Crown Royal whiskey, eighteen thousand yen at the going exchange. From the smell, it was far from full. Half-smoked Mild Sevens cluttered an ashtray.

Ozawa hurried behind his desk, then pointed at a plain wooden chair. "Sit."

Onishi, still holding the Rondon file, obliged.

"Well, what do you have to say for yourself?"

Shig felt his heart skip. Was this it? He shifted uncomfortably. "Sir?"

"That"—Ozawa nodded at the Rondon file—"has drawn the attentions of the foreign minister. Satisfied? Do you know what that means? Do you have the smallest idea? Of course you don't. You're an idiot. A Waseda man. How could it happen?"

The foreign minister was well down the pecking order of the elite group of bureaucrats who really ran Japan. The finance minister was on top, of course. What could the foreign minister want with Shig Onishi?

Ozawa snatched the longest cigarette butt from the tray and relit it. "The whole NPA struggles to accommodate itself to the new government. One to one, we make progress with them, but it is slow. All the new faces. The new secrets." He let out a long stream of smoke. "Then you, a simple *investigator,* decide to pursue shadows behind the screen. Were you directed to look beyond a simple extortion case? No. But you decided to blaze a new trail. Chasing foreigners. Is that your duty? Please. Perhaps I have made some mistake."

"No, sir."

Ozawa sucked down the smoke, then let it out. "In all the history of our organization, this has never happened. Once more, Investigator Onishi stands alone. Well, the tall nail should expect to feel the hammer now and again." He opened a new box of cigarettes and withdrew one, holding it out to Shig.

"No thank you, sir. I don't smoke."

"So." The Mild Sevens disappeared. "Do you know who controls all the tobacco in Japan?"

"It's a quasi-governmental corporation. I believe the Finance Ministry owns most of the stock."

"Correct. It earned the Ministry 200 billion last year. Meanwhile, the government spends a grand total of 2 million yen to combat the evils of cigarettes. You can't buy a decent massage parlor for that. What does this tell you?"

"I'm afraid I don't know, sir."

"Teamwork!" Ozawa shouted. "How can the Agency find a place in its heart for someone who is not a member of the team? Which is more important, Onishi? Your case or the NPA?"

"The Agency." The NPA was a uniquely Japanese institution. In America it would seem odd to combine the functions of the FBI, the state police, and the private security arm of the Republican Party. But not in the land of teamwork. "Sir, how did the foreign minister find out about my case?"

"Don't be a young fool. You think he doesn't have spies? No. I tried to save you from all this. After all, we're both Waseda men." Ozawa glanced up at his own diploma. "When the minister called, I told him you were unavailable. But even I cannot save you this time. He kept asking for you by name."

Onishi bowed his head. "I'll write an explanation. And an apology."

Ozawa slapped the desk so hard the papers jumped. "Too late! You wanted to find out where the case leads, didn't you? You wanted to catch the shadows behind the screen? The ghosts?" He glanced at the open neck of the whiskey bottle. "You have been abducted by aliens, Junior Investigator Onishi. You once worked for me. Now, you must answer to two masters. The foreign minister wants ammunition. He wants scandal. He thinks you are on the track to find some. So, it seems that I have to let you proceed."

"Sir?" Onishi didn't understand. "I thought . . ."

"You thought? I doubt it very much," Ozawa said, his face screwing up into a thousand wrinkles. "That's not your specialty, Onishi. You dress foreign. You act foreign. You behave like a yellow cab, not like an investigator for the NPA. You have been an embarrassment to me, personally, and to our university."

Shig swallowed his reply. A *yellow cab* was a young girl who sought out foreign, usually black, boyfriends. A yellow cab was a rebel. A defiant one. Not a team player.

"If you weren't Waseda, you'd be gone. You understand? And

don't think the Foreign Ministry would be kind to you. No. You might as well be a *bukaronin*." An untouchable. Ozawa plucked the bottle and poured the last of it into a tiny cup. "Tradition counts. At least in my office. Outside?" He brought the whiskey to his nose and sniffed. "Out there, everything has changed. Everything is quite upside down." He took a sip. "I have been directed by the minister himself to allow you to proceed with the Rondon matter. I have a file for you to take home and work on tonight. He wants to be kept in the loop, but you are to report directly, and only, through me. Do you understand?"

"Understood!" Shig sat up bolt straight. "But . . ."

"I will give you all the rope you need. But remember. A rope can hang anyone. Especially young investigators."

"Sir, how far can I take the case?"

Ozawa's answer was quick and unexpected. "All the way up the minister's sphincter." He took another sip. "The Japan Renaissance Party," Ozawa huffed. "They're just a bunch of toads selling wart medicine. What was so bad about the old LDP? We're the richest country on earth. They want to throw it all away? What for? So we can become poor like everyone else." Ozawa was drunk, and angry. "It's a stupid world, Onishi. You should fit right in."

"About Rondon," Shig gently guided.

Ozawa snapped back to attention. "The minister may well be someone we must learn to live with. On the other hand, he may evaporate like spring snow in the next election. Which will it be? You tell me."

"I don't know, sir."

"Neither do we." Ozawa looked down at his desk, staring silently at something that wasn't there. He grunted, then reached into his top desk drawer. He pulled out a new file, one that carried a Red Sash secrecy mark. He tossed it to Shig.

Inside, on the first sheet, were the words *Hibakusha Foundation*. The atom-bomb victims? What did they have to do with blackmailing thugs? He flipped another sheet and saw a box labeled *Nippon Aerospace*.

"Now let me offer one last piece of advice, *kohai*." It meant "young colleague," a word that usually carried more affection than Ozawa's tone indicated. "If you want to hunt tigers, be sure to bring a big gun. Don't prick him with a needle, or else you'll be the hunted one. *Wakarimasu ka?*"

"I understand." Shig closed the file. "When can I start?"

"Tonight." Ozawa sat back in his chair and stiffened. It was a signal that the interview was over.

The Hibakusha. An aerospace consortium. Blackmail and illegal transactions. Where did it all come together? What if it didn't? Maybe Ozawa had given him a last chance for success. Or he'd found a way to rid himself of a nuisance. Which would it be?

Shig packed the Red Sash file away in his attaché, grabbed his baseball jacket, and took the elevator down to the street. The Kabuto-cho train lines were the first to be reopened after the Little Big One. But people still froze when the rumble of the underground trains made the sidewalk tremble. Steel grates rattled and steam flagged up into the sky. A full moon was sailing overhead, a hundred-yen coin glinting from a blanket of dark blue velvet.

Men in groups of three staggered by. They had already visited one of the many after-work watering holes that catered to financial-district workers. Most often the one in the middle was held vertical by the ones to either side. Middle would be the high-ranking member of the troika; Left and Right were the underlings who would pour the whiskey, laugh at the jokes, and make themselves useful while they stayed away from home and wives as long as possible.

Shig was alone. No underlings walked to either side. Nor would they ever at his rate of decline. He came to the train station, passing the Kentucky Fried Chicken store, a Pizza Hut, and made his way straight to the end of the line of little food outlets. There he smelled the delicious aroma of steaming noodles. His stomach rumbled like an express pulling into the station. He ducked under the flapping banners of the *soba* stall. A few late diners were scattered around the counter, slurping noisily with a bowl in one hand and stock-option data in the other.

The noodle joint used to be packed. It had lost a lot of business to the American fast-food invaders. KFC was so successful it now required reservations one month ahead to buy a fried-chicken Christmas dinner. And even McDonald's served BST sandwiches stuffed with bacon, seaweed, and tomato.

Shig made his way to a seat at the counter. The proprietor didn't look up. He was a short, round man in stained whites. A faint white stubble marked his chin. He whipped together a Special Pork Cutlet and slapped it down in front of Shig. The young investigator began to eat, the attaché case on his knees.

Seven musical notes sounded, the simple tapping of a child's xylophone. The diners slurped the last of their noodles in a hurry as a train approached the station, all hisses and squeals. Money was thrown down, bowls clattered, and stool cushions spun as they ran to catch it.

"Everything is shit," said the proprietor. "Business is way down."

"Fried chicken is a fad," said Shig as he ate. "People will come back."

The owner snorted, then blew his nose into the hem of his apron. "The Americans are taking over, little by little. Wait and see. It was a mistake to let them open up here. They don't play by the rules."

"Free trade helps everyone," said Shig.

The owner gave Shig a pitying look. "Don't be stupid. Is it better to be poor and ..." A noise made him stop. A loud laugh, then a giggle. "Trouble," he said, soft enough so that only Shig could hear.

Shig turned.

A young thug dressed in head-to-toe denim herded a girl in a strapless silver minidress into the noodle stall. The dress clung to her body like milk to a spoon. He looked like the Marlboro Man except for his bright orange-dyed hair.

"Hey!" the thug shouted. "We wanna eat!"

The proprietor looked at Shig. Drunk, the expression said. "Why don't you go have some nice fried chicken?"

"Noodles!" Marlboro Man pushed his girlfriend down into a seat and straddled his own as if he were mounting a horse. He bumped against Shig, and the attaché case fell to the tiled floor.

"Excuse me."

"Hey! Watch out!" the orange cowboy warned. His breath fumed with enough proof to pour into a fuel tank and drive away. The girl giggled. "You better watch it! I'm a killer. A real gangster killer!" He reached into a pocket and pulled out a small black tube. With a click, a bright blade flashed out. "See?"

"Very nice," said Shig. It was a lot simpler than his Japanese Army knife. It looked a lot deadlier, too. He took three hundred yen out and put them on the counter. "I brought your tax papers."

"Thanks for your patronage. I'll take them."

"You stay!" the orange cowboy shouted. He waved the knife at Shig, then balled his other hand into a fist from which his thumb sprouted obscenely. He reached over and smeared Shig's glasses with the greasy thumb, then laughed. "What you got to do, salaryman? You stay!"

"Sorry." Shig took off his glasses and slipped them into his jacket. He bent over to retrieve the attaché.

"Hey! While you're down there, clean my boots! What's in there anyway? Papers! Not like this!" He reached into the top of his girl-friend's dress. "You got papers? I got this!"

"Stop that!" The girl giggled again. She squirmed away from his paws and rearranged her dress. "Leave me alone!"

"Whaa?" The cowboy took it as an insult. He slapped her hard. "You say what? Don't talk to me!"

"Don't do that," said Shig.

The drunk spun on him, blade in hand. "Don't you talk to me either, noodle-prick." He got up off his stool and began advancing, the knife weaving a hypnotic, swaying dance. "I cut you!"

"Don't hurt him!" the owner yelled, hoping his voice would carry out to the transit police box out by the train tracks.

Shig dropped the attaché case and felt his feet squarely beneath his weight. He tensed, relaxed, tensed again. His breathing fell into place.

"Just don't hurt him!" said the owner again, this time with genuine alarm.

"Too late monkey turd, *unka-san*. *Germ* face. I gonna hurt you," the drunk swore. He took a step and slashed at Shig's face. He laughed, then did it again.

Shig stepped aside and grabbed the knife wrist hard. He twisted and pulled. The switchblade clattered to the tile. The orange cowboy swore and kicked. It was a poor blow, but his pointy-toed boots landed hard enough to drive Shig back against the counter.

The Marlboro Man laughed an evil little chuckle and moved in to kick Shig again. It didn't happen. Shig caught him with a full swivel kick that staggered the drunk, opening his body for two quick blows, one to the kidney, one to the center of his chest. Hard enough to drop him, soft enough to keep from stopping his heart. The cowboy fell to the tiles and sprawled, gasping for air. His eyes rolled. "Oh, baby. Oh, baby," he whimpered.

The noodle-stall owner stood there shaking his head sadly. "This is what we get by letting the foreigners in. Cowboys and gangsters. This is progress?" He spat his own answer to the tiled floor.

The girl rushed over and began crying, stroking the orange hair. "Look what you did!" She sprang for the switchblade, but a heavy rubber sandal came down on it first.

The owner kicked it over to Shig. "Well?"

"Sorry, Father." Shig opened his briefcase and dropped the switchblade out of sight. "Here are the tax forms you asked for. You overpaid last quarter. There should be a refund."

The man almost smiled. "Maybe you learned something after all." He turned to the girl. "Please come again soon. And thanks for your valued patronage."

Shig put his glasses back on. "I'll see you tomorrow."

"Gamman!" his father said, then turned his back to begin closing down for the night. Endure!

Two transit police showed up as Shig was leaving.

"What happened?" they asked him.

"Drunk fell off a stool," he answered as he ran to catch the arriving train.

MacHenry was down to the end. A flickering yellow light from a single candle played across his face. He typed *CONCLUSIONS* and stopped, watching the blinking cursor flash impatiently at him from the screen of his battery-powered laptop. He wrapped his hand around the warm coffee cup and leaned back, his eyes closed. Was it a bomb that brought Arrow Air down or wing ice? MacHenry weighed the facts out one by one as though they were gold nuggets on a delicate, teetering balance.

Aviation accidents were never simple. They struck after a long chain of misfortune. By design, each link in that chain was unlikely. Yet the smoking ruin at the end was undeniable proof that the best training and the best technology in the world could only stack the deck. There were no guarantees.

Bomb or ice? Here he was trying to forge just such a chain of evidence on a case nearly ten years old. MacHenry felt the heat seep into his cold fingers from the coffee cup. Where was the truth?

The crash had happened back in 1985. Memories lapse. Minds change. More recent tragedies were still unsolved. Like JAL, he thought. In spite of all the analytical power the Federal Aviation Administration, the National Transportation Safety Board, and Boeing could apply, nobody was certain how a bomb had gotten on board that brand-new JAL 7X7 last June. In the baggage? Strapped to a passenger? Some other way not yet guessed at? Boeing itself didn't have a clue, and they surely had good reasons to find one.

MacHenry sat back up and checked his watch, holding it up to the candle. It was nearly nine. He was playing the percentages. The odds. Nothing was one hundred percent. Nothing. What did his gut tell him? He began to type again.

> Despite the results of the official U.S. Army inquiry, certain similarities exist that tend to connect the crash of the Arrow Air flight in Newfoundland with the bombing of Pan Am 103 above Lockerbie, Scotland, and the loss of a UTA Airbus over West Africa. Evidence suggests an inflight explosion . . .

The sound of a car gunning up the steep driveway came just as the wash of its high beams swept the room. It had to be Case. MacHenry heard the slam of a door, the scrape of boots on gravel. He remembered that Case used a cane. The old lawyer had a fused knee, a memento from a place the Japanese called Sulphur Island, but the world knew as Iwo Jima. MacHenry punched the F2 key to save his work. The disc drive whirred softly, then beeped.

With four sharp raps, the senior partner of Case, Rudge, McDivitt et al. announced his arrival. MacHenry got up, candle in hand, and made his way to it. Cold air rolled in as the door swung wide.

Case fired on full automatic. "Jesus, MacHenry. Don't we pay you enough?" Case stood in the weak pool of yellow candlelight, his cane under his arm. A tufted wool cap covered his bald head. He wore a dark gray tweed jacket over finely cut pants, the cuffs of which were stuffed into heavy boots. His breath steamed as he spoke, as though a cauldron boiled and bubbled inside his chest.

"Sorry about the lights," said MacHenry. "There must be a tree down someplace. Come on in."

"Your phone is out, too. Did you know that?" Case shouldered his way inside, stamping leaves off his boots.

"I wondered why it was so quiet. I've been working on the Arrow Air report."

Case looked at him. "Christ. You haven't heard, have you?"

"Heard what?"

Case whistled, but he didn't answer. Instead, he looked around the dark parlor. "By yourself?" He yanked off the cap. His high, broad forehead reflected the candle's glimmer.

"Completely." MacHenry closed the door. "What haven't I heard?"

Case's cane tapped against the polished wood floor as he made his way to the couch. He saw the blue glow of the laptop screen. "I assume that's *Henderson vee United States*?" Sgt. William Hunt Henderson was one of the soldiers of the 101st Airborne killed in the Arrow Air crash.

"Yes." Why wouldn't Case answer? MacHenry wondered what had happened out in the world beyond the pool of light shed by candles, beyond the hum of his battery-powered laptop. He had a radio, but it was never on when he was at work. "It's almost finished. I'd be able to give you something in print except for the power . . ."

"I know you will, MacHenry. I know you will." Case glanced around the darkened parlor. "I'm not here just for that. I told you on the phone. I want to talk with you about something else." He eased himself down onto the sofa, his fused knee straight out before him. "Got another chair?"

MacHenry slid his desk chair under Case's leg and then sat down on a battered leather armchair he had never found the heart to throw away.

Case looked around the room. "Candles. Wood heat. You're prepared. Not one of those survival nuts, are you?"

"No." Then MacHenry thought again. "Some people might say so."

"Some people might say a lot of things about you." Case rewarded
him with a rare smile. It flitted out of existence. "Flying for the
airlines. Must have been a nice life. Why'd you leave?"

"They wanted me to fly an unsafe aircraft. I wouldn't. So they
found someone who would."

Case's eyes sparkled. Like any good lawyer, he never asked a
question he didn't already know the answer to. "Then you hauled
freight for Flying Tigers. I imagine flying boxes around was a lot less
stressful than hauling passengers."

"Cargo flies mostly at night. I had a hard time staying awake."

"Then that business with the FAA. You bulldogged an investigation some pretty heavy hitters wanted kept quiet. You were lucky
to get out with your head on your neck. You know that, don't
you?"

MacHenry looked up. "You heard about the Aurora incident?"

"I know enough to recognize a ballsy move. The talk is, you're
a hard man to convince. A survivor." Case arrived at the inner conclusion, a verification, he sought. "The truth is, you'd fuck me and my
case if you didn't think it was legit. Am I right here or what?"

MacHenry had to think. A consultant didn't get a weekly pay-
check, after all. Facts were never hard. You could shade them one
way or the other. Some people made their living in that gray area.
"Maybe."

Case snorted, disappointed. "Maybe? Try yes. That's why I hired
you. Most so-called experts show up with a menu of conclusions.
You hand them the check. They hand you what they think you want
to hear. Not you. Truth matters to you. Am I right?"

It was as though his inner dialogue had been faxed to Case
ahead of time. What was Case getting at? MacHenry leaned over
and lit another candle with the flame of the first. The room slowly
brightened. "I'm a pilot," said MacHenry. "Or at least, I used to
be. Flying isn't like the law. In court, truth is what you can convince someone of. But in flying, there's no way to finesse a failed

engine. Wish away bad weather. Or present a good argument that a warning light is a bad circuit and not a fire. Yes, truth matters. Why?"

"Because it matters to me, too. And I have a notion it isn't getting told." Case looked around the dark parlor. "No power. No TV. No phone." He shifted in his seat. "You know that a Boeing 7X7 crashed a few months back."

"In June. A JAL ship out over the Pacific."

"Now it's two. They lost another one this afternoon."

Case watched MacHenry's face drain of all emotion. How many times had he heard those words spoken in his career? How many friends became memories with those four words as their final epitaph? *They dropped another one . . .* MacHenry felt the same cold curtain descend inside him. "Who?"

"United. It went down over Utah or some such place. The usual suspects are claiming credit for bombing it."

"Not credit. Responsibility."

"Call it what you will. Two brand-new Boeings. Both of them 7X7s. A lot of people dead. No official word out on how those *alleged* bombs got on board. Couldn't have been easy, right under the noses of all those fancy bomb sniffers and scanners. Any ideas?"

"No system is foolproof." Now it's United, thought MacHenry, wondering whether he had known the captain. He kept a binder filled with names, addresses, and phone numbers of all his airline friends and connections. A 7X7 was flown by a veteran crew. Odds were better than even he did know him. "But they've been looking now for months. I don't know why they haven't nailed them." MacHenry's fist clenched.

"Maybe they aren't looking in the right direction." Case sat back, his trap baited. "Sabotage. Bombs. It's a no-brainer. Someone farts too loud, it's Islamic extremists setting off a satchel charge. The feds go scurrying, looking in all the wrong places for terrorists."

"How do you know they're wrong?"

An arched eyebrow. "Don't you have doubts?"

MacHenry was filled with them. Even a solid case wound up with nothing more sure than the words *probable cause.* "Nothing's ever proven beyond doubt. From what I read, the NTSB came to a preliminary conclusion that JAL ship was bombed. The FAA went along with it and so did the airline. I don't know about Boeing." He shook his head. "Lots of people are looking for something, too. The best men in the business."

"The best? Not quite. There's you."

What was Case getting at? "The investigators at NTSB are good. If they say it's a bomb, I'd be willing to . . ."

"Where's your evidence?" Case leaned close. His voice descended to a whisper. "Suppose I tell you the Arabs had nothing to do with it. Nothing whatsoever. What would you say?"

"I'd say, where's *your* evidence?"

Case rewarded him with a quick smile. "Good answer. But first let me tell you a story." Case looked around the parlor. "This is a nice house. You own?"

"Rent. Why?"

"Let's say it's for sale. You know it's got bugs in the basement. Termites, say. You need the dough, MacHenry. The wolf's at the door. The sale has to go through. The house is your last chance to come out clean. So let me ask you. Do you tell a potential buyer about a few rotten timbers?"

"We were talking about airliners."

"Same principle. Different scale. You're honest. You'd reveal everything you knew. But not everyone's like you. Truth, remember? Now instead of a house, think big." Case looked up at the open rafters as though an idea hung from them like a bat. "Think Boeing."

MacHenry shook his head. The colors shifted, shifted again. Where was the pattern? "What does this have to do with those two 7X7s going down?"

Case's eyes gleamed hot yellow in the candlelight. "Boeing bet the company on this new plane that keeps falling out of the air. Am I right?" He didn't wait for an answer. "It has to succeed, or Boeing goes down the toilet. Check what Boeing stock has done since June. Check what it's going to do tomorrow after this new crash. They're ready to go over the falls. Now. See what you make of this." Case's voice fell a notch. MacHenry leaned in to his words.

"A senior inspector at Boeing calls my office a few months ago.

Why? It doesn't matter. It happened. Only I'm out. He leaves a message. I don't call back right away, and what happens when I do? I find the guy is gone. Fired."

"What for?" A sliver of kaleidoscope fell into place.

"An excellent question. All I get from Personnel out in Seattle is how the guy had a drinking problem. He's unstable. Even a little dangerous. He's made threats. Serious ones. A drum of solvent explodes at the Boeing plant in Renton. They think he did it. You know, the guy's been around for years. He has keys to everything. Now he's a boozing, disgruntled, unstable employee. A firebug. Makes perfect sense, right? Like those Arabs with their bombs."

"I'm listening."

"The fire only destroys the inspector's old office. And all his written records. Oh. Did I mention the fact that he's on the 7X7 team? A real tough break for Boeing. It used to be the best, I understand." Case watched MacHenry's eyes.

"They still are."

"With two planes down, you want to buy one for your airline?" Case's whole body was bent forward, eager, sizzling with energy.

"Did they arrest him? This inspector?"

"They wanted to. But he disappeared. Right off the face of the earth. Even the FBI can't put their hands on him."

"How does this connect with those two last planes?"

"How? I say maybe he knows there's termites in Boeing's basement. A design flaw somebody wants kept quiet until the check clears the bank. You see where this is leading?"

"What check?"

"There's a foreign outfit buying a big chunk of Boeing as soon as the weather vanes in Washington point to yes."

A foreign company. Japanese. MacHenry shook his head. "Sorry, Mr. Case. I don't buy it. I know Boeing. There's no company on earth that takes quality as seriously as they do."

"Times change. There's a saying in Washington. If you want to understand how something works, keep your eyes on the dollars." Case's eyes seemed to sharpen. "Boeing's in a tough jam. They lost orders because of that first wreck. What happens after another one

goes in? They're leaking money, MacHenry. They need a fresh transfusion. This foreign outfit . . ."

"Nippon Aerospace?"

Case stopped. "Yes," he said at last. "I believe that's their name.
They've got pockets stuffed with cash. Who wants to tell them they
might be buying a big chunk of the world's biggest flying liability
suit? Who would blow a sweet deal like that? You'd keep it quiet,
wouldn't you?"

"I don't buy it."

"You know jets? I know Washington." Case stroked his fused
knee. "Bottom line is this: I think this missing inspector smelled smoke
and yelled fire. The company's sitting on it. I want you to find out
why those Boeing jets have crashed. I want to nail the sons of bitches
who are covering up the termites in the basement."

MacHenry glanced at Case's knee. If there was a grain of truth to
what he'd alleged, if there really was a problem with the Boeing 7X7,
then the Nippon Aerospace deal might be torpedoed. "Are you sure
you're being entirely objective about this?"

Case shook his head and shrugged. "No. And nobody else
would think so, either. You know what they think of me in this
town. But I'll be damned if Boeing gets snatched up at a fire sale
because some duck-billed middle manager is protecting his ass over
a design flaw. But you they'd listen to. You find the truth. Find it
fast. Interested?"

Am I? MacHenry wondered. One, now two crashed 7X7s. A
Boeing inspector is fired. Then disappears. A Japanese consortium offering to save the last industry America still dominates by buying into
it at fire-sale prices. He looked at Case. "This inspector. What part
of Boeing did he work in?"

"Good," said Case, "now we can start."

Lawson Wheelwright waited for the rain to stop. His breath
steamed in the dimly lit pump room. He thrust his hand into his
overcoat to warm it. Instead, he felt the gun. He pulled the snub-
nosed Smith & Wesson into the light, hefted the solid weight of it.

He listened to the steady drip, drip, drip from outside the

pump-room door. A cold trickle came under it, finding its way to a floor drain. He shivered, then reached for the bottle he kept in his other pocket. The wine smelled sour. It tasted like acid etch. But it flushed his skin with warmth. He screwed the cap back on. It was time.

Wheelwright twisted the weak bulb dark and felt his way to the door. He listened. The sirens were quiet now. He'd written a letter. It was time to deliver it.

THREE

"Don't you think you'd better start taking notes?"

MacHenry pulled out a fresh pad of yellow paper and began to write. "All right. What did you say his name was?"

"Not was. Is. Lawson Wheelwright," Case answered. "A Boeing lifer. Started by bucking rivets on the assembly line and went all the way up to senior quality-control inspector. Like I said, they even gave him an award. Best division chief of the month."

"What division?"

"Propulsion Engineering. Propulsion means engines. So what do you know about them?"

"They're brand-new." MacHenry felt as though he'd walked cautiously up to the edge of a chasm, only to find himself falling in. Case was a hell of an operator, all right. "The 7X7 uses two big, high-bypass turbo—"

"Stop. Use English."

"The 7X7 has two very big, very powerful engines," MacHenry explained. "They put out almost ninety thousand pounds of thrust each. Pratt and Whitney, Rolls-Royce, and GE build versions of them. The key characteristic is that they're more powerful than any jet engine has ever been before. Five years ago they couldn't have been built. The materials wouldn't stand up to the heat and stress."

"Boeing can pick and choose what engine they put on a particular airplane? Mix and match?"

"No. The airline specifies the engine they want. Which one gets used depends on a lot of things. The deal the airline can cut more than anything else. GE's been accused of giving them away in order to nail down ten or twenty years' worth of spares and support. I wouldn't be surprised if there's some truth to it."

Case stared up a blind alley. He quickly retraced his steps and moved off in a different direction. "Okay. Let's leave that for now. If I recall, Boeing's had problems with their engines before. They fell off. Am I right or what?"

"That's right." MacHenry was on solid ground here. He'd consulted with the FAA on the emergency airworthiness directive issued against Boeing a few years back. "They're designed to hang on the wing pylon by way of something called a fuse pin. Actually, there are four pins to each engine. They're designed to break if engine stresses become too great. It's a safety feature, like a circuit breaker that pops if there's a short. The theory is, if a turbine's about to explode, you don't want it around. You want it to break off cleanly."

Case huffed. "Losing engines doesn't sound so safe."

"You may be right." The idea of tossing one engine away when you had four was bad enough. What about only two? "They never admitted they were building those fuse pins too light, but just the same, Boeing retrofitted every 747 with beefier ones. Plus they added a vee brace. That brace went into the 7X7 design right from the start."

Case brought his cane down with a sharp rap. "Bingo. So they knew they had a problem. They wised up for the 7X7. Or did they? Maybe that's our termite. What do you think?"

"Boeing didn't have a choice. You can't afford to jettison good engines when there are only two to start with. A 7X7 twin jet is almost as big as a 747. Some of my old friends were worried about that. The pilot's union came out against it, but the airlines hammered them on cost. You want more engines? We have to fire more pilots. End of discussion."

"Why were the pilots so worried?"

"This new ship could be a challenge to control with an engine out. But it was tested and given a clean bill of health."

Something sparked in Case's expression. "How do you know that?"

"I have an old friend who's with Boeing's flight-test department. Actually, he runs it. If he says it'll fly, I'd believe it."

"Name?"

"DelVecchio. Joseph DelVecchio. He was forced into retirement from the airlines when he hit sixty. Boeing snapped him up. He's a little bit wild. A cowboy. But he knows his business. I was his copilot once upon a time." A very long time, he added to himself.

"Why was he so worried about losing an engine on the 7X7?"

"It's simple. In a 747, if you lose one engine, you have three others. An MD-11 is a trijet. Losing one of them could be serious, but not instantly fatal. You remember what happened when that flight went down at Sioux City a few years ago?"

"We didn't litigate that one. But an engine exploded. In the tail, right?"

MacHenry nodded. "It severed the hydraulics. There were no checkvalves in the lines, so all the fluid ran out. The hydraulics power the flight controls. But the fact that the captain had two turning engines saved a lot of lives that day. The 7X7 is a different situation. Lose one and you have ninety thousand pounds of thrust on one side and nothing on the other. It would be like an elephant and a mouse riding a seesaw, with only the pilot to keep it level. I'm glad I'm not flying one."

It was a warm trail. No, thought Case with mounting excitement, it was hot. "So our friend Wheelwright was in just the place to discover a potentially dangerous flaw in the 7X7 design. The engines are the weak link. Fuse pins, vee braces, fixes, who knows? But something. Something."

MacHenry put his pencil down. "That's one theory."

"Where else do you start?" Case sat back. His eyes focused on something invisible up in the parlor ceiling. "Enough with the technics. Let's get down and dirty. If driving such a big airplane around on two engines is a problem, who let them get away with it?"

"The FAA worked with Boeing during the design process. They certified it. In fact, they fast-tracked it."

"What's that supposed to mean?"

"Before, you had to prove a plane was safe by flying it. You try your damnedest to break something. When it does, you fix it and try again. You keep on doing it until nothing breaks anymore. Then you fly it around on domestic runs for a year. Finally, when you think you've got the wrinkles ironed flat, you send it out over the ocean."

"This time?"

Where was all of this heading? "This time, they did almost all the testing by computer. Even the ETOPS tests." He saw Case look puzzled. "Extended Twin Engine Operations. You have to prove you can fly out over the middle of the Pacific, lose one engine, and proceed to an airport with the other."

Case looked at MacHenry, not believing what he'd heard. It took a lot to surprise Roger Case. "You mean they bet the company on the word of a computer?"

Was that what Boeing had done? "It saved them a lot of time and money."

"But how the hell did they know if they got it right?"

That was a far better question than Case knew. The 7X7 was not only designed electronically, it flew that way, too. Fly-by-wire was magic, and black magic at that. MacHenry liked a throttle that moved, a yoke that was attached to the control surfaces with braided steel cable. He didn't quite trust some flight computer's digital chattering over a hundred miles of wire. "They ran through scenarios. They also installed a complete set of 7X7's controls in another jet. A 757, I think. DelVecchio flew it to be sure the bugs were out. When the first 7X7 came off the line, they flew it, too, but just to confirm the computer's predictions. As far as I know, it did. Again, if Joe said it was . . ."

"Jesus. What a goatfuck." Case shook his head. "Number one, you'd never put a designer in charge of testing his own design. He's got too much at stake in not finding problems."

"A human, maybe. But a computer . . ."

"Number two, damned computer people, the programmers? Sneakiest sons of bitches on earth. Why? Because they can cover their tracks, that's why." Case shook his head again. "It makes no sense. Why'd the feds let them do it?"

MacHenry knew the reasons, even if they weren't very good. "The FAA's mandate is to foster safety. But it's also supposed to help the airline industry prosper. Those goals are sometimes at odds. That's one reason I left."

"I heard you were fired."

"That's the other reason."

"Crap," said Case. "But now I know why the feds haven't found anything. Don't you see? They *want* it to be a bomb. Otherwise, their own ass is in a sling for letting Boeing play video games when they should have tested the real thing. Am I right here or what?" Case was working himself up to a full head of steam. The lawsuit spread out before him like an unrolling red carpet. "They're responsible. What if they got that damned pin—what was it?"

"Fuse pin."

"What if they got it wrong? What if these planes shed engines, and you wind up not being able to fly the damned thing on one?"

It was true. Name his worst nightmare? A full 7X7 climbing out, slow, vulnerable. A fuse pin snaps as it did on that EL AL 747. Or the China Air ship. Or the Evergreen freighter. Take your pick. An engine flies off. There would be one very small chance at saving the shooting match.

Case saw all of this behind MacHenry's expression. His gut told him this was right. He was close. Now, all he had to do was prove it. "Let me sum up what we know," he said. "Not only does this whistle-blower claim to have some important information, his area of expertise overlaps an area of weakness in the Boeing 7X7. One the FAA doesn't want to find because it points right back at them."

"Mr. Case, you keep calling this inspector—"

"Wheelwright. He has a name."

"You keep calling Wheelwright a whistle-blower. That works in court. But you don't know if he's blowing a whistle or smoke. That's the truth, isn't it? Everything else is just theory."

Case gave MacHenry a reluctant nod.

"Granted the FAA might be reluctant, but they aren't the only ones investigating the crashes. The NTSB people love to stick pins into the FAA. If they found something, we'd know about it. I guarantee it. The NTSB is for real."

"Give me a quick rundown on their methodology."

It was based on what the NTSB called Go Teams, and MacHenry knew it well. He'd argued with his bosses at the FAA to set up a similar group of experts, available at a moment's notice, to secure the crash scene, recover the flight data recorders, then delve into the causes of the accident. But there was no way the FAA would be caught emulating their hated bureacratic rivals, even if it did make sense. As Case listened, MacHenry laid out the NTSB's method of accident investigation.

Within the Go Team were specialists in structures, power plants, weather, air traffic control, systems, and finally, human factors. The OSHA Orange flight data recorder, known universally and incorrectly as the black box, went to the NTSB lab at the Bureau of Technology in downtown D.C. for analysis. A mandatory waiting period kept the frantic, and often gruesome, sounds of the cockpit out of the media for two months following the accident. It was step by step with big dramatic breaks as rare as media misreporting was common. Slow and steady won the race, and the ever-improving record of airline safety proved it. Until now.

Case took it all in. He made no notes. "Okay. So they do a thorough job. But they're human. What about Boeing?"

"Boeing sends a team into every crash site, too. So do the engine makers. If there's wreckage recovered, they help the NTSB people put the pieces back together. I've worked with them. The Boeing people are very, very good. They wouldn't hide anything they found just to keep their investors happy. Or some buyout plan on track."

Case sat back against the sofa. His face glowed in the candlelight. "Look. You're the expert. Not me. I just want to know what this inspector had in mind. And I think you do, too. Am I right here or what?"

MacHenry felt a cold draft blow by. The candle flickered. "Yes."

"All right. Now, my inexpert view is that we have just two ways to proceed. One, we find Wheelwright."

"If the FBI can't find him, how can we?"

"That leaves us with the second approach. We try to develop the same information he had when he disappeared." Case reached into his overcoat and pulled out his wool cap. He parked it on top of his bald head. "That's your job. Think about it, MacHenry. Let me know in the morning." Case jammed his cane down and levered himself to his feet. "I want you to find out who's working on the 7X7 crashes at the Federal Aviation Administration. Is anyone looking at a design flaw or are they just thinking bombs? How about the engine manufacturers? They must be sweating bullets. I mean, a big new product. Hundreds of people dead. That's a hell of a liability overhang."

MacHenry just shook his head. "That's why nobody will talk."

"Sure. They'll try to stonewall you. So go to Seattle. Nose around. Use your connection."

"I doubt DelVecchio would talk to me if he knew I was collecting information for you."

"Then don't tell him." Case began to hobble to the front door. "Wait!"

Hobble or not, when Case got moving, he was hard to stop. "We need to know why the feds haven't grounded this airplane. Who bought their silence? What evidence do they have in hand? Any preliminary findings? We'll need a complete list for the discovery phase of—"

"Let me get the door for you." MacHenry jumped up after him.

"What for?" Case yanked the door open and marched outside. The air was crisp and cold. "Forget bombs. Think about those engines, MacHenry. It's going to be something small. Maybe that pin. Maybe something else, something so insignificant that nobody would ever think to worry about it. Something nobody would bother to test. Trust my instinct. And one more thing."

"What?"

"There's not much time. Nippon Aerospace is getting the green light up on the Hill to buy into Boeing. Once that happens, it'll be too late, and too expensive, to find out the truth. They'll bury it."

Case might as well be speaking in tongues. "How's Congress involved with Boeing?"

"Money. Boeing's the biggest source of export income we have. You think it's going to be sold off to some Japanese outfit without hearings? Reports? Committees out the yinyang? Congress will lead from the rear. They'll wait until someone else puts his seal of approval on the deal. That someone is Bill Regano at Treasury. He's the chair of CFIUS. The Committee for Foreign Investment in the United States. If Regano kisses the deal, all Congress needs to do is blush. Like I said. You know airplanes? I know Washington."

MacHenry followed Case out to his elderly Taurus. "I don't think you've told me the whole story, Mr. Case."

Case turned, angelic, innocent. "Oh?"

MacHenry's breath flagged white in the cold air. "Suppose it was a German company buying into Boeing and not Nippon Aerospace? Would you have come out here tonight? Would you take this case on?"

"Murder is murder." Case tossed his cane into the back and eased behind the wheel. The engine started in a cloud of steam. "We'll talk tomorrow morning." Case slammed the door shut and backed out, leaving MacHenry alone as the vapor slowly drifted away. The clouds were breaking up. The sky beyond them was black as velvet. There were a million stars. MacHenry could name a question for each and every one.

Wheelwright stayed in the shadows of the great marble buildings. At the corner of Maryland and Constitution, he took a right. The sidewalk in front of the Senate Office Building was quiet, but a scattering of lights showed that there were still people at work. Across a broad, open plaza, the Supreme Court glowed in its security lights. A temple on a pedestal of stairs.

There were cars on the street, but nobody paid him any attention. Not even the occasional police cruiser. The National Guard curfew checkpoints were easy to dodge, too. They ringed the worst neighborhoods, and if you stayed away from them, the cold, suspicious troopers were no risk.

He crossed Constitution at First, heading south again, skirting the empty Capitol reflecting pool. At Canal, he turned right. The roar of tunnel traffic was like heavy surf. Storm waves breaking on the marble pediments of power.

The small, tasteful office of CRM et al. was wedged between two claptrap commercial buildings. On one side stood a closed Indian restaurant with apartments above; on the other, a drugstore. CRM owned a floor.

The street was quiet. Deserted. CRM's offices were dark. The tunnel traffic generated a low, ominous rumble. In the stacked apartments, only a few lamps glowed from behind the heavy curtains. He walked up to the chrome-and-glass door, saw the mail slot, the pile of letters and thick envelopes inside. He slipped his own message through and left.

Wheelwright didn't go straight back to his hidey-hole. He went north along First Street, almost to the railroad station, before turning back onto E Street. Ahead, a few blinking lights blocked off the sidewalk. He stepped into the street and walked.

A wooden barricade had been thrown up across the street. He

smelled the charred odor of burned wood, the chemical stink of melted plastic, and a darker, stranger scent he couldn't quite name. Trash floated on gutters still brimming with water and clogged with foam. Where was the shelter? He stopped at the wooden barricade, trying to make sense of the progression of buildings. One was missing.

God's Love had burned to a pile of blackened timbers, glowing red clinkers, and mounds of sodden gray ash. Smoke still curled up from the ruin. He sniffed. The odd smell was strong now. His mouth watered involuntarily. It gave the smell a name: roasted meat. "Oh, sweet Jesus," he said out loud. He heard a tiny scrape. The smallest of sounds, a noise a dog might struggle to hear. He started to turn. But then it was very much too late.

"Fucking cold, ain't it?"

Two men. One tall, skinny. The other short and powerfully built. The first with a hard glitter in his eyes and a ratty ponytail; the short one had brush-cut blond hair that sizzled with high-voltage electricity. He knew them. They were the ones he'd eyed suspiciously at the shelter.

"Hey now, Pop. Some reason you aren't talking?"

Wheelwright found his voice. It squeaked out between teeth locked in fear. "Go! Go away!"

"No such luck." The small one moved in like a confident predator.

Wheelwright spun and ran.

"Get him!"

He vaulted over a wooden barricade and ran for the safety of an alley. Brick walls hemmed in, fire escapes dangled overhead. The heavy tread of running feet sounded close behind. A chain-link fence blocked off the far end of the alley. He hit it running, scrambling straight up and over, down to the far side, running, running.

"Shit!" The voice behind echoed off brick. The fence rattled.

Wheelwright came to a street. Ponytail appeared at the corner. "Sturgis! *Aquí!*" He began loping in Wheelwright's direction in fast, purposeful strides. "Hey, bro. *Calmate,* okay? We just want to talk."

Wheelwright turned.

The other one emerged from the alley breathing white steam into the cold air.

Wheelwright stood as the short man approached. He watched his hands. He ducked as a fist hurtled out of the night. But it was a feint. His legs were kicked out from underneath him. He fell to the street, arms flailing for balance. A glass bottle shattered in his pocket, spilling cold wine. He rolled away and his other hip struck the pistol. He made a grab for it. A boot came down onto his wrist, crushing, harder, harder. He felt the bones bend, bend, then snap.

"Oops." Laughter.

Wheelwright drew in his breath to scream, but it was driven out by a vicious kick. The world narrowed to a tiny circle of light. A pinprick, a camera's eye, surrounded by black. He heard the sound of a car approaching.

"This is gonna be one happening party, sport," Sturgis said with a chuckle. "You're the fucking honored guest."

The car glided up and stopped. A door opened. A cascade of perfume. The whisper of nylons.

Wheelwright moved his head to see. The short one stepped in close and kicked him in the kidneys again. The pain was unbelievable. An animal tearing at his guts.

"No peeking," said someone.

A new voice struggled through Wheelwright's senses. A smooth voice. ". . . check him?"

They found the snub-nose and examined it with professional interest.

Wheelwright's chest heaved. His smashed wrist ballooned. It filled the end of his sleeve like a cork, a stopper made of pure agony.

"Bring him up here."

They hauled him upright and shoved him against the cold flanks of a car. He heard a faint sound. A metallic sound. He opened his eyes.

She was dressed for an inauguration. Black silk. Sparkling jewels. Heels. And a knife. "You've given all of us a very bad time." Her voice had a slight accent. "What shall we do with you?" She moved close, her perfume strong in his flaring nostrils. She tugged at his clothes.

Wheelwright struggled. He managed to move his head enough to see that his entire jacket had been opened. No. Not opened. Cut.

The blade drew close to his face. The needle-sharp tip filled

Wheelwright's vision. A flick and his nostril began to bleed. Then came a laugh. Not from the men. A woman's laugh. He smelled the red, rusty scent of his blood as it streamed across his face, swirling with the scent of her perfume.

"Now, don't be stupid. There's no reason not to give it to us, is there? Not anymore. We paid you before. We can pay you again. You know that, don't you?"

He snorted warm blood. "I don't have anything!"

The blade flashed by his face. His face flushed warm. More blood. "Well?"

"Park . . . ," he gasped, a sob. "Stanton Park. Pump room. Under the statue . . . a room. A pump room. I left the . . . everything . . . Please. It's all there."

"Hold him."

There was a sharp jab in his stomach. His whole body recoiled against it. They'd stabbed him anyway! *Christ!* He felt the cold metal turn warm with his blood. Three words rose up behind his eyelids, then faded like luminous clouds at sunset: *All for nothing.*

FOUR

Arthur Dean Bridger was ushered into J. William Regano's outer office by a long-legged beauty: last year's Miss Texas. The warm incandescent lamps turned her hair the color of spun gold. "The boss working you late tonight?"

"There's always so much to do before Congress heads home for the holidays," she answered. "Can I take your coat?"

"Thank you, Miss . . . ?"

"Just plain Charlotte is fine."

Plain? Not a chance. Washington was a town full of trophies, but the director of the U.S. Treasury's Office of Investment clearly had one of the choicest.

To say that J. William Regano was powerful was like calling the Washington summer muggy. It was self-evident. At forty-nine, he'd held a wide array of increasingly influential jobs. Labor representative on the Competitiveness Council. Clinton campaign adviser. Member of the transition team.

When the '92 elections washed the Republicans from the Oval Office, his name had been high up in what Capitol insiders called the Plum Book: a list of Democratic Party heavies who deserved special thanks. To the victors went the spoils.

On the surface, Regano's plum was a rather small one: as director of the Office of Investment, he was entitled to little more than a two-window corner office. But the directorship also put him in charge of CFIUS, the Committee on Foreign Investment in the United States.

When a foreign company wished to buy into a critical American industry, CFIUS blocked the way. CFIUS was a kind of tollbooth, an obstacle that could be removed given the correct set of circumstances. So long as foreigners wished to buy into America, Bill Regano was one of the most powerful men in the capital. A rainmaker.

The secretary reappeared. "The director will see you now. Follow me, please." The dark oak door swung wide.

"Thank you, Charlotte," said Regano, dismissing her. A framed photo on the wall showed Regano and the president shaking hands. Regano looked at Bridger. "So, Arthur. What's doing? You working Tokyo hours these days?"

"I'm glad you were able to make time for me tonight, Mr. Director. It's been a very busy day in a very busy week."

"Tell me about it. Our approval rating's down another ten. If it keeps going, Clinton might have to quit and run against the incumbent to win."

Bridger smiled.

"No joke, Arthur. We've got quarterly trade figures due out next week, and I can tell you they will not help. The Republicans are hammering us, and the rats are starting to panic. I'm getting screams from the Schedule C community to burrow them into Schedule A jobs before it's too late. One year before elections. It's not good. Not good at all."

Bridger nodded. Schedule C was the realm of the political appointee. Schedule A was civil service. If the politicals were running scared, it was because they were hearing water rushing into a sinking ship. "You heard about the crash?"

Regano grimaced. "Tragedy. Came over CNN a couple of hours ago. Thank God it wasn't another Jap plane." He paused, testing the air like a bear smelling woodsmoke. "Any idea how it's gonna spin in Tokyo?"

The opening move. "The management at Nippon Aerospace is very concerned. They wish to express their condolences to the families." Bridger shifted gears without a pause, without so much as a twitch. "What's the mood up here on the Hill?"

Regano sighed, took off his glasses, and rubbed his forehead. "I'll tell you the naked truth. I hate to say it, but I wish to hell they'd bomb an Airbus next time. Your boss. Is he nervous?"

"Everyone's still gung ho. But that could change." Bridger let out a bit more line. "Things are still uncertain on the financing side. That's why I'm here tonight."

Regano decided this was worth his time. He pointed to a leather-padded oak chair. "Sit."

Bridger settled himself, careful to keep the creases on his slacks sharp. Bridger had the Beltway Bandit look down cold: the costume of a successful and wealthy academic. The dress of a university president, Ivy of course. He'd run in the right circles now for nearly thirty years. A technical degree from MIT, research staffer on the Hill; assistant deputy director out at Langley for Science and Technology. But the CIA had been too claustrophobic for Bridger. Too much a middle-aged institution concerned only with not being wrong, and not at all interested in taking the risks necessary to occasionally be right. When CNN broke the Iraqi invasion of Kuwait ahead of the Agency, he quit. In a town that showered wealth on the purveyors of timely information, what good was the CIA?

Now he stood squarely between an avalanche of money and the goal that money sought to make its own. It was risky. It was like dancing with elephants. But Bridger was smart, and so far, nobody had stepped on his toes.

"So? Time's wasting, Arthur. What's the rumble?"

"You just said it. Time. In my opinion, it's our common enemy. The Japanese are still quite upset about the first wreck, the JAL plane. This new crash will raise more questions among the Consortium's investor pool. As you know, they're under a great deal of pressure on that front. If this is allowed to fester, there may be problems securing the necessary package."

"Hell, they're all in bed with each other over there, aren't they? They own their own banks. They write their own loans, the way I hear it. What gives?"

"There's talk. Why should Japanese money come to America? They got burned on our real estate. They got burned in Hollywood. They're looking harder at overseas investments."

Regano snorted. "Horseshit. Your Japanese friends are getting cold feet? Is that it? Tell them to keep their heads down and their noses clean. Tell them to quit making problems for themselves."

"Sorry?"

"This dedication on Friday you invited me to? One *very* dumb move."

"The *Enola Gay* is a very potent symbol to the Japanese, Mr. Director."

"And it isn't here? First, your boss is buying a very big chunk of the last industry we still like to think of as our own. They're stirring up the yahoos right there."

"There's been some Japan bashing over NAC's investment plans, yes."

"So now what do you do? You schedule a goddamned ceremony over pulling that old WW Two bomber out of the Smithsonian. Who shows up? The Japs. Where is it going afterward? Tokyo. Dumb."

Bridger looked at Regano and spoke slowly, emphatically. Even, it had to be admitted, with sincerity. "I think it's important we keep in mind that NAC's pumping a lot of cash into Boeing. That spells jobs." He shifted his attack, coiled his line, and cast again. "But I'll be sure to speak with the Foundation officers about the ceremony. By the way, how's the head count on the Select Committee looking?"

"So-so. It could fall either way. You know how Congress works. Nobody's gonna take a stand that could blow up in their faces."

"Politics as usual," Bridger said with a shrug. "How will the CFIUS recommendation read?" It was literally a billion-dollar question.

Regano smiled. Would CFIUS approve, disapprove, or approve with conditions? That was information worth more than just a casual drop. "Let's just say I don't screw my friends. How about you?"

"We all would like to put this behind and get down to business. That's why I'm here."

"Business." Regano shook his head. "You watch the monthly trade figures. Care to guess who's the long pole in the tent?"

Bridger knew. "Boeing."

"They sold four hundred jets in 1993. They may, and I emphasize *may*, sell a hundred this year. Hell. Even the Chinese have backed off. I mean, we have to run a reelection campaign. We can't afford to let the doors shut at Boeing. You know how many jobs that means? With subcontractors, more than a million nationwide. They're already mad as hell over NAFTA and the Mexicans. Now this."

Bridger knew the numbers. "That's why my client's first priority is helping Boeing restore its reputation for quality."

"Yeah. Sure. But what happens in the meantime?"

Bridger shifted in the chair. "What would you say to bumping up the hearings?"

Regano jerked his head as though he'd been stung. "Bump? What for?"

Bridger leaned forward. "I think we all know why the hearings were scheduled for the holiday season."

Regano awarded him a wary smile. "The Japanese are buying a nice juicy chunk of our biggest source of foreign trade. You want that done on page one? All over the papers? It has to be balanced."

Not balanced. Buried. "I work for the Consortium. You and CFIUS are the last hurdle prior to the deal going through. Can't we find a way to make this happen?"

"We? I don't see *you* volunteering to take the heat. You know the phrase *honban manaito*?"

"I don't believe I do."

"It means 'real chopping block,' if my Japanese doesn't fail me. *Honban manaito*." Regano brought one hand down onto the desk in a karate chop. "It's those live-sex stage acts where the gal takes on all comers from the audience. Well, I'm not anxious to put on a show. It's lonely up onstage. I need protection. So how big a bump are you looking for?"

"We think CFIUS should offer its final assessment immediately. Convene the Select Committee and go for the vote before adjournment. Take the high ground. Next week would not be too soon."

"Before Thanksgiving recess? Impossible."

Bridger sighed. Deep and for effect. "In that case, I'm authorized to inform you that NAC's management team may wish to pull back and reexamine the entire undertaking. Run the numbers out and see if they still add."

Regano stared. "Don't fuck with me, Arthur. I won't go down as the guy who stalled this deal into the ground."

Bridger gave Regano a look of sympathy that could freeze brine. "I can see how it would make things uncomfortable for you."

Regano leaned across his desk and pointed a finger at Bridger's face. "You may be riding high now, but think of your own reputation.

Arthur Bridger: his deals fall through. Who's gonna hire a guy like that next time?"

One deal like this was all Bridger would ever need. But he didn't say as much. "It comes down to this: the Consortium can't write a check for three billion dollars. It needs its financing package in place. If NAC backs out, Boeing folds. Will it have an effect on the economy today? The elections next year? I think we both know that it will."

Regano had the look of a wary animal that hears the first faint click of a trap and knows it's all over except for the swift conclusion of springs and steel.

Bridger gave him an empty, cold smile. "But of course, that's putting a negative spin on it. On the plus side, the deal going through means jobs. Millions of jobs are at stake, Mr. Director. They're in your hands. Now, can we work on this together?"

"And all I have to do is round up a bunch of scared congressmen and tell them they have to vote something up that could backfire on them big time." Regano chuckled, but only with his mouth, not his face. "And if I don't?"

"The deal might go down, and everybody would know that Boeing shut its doors, a million jobs down the drain, because this administration let it happen. That it didn't care for the average American who works hard and plays by the rules." Bridger smiled. "That's how I would frame it, if I were asked to offer an opinion."

Regano's eyes glittered with a curious mixture of fear and defiance. "You know, those *honban manaito* gals? The Japs have this thing about fucking American women. I always wondered why an American would lie there up on that stage and open her legs for a bunch of gooks. I figure it must pay pretty good. What do you think?"

"I wouldn't know, Mr. Director."

"That surprises me greatly, Arthur. Greatly." Regano jabbed the intercom button. "Charlotte?" he said into the speakerphone. "Could you bring in a copy of the Boeing hearings schedule? . . . Yes. And find out where everybody's hiding out. The private numbers."

Bridger snapped his attaché closed and stood. "It's a pleasure doing business with you, Mr. Director."

"Yeah," said Regano. "Anytime, pal."

★　　★　　★

The street was choked with traffic as Tokyo went to work. Cranes stood everywhere, turning the city into a convention of long-legged storks. Some hauled mangled chunks of concrete away from quake-damaged buildings. Some pulled fresh red steel from stacks, setting the beams into place on the skeletal frames of new office towers.

Out on the street, things appeared much more normal. Motor scooters engaged in hand-to-hand combat with taxicabs; the cabs swarmed like yellow mayflies. A stampede of pedestrians barely parted for Shig as he stood, checking the address against the big new building in front of him. It was supposed to be the headquarters of the Nippon Aerospace Consortium. He watched as a few people drifted in through the glass doors. They moved slowly, as though they had no worries about being the last ones to their desks. Shig noticed a few glass watchers posted outside the ground floor. They gazed up at the facade with special polarizing binoculars, ready to shout a warning if a sheet of plate glass loosened in the Little Big One began to fall.

All in all, it was a fairly typical building, a thirty-story box of steel and glass with a marble entry lobby and banks of elevators waiting patiently for riders. Built during the speculative bubble economy, it was obviously far from fully occupied. Entire floors were empty from the look of the shadeless windows. What did the Americans call them? See-through buildings.

A pet store occupied the ground floor. Small cages were displayed in the front window. They seethed with glistening tangles of snakes. Bat houses hung from the interior walls in every imaginable style, traditional to prismatic modern.

He checked his watch. It was well past the time a good employee would be at his desk. He straightened his tie and walked into the lobby.

It was like a memorial. A mausoleum. His steps echoed from the hard surfaces. A uniformed guard eyed him as he walked by. A bank of security monitors blinked behind the guard, the screens filled with more empty corridors. He put down his *manga*, comic book. Shig saw that it was the ever-popular *Rape Man*. The guard had a mass of black curls falling from beneath his cap. Shig noticed the beginnings of a tattoo on his wrist. Permed hair and tattoos. Had the *yakuza* taken over the job of guarding buildings from themselves?

"Who are you looking for?" the guard asked boldly. It was unusual for them to speak at all, at least to speak anything more than a formal greeting. He rolled up his *manga* and began slapping his palm with it, truncheon style.

"Nippon Aerospace."

"Floor seven," the guard grunted, and returned to his *manga*.

All six elevator cabs were available. Shig noticed the pressure-sensitive pad installed in front of each door. When he stepped on the rubber, a woman's voice beckoned him to a particular elevator.

"This way, dear people." He punched the seventh-floor button. "Thank you for sparing the time to visit our building. Please enjoy your ride. Next stop floor"—there was a slight pause—"seven."

Seven was the luckiest number. A prime location. It was what you'd expect. The elevator went straight up to the seventh floor without a stop. Shig wondered, would there ever be tenants for all the buildings built during the bubble? The cab slowed so gradually he wasn't sure when he'd arrived. It was one of those new, fuzzy-logic elevators. So smooth you could hardly tell you were moving at all. The voice thanked him and the door opened to reveal a dark-paneled lobby.

"Consortium. Please hold. Yes?"

Pictures of aircraft adorned the walls. Soft music filtered in from hidden speakers. The floor was thickly carpeted.

"One moment, please. I'll transfer the call." A pretty receptionist stood guard behind a swooping white desk. She was dressed in standard navy and gray and wore the harried expression of a person with too much to do. Telephones blinked constantly for her attention. Her fingers danced over the control pad, fast as a concert pianist's, punching numbers, switching calls, taking notes. Two doors were behind her, one to either side. One was closed, the other open a crack. Shig saw the bustle of a typical Japanese office in thin section.

He stood, holding his card, waiting to be acknowledged. The phone calls abated enough for her to look up. "Yes? What is it?" Her accent was clipped, sharp enough to etch glass.

And rude, he thought. He approached her and held out his card. She took it as two calls came in at once. "One moment, please. . . .

Yes? Can I help you?" She read the card as her red nails flickered across the face of her telephone. She looked up. "Do you have an appointment with someone, Mr. Onishi?"

"No. I'm conducting a study for the Ministry on new—"

"Just a moment, please." She fielded a blinking light. "Consortium. . . . Yes. Hold on a moment. Thank you." She looked up. "You'll need an appointment," she said, again with more directness than any office lady Shig had ever met. "Call ahead next time." She punched a flashing light. "Consortium. Yes. Please hold." She looked up again.

"Is there someone I can speak with? I won't be long." Shig watched as the shapes of busy men and women flitted across the narrow slot of the partly open door.

"No. Everyone is very busy." She returned to her phone, ignoring Shig as best she could.

Very odd. She was giving him the brush-off. An office lady! It was unheard of for an OL to block even a junior investigator from the NPA. Still, unless he was willing to rush by her through one of those doors and grab someone by the scruff of the neck, this was as far as he was going to get. He turned his back on the rude woman and returned to the elevator. It was waiting for him.

"Thank you," it said as the door shut. "Floor, please?"

Shig was about to punch the ground-floor button, but stopped his finger just in time. Instead, he pressed eight.

"Thank you. Next stop, floor"—there was that pause again—"eight."

The elevator rose quickly, then came to a soft stop. The door opened on a tangled landscape of concrete floors, hanging wires, ducts, and bare windows. He got out as the elevator door closed. Over the door, a security camera gazed down, its red, unblinking eye accusing him of trespass.

Shig had two things in his favor. He was tall, and Japanese designers of building security systems never suspected anyone would try to blind their eyes. He slipped a business card from his jacket, curled it slightly, reached overhead, and popped it in front of the lens. Now, he thought as he surveyed the empty floor, let's see what is going on here.

Directly across from him on the far wall was the freight elevator. He could see out three of the four faces of the big new office tower. There was nothing but structural columns to block the view. The air smelled of concrete dust. Stacks of wallboard were piled around the perimeter. As he walked, his shoes left prints. Nobody had been up here in quite some time. When he came to a pile of wallboard, he saw it was half-rotted with moisture, expanded and crumbling.

He came to the freight elevator. The control panel was hanging by its wires. Next to it were two more doors. He checked them. They led into unfinished rest rooms. One final door piqued his curiosity. He tried the knob. It was locked.

He pulled out his Japanese Army knife, selected the Phillips-head driver, and quickly pulled the four mounting screws from the lockplate. The handle fell apart in his hands. Knife stashed away once more, he pushed, and the door swung in, opening up to a gloomy, unpainted gray stair tower. A gust of warm air rose by him. Why not? He let the door close behind and quietly eased his way down two flights of red steel stairs.

Another door faced him now. It had to open up onto the seventh floor, on the far side of the building, away from the dragon lady guarding the gate. He tried the knob. There was some resistance. He twisted harder.

There was a loud click, followed by the shriek of an alarm. He froze for an instant as the noise echoed down the concrete tower, then pulled.

What? Where . . . The room was a dead ringer for the one he'd left behind. Dangling wires. Concrete floor and dust. The seventh floor was a mirror image of the eighth! The alarm shrieked, but Shig didn't hear it. He was stunned. One wall partitioned off the main elevators. Two doors led into that busy little reception lobby. A computer on a rolling cart sat next to one of those doors, its cables snaking underneath. The partly open door had a screen mounted behind it. A projector sent the images of busy workers scurrying across it. Footprints left a trail connecting one of the doors with the rest room beside him. It suddenly opened. It was the pretty OL. She saw Shig, eyes locked wide open. Then she screamed.

Shig slammed the fire door shut and ran down the stairs, taking them three at a time. Sixth floor. Gravity was pulling his upper body down faster than his feet could catch up. He had to hold tight to the rail to keep from falling. Round the corner and run. Fifth floor. Voices came from above. He didn't stop to listen. Round the corner, run. No. Not above. From below. Round the corner. Run. Fourth floor.

As he swung himself around the landing, he smashed straight into a wall. His momentum sent him flying. Who would put a wall across the fire stairs! It was impermissible! His vision doubled as he bounced once, twice, again. The alarm faded. His brain came loose. Only as he looked up at the legs of the guard did he realize it hadn't been a wall he'd hit. Not at all. The alarm came back, louder than before. There was a reason for that. It was ringing inside his skull now.

"You," said the guard. He was carrying a blackjack, slapping it against his palm the same way he'd done with *Rape Man*. He'd struck Shig on the fly, sending him down the stairs until he came up hard against a real wall.

Shig counted the stairs between them. Why? He was an accountant. It was a natural thing to do, if not terribly smart. He fought to focus. There were four. The guard's polished shoes scuffed as he descended. He sensed the blow coming. When it did, the blackjack slapped the concrete where Shig's head had been an instant before. The kick was unexpected.

Once more he was falling, thumping down the steel stairs, those black shoes scuffing in pursuit. He scrambled back as the truncheon whizzed by and struck the wall. A small chip of concrete came loose. What would it do to bone? He moved fast enough to avoid the steel toecap he knew would be next. The thug was unimaginative. He seemed to be able to count only to two. So far, it had been enough.

"Hold still, you little germ," the guard growled as he moved in, the blackjack way behind him as he wound up for another strike.

It was time to graduate to higher mathematics. "Sorry to inconvenience you." Shig saw the muscles tense, the blackjack begin its arc. This time, instead of avoiding it, he grabbed the guard's forearm with one hand, the elbow with the other. His knee came up to supply the fulcrum. The momentum of the swing did the rest.

A double crack echoed in the stair tower. One from the blackjack falling, the other from bone. The guard squalled. Shig slammed him against the wall face first. There was another snap, softer than the first. The guard left a smear of bright blood as he slid to a heap.

The alarm was still ringing. So was Shig's head. He wobbled as he took the stairs down to the ground level, straightened his tie, and entered the cool marble lobby. In a minute, he merged with the crowds out on the street and was gone.

FIVE

The sun was still below the eastern horizon. The main runway at Dulles International was a dark river outlined in blue edge beacons. Beyond it, a big hangar stood out like an island rising from a black sea, bathed in brilliant yellow sodium security lights. It cost an $8-million donation to the Smithsonian's Air and Space Museum to erect; the airplane it housed, though half a century old, had cost the Hibakusha Foundation even more. Inside the steel structure, the *Enola Gay* was finally ready to emerge.

Its dedication on Friday would be attended by members of Congress who could not afford to miss it: those with Japanese plants in their states and those who hoped to lure them. The surviving members of the *Enola Gay*'s crew had been invited as guests of honor, though they declared in no uncertain terms that if the *Gay* was headed for Japan, they wouldn't be around to bless it.

A lot of Americans agreed with them. It was bad enough for the artifact to be brought back to life by way of Japanese money. It was something else again for it to head off on temporary loan to a Japanese museum.

The controversy was duly reported in the Japanese press with an air of indignant noncomprehension. Why all the fuss? The bomber was a potent symbol for all the old hatreds. The Americans had let the plane rot in the shadows for almost half a century. It was yen that had brought it back to life. Didn't they understand gratitude?

Built in 1945, the *Gay* was a Special Mission variant of the B-29 Superfortress, registration number 44-86292. Stripped of all its guns except for the tail turret, it flew just one combat mission: August 6, 1945. Hiroshima. The world's first atomic bomber; the airplane that had ended the Second World War in a dazzle of nuclear light and thunder. Its one moment of deadly glory.

While GIs paraded under blizzards of ticker tape, while victorious fleets filled the berths of war-weary ports, the *Enola Gay* sat all but forgotten under the desert sun near Tuscon, Arizona. Finally, in 1953, it flew again, this time to Andrews Air Force Base outside Washington, D.C. Given by the Air Force to the Smithsonian Institution, the bomber was to be exhibited at the National Air and Space Museum after a complete restoration.

She sat in pieces, stored away in musty old sheds, for the next thirty years. No guide to the capital included it. Still, a few people each day managed to find her. The visitor's registry filled with names over the years, many of them Japanese. The plane rusted while the promised restoration was put off again and again.

As the fiftieth anniversary of its one and only mission approached, the federal government simply had no money to spend on such a controversial memorial. None to build the annex, and none to hire the craftsmen able to put the disassembled B-29 back together.

But the Hibakusha Foundation did.

Work began again. The *Enola Gay* came together, as good, even better, than new. America would have only a brief time to appreciate her: After the dedication, it would be disassembled, crated, and shipped to a second ceremony marking the opening of the $120 million War Memorial Museum just outside Tokyo. After half a century, the plane was ready for its last mission. Thanks to Japanese money, its bright aluminum would once again feel the touch of the rising sun.

"Juliet Hotel Fox Seven, Dulles Tower. Runway One Niner Right, cleared to land." Juliet was the letter applied to all Japanese civil aircraft. The *H* and the *F* stood for Hibakusha Foundation. Seven was for luck.

"Cleared to land, Fox Seven."

A bright star appeared in the north as a jet curved onto final approach. Landing lights blazed out a trail ahead of the descending jet. A flashing strobe added to the dazzle. Red and green wingtip lights joined the constellation.

The scream of its engines grew as it swept in toward the runway. The twin-engined Gulfstream touched down and immediately roared in reverse thrust, slowing. It pulled off the runway, heading for the dark United Parcel Service hangar. Overhead, the black sky turned pale white as the new day neared.

The posh jet came to a halt in front of the UPS building. The Smithsonian compound was just next door. Two men in dark, insulated coveralls rolled a red-carpeted airstairs against the jet's smooth skin. Shintaro Ishii heard the thump.

So did Yoshi. The bodyguard bowed slightly, then stood up. His limbs didn't seem stiff, even after the long flight. He made his way toward the front of the cabin. Anyone coming in would have to get by him first.

Shintaro regarded him as a piece of furniture. Yoshi never talked much. He never got in the way. He was a presence. A reminder of his father's dangerous ways.

He tried to remember back to the days when his main worry was how late he could sleep, what he might have for breakfast, or what color to select for his new car. Damn his father's ghost! He'd wished for money, not responsibility. I will help you find your place in the world, his father had whispered on his deathbed. I will correct the mistakes I made. Old Susumu Ishii, lord of the *yakuza,* had never been much of a father while he was alive. Why had he warmed to the role as he lay dying?

Shintaro peered out through the broad oval porthole at America. What a big, empty place. So alien. So out of scale. It had been a long flight from Tokyo to Washington. He hoped it was worth it. Kazuo Ibuki said it was necessary. Ibuki was supposed to be his navigator, his helmsman. But Shintaro was a modern man. He knew enough to value hard, even unpleasant, truths. And the truth was simple. Ibuki was not his guide. He was his master.

He unbuckled his seat belt and looked around the interior of his flying command post. The G-5 was the largest executive jet built. Made to span whole oceans nonstop and equipped with every luxury. The main cabin was fifty feet from cockpit bulkhead up front to the door that opened onto Ishii's private chambers at the tail. The jet had cost $30 million. Fitting it out had nearly doubled the cost. He wanted for nothing. Yet nothing, not even sudden and unimaginable wealth, came without a price.

The forward hatch opened. Arthur Dean Bridger appeared with

Yoshi right behind. They walked down the executive jet's wide center aisle. The elegantly attired American was like a small bullet propelled by the charge of the wide, unhappy-looking bodyguard.

"Good morning, Mr. Ishii," Bridger said with a slight bow. He looked up, not knowing to wait for Ishii's reply. "I'm glad we finally have the chance to meet."

Ishii nodded. Americans never got bowing right. Why do they even try? "Yes, Kazuo Ibuki has told me all about you. I understand you have been very helpful to us."

"I do my best."

"I suppose we should start with a tour of my father's favorite charity."

Bridger's pale skin was flushed. His gold, wire-framed glasses steamed over and he took them off. He unbelted his raincoat and draped it over a seatback. Underneath he wore a dark suit, cut through with tiny, silver pinstripes so narrow they might have been applied with a razor. "I think we'll want to leave the airport as soon as possible and get you settled in. The Hay Adams is ready for you."

"Thank you for making the arrangements, but I'd hoped to see the *Enola Gay* first."

Bridger looked uncomfortable. "It may not be the best time. This morning, I mean. There's a certain protocol I would recommend you follow."

"Please be direct, Mr. Bridger. I have had a very long flight. What are you trying to say?"

Bridger seemed to be weighing something. "I work with appearances, Mr. Ishii. The dedication ceremony on Friday will not be universally seen as a positive. Not for you, not for America. That's a problem. I've orchestrated your visit to present an alternative image."

Facts were one thing. Image was something Ishii understood.

"Later, we can . . ." A sound made Bridger freeze. He turned. The forward cabin door opened again, and a redheaded stewardess wearing a dark green kimono brought a silver carafe of coffee. A fan of sweet cakes was artfully arrayed on a china plate. Thick cream chilled a silver server, beading it with moisture. She placed the tray on the table across the aisle from Ishii and Bridger.

"Thank you, Mikki," said Ishii.

"*Hai,*" she said with a small bow as she poured two cups. "Do you take cream, Mr. Bridger?"

"Black. Thank you."

Ishii took his regular, cream and double sugar. Green eyes were his favorite. Mikki retreated silently toward the front of the jet. "What you are trying to say, if I may paraphrase, is that you want to show official Washington that I am not some greedy Japanese out to steal the industrial heritage of the United States. Is this so?"

Bridger smiled his reply.

"Well, you're the local expert," said Shintaro. Americans were so difficult to understand. "You have a car?"

"Waiting outside."

Understanding gaijin was such a chore. He raised the coffee in a toast. "To our efforts together."

"To success."

When the cup was drained, Shintaro spoke to Yoshi. "You wait here and supervise. I'll go into the city with this one."

"He's lying," said Yoshi, his face a perfect mask.

"I know. But what about?"

Yoshi shook his head.

Shintaro turned to Bridger. "I am ready. Lead on."

Ten minutes later, the black car was speeding east through early Wednesday traffic, on its way downtown.

"Hey, Pop. Time to shit and shave. Up and at 'em."

There was a pause, then the other one spoke. "You're right. He's out. What she hit him with?"

"Major medicine. Fucker'd sleep through his own funeral."

Wheelwright listened to the two men. He knew them. Little and Big. A Latino—was his name Ramón? And someone named Sturgis. They'd stabbed him! Why was he still alive? He kept his eyes shut. Where was he? Flat on his back. Warm air circulating. Gentle breeze. His side felt kicked in. His brain cleared. His broken wrist was a cannonball pulsing with each beat of his heart. He bit down on his tongue and tasted iron blood. Iron. Steel. He would be a man of metal.

"How about some fresh air? Smoke?" The man spoke with a drawl. Sturgis.

"Leave him by himself?"

"He ain't goin' noplace. Come on."

Wheelwright listened as the footsteps receded. A chain rattled, and then the sound of a heavy motor rumbled. A few moments later, a cold breeze fresh with the promise of escape washed over him. He opened his eyes.

The ceiling was high. Bare metal trusses spanned a wide-open space. Painted corrugated metal. Fans turning to push the warm air back down. Bright orange sodium lights. He was above the floor. Not on a bed. A table. Wooden partitions blocked his view in the direction the two men had taken.

He reached down into his wine-soaked pocket. At first, he missed it. He dug his fingers into the stiff cloth. A piece of glass jabbed back, but he hardly felt it, for beyond it he felt the slight heaviness, the barely perceptible wedge of fabric. God and his miracles. The cloth sack was still there.

The smell of oil, new rubber, hydraulic fluid, was familiar. Where had they taken him? He moved his head. A wall was split by darkness. Beyond it he could see distant orange lights, small and bright as stars. He was seeing through the wall somehow. No! The wall was open a crack! Not a wall. But doors. Big sliding doors. A hangar?

Yes. There, within spitting distance, a huge silver airplane sat behind a perimeter of velvet rope. A small white sign was on a stand, but he couldn't read the words on it. He breathed again. He was in a hangar. They'd brought him to an airport! Only the sweet odor of kerosene was missing. How do you have airplanes without jet fuel?

Wheelwright eased his head farther around. The body of the airplane was perfectly smooth. It glittered in the lights. And she was big. From the high, rounded tail to the glassed-in nose, the ship barely fit from one corner of the hangar to the other. There was writing under the canopy windows. He couldn't quite make it out. What was she? He squinted at the white sign and saw the word *Foundation.*

Her tail was marked with a black circle enclosing the letter *R*. She had lean, greyhound lines. Massive wheels were chocked against yellow blocks. And propellers, of all things. There were two that he could see. Two more on the far side. Four black, paddle-bladed props.

Four radial engines stubby and fat as an old cigar. They looked like Wright 3350s. Eighteen cylinders. Over two thousand horsepower each.

He rolled his eyes up. A big blue banner hung against the far wall: *Fifty Years of Peace: 1945–1995*. It shifted uneasily in the slight draft of the fans. Then he knew.

Black-circle *R*. The slender body, the burnished pewter skin. He knew where he was.

He felt his brain shift, tilting. Why was he here? What was . . . his heart surged. A voice. A laugh. ". . . dumb-ass cherry goes for a smoke and leaves his lighter behind."

Big and Little. Ramon and Sturgis. They were coming back.

The thought of them blasted through him with a high-voltage sizzle. He had to get away. Had to. He swung his legs out into space and tried to sit up. His stomach muscles refused. *Iron. Steel.* He strained. *Run!*

He rolled onto his bruised side and fell to the cement floor. His knees struck, his good arm thrust out to keep him from falling flat on his face. The pain screamed in his ears. He couldn't stop. *Run!* Wheelwright struggled to his feet. They were coming. Louder. Nearer. He turned. Where to go? They'd left the doors open. Stooped in agony, he fell toward the old bomber just as the two guards came around a partition. He grabbed the sign with his good hand. The heavy metal base screeched as he dragged it. The words written on it finally registered.

Gift of the Hibakusha Foundation.

"What the fuck was . . ."

"Shit!"

Mouths open in shock, they were standing between him and the freedom those cracked-open hangar doors promised. The moment hung like a weight out over a sheer drop.

Then it fell.

Wheelwright forgot all the pain. He grabbed the sign and swung it like a mace as Sturgis charged him. The heavy base thudded against his chest. His breath blew out in a grunt and a gasp as he fell.

Wheelwright dropped the weapon and ran away from the two, turning his back on those open hangar doors. He ran around the tail of the *Enola Gay*, slipping on the painted concrete floor. He ducked under the wide tail and ran full speed along the slim metal body of the bomber. The big Latino showed up right ahead, blocking him. He wasn't going to make it. The boarding ladder leading up into the belly of the *Enola Gay* all but shouted his name. He crouched low and dove for it.

"I got him!"

Wheelwright scrambled up one-handed. Voices. Shouts. Wheelwright was in the cockpit. The big metal door hatch at his feet stood open, hinged on its side. The boarding ladder shook. He kicked the hatch free. A blond head appeared. Sturgis. The door fell slowly, heavily, a ponderous swing that ended in a heavy thud, then a clang as metal met metal. A squawl, then the ladder clattered to the concrete.

He turned. Orange light filtered in through the many panes of the cockpit windows. Beyond, he saw the cracked-open hangar doors. But how could he get there? Not down. That was blocked. He turned. The aft cabin bulkhead was perforated by two holes. One was a high, circular tunnel that ended in blackness back at the tail. Below, nearly at floor level, a second small hatch opened into the *Enola Gay*'s bomb bay.

". . . gonna *kill* you if he messes with anything." The boarding ladder scraped across the concrete floor.

Now. Wheelwright stuck one leg through the bottom hatch, swung his shoulders in, and then his other leg. He pulled the round hatch closed behind him. He was perched on a narrow catwalk.

It was like hiding in a closet. Dark, his blood pounding in his ears, his breath coming in shallow gasps. At his feet, a thin line of light betrayed the imperfect joining of the bomb doors. A trapeze of metal structure was overhead. A massive steel hook dangled from it. He knew it had to be the bomb shackle. The old plane swayed as the guards swarmed up the boarding ladder.

"Where'd he go?"

"He's here someplace."

There wasn't much time now. None. He reached into his pocket and ripped open the false seam at the bottom. The cockpit floor hatch slammed back on its hinges. He pulled out the small bag. It was stained with old wine and fresh blood.

"Where the fuck?" The voice was barely muffled. It was Sturgis. He was right beyond the small hatch. Close. Boots stomped on the cockpit decking. Hunting.

Lawson Wheelwright reached up in the darkness—it reminded him of the abandoned pump room—and wedged the bag into a crevice where the bomb shackle met the fuselage wall. He shoved it back behind the aluminum girder. His arm was still raised up when the round hatch was yanked open.

A flashlight pinned him like an animal caught on a freeway. "You sorry son of a bitch," said the voice behind the light.

Wheelwright jumped down off the catwalk and landed in the belly of the bomber. He dug his fingers into the crack separating the bomb-bay doors, but they were locked.

Sturgis started laughing.

He scrabbled away from the laughter, away from the light, back, deeper into the darkness. Up and over a metal beam and into a second empty bomb bay. At the back, dim in the faint light shed by Sturgis's beam, he saw another low hatch. Where did it go? He was beyond such questions. Wheelwright pulled it open and dived through. He landed in a wide cabin in the waist of the B-29. The sound of slow, stealthy footsteps came from the bomb bay. He pulled the hatch shut and ran a lock bar across the operating mechanism. Above it was the terminus of the long tunnel that led up to the cockpit. He chanced a look. It was like peering down the barrel of a howitzer.

The hatch leading into the bomb bay banged, then again.

"Open the fucking door!" This voice came from below.

"Where did he go?" This voice caromed down the tunnel from the cockpit. A bright beam shot down it and caught Wheelwright square in the eyes.

"*Aquí!*" Ramón scrambled up into the tunnel and began fast-crawling right at him.

Wheelwright spun. Think! What was the layout of a B-29? There had to be another way out! He staggered back toward the tail and into another, smaller cabin. A final pressure door beckoned him on. He got down on his knees, forgetting the pain, and yanked the hatch open. He dived through into total darkness as Ramón thumped down from the tunnel and stood where Wheelwright had been not seconds before.

He slammed the last barrier shut. The blackness was total. He crawled by feel alone through what seemed to be a narrow corridor of metal tanks and rubber hoses. The floor was webbed by taut steel control cables. He clambered over them like a broken spider, hitting his head on invisible obstacles, slamming his shoulder against the skin of the bomber.

"Watch yourself! Don't let him get to the doors!"

Wheelwright came to the end. He leaned against the tail bulkhead, knees drawn up, shaking from adrenaline and fear. He was in the tail. There was no way out. He . . . wait! The bomber had a tail turret! Where was the tail gunner's cabin? This wasn't it. How . . . He turned, his fingers searching the bulkhead. They found a handle. An ax handle. He grabbed at it, but it was secured in some way he couldn't see. He kept searching. There had to be a . . . he found another. This one was cold and made of metal. He leaned on it, the bar squealed, the door swung in, and the blackness was flooded with bright light.

Just then, Sturgis's voice boomed so close it sounded like a shout.

"I can smell him!"

In the light coming in through the tail turret, Wheelwright saw the ax's catch and flipped it open. It dropped to the deck with a loud clang.

"He's right back here!"

Wheelwright grabbed it and rolled through the tail gunner's door. The hangar lights flodded in through the bulletproof glass. There had to be . . . there was! A door in the side wall went outside! He shoved it open and fell through, dropping four long feet down to the concrete floor. Exhausted, he didn't feel anything. Nothing. His nerves were sawdust dead. He was on his feet in a flash, heading for the hangar doors again. He ducked under the plane's wings. The nose was dead ahead. The doors. They were right there. Right there. Black stripe of freedom. Cold air. Outside. If he could just . . .

The big Latino jumped down from the cockpit hatch.

From behind: "You see him? You see him, Ramón?"

"Yeah. I see him, Sturgis. I see him real good."

Sturgis came up puffing as he ran. They had him sandwiched! He feinted once more, than ran right, reaching the hangar door but not the opening. Sturgis was coming for him. He backed up against a drum of solvent. A welder's torch on a wheeled dolly was right next to it. He raised the ax.

"Whoa now, boy, don't get upset. This ain't what you think." Sturgis kept his distance, eyes flicking back and forth.

Panic finally seized his muscles. He couldn't think, he couldn't move. His nostrils flared as he gasped for air. He smelled the sharp scent from the solvent drum again. It woke him up. He grabbed the sparker from the welder's dolly, then brought the crash ax down on the dripping spigot. It snapped off and a gusher of pungent petrochemical flooded out across the floor.

"God damn it!" Sturgis shouted.

"Stay back." It came out a croak. He snapped the sparker near the pool of flammable MEK. Hot sparks drifted down close to the chemical. It was flooding all around his feet now, running up his shoes. He could feel the cold vapors evaporating against his ankles.

"Come on, pops. Be fucking careful with that!" said Sturgis, keeping his distance now.

"Stay back," said Wheelwright as he backed up against the massive hangar door. "Stay back."

"We're just—"

The overhead lights went out. The darkness was heavy as a curtain. A new sound came from above. A crackle, a pop. The loudspeakers were on. A voice drifted down from the invisible rafters. A woman's voice. "He lied to us. Keep him where he is. I'm coming down."

A motor whined. Suddenly, from behind Wheelwright's back, the hangar doors he'd give anything to move began to do exactly that.

"Honey? Are you awake?"

"Hmm?"

"The camera. I'm not sure it's working."

"It's brand-new." A nudge in the ribs woke him up. Who could sleep in one of these damned chairs, anyway? The airlines must have bought their waiting-lounge furniture from old McDonald's franchises. "What?" he said, his eyes still closed. It couldn't be their flight. It wasn't for another hour or two. Why the hell did she insist on getting here so damned early? Her rule was that for every day of scheduled vacation, two should be spent preparing for it, and another one worrying over what she forgot. It was a sickness. A disease. She was standing by the big plate-glass window of the departure lounge, pointing their new camera out at something.

"I'm not sure the zoom thing is right. I've been using it and it looks funny. Just try it, okay?"

"It's fine." She was always worrying. Traffic jams. A flat. Aliens taking over the tollbooths on the Dulles access road and demanding payment in interplanetary tokens. Who knew what she'd think up? He bunched up the down coat that served as his pillow and tried to put himself back to sleep.

"Maybe the store sold a lemon to us. Or maybe it's bad batteries. Do we have any extra batteries? I wouldn't want to get to Mexico and have dead batteries."

"They sell camcorder batteries in Mexico."

"Maybe." She panned the camera across the cold expanse of the plate-glass window. It was very dark out, and there was nothing to see except her reflection and a brightly lit hangar on the far side of the runway.

"Keep playing with it and it'll break for sure."

"I'm not playing. I'm testing." She was about to switch it off when a new light blossomed on the tiny eyescreen. "Uh-oh. Wait. I *knew* it. It's broken." She zoomed in on a bright red dot. "Something's wrong. There's a funny light." But it wasn't broken. "No, wait, maybe it isn't. I think there's a fire over there. By that building."

"Okay."

"No. I mean *really*. A real fire. What if it's our plane?"

"They have other airplanes."

She kept the camera running. The tiny orange dot swelled to a bright globe. She focused. She ran the camcorder's zoom in to maximum magnification. "Oh, my God," she said as the image grew to a bright orange flower with a black, writhing heart. "It's . . ." She couldn't take her eye from it. "It isn't a plane! Oh my . . . it's a man!"

★ ★ ★

The first light of the new day filled the kitchen windows of the old Virginia farmhouse. MacHenry stood up from his desk and fed another log into the woodstove, then swung the iron door shut. *Who can I get to talk?*

Joe DelVecchio out at Boeing, maybe. He hated to think he'd lie to his former captain about working for Roger Case. Could he do it? His thoughts stopped short when his telephone rang.

"MacHenry here."

"Brian! It's Julia!" Her voice was as clear as if she had called from the next room. "I tried before, but they said that there was a problem in the lines."

"Aloha. You're up early. How's the conference?"

"I haven't gone to bed yet. I wish you could have come. Is everything okay?"

"We had a windstorm. It knocked out the power and it must have taken some telephone lines down, too. I'm working pretty hard here. No time for fun, I'm afraid."

"You work too much." Pause. "Maybe I should have stayed home."

"I don't know about that." MacHenry looked outside. "It's about thirty degrees. The power's still out. I'd stick with that conference as long as you can. Kona's a lot warmer than Hound Hill."

"Thanks. I miss you, too."

Here we go, thought MacHenry as the line popped and whistled. Why did everything come out wrong? "You know what I meant. It's just . . ." Suddenly, the lights came up and the refrigerator began to hum. "Hang on. Power just came back." A loud, excited voice came from the television in the kitchen. "Julia, can I call you back? I must have left everything running last night when the electricity died."

"Sure. It's been nice talking with you."

"I didn't—" The line to Hawaii went dead with a determined click. MacHenry hung the receiver back on the wall. Fifty-six and thirty-six. There was a hell of a lot more than time stretching between those two numbers. And now, just as events had thrown them together once before, the whole world seemed to conspire in their drifting apart. Maybe it was all for the better. Some days, giving up seemed more than just natural. It felt inevitable.

The television audio boomed. He walked into the kitchen and

turned it back down. Far from the woodstove, the room was cold as a morgue.

The screen showed a flat, desert salt pan. But not empty. People were walking slowly across the terrain. Small flags on metal stakes whipped in a strong wind. Objects were carelessly strewn across the landscape. Bundles of wires, insulation, shiny metal twisted into jagged, dangerous shapes. Then, eerily, a landing-gear leg standing upright on its tires, the massive steel looking remarkably intact except for the torn fittings at the top. Behind it, a row of seats. The camera zoomed in to show the looped belt buckles all neatly fastened. It looked like opening day at an aviation landfill.

But MacHenry knew better.

It was a crash site. The shattered plastic, the twisted wires, the metal shapes too bizarre to have ever fit together, they were all pieces of a giant puzzle that had once been a Boeing 7X7, not that the casual eye could tell. But MacHenry could. The orange flag was a marker of the sort MacHenry had stuck into the ground too many times himself. It marked the place the rescuers had found a piece of the puzzle. A tube. A ball bearing. A body. The scene flickered out and was replaced by a map.

Southern Utah, he thought. A bad place to go down. Not that there were any good ones. The distribution of the puzzle parts told him the plane had come apart in midair. The pieces had undergone a crude sorting by wind and gravity. And from the look of those seats, no fire. How do you blow up a jet without there being a fire?

The screen flickered again to a blow-dried talking head. Mac-Henry recognized him. He'd once been MacHenry's boss at the FAA. The man who'd fired him. He'd done well in the agency, rising to the topmost tier, right beneath the political appointees. MacHenry turned the volume back up.

". . . effort is being made. I can promise the traveling public that security measures are being beefed up at every airport in America and abroad."

"Is there any idea how the bombs are getting on board?"

The talking head nodded, but said, "No. Not yet. But we are working on a number of leads I can't discuss."

"It's been nearly five months since the first sabotage of the Japan

Air Lines plane. Why can't we keep terrorists from planting bombs on jets?"

"We have to win every time a terrorist tries to smuggle an explosive on a plane. But the terrorists have to get lucky just once. It takes a great deal of teamwork . . ."

MacHenry listened to the long, looping answer. *In other words, he doesn't know, and it's not our fault. He doesn't have a clue.* Out in the parlor, the telephone ran again.

"God damn it," Case swore as he punched in MacHenry's number on the autodialer. The phone trilled. "Where the hell are you?"

It was barely seven. Nobody was in at Case, Rudge, McDivitt et al. A Styrofoam cup of coffee steamed next to a wax-paper bundle containing a sticky Danish.

"Come on, MacHenry. Answer the damned phone." His desk was piled high with papers. They threatened to topple over and swamp the small square of clear space he had left. He hung up. He fingered the note he'd found wedged through the mail slot this morning. They wouldn't have to find the missing Boeing whistle-blower. He'd found them. He punched redial. The telephone clicked.

"MacHenry here."

"Where the hell have you been?" Case demanded. "Never mind. Can you be down at my office by nine? I have some very important news. For a change it's good."

"Yes. I can be there. What is it?"

"You'll see. Get over here as fast as you can. I'll be waiting." Case hung up and reread the note: *JAL 6-22-95 I know why our A/C went down* . . . "You sneaky sons of bitches. I've got you."

Shig shifted in his chair to ease the aching in his ribs. It was amazing nothing had broken, but he was bruised to the bone.

He tapped in the key words *Hibakusha Foundation* and *Nippon Aerospace Consortium*. The NPA central computer began rifling through millions of pages of documents stored on CD-ROM discs. Cross-referencing thousands of entries, the search took a while to complete.

One thing was clear. Rondon-Nomura was peanuts. Gangsters

looking to wash a few hundred million yen. Nippon Aerospace was far bigger. How far would it go? There was a time-honored collaboration between bureaucrats, politicians, and industrialists. Perhaps the *yakuza* was looking to turn the trio into a quartet. Why not? They were the ones who still had money.

A chime sounded. Shig issued the print command. Across the busy room at NPA Records Division an industrial-strength laser printer began to hum. Sheets spilled out from it into a waiting basket, one after the other, filled with selected newspaper articles, court testimonies, and police-case histories, all organized around his key-word search. This was the easy part. The hard part would come tonight when he tried to digest the information and make something of it. He watched page after page fall into the printer basket. It would be like taking a drink from a fire hydrant.

Ten minutes and one change of paper later, he had a stack of material half a meter thick. He went over to the nearest desk with a phone, then thought better of it.

He waited for the elevator to take him down to the street. The signal dinged and the light beside the door switched on, but no elevator stopped. He was the only one waiting, and pressure-sensitive tiles beneath his shoes measured his solitude. Why stop for just one? It would only break the efficient flow. The group was more important than the individual. It was a message that came in many forms.

Finally, the steel doors opened. He took the elevator down to the street. Was there time to stop at the central office of the Manufacturers Credit Bank? He checked his watch. No. Probably not.

A bank of phone booths stood in front of the National Press building. Only one was free. It was one of the new "fragrance phones" that piped in a scent, either honey-lemon or fermented seaweed. They were not equally popular. He closed the door behind him, sealing off the clamor of Hibiya Street, and heard the faint hiss of gas.

Now he knew why it was empty. Fermented seaweed. He slipped his prepaid phonecard into the receiver slot. A little window displayed how much time he had left on it. Phone calls all over Japan were absurdly cheap, all because of a war between the Telecommunications and Finance ministries. Finance owned the national phone system, but

Telecommunications set the price. It was one way the smaller ministry could stick pins into its big, powerful brother. And foreigners thought Japan was one big company! Shig punched in Ozawa's direct number.

"Yes?"

"Investigator Onishi here, sir. I have the material from Records. Would you like to review any of it?"

"Where are you calling from? Not from Records I hope."

"I'm in a phone booth outside the Press building. I can . . ." He stopped when he noticed someone hovering just beyond the phone booth's door, an impatient look on his face. Japanese phone booths came equipped with signal lights; hit the red button and it informs the person waiting outside that you'll be a while. The green means, I'll be through in a second, don't worry. Shig hit the green. "I can come to the office now if you'd like."

"No. Don't. Review them at home tonight by yourself. I want your best thinking, Onishi. Your job depends on it. Did anyone notice you at Records?"

"Not that I saw. I had an interesting experience at Nippon Aerospace."

"Save it for tomorrow. We'll talk in private. Understood?"

"Understood." The line clicked dead. Shig opened the door. The street sounds flooded back in. He saw the man waiting to use the phone. "Seaweed," he warned him.

"Ah. Thank you."

"*Do itashimashite.*" Don't mention it. Shig headed off for the subway. The man turned and waited for another booth.

SIX

The whole office fell silent as Shig walked in from the elevator lobby. Eyes flicked up from computer screens. Telephone conversations sputtered out. One of the office ladies giggled, spilling the tea she was pouring. In an office that was a sea of navy blue jackets, white shirts, and charcoal gray skirts and slacks, Shig wore drawstring pants, Nikes, and a Yomiuri Giants baseball jacket.

He ignored the hard stares and headed for Ozawa's office. A new poster had been hung on the wall beside the watercooler. A famous TV actor smoked a Mild Seven with one hand and cradled a blonde with the other. Behind him, a huge orange fireball erupted from the top of a very artificial-looking volcano. *Smoking Mild Sevens keeps my creativity at peak levels!*

The section chief's underling rose to intercept him as he headed for Ozawa's office. Instead of berating him for his appearance, the section *bucho* hurried him through Ozawa's forbidding oak door. The office buzz resumed.

Ozawa moved a file to the top of a teetering pile. He looked up. "What took you so long? It's almost ten."

"There was a lot to read." Shig had been up all night as it was. He held up the thick stack of printout.

The chief of the NPA's Economic Crimes Section switched on a microrecorder, then sat back in his chair. "You must learn to work faster, Investigator. Now, close the door. Sit down and tell me everything you've learned."

Shig Onishi shut the door. He glanced at the chair. After reading all through the night, he had the feeling that, once down, he'd never rise. "I'd prefer to stand, sir."

"State your name and rank, then let's have it."

"Shig Onishi, investigator, Economic Crimes Section of the National Police."

"*Junior* investigator. And the case assigned?"

"Rondon-Nomura. It began as a simple extortion case involving Nomura Securities. In the course of looking into the financial background behind Rondon, I found links to the Manufacturers Credit Bank of Tokyo. It's one of the least secure of the big banks."

"The record will note that Manufacturers Credit is on the Section's official Watch List," intoned Ozawa. "Go on."

"Manufacturers Credit Bank is in very bad shape. They were especially hard hit by the earthquake. Many of their mortgaged properties no longer exist. But given all of this, they still were able to loan a large sum of money to the *sokaiya* gangsters. I found that these loans were made possible through a large infusion of money from overseas deposits. I brought these findings to the section chief's attention and was given additional information on two other entities, the Hibakusha Foundation and the Nippon Aerospace Consortium."

"At the direction of the foreign minister," said Ozawa, eyeing the spinning tape cassette.

"Yes. Both the Consortium and the Foundation have large accounts at Manufacturers Credit. Nippon Aerospace was organized with Manufacturers Credit as the lead lending bank. All in all, a lot of activity for a bankrupt bank." Shig felt his knees begin to tremble. His chest throbbed. There was a hard knot of bruises under his skin. "Maybe I should sit."

"Please. Take your time. What else do I have to do but listen to you?" Ozawa reached for the butt of a Mild Seven and got it smoldering again.

Shig settled into the chair. "When I left the office after our meeting, I thought Rondon-Nomura was the most important part of the case. It's not. It's only a piece of the puzzle. In fact, it's not even a big piece."

Ozawa looked as though a foul odor had suddenly appeared in the tiny room. "Really," he said. "So Manufacturers Credit Bank is the real problem?"

"No, sir. The bank is vulnerable, the weak member of the herd. Their weakness drew the attentions of the wolf pack."

"Even thieves can't make an honest living. Is that what you've discovered?"

"No, sir. Manufacturers Credit of Tokyo was the conduit for a number of very big, and very suspicious, transactions. The one thing that seems to knit the puzzle together is Nippon Aerospace. The Consortium. Half of the companies that belong to it are Japanese, the rest are from Malaysia, Thailand, South Korea, and China."

"So. The foreign involvement the minister suspected is real?"

"Technically, yes. The Consortium's member firms are spread across half of Asia. But its funding, and its purpose, seem to be entirely Japanese."

Ozawa sighed. "The foreign minister hoped you might discover something a bit more useful." Ozawa looked at the microcassette machine as though the minister himself was riding those tiny reels round and round. "Well, go on. Tell me about this Consortium."

Shig winced as he leaned over the desk. "It consists of thirty small manufacturing firms bundled together under one name. Its Japanese members come from different *keiretsu*." These were the giant, interlocking tribes of companies that gave Japanese industry its substance and structure. The bones of the "miracle economy." Shig continued, "But NAC, the Consortium, theoretically brings them all together under one roof."

"Sometimes sworn enemies find it profitable to work together against a common foe." But Ozawa stopped. "Why do you say theoretically?"

Now it was Shig's turn to hold back a little. "I'll come to that in a moment, sir." Shig shifted in his seat. "The Consortium was funded through a loan from Manufacturers Credit Bank of Tokyo. The loans were backed by a series of very large institutional deposits. A significant sum came from the Hibakusha Foundation. When I checked, the transfers arrived from the same offshore holdings that funded the original blackmail attempt against Nomura. These transfers were made in late 1994. They were big."

"Big?" Ozawa sat up. "How big?"

Shig paused. "Nearly two hundred billion yen."

"Million?"

"No, sir. Billion."

Ozawa drew in a short, sharp breath. It *was* a lot of money.

Especially these days. "You have reached a private conclusion, Investigator?"

Shig nodded. "NAC is a shadow corporation. It lured members of three different *keiretsu* together through the promise of private funding for a very special project that even sworn enemies would find it worth cooperating over. Large institutional investors were drawn into the effort, probably by the big corporations themselves. Company retirement funds are often invested in company projects. You know how that works."

"But in a bad bank?"

Shig nodded. "That was the red flag. The Hibakusha Foundation doesn't seem to care whether it loses billions on a project so risky no solid bank would underwrite it. But there are other sources of capital." He eyed the recorder again. "I checked the account records at Manufacturers Credit for NAC. The Hibakusha Foundation is the largest single depositor. But there are others. Some of the private investors have very prominent names, sir. For example . . ."

Ozawa's hand shot out and snapped the recorder off. "Go on."

"Most of them were big names in the old LDP. But some are in the new government, too."

"Are they now?" Ozawa broke into a huge grin. Finally, here was something worth listening to! A lever that could be applied to those smug bastards in the Japan Renaissance Party. Yes, indeed. Ozawa switched the microcassette back on. "I'll need copies of everything you found. A complete list, so don't bother reading names onto my tape. Please continue, Junior Investigator. What about the Consortium itself?"

"The headquarters of Nippon Aerospace is not far from here. I decided to visit it."

Ozawa's eyes sparkled even as his face remained immobile. He looked like a frog watching a fly buzz closer, closer, lighting on a leaf.

"It was very enlightening." Shig let the last bullet fly. "NAC occupies a floor in a new building. A see-through building with very few other tenants."

"There are a lot of those these days."

"Sir, the Consortium's backers are some of the biggest industrial concerns in the world. Almost a quarter of a trillion yen flows through their books, and they live in an unfinished office with one employee."

Ozawa nearly swallowed his cigarette.

Shig hit his second wind. Or was it his twentieth? He was too tired to count. "There's a receptionist. No office furniture. Just a computer generating phony telephone calls and a screen with ghosts projected on it. Nothing at all."

"You saw all of this? You can prove it?"

"Yes, sir." Shig felt his bruised chest throb. "Nippon Aerospace is a front. What it is a front for, I don't know. Not yet."

Ozawa put his index fingers together and tapped them against his nose. He growled as though arguing with himself, then looked up. "Let's concentrate on another matter. The Hibakusha connection."

Shig had done his homework. "The Hibakusha are survivors of the two atomic attacks. There are about three hundred thousand left. About four thousand die each year, some from old age, some from the effects of the radiation. They use their investment portfolio to fund charitable projects. Clinics, retirement homes, research into radiation safety. But until now, never aerospace. I believe they are a clean organization."

"Amazing." Ozawa clapped his hands together. "Imagine. Something that I know and you do not. What a surprise!" His expression sharpened. "You run around chasing ghosts, Investigator. But why not go straight to the devil himself? Does the name Kazuo Ibuki mean anything to you?"

A small light blinked on. "The lawyer?"

"The rich, powerful old lawyer. Adviser to"—Ozawa paused, glancing at the recorder—"to many high-placed individuals. He ran the Hibakusha Foundation until it passed to a young man by the name of Ishii. That happened in late 1994." Ozawa paused, waiting for a reaction. "Well?"

"A man named Ishii is listed as CEO of the Consortium. He's young, but I don't know him personally."

"Well. You have finally graduated from first grade." Ozawa picked up a folder. "Now listen and open up the wood slats inside that head. Susumu Ishii was the top dog in the Inagawakai for two decades. Shintaro Ishii was his only son. Pure as the snow on Fujiyama. The old devil Ibuki has seen to that."

Shig rocked back in his chair. He remembered the tattooed arm of the thug guarding the empty office tower. "Then there is a connection between the Inagawakai and the Consortium?"

"Now you've reached second grade," said Ozawa as he sucked down another lungful of smoke. He let it out slowly, pleased with himself. "But knowing and proving are very different things. As for this front, this Nippon Aerospace. What is its role?" He stabbed out the last remnant of his cigarette and looked for another.

Shig's brain was firing at full RPM in a different direction. The Inagawakai buying up a false-front aerospace company! Was it money laundering, or was it something more?

Ozawa looked sour as he broke into a new pack of Mild Sevens. "Well?"

Shig's eyes refocused. "NAC is an umbrella organization. Almost like OPEC. They're supposed to negotiate favorable terms for Asian aerospace contractors. One large voice instead of thirty little squeaks."

"And what are they really?" Smoke billowed.

That was a good question. Shig didn't know the answer. "The Consortium is a front, but the manufacturers that belong to it are real enough. They make a lot of critical hardware for several big companies. Without their cooperation, aircraft production would come to a stop." Wait. Wasn't that just like the gangster's threats to Nomura? Was that the connection? "They are also involved in a plan to buy into one of those big companies."

"Which one?" asked Ozawa as he tapped a finger of ash from the tip of his cigarette.

Shig looked up. "An American company. Boeing."

Ozawa dropped the smoke and hissed like a leaky valve. He punched off the recorder again. "No wonder the foreign minister is so interested. What nerve. Boeing? You're certain?"

"Yes, sir. It's creating a big controversy in America."

"A fart in Tokyo makes them sniff in Washington." Ozawa looked distant. "The son of the Inagawakai maneuvers to buy into Boeing. With Kazuo Ibuki at his side. The old lawyer comes from a world of blackmail, threats, and dirty money. Only now—"

"Sir?" Shig interrupted. "What if this whole matter, the Consortium front, is a giant money-laundering scheme? A quarter trillion yen in dirty money for a clean piece of Boeing?"

"Another Pebble Beach, only this time not for golf fees."

Pebble Beach. The world's premier golf course had been bought by the Isutani mob with dirty money. Hundreds of millions in membership fees, all clean, were funneled back to the Japanese investors. When the scandal broke, it took down more than a few LDP politicians with it. Some of them were still in jail. Most had abandoned their old political affiliations, declared themselves new-faced reformers, and gotten elected again.

Ozawa shook his head and pursed his lips. "A golf course is one thing. Even Kazuo Ibuki wouldn't dare take on Boeing. It's too big. Too powerful. Too important to the Americans. Look how they complained when we spent a fortune on a bunch of worthless buildings. As if we would pack them up and ship them to Tokyo."

"Maybe Ibuki would try if the *keiretsu* were standing behind him."

Ozawa looked up, interested. "Go on."

"They have never been able to crack the market for airliners on their own." Shig leaned over the desk. "Sir? Perhaps Boeing is like the Manufacturers Credit Bank. They can't say no to money, no matter where it comes from. Boeing is in great difficulties. I called an old classmate over at Kokusai Securities. Take a look at this." He opened a folder and slipped a computer-generated line chart across the desk.

The line tracked the sale price of Boeing common stock over the last year. It was a slope that began at $56 a share and was now trading at $17.37.

"You've been very busy, Junior Investigator," said Ozawa.

"Boeing's reputation has been damaged by the crash of a JAL plane last June. See what it did to Boeing stock?"

"JAL was very foolish. Who would buy a jet airplane from a country that can't even build cars?"

"Yes, sir." Shig knew this was a common belief in Japan. He didn't share it. Was that his problem? "They make better cars now, but they've always built the best airplanes."

"Then why do they fall out of the sky?"

Shig had no answer for that.

"So we have a Consortium offering a pile of money just when the Americans need it most." Ozawa began tapping his fingers together again. "The big Japanese industrialists know they cannot buy into Boeing outright. The Americans would drop another bomb on us. So they let Kazuo Ibuki take the lead. And maybe the heat." Ozawa wondered what it might be worth to his section to make such an allegation stick. With Ibuki's connections, even an incomplete case would be worth a lot to bury. "An interesting path, Onishi. A very interesting path. But where does it lead? Any ideas?"

"In a typical blackmail case, the target company's cooperation is necessary for a conviction."

"My very thoughts, Investigator. I believe Boeing headquarters is in Seattle, Washington." Ozawa drummed the desktop with his fingers. "I think you'll like Seattle." He scowled. "Be sure you dress appropriately. I don't want Americans to think we all come to work in our pajamas."

"Yes, sir." Shig slowly got up, his legs stiff as two pipes. He opened the door to the office. Once more, a dozen conversations came to a sudden halt.

"And, Onishi? One more thing."

"Sir?" Shig stopped at the door.

"Watch yourself over there. Americans seem stupid and simple, but they love to blame all their troubles on us. And they can be very sneaky. Now, get going."

"Understood!"

Out on the teeming Kabuto-cho street, a crossing light had failed. The WALK signal sounded, but instantly changed to STOP. A crowd of pedestrians waited less and less patiently to cross over to the train station. From across the river of traffic the seven-note sequence of tones announced the arrival of yet another train. Still nobody challenged the tyranny of the light.

"It must have broken in the earthquake."

An indignant voice rose about the general buzz. "Someone should report this!"

"It wasn't like this before," muttered someone else.

"Everything is worse now."

Shig pushed his way to the front of the crowd. When an opening in the traffic appeared, he sprinted across the street.

What does Case have? MacHenry wondered as he let the engine in the Wagoneer warm up. He switched on the radio, but there was nothing but static. It was a typical autumn morning, cool, clear, and blustery. The sky was the hard-edged color of new steel. He wore a heavy wool shirt and a windbreaker on top of everything. His old leather flight bag, filled with a change of clothes and his all-important notebook, was on the seat beside him. The book contained the names, addresses, and phone numbers of a worldwide fraternity of aviators who could be called upon to supply what he might need. It had come in handy more than once.

The steering wheel groaned as he turned it one way, then the other, loosening the old Jeep's joints for the drive into Washington. Was Lawson Wheelwright there with Case? That would be a break all right. MacHenry figured that five minutes of questioning would reveal whether the Boeing inspector was the real thing or a nut case.

The temperature gauge stirred off its peg. He put the car in gear and rolled down the steep drive. At the bottom, he turned toward town.

He tried tuning the radio as the elderly Jeep bounced over the potholed blacktop. ". . . from sources at . . ." The signal faded to static again as he rounded a hill, then clarified.

". . . ended in apparent suicide this morning at Dulles . . ."

What about Dulles? MacHenry quickly turned the tuning knob one way, then another. The voice faded, overpowered by the thump thump thump of an adjacent station's music. Then the voice returned. "Wanted in connection with a previous case of arson in . . . identified as . . ." Thump thump thump. ". . . dental records will be used to . . ."

MacHenry spun the wheel and stomped on the brakes. The Jeep wagon skidded to a stop. What had they just said? Arson?

". . . representatives of the Japanese foundation that funded the restoration deplored the violence, stating that they were here to help, not hurt, America. Now, on the worsening political fortunes of President . . ."

MacHenry threw the Wagoneer into Drive.

The Wednesday commuter traffic was thick, and it took an hour and twenty minutes from the moment MacHenry left Round Hill to when he rolled across the Roosevelt Bridge and into the capital. He found parking space outside the offices of Case, Rudge, McDivitt et al. There were some suspicious-looking characters lurking in the alley beyond a shuttered Indian restaurant. They were sharing a bottle. Laughing. Breath steaming in the sharp air. MacHenry grabbed his bulging flight bag. There was nothing in the Jeep worth stealing. He left the doors unlocked to keep anyone from breaking the glass. Winter was coming and it would be too damned cold to drive without a window. He walked up to the door and pressed CRM's button.

"Who is it?"

"Mr. Case? It's—"

"MacHenry! Get up here fast." The door buzzed. He pushed inside. Would Case know about the incident at Dulles? That his star witness was dead? He punched the elevator button and the door slid open. A musty old smell issued from the cab. He stepped in and hit three. Case had sounded pleased when he'd first called. He didn't sound that way anymore.

"After what happened early this morning, I'm very happy you suggested I check in at the Hay Adams," said Shintaro Ishii. He looked shaken. A man burns to death on your very doorstep. A life reduced to ash and a dark stain on the concrete. What if he'd been there when that fool set himself on fire? Imagine having to see such a thing. Or explain what you saw to the local police. "I'm still a bit shocked." The limo was so hushed the engine was impossible to hear. The car seemed to float a few feet above the highway.

"He must have been desperate," said Bridger. "Security caught him trying to break in. You know he set some fires out at Boeing? He was wanted by the police."

"I don't doubt it."

"Our men called them. If they'd only come right away . . ." Bridger shook his head. "He got loose and tried to burn the hangar down. Security caught him just as he was about to light the thing off. Thank God there was a fire extinguisher there."

"Yes, well. Now that is over, isn't it?"

"Absolutely." Bridger shook his head. "A man like that, an arsonist, a blackmailer, well. You just can't predict what his state of mind might have been."

"Blackmail?" Shintaro swore he heard his father's chuckle. He sat up straighter.

"Didn't Kazuo tell you? This man had made threats against Boeing and the Foundation as well. He was a real Japan-basher."

Kazuo? That was very familiar of him. "He never mentioned it to me."

Bridger turned. His raincoat whispered against butter-soft leather. "Kazuo's a very busy man."

How well did this foreigner know Ibuki? "So it seems."

MacHenry had barely touched the doorknob when it was yanked open. Case stood there, cane in hand. He was furious enough to set off a Geiger counter.

"Get in here." He spun on his cane and marched back to his desk. He yanked a cord and the window blinds went dark. A special ottoman, worn to threads and faded almost pink by use and time, stood next to his chair.

MacHenry followed. A metal cart had been wheeled into the office. A television was on top. A VCR on a middle shelf. A tape of a television news program was running.

"I heard on the way in that—" MacHenry began, but Case cut him off.

"Don't talk." Case sat down and raised his leg onto the ottoman. He glanced at the screen. "Watch."

The talking heads dissolved to a black screen with a lit hangar in the center of view. A jet's sharklike tail drifted by left to right. Was it Dulles? "Where did you get this?"

"I taped it off the news. Some person with a video camera caught the whole thing, and the networks just sucked it right up. Probably paid a hundred bucks for it. Now be quiet and watch."

The image bounced a little, swung one way, then the other. Suddenly, a tiny red dot appeared where the two doors were ajar. It flickered like a windblown candle. "Is that—"

"Sssh. Here it comes."

The view zoomed in on the dot. It became a fuzzy orange globe. Then the focus became sharper, though still imperfect. It was good enough for MacHenry to see that the orange globe was a fire. And at the center of the angry boil of smoke and flame was a human being. The figure stumbled, fell, then seemed to half-rise again before falling a second time. A white cloud of fire retardant billowed out the open doors.

Case hit a freeze button. "Look very closely." He rewound, then went forward again. Red dot. Orange globe. Focus to the opening flower of fire streaming from a man's body. A man who was burning alive. The human form struggled inside the flames, stumbled, rose on one knee, then fell. The fire extinguisher.

"I heard it on the radio. They said it was attempted arson. Why would he do it?"

"I doubt very much that he did. Watch again." Once more the action reversed, stopped, then ran forward.

"What am I supposed to see?" MacHenry squinted. The tail fin drifted by. The hangar doors had been open a crack. Now the crack was wider. Was it an illusion? No. "Who opened the doors for him?"

Case smiled. "Now that's a very good question, MacHenry. The man's on fire. How is he going to start those doors opening?"

"Someone else was there. The one with the extinguisher?"

"They waited until he was dead before hitting him with it. Yeah. The report said security found him. But what kind of security officer opens the doors, shoves him outside, and watches him burn? Helpful son of a bitch, wasn't he? You might call it assisted suicide. Then again, you might call it murder." Case let the sequence run forward again, right to the point where the human torch collapsed to the ground. He froze the image.

Case pulled a paper from a pile on his desk. "Okay. We can't do anything more ourselves. I have an old friend at the FBI. If I can get him to do it, I'll ask them to work up that image and see what they can see. It would take a Richardson Table. Spook stuff. I don't suppose you have access to that kind of equipment, do you?"

"Not anymore." MacHenry was surprised. How did a lawyer know about Richardson Tables? They were exotic gear designed to work with satellite imagery. He'd managed to get the National Reconnaissance Office to use one to find parts of a crashed airliner in a jungle, but that was long ago.

"Now, what do you make of this?" Case shot the paper across the desk to MacHenry.

It was a sheet torn from a small lined notebook. Cheap and completely untraceable. The writing, MacHenry decided, was not that of a crazy man. It was meticulous. Slanted uniformly. The hand of a person who valued order. Someone he could imagine knowing. Someone like MacHenry himself. He read.

> JAL 6-22-95 I know why our A/C went down. Nonspec TMC components have been used at assembly. They were passed through testing. I have five samples. Leave a letter here tonight if you want to take this on. I hope you will. It has to stop.
>
> L. Wheelwright IA10984

MacHenry looked up. "When did he leave this?"

"Sometime last night. Somehow he got from here to Dulles. You're the aviation expert. What's it all mean?"

"June twenty-second. The date is obviously the first 7X7 crash. The numbers are from his FAA inspection-authority license. It's a low one. He's been around. I'm not sure whether this TMC he refers to is a component or the initials of the company that makes it."

"Those pins you were talking about? The bolts that hang the engines? What if some bad bolts got mixed in and installed? What's with this 'nonspec' business?"

"Everything that goes into an airliner has to have complete documentation. 'Nonspec' could mean the record is incomplete. That happens all the time. But it could also mean they're counterfeit."

"You mean bogus." There was no deflecting Case. He was like

a gale that swept everything, even MacHenry's objectivity, along for the ride.

"Boeing would never let counterfeit bolts slip into the assembly line. Maybe a bankrupt airline. But not Boeing."

"Take a look, MacHenry." Case nodded at the frozen image of a man on fire. "What do you believe?"

It looked like a bright flower caught unfolding against a dark backdrop. Only at its heart, a man had died a horrible death. The man who had written the note he held in his hands.

"What do you know about bogus parts?"

MacHenry shifted his eyes away from the screen. "The worse the economy, the more incentive there is to use them. Certified parts are expensive. Remember the thousand-dollar toilet seat the Air Force had on one of its planes? The seat was cheap. But the paper trail that proved it was everything it was supposed to be was what cost so much. Bogus parts look like the real thing, they come packaged like the real thing. But they aren't."

"Who's supposed to guard against them?"

"The FAA. But the FAA has a fleet of planes, and they discovered bogus parts on them, too."

"Figures. Lawson Wheelwright seemed to think he had his hands on something. Assume for a moment that some crappy part, a bad fuse pin, slips through. Who would know the difference?"

"If it passed testing and never caused a problem in the field, then just the financial officer who sees a widget coming through the books at half-price. It might not be the kind of mistake he'd raise a flag over. Not these days. But after the first ship went down, I guarantee you, the FAA was looking."

"Maybe they don't want to find a problem. They put their seal of approval on a plane that hadn't even flown yet, remember? Who else?"

"The FBI. The Quantico lab would get involved in a case of suspected sabotage."

"They say it's bombs. Who else?"

"JAL. The Japanese civil aviation authorities. Now United. And of course, Boeing. They know their own plane better than anyone."

"And Boeing had the most to lose if the world discovers they screwed up. The most to gain by burying their mistakes."

"Never."

Both their eyes went to the frozen image on the screen.

"Look with your eyes, MacHenry. Not your heart. You said you knew someone out at Boeing?"

"It's not Boeing." MacHenry shook his head.

"Okay. Forget Boeing for the moment. Who makes these bogus parts?"

"Counterfeit shops have sprung up all over South America. Even here in the States."

"They come from Asia, too?"

MacHenry nodded. "The problem is enormous. The counterfeit shops get caught only by bad luck."

"Or when something breaks." Case breathed in deeply, let it out slowly. "So maybe it's not Boeing. Maybe it's one of these counterfeiters. Maybe Wheelwright knew some names and they came after him. Can you buy that?"

"Maybe." MacHenry reread the note. "I don't know what a TMC is. I could probably find out." He looked up. "That means going to Boeing. To Seattle."

"Did I mention it?" Case looked up. His half-glasses were perched on his nose. "I've booked you on the afternoon flight out of Dulles. I assume there's no reason you can't be on it?"

MacHenry shook his head. Case was a confident old bastard. "I'll call my contact out there." He checked his watch. "I doubt they're open for business yet."

"Then there's time to look at the tape again."

Case busied himself at the VCR while MacHenry popped open his flight bag and pulled out a thick binder. It was filled with names, some entered in pen, some pencil; others were just business cards taped to an appropriate place. He'd jotted down some saying he'd picked up from each one. Some stray wisdom. More than once, remembering those pieces of advice had saved his life. A star beside a name meant the person was dead. MacHenry had kept it from the first day he began flying for a living. There were plenty of stars in the book. He opened it to the *D* section.

"Don't tell your pal what you're up to," said Case. "He'll dummy up on you if you do."

He hadn't spoken with Joe DelVecchio in quite some time, and he'd never lied to him. Not once. MacHenry's world was held together by personal honor and trust. "I won't mislead him."

"You'd make a lousy lawyer, MacHenry."

"Thank you, Mr. Case."

SEVEN

TMC. TMC. What could it mean? His breath steamed, condensing against the cool glass of the windshield. He put the Wagoneer into Drive and moved off from the curb. A battered Ford Escort started up and followed four cars behind.

JAL. Now United. What was the common link? Both ships had crashed from cruise configuration, from high altitude, the safest place for an airliner to be. What was a TMC? The fact that it passed quality testing meant either that it functioned enough like the real thing to get a passing grade, or that the inspector wasn't doing his job. Inspector. Wasn't Wheelwright responsible for QA at the Boeing engine facility?

MacHenry slipped in behind a brown UPS truck and let it clear the path through the afternoon traffic. He was driving on automatic pilot. It worked until he followed the truck into a delivery zone. He sheepishly pulled back out into the street; the UPS driver gave him a strange look as he passed.

TMC. It could stand for almost anything. Narrowing it down to the area of Lawson Wheelwright's expertise helped some. TMC. Something to do with the engines. Or with the systems that served them. Hydraulics? Fuel? Power? Controls? That bumped the parts count into the millions. What was a TMC? Was it as big as a system? Or small as a gasket?

He considered it. If Wheelwright possessed five samples, they had to be small. A bolt? There were millions on each airliner. Some were common. A few were critical. These were known as Jesus bolts. As rare as they were, an airliner as big and as complex as the Boeing 7X7 might have hundreds of Jesus bolts. The failure of any one was capable of causing a fatal crash.

The drive out to the airport brought him nearly halfway back home to Round Hill. He felt a kind of cold dread as he neared the airport. Dulles. This was where Lawson Wheelwright had died this very morning. How did Wheelwright get from Roger Case's office all the way out here? Who drove him?

He remembered that he was supposed to pick Julia up in a few days on her return from Hawaii. She was coming into Dulles, too. What would he say when he saw her? Somehow, he could imagine the words *I'm sorry* coming from both their mouths at the same instant. Sorry for the time spent trying. Sorry for the time wasted. Sorry for the hopes too fragile to bear up under their own sodden weight. He'd lived much of his life alone. He could get used to it again. But is that what he wanted? Figuring it out made solving the Boeing mystery look trivial. It would be easy to just stop. To just let it go. Easy.

The Dulles toll road was quiet. It was just as well. He was too busy sifting through the meager horde of facts he and Case had managed to squeeze from theory. Nothing was ever known beyond doubt.

At Dulles, MacHenry turned into the short-term parking lot. A terminal addition was under way, and long-term was filled with construction equipment. He found an empty slot and pulled in. As he got out, the crackle and roar of a departing jet made him look up.

A 737 rose from the runway, swept over the trees, and banked west. It had the new, big-fan engines on it. They were remarkably quiet for all their power. There were only two of them, just like on the 7X7. A proven design. One that had been wrung out through hard trial and error. Very few had ever been lost. What was different about the new, 7X7 twinjet? He slammed the Wagoneer's door shut. What was different about the Boeing 7X7?

The one man who knew for sure was dead.

Roger Case stared out his window as he flipped the telephone to his other ear. "Aaron, that's bullshit," he said. "And we both know it."

"So what do I know? Maybe he caught a bus or a cab." It was Aaron Freeman, the one agent at the FBI who would still talk to him. "Hey. Come on, Roger. Lighten up. I just put a file to bed on this felon friend of yours."

"He was *here* sometime in the middle of the night, you know.

He couldn't walk thirty miles to Dulles. So you tell me. How'd he get out there? Flap his arms? Someone took him. Who? How come this doesn't interest you?"

Freeman sighed. "What, he was your client or something?"

"No. He's not my client. He's dead. And I don't know everything yet. But do me a favor. Pull that videotape apart. You have the labs. Look at it, for Christ's sake. Somebody opened the hangar doors for him and then waited until he was dead before they used the fire extinguisher. Did you talk to those security people out at that hangar?"

"Now you're offending me, Roger."

"So? Who are they?"

"Two *Soldier of Fortune* clones. I wouldn't be surprised to find out they've got yanked credentials from across the river." By this he meant the Agency.

"That doesn't get you interested?"

"Why should it? I'm *glad* there's a place they can go to make an honest buck. They can't all sell their memoirs and hawk bulletproof vests, can they?"

"You aren't taking this seriously."

"I am. Look, Counselor. They did their job and they handed me my case all wrapped up in a nice big bow. What do you want from me?"

"Take the videotape to the lab and pull it apart. Then I'll shut up. Is that a lot to ask? Send a courier. I'll have the tape ready. Or you could get your hands on the original over at—"

"The station won't hand it over voluntarily. We've been down that road. I'd have to subpoena it. You got that much time?"

Case paused. "There could be a real lead in it."

"Lead? What lead? You got crap."

"Prove it. Send a courier. Pick up this tape. Pull that image apart and call me back." Case hung up.

"Flight 51, service to Seattle, is now boarding at Gate Thirty-two. All passengers should . . ."

MacHenry got in the boarding line. It moved quickly. The afternoon flight to Seattle wouldn't go out full. Not by a long shot. What equipment are we flying? he wondered. Dulles to SeaTac was a long-haul route. Probably a DC-10 or its modern cousin, the MD-11. Maybe a 767. Jumbos. Both were going to feel mighty empty unless . . .

All his thoughts came to a sudden stop when he looked out the lounge window.

It was a Boeing 7X7.

"Ticket?" asked the agent at the gate.

MacHenry handed over the envelope with the same leaden motion a man might have after spinning the barrel of a revolver and placing it next to his temple. Would the next sound be a click or an explosion?

The agent tore off the boarding pass with a tiny rip. "Thank you, sir. Next?"

He found his place in the nine-abreast ocean of dark red seats in the middle cabin. A window seat. Once, when he was flying as a captain of the line, he'd refused to take a plane that had not been properly serviced. It had cost him his job when the problem turned out to be paperwork and not real. But how was he to know?

What should he do now? He knew there was a real chance there were problems with the new Boeing. He didn't know what they were. Was that reason enough to get off and fly on a different plane? He looked around. The 7X7 was big. Everything about it had the same outscale feel of the 747 jumbo. But there were only two engines. He looked out his window and saw the port turbine extending far ahead of the wing's leading edge. TMC. What was it? A shadow fell across him.

A trim blond woman came to a stop in the aisle. Her short hair was glossy and thick. "Is this Twenty-eight D?" she asked. There was only the slightest trace of an accent. Not enough to pin down. She seemed perfectly ordinary in her jeans, black silk turtleneck, and tweed jacket. Her gold wire-framed glasses seemed a size too large for her small face. Her lace-up shoes were flat and sensible. She looked like a graduate student. A librarian. She held her ticket against the number stamped above the seat.

MacHenry moved his papers for her to sit. "Lots of empty seats," he said as she placed a soft-sided bag under his feet. "You could have a whole row to yourself."

"No, this is where I'm supposed to be."

"Your choice." There was something odd about her face. It was wide, her eyes far apart, her skin almost translucent. Her eyes were dark brown, almost black. That was a little unusual in a blonde, wasn't it?

She buckled in. And odd scent wafted over from her direction. A perfume. Not a bad one. He couldn't put a name to it. Part sweet, part dark, a flower blossoming at midnight.

The lights flickered once. A tone sounded. A tug began pushing them back from the gate. A deep rumble rose to a roar as first one, then the second engine spooled up.

"Welcome aboard Flight 51, nonstop service to Seattle. The captain asks that you take the time to check all . . ."

MacHenry was flying this beast to Seattle. He decided to make the best of it. He reached into his jacket and pulled out his wallet. He still had his old FAA ID card, but more important, his Airline Transport Pilot license. It was out-of-date, too, but it carried type ratings from the Martin 404 up to the stretch DC-8, the freighter version of the venerable Douglas jet. An ATP identified him as one of the fraternity. He slipped both out as a flight attendant came by.

"Excuse me," he said to her. He reached across the quiet blonde sitting next to him. "Could you pass these along to the flight deck? I'd like a word with the captain when he can spare a minute."

She gave a close look at MacHenry's credentials, then glanced at him to see if the picture and the FAA ID card matched. They did. Still she was wary: "I'll let the captain know after we take off."

"Thank you." MacHenry watched as she retreated up the cavernous cabin.

"Are you a pilot?" asked his seatmate.

"I used to be." The engines throttled up, then back down as the jumbo jet began to taxi out for takeoff. She looked too young to be a nervous flier. But she did look uneasy. Her hands were roped with tendon and muscle, strong looking. "My name's MacHenry." He offered his own hand.

Her grip was mannish and firm. "Maria. This looks like a brandnew plane. Yes?"

The 7X7 squealed to a stop for the briefest pause, then turned out onto the active runway.

"It is. Probably no more than a few months at most." Here it comes. He knew the takeoff was an instant away. The moment of maximum vulnerability. Yet neither crash had occurred on takeoff. That was odd all by itself. Cruise was the safest portion. . . .

The engines wound up into a tremendous shout. The brakes released. The lightly loaded jumbo leaped forward like a greyhound bounding from the gate. The nose came up smartly. The wings clawed for lift. With none of the saggy feeling so common in the old days, the 7X7 ramped solidly up into the night, banking west by northwest.

TMC. What could work so well under such tremendous pressure, yet fail at altitude when so much less was asked of it? What sabotage worked when the regular gremlins were fast asleep?

All MacHenry could say with certainty was that the TMC, whatever it was, seemed to be working.

Shig had to hand it to Boeing; they were waiting for him at the SeaTac airport, ready to whisk him straight from his flight from Tokyo to corporate headquarters. But the effect was unsettling. He felt cut adrift in time and space. The dateline crossing. The hours spent aloft. It was all he could do to focus as he sat in the conference room, staring out the window into the late afternoon gloom.

The conference room was as formal as a chessboard prior to the first move. Shig was in a rumpled navy suit. Two men in charcoal suits sat across a polished cherry table from him: Sam Nakamoto, Japanese liaison, and Walter Abrams, a VP from Boeing's Legal Affairs. Nakamoto was as young as Shig, Abrams a few years older. There wasn't an ashtray in sight.

"I don't believe I've ever met a Japanese policeman," said Abrams as he fingered Shig's card.

"Economic Crimes isn't like the real police," Shig answered. "They don't let us carry guns or make arrests."

"Still, Japanese police methods must work. Your crime rate is the envy of the world."

"We manage our statistics as well as our criminals."

Nakamoto launched into a discourse on why Japanese society was so secure and lawabiding. Shig looked away.

Three tumblers filled with ice water sat untouched and sweating. A computer screen stared blankly back, a tiny cursor symbol blinking over and over. Spotlighted photographs hung on three of the walls, arranged chronologically.

The first photo was an old silvertint. On it, two men shoved a spidery seaplane into shallow water, a big wooden barn behind. It must be the first Boeing, thought Shig. Was one of those men the founder himself? He'd noticed that like most big Japanese companies, Boeing bore the stamp of its founder. Portraits and busts and historical artifacts were displayed all over the place. Mostly though, there were airplane pictures. The last photo on the wall was in full color: a Boeing 7X7 with Mount Rainier glowing in gold, sunset light.

Out the plate-glass window at the end of the room, the traffic on East Marginal Way flowed heavily in both directions. The afternoon light was absorbed by the clouds and the rain; the world was awash in a wet gloom. It was the precise moment when a window begins to fill with interior light, with reflections, turning its back upon the outside world and itself into a dark mirror. Streetlights were on, and rain spattered noiselessly against the insulated glass.

Shig wondered, how are they recording this?

Nakamoto wound down, then stopped. Abrams put both hands flat to the table. "Sam is a real fan of all things Japanese," he said with a smile. "Now. Perhaps you could tell us exactly what the National Police Agency is looking for, Mr. Onishi?"

In Japan, he'd have to ease his way into it. He decided that here, in America, he could be more direct. "I'm here to investigate a case that involves elements of Japanese organized crime."

"The *yakuza*," Nakamoto piped in, eager.

"If not the *yakuza*, then at least their money," said Shig. "Specifically, the second-largest criminal organization in Japan. The Inagawakai." Shig rubbed his eyes and took a drink of ice water. It woke him up some. Maybe he should start smoking, after all. As the poster back in Tokyo said: *Mild Sevens give you the competitive edge!* He put the glass down and continued.

"The *yakuza* made lots of money during our big-boom time. All that accumulated money has to be converted into a profitable, legal business before it can be used. We think Boeing may now be the target."

"Profitable?" Abrams shook his head. "I doubt it. You must understand. Boeing is going through some tough times. We've launched a brand-new aircraft into a very challenging market. There have been tragic incidents as well. They've created great difficulties for us."

Shig nodded. There were two wrecks now. Almost a thousand people dead. A society run by hungry lawyers. I bet it does.

"It's had a terrible impact on our order book," Abrams continued. "So long as Boeing remains targeted by terrorists, who wants to order a plane from us? So, you see, we aren't a very lucrative target for a blackmailer."

Just the opposite, thought Shig. A powerful company would be much less vulnerable. "Still, my agency believes that evidence of blackmail exists."

"What are the particulars of your case, Mr. Onishi?"

Shig took a deep breath and began. When he was done, the silence that followed was so pronounced he turned to see if someone new had entered the room. The door was closed.

"Investigator Onishi," said Abrams. "I have visited the offices of the Nippon Aerospace Consortium. When we were drawing up contracts for the 7X7, I had the chance to stay in Tokyo with some of their legal staff. There is no possibility whatsoever that they are engaged in any sort of shadowy deal."

"You visited their offices?"

Abrams nodded. "I was frankly very impressed at how hardworking and diligent they all were. I can say without hesitation that the Consortium is completely untainted by any money laundering."

"Forgive me, but I am personally convinced this is so."

"Come now," said Abrams with a smile. "If you were really sure, why are you here asking for our help?"

Shig blinked. Abrams had a point. "We don't know enough to bring a case against them. We need your help for that."

Abrams shook his head. "Investigate one of our most important subcontractors? Can you imagine what bad blood that might create? And on what evidence? A failing bank you won't even tell us the name of?" He paused. "Are you sure this isn't about the first incident? The JAL loss? I know it's upset a great many people in Japan."

"I work for Economic Crimes Section, not the Civil Aviation Authority."

"Well." Abrams sat back, a nervous tic on his otherwise bland face. "I would think your agency could look into Japanese criminals much more easily in Japan. They aren't here at Boeing."

"Has Boeing received any direct threats?"

Abrams scowled. "To be honest, I wish we had received something. It would be easier to trace who's responsible for bombing JAL and now United. The only threats we got were after the fact. Our FBI considered them inauthentic."

"There's been no note, no"—Shig paused—"*authentic* threats then?"

"None. Boeing is a big family. One hundred and twenty thousand men and women. I can't say everyone is happy. We've been laying off, you know. But other than a few isolated incidents, we've had no cause for concern."

"How isolated?"

"One," said Abrams.

"A lunatic," piped in Nakamoto. "Every company has one."

"That's right, Sam. We had a little incident last May with a disgruntled employee. But I imagine you have those in Japan, too."

More than you know. "What did he do?"

"He set a small fire," said Abrams. "Some project records were destroyed. But nothing valuable was lost. The police were notified. That was all."

"What kind of project records?"

"I'm not entirely sure."

"Was he involved with Nippon Aerospace products?"

Abrams shook his head. "He was in Propulsion Engineering. That's where engines and engine parts come in from our suppliers for testing. Nippon Aerospace doesn't build engines. None of their products ever went through Propulsion Engineering."

"We wish we could be of greater assistance," soothed Nakamoto. *"Itsu made o-tomari desu ka?"*

"I'll be here until I find something," Shig answered testily. Be patient, his father would be saying. Watch it, Ozawa had told him.

Americans are sneaky. "Are there copies of these lost records anywhere?"

"I'd have to check. But they were nothing vital. And I don't see how they relate to your investigation."

In other words, forget it. "I see," said Shig.

"Is there anything else we can do?" asked Abrams. "I feel badly that you've come all this way for so little."

Me, too. "What about records on Boeing's trade with the Consortium?"

Abrams chuckled again. "Please don't take this wrong, but I don't think you know what you're asking for. Take the new plane. The 7X7. Nippon Aerospace supplies us a third of the basic structure. Fabricated assemblies arrive in Seattle every day of the week. In some ways, the record-keeping task is just as big as building the plane itself."

Record keeping was something Shig could respond to. He was a Waseda-trained accountant, after all.

"Everything that goes into a Boeing airplane has a complete pedigree," Abrams explained. "From the time the metal was refined to the last coat of paint before it gets shipped. We know who made what, where it came from, and what tests it passed along the way. An unbroken chain from beginning to end. It all goes into the Master Project Archives."

Shig imagined an airliner had millions of pieces. Each with its own, documented history. The record-keeping demands would be staggering. "Everything has this—what was it? Pedigree?"

"Everything. That adds up to a lot of records. Enough," said Abrams, "to fill this room with data discs and tape reels. I can see that you get a look at whatever you want, but sifting through all of that with no notion of what you're hunting for seems like a pointless exercise."

Shig scowled. Why were they acting like a sack of cement, utterly yielding and so difficult to pick up?

Abrams supplied one answer without being asked. "You must understand, the Consortium is a valuable partner. We wouldn't want even a hint of mistrust to creep into our partnership."

Shig nodded. "Teamwork is vital."

"And," Abrams went on, "Japanese airlines are some of our very best customers. They specify that each Boeing-built plane contain a certain percentage of Japanese-made parts."

"And if the plane does not?"

"We're careful that they do."

"I see." Shig could imagine they were. When it came to saying yes and acting no, nobody did it better than the Japanese. If they wanted domestic parts, they'd get them. One way or the other.

"We can't afford to make wild accusations of criminal involvement."

"Certainly not." Shig tried a new angle. "Have there been any problems with delivery of items built by the Consortium? Any slow-downs? Examples of poor quality? Sometimes threats can be subtle."

"Just the opposite. The Consortium is on time, on budget, and to be completely frank, their product is superior to what we could build right here in Seattle." Abrams opened a calendar. "Tomorrow morning at eight there's a shipment of fuselage panels due in. Would you like to see them for yourself?"

Shig thought of the stacks of papers, discs, and reels of tape. And one little unimportant mound of ash. A disgruntled employee. He looked up and nodded. "All right."

Abrams looked to his liaison. "Make the arrangements for seven-thirty in the morning, Sam." He turned back to Shig. "We value our relationship with all our subcontractors. Everything has to fit together properly. Not just materials, but people, too. That's the Boeing way."

"In Japan," said Shig, "we call it a *keiretsu*. Your government is very critical of us for it."

"Competition is good to a point," said Abrams, "but cooperation is even better."

Ozawa couldn't have said it any better, thought Shig. He gathered his papers and stood. "I'll be here to see the shipment arrive tomorrow morning. And those records that were lost? The ones that were burned? I assume there are copies someplace?"

"In Project Archives," said Abrams. "But I can't promise they'd be available by tomorrow morning."

"Then tomorrow afternoon would be fine," said Shig. "I appreci-ate your efforts to assist us in this investigation. As you said, cooperation is the key. We need to work together to solve this. Like one big family."

Nakamoto bowed. "*Kom ban wa.* The liaison staff would like to invite you to dinner, Onishi-san."

"No thanks," Shig broke in rather rudely. It was not a very Japanese thing to do, and even Nakamoto noticed. "There's a baseball game tonight at the Kingdome. I'll see you both in the morning."

The cabin lights dimmed automatically as the twinjet jumbo leveled off at forty-seven thousand feet. Far below, MacHenry could see the first lights come on in the tiny West Virginia hamlets sweeping below the 7X7's long, elegant wing. His seatmate seemed absorbed by a book. MacHenry noted it was in German, so maybe he'd been right. She was a foreigner with a good command of English. Maria could be a German name. But her bones didn't seem right. They were too delicate. She was pretty. Very pretty, even. But there was an odd sense of uncomfortable mixture about her.

A flight attendant came by and leaned over. "Mr. MacHenry? The flight deck is available, but don't make a big fuss about it. We aren't supposed to do it these days. Security. You know."

"Thanks." MacHenry unbuckled and placed Roger Case's notes on the seat. "Excuse me," he said to Maria. He eased by her, then remembered Case's warning to trust no one. He reached back, picked up his work notes, and slid them carefully into the overhead bin.

MacHenry followed her forward, feeling the vibrations coursing through the big jet's floor. The decking was made of a composite, some kind of stiff plasticlike material. It was supposedly fireproof, insulating, and far lighter than the old metal floor structure. But it shook. Or was the entire plane shaking? Shake it off, he told himself.

First class was dead to the world, the big reclining leather seats all the way back, a scattering of lamps shining pools of light over a few readers. Three attendants were gathered at the forward galley, making small talk that stopped the instant MacHenry appeared.

The cockpit bulkhead door was locked. It took a call and a buzz to gain admission. "Call when you're ready to go back to your seat." She turned and left. The door locked shut behind her.

MacHenry entered a softly lit, humming chamber that was at once completely familiar and totally alien. He stood there for a moment, watching.

The 7X7's cockpit was a study in tans and off-whites. Sheepskin pads covered both pilot and first officer's seats. Five big screens were arrayed across the instrument panel, alive with bright blue data. Smaller screens were mounted on the center console between the two pilots. Very few conventional switches or instruments were in evidence. It gave MacHenry the eerie sense of seeing something superficially simple, yet impossibly complex.

"Roger, Indianapolis," said the first officer. "Heading three three zero for United 52 heavy." The big jet banked to the right, then leveled.

The first officer on the right had his hands on the yoke. The captain on the left was entering data into a keyboard on the cockpit center-aisle stand. They both looked barely old enough to be allowed to glue plastic model airplanes together, much less guide a half-million-pound transport through the night at .85 Mach. MacHenry cleared his throat.

The captain looked up. "Hey. Welcome aboard, Mr. MacHenry." He held up MacHenry's ATP license and FAA identity cards. "We aren't supposed to do this, but I thought with your background, we could make an exception. My name's Marston. Mr. Bates here will do his best to keep us flying while we chat." The first officer turned and nodded.

Bates looked nervous, thought MacHenry. But then, what copilot doesn't? He collected his license and ID. "I appreciate it, Captain." The word tasted odd when used to identify someone so young. Yet, MacHenry had once looked like this himself. What had the old pelicans said behind his back? He could guess. "Where are we?" he said, looking down at the dark ground. "Lost again?"

There was only one permissible answer: *certainly*. MacHenry waited for it. Airline pilots were loathe to brag, to take credit. They elevated modesty to a religion.

"Lost?" The captain tapped the navigation screen. "No, sir. We couldn't get lost if we tried. This ship has triple-redundant navigation computers, plus a satellite feed to keep them all honest. To tell you the truth, it's easier to fly and navigate than a little private plane."

Marston pointed to a jump seat. "Take a chair and I'll give you the nickel tour."

MacHenry pulled down a folding jump seat. "I've never had a chance to see the front office of one of these before."

"It's a real treat. I came up from the 767. I tell you, this ship hardly needs us at all." The captain pointed to the five screens that took up most of the instrument panel. The blue light rising from them gave his skin an odd pallor.

Flight data was displayed on one; radar and course information on another; engine and systems parameters in the middle; and a complete backup set over on the copilot's side. A separate screen was dedicated to checklists, plus two more for the communications gear. "It's just one big video game the Octopus plays by itself," the captain said when he'd identified them all. "We just kind of watch over things."

"Octopus?"

"Officially it's called AIMS. The Aircraft Information Management System. It used to be the Aircraft Integrated Data System, but you know what that spells."

"Yes. What does this Octopus do?"

"The ships you commanded were mechanically controlled. Pull the wheel and steel cables connected you to the control surfaces. Even the hydraulic systems were basically mechanical. They just used fluid instead of cable. That's all gone." The captain patted the glareshield. "We're a fly-by-wire transport. Everything is hooked up by way of a central ship's data system. Move a switch up here in the cockpit and a signal gets sent down a pair of wires. AIMS is what they call it on the ground, but it's the Octopus to us."

"Interesting. Ever hear of something called a TMC?"

The copilot turned.

"TMC?" the captain said. "Let's see, you mean terminal maintenance chaos?" He chuckled. "That's what we've got on this ship. Mechanics used to spend hours chasing squawks. They depended on it for overtime. Now the Octopus tells them what's wrong, when it happened, and what to do about it." He smiled a warm and not altogether genuine smile.

"The central ship's computer, this Octopus," said MacHenry, "are the maintenance files downloaded after every flight?"

"The Octopus doesn't wait that long. It transmits it in real time over ACARS." By this he meant a dedicated frequency monitored by the airline. "I'll show you what I mean. Tom, kill your standby horizon for a second, will you?"

MacHenry watched as the first officer powered down the small gyroscope. The peanut horizon was designed to give the crew emergency altitude information in case the big screens all failed at once. Its own battery was kept constantly charged.

A red light went on beside the small instrument. Almost at once, an error message scrolled across one of the systems-advisory displays set into the center-aisle stand.

B/U Horizon 2 Fail Internal Pwr ACARS Comm Select?

The captain punched in a negative response. He turned. "If I hit yes, the Octopus would automatically transmit the fault message. It gets routed to Seattle, and some mechanic would be waiting with another horizon as we pulled into the gate. Tom? Power it back up."

The fault message blanked out.

"Very impressive. What if a major system failed?"

"Same thing."

"What if you had to shut down an engine? Would they be waiting with a new one?" MacHenry said it as evenly as he could.

Marston paused a few fractions of a second too long. "Well, we don't really worry too much about that. These engines are light-years ahead of the old Hoovers you had to fly with. Can't figure how you kept watch over all those dials and switches."

"We had flight engineers."

"Those were the days. The Octopus handles that all now, and it doesn't ask for overtime or make passes at the stews." Marston chuckled again. "I noticed you were with the FAA once. Are you retired now?"

Lie and maybe find out something. Tell the truth and they'd clam up. Which? "No, I can't afford to retire. I'm an accident investigator. I freelance."

The copilot looked over his shoulder again. "Any money in it?"

"Some," said MacHenry with a smile. Cockpits had changed, but copilots hadn't.

"Freelance investigation," the captain repeated. "That's interesting. I bet you hear all kinds of theories."

Was he fishing? "Theories are easy. Facts are hard."

"True enough. What are you working on now?"

Why not go all the way? MacHenry had nothing to lose. "I'm working on the 7X7. That's why I'm headed to Seattle. I'm meeting the chief of flight test at Boeing."

"No sh . . . Joe DelVecchio?" Marston grinned. "He's a real character. We had him with us for the acceptance flight on this bird. Is it true he once barrel-rolled a dash 400 737?"

"At the Paris Air Show, and in front of Boeing's CEO. When he landed, he told everyone it just got away from him."

Marston laughed. "How'd he stay out of jail?"

"Boeing sold a dozen jets after that demo flight."

"Well, I sure do hope you find out something." Marston leaned close, as though the Octopus might overhear him. "You might want to tell the company about something we discovered. Just for laughs."

MacHenry's ears all but bent forward. "What is it?"

"An Easter egg."

"What?" MacHenry was spring-loaded alert. He watched as the captain reached down to the data-entry pad on the center-aisle stand and pressed three buttons at once. The screen dead center on the instrument panel, the EICAS display, went blank, then the word OUCH! appeared. It faded away so fast MacHenry wasn't sure he'd seen it. The normal display appeared a microsecond later. Marston picked another three at random. The same thing happened again.

"What was that?"

"The Easter egg. Programmers like their little fun and games. I know. I used to hack back at school. You'd hide something in the code and see if anyone was smart enough to find it."

"Like a virus?"

"A virus is just the dark side of an Easter egg." The captain looked at the innocent keypad. "They figured nobody would ever press three buttons at once, I guess, so the software people put in a little message of their own. Just a joke. . . . Freelance means you're working for who?"

Now MacHenry paused. "An attorney."

The room temperature immediately went frosty. "For JAL or United?"

"Neither. TMC doesn't sound familiar to either of you?"

"TMC," said the captain. "It sure doesn't ring any bells. But I sure hope you find what you're looking for."

He knew he'd been dismissed. "Thank you, Captain." MacHenry walked back to the door.

"My pleasure, sir," said Marston. "And have a nice flight."

EIGHT

The low moon was still nearly full, and it burned yellow as a kerosene lantern, washing the deserts of eastern Washington in ruddy light. MacHenry put his forehead against the cold plastic porthole and felt the power course through the 7X7's skin. Somewhere in those vibrations was an answer. A range of black mountains snagged the setting moon, taking bigger and bigger bites even as he watched. MacHenry pressed harder, as though by sheer force the answers he sought might flash directly into his brain.

"Feels like we're almost there. Don't you think?"

MacHenry turned to his quiet seatmate.

"You worked almost the whole way," she said.

"It was easier than trying to put myself to sleep."

The engines throttled back and the 7X7 began a long, fuel-efficient descent to Seattle. He'd talked to her remarkably little for such a long flight. Sometimes conversations just naturally built. Not this one. They'd covered the polite basics. She was a language teacher at a Maryland private school, an immigrant from East Germany some years back, well before the Wall came down. She'd left her seat only twice. Once to use an airphone to place a call. The other time she simply disappeared into the darkened cabin.

"Seattle is supposed to be very nice. I'm anxious to see the waterfront," she said, flexing her arms as she stretched. They were roped with powerful muscle. She obviously worked out, and hard. "I've heard it's quite beautiful. Will you go there, too?"

"Not this time. I'm here on business."

"All night, then all day. Are you sure you aren't German?"

He smiled. "Positive. Sometimes I go weeks without anything to do. Everyone thinks I'm retired."

"But you're too young."

"Thank you." It was nice to hear from a young woman. Especially a beautiful one. It reminded him of Julia. He thought of her in her bikini, running along some beach in Kona. She had magnificent legs, there was no other way to describe them. An athlete's body, though without the musculature this young woman next to him possessed. Trouble was, when he thought of Julia, he couldn't imagine her alone.

The PA system popped on. "The captain advises we are beginning our descent into the Seattle area. Please return to your seats in preparation for landing."

Captain, thought MacHenry, remembering the blond youngster he'd spoken to earlier that night. He'd reacted when he said the letters *TMC*. He thought of Joe out at Boeing. How honest could he afford to be with him?

"The SeaTac weather is cloudy, temperature fifty-one, with light drizzle. On behalf of all our crew tonight, we . . ."

"So you're here on business," she said, looking at MacHenry's open workpad. "You said you work with airplanes. What do you do with them?"

"I investigate accidents."

Maria pursed her lips. "That's a very sad kind of business to be in."

"Only if you don't find what you're looking for." He saw that she wore a small enameled flower pinned to the black turtleneck. "What brings you to Seattle?"

"It was time for an adventure. Besides, it's the only American city with decent coffee." She smiled, but it was strained. "I have a rental car waiting. If you aren't meeting someone, I could give you a lift?"

"Thanks. But I'm supposed to be meeting someone." I hope, he added to himself. He'd used the airphone himself to call ahead to Boeing. He hoped DelVecchio would send somebody to meet him at the gate. "That's a very pretty pin you have there." He nodded at the small flower. "What is it? A rose?"

"No. It's just a blossom."

What did I say wrong? He turned and peered out his window. "Lights. We should be getting ready to land any minute."

"I hope you find what you're looking for in Seattle." She rolled down the sleeves of the black turtleneck.

"Thank you. So do I. And good luck with your adventure."

The landing gear popped out with a whine and a thump.

"Who knows?" she said with a smile. As she spoke, she unclipped the enameled pin with its red blossom and put it out of sight.

The ringing phone shattered a pleasant dream. Shintaro Ishii was in his old roadster, purring down the Ginza, the top down, trolling for fun. Not a care in all the world. No fortune to manage. No responsibilities. And nobody hated him. He was friends with the entire . . .

"Shin? The phone," said Mikki.

"Mmmm. Just let it ring."

But the young stewardess was well trained. "Maybe it's important."

"Sshh." Shintaro Ishii clumsily grabbed the phone. It fell to the thickly carpeted floor of their hotel room. "Ishii."

"Lazy boy! Why haven't you called me!"

Ishii recoiled at the sudden assault. "It's late."

"I served your father. I serve you. Do I have to hear of problems from *gaijin?* Where are your brains?"

It was Kazuo Ibuki.

"Problems?" Ishii was now wide awake. "What kind of problems?"

"Bridger called me. He told me what happened."

"There was a fire. A man." Ishii was hung over. He'd had a lot to drink on his first night in Washington, D.C. And Mikki had been especially playful once they returned to their room. Black lace was still knotted to one of the bedposts, stockings to another. He looked at his watch. Why was the hour hand moving?

"A fire. A man," Ibuki repeated, his voice a scornful singsong. "You look at water and you see only the surface. Idiot! What is beneath the waves, eh?"

Shintaro willed it to stop. "I'm sorry, but I don't understand."

"I should have known. I will have to attend to it myself."

"All right." *Then why call me?* he thought groggily.

"I'll be there as quickly as I can. Do what you are told and try not to make any more mistakes. Understood?"

"Here?"

"Do you understand? *Do as Bridger says!*" The line went silent again. This time, it ended in a click, then a dial tone. Kazuo had hung up on him!

Shintaro Ishii put the phone down onto the table. What had Ibuki said? He was coming here? He tasted the whiskey in his mouth, smacked his lips, and flopped down on the bed.

When MacHenry had called Boeing Flight Test to leave his arrival plans for his old captain, he'd hoped DelVecchio would send someone to ferry him to the airport Radisson. What he got was a bit more.

"Joe!"

DelVecchio looked up, smiled, blinked like a lizard. He was a pasha, a five-foot-three dandy in Gucci loafers, gray slacks, and a navy blazer; the very image of elegance, straight from a 1973 issue of *GQ*. His silk shirt was worn without a tie, open at the neck. Even with his utterly bald head, he looked an athletic fifty. It was all the more remarkable given he'd just turned sixty-four. A pirate's black mustache sprouted from beneath a prominent, fleshy nose. He eased himself to his feet. A glint of gold came from the open neck of his shirt, embedded in thick curls of black hair. He walked as though his gleaming loafers had springs.

His pretty companion watched. She was a raven-haired beauty, mid-thirties by MacHenry's eye, heels, slim legs crossed and revealed by a very short black skirt.

DelVecchio bounced up to meet his old copilot. None of the easy-gliding motions affected by so many airliner pilots; Joe DelVecchio was nothing, if not eager, even at this hour. When was it, anyway? He checked his watch. It was eleven eastern, eight local on a Wednesday night.

"Well," said DelVecchio. "Look what the breeze blew in." He reached out and grabbed MacHenry's hand like a locomotive coupling up to a car. He winked as he pumped MacHenry's hand. "So? What do you think of her?"

MacHenry peered over DelVecchio's polished skull at the woman. "You run to type, Captain. Dancer?"

"Nah, she's a spokesmodel or some such nonsense. I met her when she was temping in the Flight Test Office. Her name's Dyonna. With an o, not an a." DelVecchio turned and ogled her. "How's . . ." He shook his head. "I'm terrible with names."

"It's a shame to see what age will do to a mind."

"Julia. Am I right? Age hell. Some kind of professor."

"Meteorology."

"So, what, she gives good weather reports?" DelVecchio shook his head. "Who's the blond?"

"Who?"

"The little number in the black turtleneck. I saw her walk out behind you. I think you made an impression, MacHenry. She looked like a student or something. Just your type. She was giving you the eye."

MacHenry turned. The stream of passengers coming down the tunnel had slowed. He must mean the German teacher. "Must be the one I sat next to." MacHenry shrugged. "I'm sorry to show up so suddenly. I tried to call from D.C., but they said you were out flying at Moses Lake."

DelVecchio snorted. "They picked four green planes right off the line and assigned them to flight test. That's in addition to the bastardized test ship we made out of a 757 and the Iron Bird. Asshole engineers think you get nine women pregnant, you can get a baby in one month. Well, it's not that simple."

"I heard about United. These four new test planes. They're 7X7s?"

"What else?" DelVecchio glanced at MacHenry's battered leather flight bag. "Jesus H Christ. I thought I'd never see that old thing again," said DelVecchio. "You have that notebook in there, too? The one you used to write in all the time when you were supposed to be working?"

MacHenry nodded. Joe wasn't anxious to talk about 7X7s.

"You know, MacHenry, you'd have been a hell of a better pilot if you'd only stopped scribbling and paid attention." DelVecchio nodded in the direction of his companion. "Come on. Let's grab something to wet the whistle. I have to be on the flight line in the morning, but the night is young."

"I reserved at the Radisson."

"Hotel? No way. You'll stay with me. But remember. It's not

Di-anna. It's Di-yonna. She's very sensitive about her name. And no moves. Got it?"

"Lead on." As they neared DelVecchio's latest conquest, Mac-Henry could see her beauty was real enough. How did an old geezer like DelVecchio do it?

DelVecchio introduced them: "Meet my old copilot MacHenry."

She held out a hand. MacHenry noticed a ring. "Pleased to meet you," she said, her voice husky from smoke. "Joe has told me a lot about you."

"War stories," said Joe. "I remember his navigation. Without me to tell him where he was, poor MacHenry here would stumble around the terminal looking for a star to get a fix on. That's the game he used to pull on me before I wised up."

MacHenry smiled. He remembered gazing up the inverted bowl of stars, his head crammed into the astrodome of a Lockheed Constellation, the sextant all but forgotten as he stared at the blaze of glory overhead.

"They should have given us *combat* pay to fly with copilots like you." DelVecchio jabbed his thumb at MacHenry. "He was just a kid when he showed up on my flight deck. Still on ninety-day probation. He didn't even know how to buckle his seat belt. Remember? You got so turned around trying to sit you *crawled* into your seat on your hands and knees."

"The dispatcher warned me about you. I was praying."

"Hell. How many times did I save your ass?"

"Joe, watch your language," said Dyonna.

"Come on, honey. You aren't a Mormon anymore. MacHenry and I were kids together. You ready to paint the town?"

"Actually," said MacHenry, "I'm beat. I worked all the way out here. I even got a cockpit tour."

"I noticed it was a 7X7," said DelVecchio, but his tone was worried, not proud. "I delivered that ship to the line. It's a good one. Come on. Let's get something to drink before I fall over with sentiment."

Dyonna fell in behind as they walked out of the terminal toward the parking lot. A fine mist fell, too light for rain, too heavy for fog.

"So. What's the bad news, MacHenry? Last time you were out here to chew on the company over some fuse bolts. What's it this time? Tell old Captain D your tale of woe and intrigue."

How could he lie? "I'm working on the 7X7, Joe."

DelVecchio grimaced. "Yeah. That's the way I had it figured. FAA? Or United?"

"I'm freelancing this one for an attorney. Roger Case is his name."

DelVecchio sniffed. "Who farted?"

"It isn't what you think."

"Whooee. Lawyers and busted bolts. Fresh meat and the vultures are circling. Forget the bolts, *paisan,*" he said, "they're so overengineered they wouldn't break if you piled all the lawyers in the country on top of them. Which, come to think on it, is not such a bad idea. No. Forget *bolts*. Think *bombs.*"

"I know the FAA is moving that way. But what about the Safety Board?"

"The NTSB always finds a way to blame the FAA. Asshole flies into a mountain at night, in stinko weather, and the Board'll blame it on FAA training requirements. I mean, so what's new? Now, about you and your lawyer pal. Who's paying the bills? JAL? They still won't talk to us, you know. Pissed those little people right off we did."

"No. Not JAL." Was it time? MacHenry was wound too tight to make fine measurements. "Joe, I need some inside information. I think there's a problem with the 7X7. It may be in something called a TMC. I don't know what it is. Can you help?"

"TMC?" DelVecchio stopped. His smile was utterly frozen. "Where'd you hear that bullshit?"

MacHenry paused. "From someone who was inside."

"Was is right."

"What do you know?"

"Hey!" DelVecchio brightened. "Remember that first flight we took into LaGuardia? I gave you the landing to see how you would handle things. Remember?"

It was a deliberate diversion. But a good one. MacHenry remembered all right. It had been a near disaster. Too high, too fast, and a wet runway ready to skid them off into the water at the end.

DelVecchio had to take over and wrestle the Connie to a stop. When they turned off onto the very last taxiway, the brakes glowed cherry red as one wing pivoted out over black water. But MacHenry wasn't going to let the subject veer. DelVecchio looked as if he'd been stuck with a straight pin at the mention of a TMC. "Ever hear of a guy named Lawson Wheelwright?"

"Never."

"He was a quality inspector in Propulsion Engineering."

"You know how many people clock in at Boeing? One hundred and twenty thousand. I don't know everybody."

"About that TMC. Have you—"

DelVecchio swerved and caught MacHenry's collar up in a playful grab. "Listen," he said as he tightened his grip incrementally, "your asshole buddies at the FAA said I was washed up at age sixty. The airlines kicked my ass out. Now you want me to fuck over the guys who took me in?"

"Joe . . ."

"You know what I say? I say fuck you, MacHenry. Friends or no friends. Fuck you. 'Nuff said." He let MacHenry go. "Now. Let's go have a little fun. I know a place you'll die for."

They walked in silence until they came to DelVecchio's car. It was his usual: a two-door sports coupe, a bright red Lexus with a minimal backseat. He opened the door for Dyonna and pointed.

"Back there?" she protested.

"Honey, you know it's bigger than it looks. In you go."

She folded her long legs and made herself as comfortable as she could. Her perfume was intense in the close confines of the car.

The engine came to life. "So," said DelVecchio, revving it, making the needles on the instrument panel dance. "What's it to be? Hit the sack like an old fart or hit the town like the young studs we are?" His harsh words were all but forgotten.

"The sack," said MacHenry.

DelVecchio shook his head sadly. "Listen to him, honey. His friend the doc must not feed him his Wheaties."

"She's in Hawaii." But MacHenry kept coming back to those three letters: TMC. Joe knows what it is. The flight crew last night knew. Why was everyone clamming up over those three letters?

The car merged with traffic on Interstate 5. MacHenry noticed all the new industrial buildings just off the freeway. He mentioned it.

"It looked like a real boomtown for a while," said DelVecchio. "Boeing owned the land and sold it off hand over fist. Contractors, subcontractors, the whole nine yards." The signs carried familiar names like Grumman, Honeywell, and General Electric. Others bore less familiar titles: Menasco, Alenia, and some anonymous conglomeration called TSA. MacHenry noticed the buildings that wore the Boeing logo were still lit, their parking lots full. On a Wednesday night?

"Yeah," said DelVecchio. "It used to be we were living fat. Before scavengers like your lawyer boss got into it. Can't let anybody make an honest living, no. We've got to make those successful bastards at Boeing pay their way, and our goddamned way, too. Now everybody's working flat out just to stay in one place. It's like the *Titanic*. The ship's going down and they hand out mops." He looked at MacHenry, his face tinted green by the dashboard lights. "You want answers, MacHenry? Join the crowd. Nobody knows how those bombs are getting aboard. How come your lawyer friend isn't looking into *that*?"

"He doesn't think that it's bombs."

"He's so smart, he can tell the FAA, the NTSB, JAL, and even poor dumb Boeing how it's happening."

"He may do just that." MacHenry watched as DelVecchio sped through traffic as though the whole world operated at half speed while he ran at warp factor four. MacHenry found himself gripping the armrest. He forced himself to let go. "Joe, has the NTSB recovered anything that points to a bomb?"

"What else could it be?"

MacHenry remembered the little Easter egg the captain had shown him on the flight to Seattle. Three random buttons pushed together and the word *OUCH!* appeared on the multifunction display screen. It was innocent enough. But maybe it was a way into, or under, DelVecchio's personal armor. He described it.

"Impossible," said DelVecchio. "I don't know what you *thought* you saw, but what you've *described* is impossible. I've been through the control laws on this beast, MacHenry. From A to Z. I know whereof I speak. You think I'd let something get by me?"

"Not on purpose, no." A to Z. *What about TMC?* thought Mac-

Henry. "The captain said he'd seen it on other 7X7s. He said it was because the Octopus was too complicated to wring out. There were places in the computer code nobody had ever looked."

"Nope. Not so. We've washed down every square inch of the Octopus, which, by the way, the natives prefer to call Aircraft Information Management System. It's more dignified, you understand."

"AIMS." MacHenry decided to test the waters again. "Joe, this Easter egg. Virus. Call it what you like. I could show you what I saw."

"Christ. You're a stubborn old pelican. Ain't it enough I spend all day working, you want me to clock in all night, too? Wednesday night, and MacHenry wants to go on an Easter egg hunt."

"What about first thing in the morning?"

"I'm due on the flight line at nine, but we can play around with the Iron Bird if we get in early. Even Boeing engineers don't like to show up early. Clock punchers."

"Iron Bird? You mean, the simulator?"

"That's the one. It's in the Systems Integration Lab. That's where we test the hardware and software before we go fly it. But don't worry, MacHenry. If you saw an Easter egg on that 7X7 you flew in tonight, it's gonna be on the Iron Bird tomorrow. It's a one hundred percent, high-fidelity simulator. It's so real that if you crash it, the Bird's programmed to spit out an FAA inspector to confiscate your license."

"I'd rather demonstrate it to you on a real aircraft."

"MacHenry," said DelVecchio, "the Iron Bird is what I'm offering. The Iron Bird is what you get. Now," he said more brightly, "remember that time we were flying the Mecca run on charter?"

"Mecca?" said Dyonna. "As in Egypt?"

"Saudi," MacHenry corrected. This was his payback for not staying at the Radisson. A night of wild stories, and most of them true. "I thought we had a malfunction in the cabin fire sensor."

"So did I," said DelVecchio. "Until I smelled shish kebab. Jesus. Who would have believed someone would build a cook fire in the goddamned aisle?"

MacHenry sighed. It was going to be a long night.

NINE

Sam Nakamoto was waiting first thing Thursday morning for Shig with a pile of computer printout. The translator from Boeing's liaison staff bowed as Shig walked into the lobby of the Systems Integration Laboratory. *"Ohayo gozaimasu,"* he said as he stared at the floor. His hair was dense and black as a cobalt helmet.

"Good morning," Shig answered. "What's all the paper?"

Nakamoto straightened. "The printouts you requested." He held up a wad of accordion paper six inches thick. "These are the acceptance records for all items shipped by Nippon Aerospace." He handed them to Shig.

"All?"

Nakamoto smiled. "For the last ten days. I think you'll find them very complete."

Shig took one look at the first page and decided there was little information for him on it. Or rather, too much. You could barely see the green paper for all the ink. Numbers crawled across the page like an army of highly disciplined ants. If anything, they looked too good. But he couldn't sound an alarm over perfection. He put the stack under his arm. "Shall we go see the delivery?"

"Please follow me."

The SIL visitors' entrance was quiet at this early hour. Shig saw a sign that warned all employees not about security, not about doing their very best for the company, but instead that the plant was a nonsmoking facility. He could get along with a rule like that. Clearly, aspects of the American way of doing business were worth copying.

He followed Nakamoto back through a security checkpoint. The guard reminded him of the one stationed at Nippon Aerospace. Low, thuggish brows, tight black uniform. He looked for the truncheon, but there was only a lineup of radios in a recharging rack behind the desk.

"Did you get to your baseball game last night?" asked Nakamoto.

"Yes. It was very exciting. I thought there would be a fight."

"On the field?"

"No. In the stands. In Japan, everyone roots for the hitter, no matter what team he's on. Say you're a Carp fan, and a Yomiuri Giant comes up to bat. Everyone stands and yells, 'Hit it well!' It doesn't matter which team you favor."

"They don't do that kind of thing in the States."

"No." Shig paused. "What about those lost records? The ones that were burned? Any luck?"

"They may take some time to assemble," said Nakamoto delicately. "It happened down in Renton. They don't have any connection with the Consortium, you know."

"I see." Shig wondered why it sounded so formal, so rehearsed. "But they did have something to do with the 7X7?"

"Perhaps. But we are sure the Consortium is not involved with criminals."

"Well, that's great news."

The corridor opened onto a high bay. A complicated truss of blue steel spanned its length and width. Red lights flashed from the ceiling, warning that the Iron Bird was in use.

The whir of motors came from various places along the framework. A cabin stood at the end. Two men stood by a closed door, one tall with iron gray hair, the other short and bald.

"What is happening here?" Shig stopped to watch. A skeletal aileron rose from the metal trusswork, then fell. Leading-edge flaps deployed, then retracted.

"Routine testing." Nakamoto motioned for him to follow. "We call it the Iron Bird. Please follow me. The truck should be arriving any moment."

They came to a balcony overlooking another tall bay. More red lights flashed from the girders. Cranes and hoists ran on a complex overhead railway system. Shig noticed that they were all manned and ready.

Below, a crew waited like a football team tensed for the kick. A yellow Komatsu industrial tug idled, its exhaust drawn into floor grates placed for just that purpose. It looked very tidy. Almost Japanese.

"This is as far as we can go," said Nakamoto. "But any . . ."

The outside doors began to slide open. The beep-beep-beep of a backup signal sounded as the words OVERSIZE LOAD loomed into sight. The smell of rain came in along with a gust of cold, damp air. The tall shipping container eased back, then shuddered to a stop with a hiss of air brakes. The yellow tug moved up and the receiving crew got to work. The tug advanced like a crab, pincers up and ready, grabbed on to special lugs on the back of the shipping box, then slowly pulled back. The cargo box slid back on rollers built into the floor. Like a snail, it left a dark rainwater trail behind as it came. An overhead crane maneuvered directly above it, trailing cable like a jellyfish trolling for supper.

"Very impressive," said Shig. It was like a ballet. Everybody was doing something necessary. Workers with special tools unlocked the sidewalls of the container as steel cables snaked down and clipped on to eyebolts, ready to catch the panels as they came loose. The background noise swelled as engines revved and cranes rumbled.

Nakamoto had to raise his voice. "These are the largest shipping containers ever used for aircraft manufacturing," he said proudly. "Watch." The shipping container's sidewalls slowly dropped like flower petals, revealing a piece of an airliner resting on an elaborate cradle.

The component emerged, a work of sculpture on the morning of its unveiling. It gleamed in the bright worklights, an aluminum ring with portholes already in place. It was dazzling, so perfect it might have come straight from the mind of the designer without ever feeling the touch of an assembler's rivet gun. The container sides were pulled away and the overhead crane now dropped a complex cradle that the workers below fastened on.

"Where will it go?"

"Into the final-assembly area. But first, it has to be checked."

An inspector with a clipboard approached and unclipped a laser from his belt. He scanned a tag attached to the metal, then reholstered the laser.

"The bar code is automatically entered into the database," explained Nakamoto. "This is what generates the records you have in your hands. We track each part every step of the way."

Shig watched as the acceptance inspector began doing something odd, something Shig could not identify.

"What's he doing now?"

He seemed to be lightly striking the huge ring with something too small to see.

"Quality control," said Nakamoto. "It's not really much of a problem. One look at how the Consortium builds things will tell you that much. But we test anyway. He's tapping bonded seams."

"Tapping?"

"With a coin. To test them. A good seam rings. A bad one has a hollow sound. We used to find lots of bad seams when we made our own structures. But not anymore."

Shig watched, disbelieving. No, this was not Japan after all. Testing a piece of a jet with a coin? In Japan, there would be machines, X rays, robots swarming over such an assembly. Especially if it came from someplace overseas, and particularly if it came from America.

There were still angry editorials over the crash of a Boeing 747 that took place years ago because of faulty American maintenance. A bulkhead had ruptured at a splice, the cabin had explosively depressurized, and the jumbo jet, minus its tail, struck a mountainside. Shig shivered at the memory. The passengers did not die quickly, unsuspecting. Death notes had been recovered, written as the jet spiraled down to the rocks. It was like a buried ember. When the JAL 7X7 went in over the Pacific, the coal had flared white-hot in the national press.

"As I said, we used to build these components here," said Nakamoto. "They were all perfectly serviceable, but not like this. Not like the Consortium's."

If you built them the same way you test them, no wonder, Shig thought. "You mean they had more bad seams?"

"I mean everything. American-made parts had scratches. People would write messages on them for the factory. There would be grease. Dirt. They were usable, but very ugly." Nakamoto looked at the giant ring as the Komatsu tug began pulling it away. "The parts the Consortium builds for us are not just acceptable. They are also beautiful. They're art. You can hang them on a museum wall." He turned to face Shig. "Now do you see? There is no quality problem with anything we receive from NAC."

Finished with his testing, the inspector stood back and circled a hand over his hardhat. The overhead crane hoisted the ring up, slowly, then, once it was clear of the factory-floor clutter, faster. The crane rolled off into another part of the huge facility, the bright aluminum flashing as it went.

"Well?"

Shig turned to Nakamoto. "Masahide was also famous for making aesthetically beautiful products."

"Masahide?" Nakamoto looked puzzled. "Electronics?"

"Swords." Shig turned away. "Now let's go find out about those burned records."

The Iron Bird hummed as it was put through its paces. The steel trusses mirrored the outline of a full-size Boeing 7X7. Actuators, wires, cables, and computers were installed on it just the way they would be on the real plane. A small enclosed room duplicated the cockpit. Move the yoke in there, and far out on the steel beams, an aileron would rise. It was a safe way to test the fly-by-wire transport without risking catastrophic error.

"I thought you said the engineers didn't come in this early."

Joe DelVecchio tapped his loafers in impatience. He checked his watch again. "They should be finished any second," he said to Mac-Henry. "Then we'll jump in and you can show me this Easter egg of yours. Then I have to run. I'm due on the flight line in an hour."

"The captain last night said an Easter egg was just like a computer virus. He said it was two sides to the same thing."

"We don't get viruses at Boeing." DelVecchio drummed his fingers on the door to the Iron Bird's control center. It was locked. "Tell you what. While we wait for the engineers to finish playing in there, let me show you some real miracles. Follow me." DelVecchio bounced in the direction of a side door off the Iron Bird's bay. There, in a specially conditioned clean room, a computer workstation hummed next to a strange, complicated piece of equipment. It was an odd contrivance, some kind of vat of liquid but with unusual-looking apparatus set atop it. Like an aquarium built for robot fish.

"What is this?" asked MacHenry.

"The 7X7 is real whiz technologically, but this, this is 'Star Trek.' " He hopped into the chair set before the computer screen. The cursor blinked patiently. DelVecchio entered a personal code number, and the screen changed. He looked up at MacHenry. "Say you've got a 7X7 AOG in the boonies." AOG meant "aircraft on the ground." Usually with something broken. "You're in Bonga Bonga land, a continent or two away from a spare-parts depot, but you need a spare part pronto. A major headache, yes?"

"Sure."

"Pick a part. Any part."

MacHenry cocked his head. "Where is this headed?"

"I'm going to demo how a critical piece of hardware can get faxed to any place on earth."

"Faxed? What's that mean? You mean the drawings?"

"Negative. I mean the *part*. Name it. I don't have all morning."

MacHenry considered. "You mean, anything I want can come up on that screen?"

"If it's on the 7X7." DelVecchio nodded. "This is part of the dog-and-pony show we run for the VIPs."

"Interesting." MacHenry took a moment to consider. A part. There were millions. But how many could there be with initials like TMC?

"Well?"

"Okay. Say one of the main-gear trunnion pins snapped. We're stuck until we get another one."

DelVecchio grinned. "Not for long. Watch." He tapped his way through a menu of commands until he came to a parts list. He entered *TRUNNION, MAIN GEAR*. A page filled with rows of numbered items appeared. He used a mouse to snap a box around the entry. He hit EXECUTE and swiveled away from the terminal to watch the vat of liquid.

MacHenry stepped over to the screen. "It's hard to believe everything on the 7X7 is in here." He reached over DelVecchio and touched the scroll key. The list shifted one entry up. He hit it again. A new row appeared.

"Everything down to the last rivet and screw," said DelVecchio. "Any second now."

TRUNNION, MAIN GEAR sank to the bottom of the screen as MacHenry kept pressing the scroller. Suddenly, at the top of the screen, almost lost to the edge, was a new entry. Not for a single part. But for an entire system.

THRUST MANAGEMENT COMPUTER.

"Watch this," said DelVecchio.

MacHenry looked up. A loud beehive buzz startled him. Something was happening in the tank of liquid. Beams of light lanced down from the top of the tank, steered by mirrors and prisms. He looked back at the screen, but it had blanked itself dark.

DelVecchio explained what was happening. "The computer's sending data to the lasers. The lasers are making you a new trunnion pin right before your eyes. The light goes through some kind of filter so that it hardens up the plastic in just the right shape. You have one of these babies at every airport, and new parts are just a phone call and a modem away."

Thrust Management Computer. TMC, thought MacHenry. A computer!

The pin was materializing from the vat of liquid as though it had been beamed down from the Enterprise.

"Like I said, this is just a demo setup. The pin comes out in plastic. The real gizmo will work in aluminum, steel, even carbon carbon. Imagine faxing a new turbine blade halfway across the world." DelVecchio looked proud. "It's this kind of stuff that makes working here a real pleasure. Boeing knows you can't just improve your way to the top. You have to innovate. The Japs don't even have this technology yet."

But they will soon, thought MacHenry. Or was that Roger Case beaming himself across the country and into MacHenry's skull? TMC. Thrust Management Computer. Lawson Wheelwright. What was wrong with the Thrust Management Computer on board Boeing 7X7s?

The lasers went dark automatically. DelVecchio opened a door in the top of the vat and used a wire to fish out the plastic trunnion pin. It looked just as it should, all the machined edges and grooves perfectly reproduced out of thin air, or thin plastic. He held it up to MacHenry. "Take it for a souvenir. Now let's go take a quick flight in the Iron Bird."

MacHenry took the magic pin. It was warm, almost alive to the touch, but definitely plastic. He put it between two fingers as he followed DelVecchio back out into the tall bay. *I know why our A/C went down . . .*

The pin snapped like a dry pencil.

The door to the Iron Bird's control room was open. An engineer emerged, blinking as his eyes adjusted to the bright lights. A mole rising from his mound.

DelVecchio shouldered by the perplexed engineer.

"Excuse me, sir, but we're scheduled to—"

"Keep your pocket protector on, son," said DelVecchio. "We need to borrow your little toy. I promise not to break it. Come on, MacHenry."

MacHenry followed him into the simulator cab. DelVecchio closed the door behind them. It was dark inside. The only lights came from the flat-panel displays arrayed across what looked very much like the instrument panel of a Boeing 7X7.

Beyond the windows, runway lights made a vee that ended on the horizon. Lights drifted across the simulated night sky as airplanes lined up to land on the electronic runway. A beacon flashed from a control tower that looked a bit like LAX. It wasn't a full-fidelity simulator, not like the ones that made you break out in a sweat. But it was damned close.

DelVecchio hopped into the left seat. It was cushioned by sheepskin, just like the real thing. "Okay, MacHenry. What's with this Easter bunny?"

"Egg. Easter egg." MacHenry eased into the right seat. He looked at the empty EICAS screen on the center console. The Engine Indication and Crew Alerting System displayed the status of each of the Boeing's big engines, the thrust as measured by exhaust pressure ratios, the temperatures inside each combustor as well as engine rpm. It obtained its critical data through the Aircraft Information Management System. That made EICAS another arm of the Octopus. "Watch." He picked three buttons on the center console and pressed.

Nothing happened.

"Uh-huh. I'm looking, MacHenry, but seeing I ain't."

MacHenry jammed the flat of his palm down across the rows of buttons. Nothing. "Is this setup absolutely the same as on a real 7X7?"

"One hundred percent. That's the whole idea. How can you test it if it's not the same? We can take any item off the Iron Bird and plug it into a 7X7 out in the fleet. It will fit, and it will work. In fact, we do it all the time just to prove the point. Anything else, professor?"

"Wait. Maybe this Easter egg only shows up if we're under way. Can you do that?"

"What a question. There is nothing I cannot do with an airplane." DelVecchio pressed a button and the view out the windows dissolved. The panel came to life. One moment they were on the runway at LAX; the next, thirty thousand feet eastbound at Mach .85. The sound of engines came from hidden speakers. The EICAS screen registered two healthy turbines putting out cruise thrust. The mode symbol read CRZ.

"Your airplane, Mr. MacHenry. At least you can't bust this one."

He took the wheel and felt the live touch of a big jet in flight. He had to convince himself that out on those blue steel trusses, control surfaces were moving as he swung the wheel one way, then the other. That this little enclosed cabin was bolted to the ground. The nighttime horizon was spattered with city lights, the sky with stars.

"Well? Are we through? Can I get to work now?"

MacHenry reached over to the center console. I need DelVecchio on my side, he thought. Make this work. He chose three buttons. One was marked INIT REF. The second was PREV PAGE. The last was labeled CRZ. He spanned his fingers across the buttons and pressed all three.

The EICAS screen flickered.

"I told you that . . . *son of a bitch!*"

The word *OUCH!* appeared, then, when MacHenry let go, the illegal letters evaporated.

DelVecchio did it himself. The message came up again. "God

damn it." He looked up at MacHenry. "This system has been through three years of testing." He pressed three more buttons as if to prove it was a mirage. *OUCH!* came up again. "I wouldn't believe it except . . ."

"It makes you wonder what else might be in there," said Mac-Henry. "Maybe we should both press three buttons at the same time."

DelVecchio looked worried. "More Easter eggs?"

"On my mark. Three, two, and one."

They each hit a row of buttons. EICAS registered OUCH!—but then, a new message flashed into view.

The Warelord.

"Somebody's gonna fry over this. That's a promise," said DelVecchio as the illegal message faded. "My life's on the line every time I run the throttles up. And they're playing games?" He powered the simulator down with a swat of his hand. "Enough. The flight software project office is upstairs."

"This early?"

"Programmers? Hell. Those green-faced assholes *live* up there like a bunch of squirrels. Talk about not having a life."

He stopped DelVecchio, hand on his old captain's broad shoulder. "Joe, why won't you talk about the Thrust Management Computer?"

DelVecchio's face shifted through anger, through worry, all the way to indignation and back to a cold fury. "I think it's time we pay Tom Kelly a visit. He's the chief squirrel. You can ask him that question yourself."

TEN

Shig sat down at an unoccupied computer carrel in a quiet corner of Central Archives. Library stacks filled with reels of computer tape divided the room into a maze of narrow corridors and niches. Plain fluorescent tubes buzzed overhead. The library was a sealed and specially conditioned room in the basement of the Systems Integration Lab. It had the dead, heavy feel of a bomb shelter.

The computer in front of him was a dumb terminal, capable of reading material from memory but not changing any of it. The truth of it was, Shig felt pretty stupid himself. It was as though he'd found a loose thread and pulled, seeking its source, only to discover himself standing naked. He placed the stack of printout Nakamoto had given him beside the keyboard. "So everything, every part of the Boeing 7X7, is in this system?"

"Everything is here," said Nakamoto as he reached over and entered his personal access code. With an insolent little beep, the screen went blank, then the words *GOOD MORNING, MR. NAKAMOTO* came swimming up from the dark green glass. This message disappeared, to be replaced by *READY*. "An airliner is like a big jigsaw puzzle, except you don't start out with all the pieces. They keep showing up as the work goes on. Sometimes, you have a two-year lead time from when you place an order for a part to when it shows up here in Seattle. So a good tracking system is really important. Otherwise . . ."

"The puzzle doesn't come out right. Good records are important," Shig agreed solemnly. "Was the information on those lost records entered into the system before the fire?"

"I'm no expert in data processing," said the worried-looking liaison officer. "They were down in Propulsion Engineering. They involve an American vendor, not the Consortium. The Consortium doesn't build engines, after all." He said it the way a child recites a simple theorem. There. Isn't everything clear now?

It wasn't. It was a little bit too much like the printout Nakamoto had handed him. Complete, and a bit too nicely constructed. "I see," said Shig. "An American vendor. Then you do know what was lost?"

"Well . . ." Nakamoto hesitated. Had he said that?

"The lost records involve which vendor?"

"I'm not sure, but I think Norton Aerodyne. They manufacture electronics." Nakamoto recovered. "I don't know why they don't use Japanese companies for them. Japanese electronics are the best."

"What kind of electronics does this Norton Aerodyne supply?"

Nakamoto licked his lips. "Maybe I should ask Mr. Abrams from Legal Affairs to join us. He can explain it better."

Shig smiled. "I'll stay right here and wait."

Nakamoto's footsteps faded down the aisle. Shig typed a command on the keyboard. He called up the index page, then selected the *Propulsion Engineering* subgroup.

The screen flickered, then a new index appeared. He selected *May.* The month of the fire. The gap in the otherwise meticulous records. What was drawing him there? Nothing specific. But many little things. Things a Japanese investigator with an eye for subtlety and detail found interesting.

The screen brightened. Shig scanned the neat rows and columns. May had been a very busy month. Page after page of acceptance records, test results, and shipment dates scrolled across the glass. Items came from all over the world. General Electric. Rolls-Royce. AirResearch. Norton Aerodyne, too. It certainly looked complete. But then, what had his wary old Waseda professor told him? Beware the books that look too good. Nothing is perfect.

Shig began sifting through the data on the screen. Surely where there were so many questions and so many numbers, a good accountant could find at least one answer.

The young woman jumped up from behind her desk. "Excuse me! You can't go in there without—"

DelVecchio marched right by her and straight into the project manager's office. MacHenry was close behind. DelVecchio walked straight up to the man in charge of programming the computers that drove the Boeing 7X7. Some men at Boeing might point to a particular curve, a piece of metal, that was uniquely their design. But Tom Kelly was the man behind the Octopus. He was head down in front of a powerful laptop computer, totally absorbed despite the noise they'd made barging in. "Put it over there, please," he mumbled distractedly.

DelVecchio picked up a thick binder, then dropped it to the desk with a *thwap!*

"Right. Hang on for just a second." Kelly spoke without looking up from the foldup screen. He maneuvered a button-studded mouse with one hand, clicking, moving, clicking again.

MacHenry noticed posters of a brightly hued aerobatic airplane, a Christen Eagle. It was a high-performance aerobatic plane, one the pilot had to build for himself. A cluster of photographs showed the biplane in stages of assembly. Marathon-race medals were hung in a wooden cabinet by the window.

"Okay. Saved." The director looked up. "I thought you were Janet. How's it going, Captain Joe?" He had a thin runner's face, not much hair, and the expression of a kid with the keys to the toy store in his hands.

"What do you know about a programmer by the name of Warelord?" DelVecchio glowered down at him.

"I'm sorry. Who?" Kelly glanced at MacHenry.

"The Warelord." DelVecchio turned. "This is *Mister* MacHenry. He's an airline-accident investigator. He thinks there's a little problem with the 7X7's computers."

"Gee, I'd really like to help but I'm wrapped up in—"

"I don't think you're hearing me." DelVecchio reached over and folded the screen of the laptop down with a snap. "Two of our ships have gone down, Mr. Kelly. MacHenry here thinks you might know why. He asked me about the TMC. Now, what do you think I should tell him?"

Kelly swallowed, his Adam's apple prominent as a hamster heading down a snake's gut. "We're not supposed to go into that aspect," he said obliquely. "What exactly are you worried about?"

Not supposed to? wondered MacHenry.

"The Octopus has a bug," said DelVecchio. "I saw it with my

own eyes. We've got a virus on board and I want to know how it got there and who put it there."

"Virus?" Kelly kept switching his gaze back and forth between them. "What kind of unauthorized code did you find?"

MacHenry described what he'd found, both last night on the flight to Seattle and this morning, right downstairs on the Iron Bird.

Kelly chuckled, relieved. "That's no virus. That's a hacker's tag. Like the captain told you. An Easter egg. It's unlikely to be a safety-of-flight issue. Just a little—"

"Unlikely?" said DelVecchio. "We're flying a computerized jet with bugs in it. *Again.* Or have you forgotten what happened last time?"

Again? wondered MacHenry. Last time?

The project manager swallowed. "What do you want to know? I won't discuss proprietary items or matters we've been directed to keep quiet about, but I can generalize."

You can start by telling me what's the deal with the TMC, MacHenry thought, but he decided to come at it from an angle. "Where does the software for the 7X7 come from?" he asked. "Are you responsible for it?"

"Yes and no," said Tom, his tone much more serious now. "We establish what the equipment is supposed to do, how it's supposed to work, its physical dimensions, and we spec it to our suppliers. They write the programs. But we test them to make sure the boxes they ship are in compliance with our specs."

"You only do the specifications?" That sounded like an important distinction. One link in an ambiguous chain. "Who else is involved?"

"A lot of subcontractors."

"Which ones?"

Kelly shook his head, his spine stiffening. "That's not the sort of thing I think I should discuss."

"Why the hell not?" demanded DelVecchio. "We put out media packets with all that stuff in it!"

"Maybe you should go down to PR and get one."

"Crap!" DelVecchio turned to MacHenry. "Honeywell is our prime for electronic systems. Rockwell builds a lot. So does Norton Aerodyne."

"So this Warelord isn't Boeing?" asked MacHenry. "He's Honeywell?"

"Not necessarily," said Kelly. "You see, Honeywell and Norton don't do much programming in-house. They farm out the chips and the tuning to others."

MacHenry looked up. "Tuning?"

"We give them a physical space for their computer. They write the code in a convenient language. Usually C. But C is a fat language, easy to program but tough to fit on a chip, so they get the program translated into Assembly Language, which is real compact. That's called tuning. Dimensionally, it saves fifteen, twenty percent on each chip. Each box has hundreds of chips, so it adds up to a big space savings."

MacHenry committed the information to memory and recomposed himself. "Who does this tuning?"

"The chip makers are responsible, but they sub it out to a bunch of little firms in Great Britain, India, a couple in Thailand. Whoever has an open slot. They beam it to them by modem in the morning, they get it back by the afternoon ready to burn onto the chips. The chips are loaded onto the boards, they build the box and ship it to us. We test it, plug it in, and the bird flies away."

A subcontractor subcontracts to another subcontractor. From Boeing to India and back. This wasn't a system. It was a swamp. MacHenry felt as though he were up to his waist in murky brown water, grabbing at things just beneath the surface, looking for an answer. "Who checks all the work?"

"The manufacturer is responsible for debugging."

"No. Wrong," said DelVecchio as he wagged his finger back and forth. "*You* are responsible for a clean product."

"That's exactly what we've delivered," said Kelly.

"How can you be certain?" asked MacHenry.

"Look. This is getting into some hairy stuff. I'm not sure I can—"

"Answer Mr. MacHenry," said DelVecchio. "Because if you don't, I will submit his questions to you, through the second floor." That was shorthand for Boeing's senior management.

"Okay. On your authority, then." Kelly looked at MacHenry. "We specify a series of built-in checks that keep the programs clean. We have our suppliers hide encrypted numbers all through the code. It adds up to a total only Boeing knows."

MacHenry shook his head. "Who at Boeing?"

"Well, only I know all of them," said Kelly. "Then, when the computer comes to Seattle, we run what's called a checksum program. It makes sure the totals are still the same as the ones we hid originally. If they aren't, we start looking for errors."

"There's no way these translators, these tuners, could alter the totals so they come out right even if something's wrong?"

"Well, sure, I guess they could if they spent the time," said Tom, "but why would they?"

"The Warelord did," said DelVecchio. "He got his little virus by you no sweat. What else is in there?"

"There's no reason to be upset, J . . . Captain. A virus is destructive," said Tom. "This is not. To be honest, we kind of expect to find little things stashed away now and then."

"You *expect* people to screw around with the black boxes?" demanded DelVecchio.

Kelly flashed an easy, almost disarming smile. "Sure. Software people never get recognized for what we do. So we like to personalize our work somehow, even if it means pulling a little prank."

DelVecchio was not disarmed. He was spring-loaded to the explode position. *"Two ships down is not a goddamned prank!"* DelVecchio shouted. "This is *not* a game. This is for *real*."

"Joe . . ."

DelVecchio didn't stop. "Every day, thousands of people, real live human beings, come aboard Boeing aircraft expecting to live to see tomorrow. Some of them have been sadly disappointed in this expectation. The entire company is turning itself inside out to find out what's wrong, and you're talking to me about pranks? That you *expect* some sneaky little son of a bitch to hide personal messages in my airplanes? I want that program swept *clean!*"

Tom's ears flattened back from the blast. "Joe, do you know how many lines of code go into the 7X7? I'll tell you. Over forty million. It's tough to make sure each line is clean and does what it's supposed to do, but we did it. Now, most of those lines of code interact with other lines of code. Think of it as a grid with millions of wires crossing one another. Every time two wires cross, there's a node. A couple hundred million of them. But we've certified each and every legal node. Every legal interaction has been completely debugged. There is nothing to worry about. There are no viruses."

MacHenry's ears pricked up. There was something a bit too specific about Kelly's explanation. "What do you mean by 'legal interactions'?"

"Remember how you activated this Warelord's Easter egg?" Kelly asked. "Hitting three random buttons was not a legal operation. It's like asking what would happen in the first-class galley if you try to fly a 7X7 while rubbing your ear. Who cares? It's not in the legal universe, softwarewise. So there was no reason to test for it. This Warelord knew that and hid his message, this Easter egg, where only a random accident would activate it."

"You mean you only checked the things that were supposed to work together?" asked MacHenry.

"Correct." Tom nodded. "The truth of it is, we can't check all possible software interactions. We could run tests twenty-four hours a day for years and we wouldn't get to the end of them. The 7X7 has been a fast-track project from the beginning. So I designed a hard wall around all the really important stuff, and then we issue software updates as we Beta-test it in the field."

" 'Beta-test'?" asked MacHenry.

"Operational feedback from our first customers. Like this Easter egg. The next software update, we'll be sure to erase it. That kind of thing. Does that answer your questions, Mr. MacHenry?"

No. It didn't. It opened them up a thousandfold.

Kelly sensed victory. "Look. This message, this Easter egg is important because we didn't know it was there. But airliners aren't going down because of a little message over the EICAS screen."

"Maybe he's right," said MacHenry.

Joe gave him a shocked look. "What?"

"When the captain pressed those buttons last night, we didn't fall out of the sky." Good cop, bad cop. Maybe it really worked. Now, thought MacHenry. Let's dig a bit. "Tom, I asked you about the TMC. The Thrust Management Computer."

"Jesus, MacHenry," said DelVecchio.

Kelly's forehead popped out in a faint sheen of sweat. "I don't think the TMC is something we can discuss at this time."

"I don't understand. Why?"

"You'd better talk with Legal Affairs. It's their area of . . ."

"MacHenry, listen," said DelVecchio. "He's right. There's a lot of legal mumbo jumbo over something we may have screwed up on in the 767. It doesn't have anything to do with this."

"A problem with the Thrust Management Computer?"

"Yeah. Trust me. That unit's swept cleaner than a virgin's conscience."

"Correct," said Kelly. "After what happened on the 767, we made triple sure."

MacHenry hit a full stop. Do I press my old friend? He knows more than he's saying. But I need to know what he knows. People have died. Maybe more people will if I let it pass. He looked at his old captain. "Joe, you have my word. Whatever you want kept quiet, I'll keep quiet. I'm not interested in the 767. But if there's something there that can help us solve what's ailing the new ship, then I think we'd all be ahead if you told me what you have on this TMC."

DelVecchio squirmed. "Damn it, I can't."

"Why?"

"Damn it!" DelVecchio shook his head. "Look. The TMC unit is a little black box about yea by yea." He held his hands out to encompass a space one foot long. "We had a little problem with it on one ship, a few years back. There was a hull loss. We learned our lessons. End of story."

"What kind of a problem, Joe?"

"Captain," said Kelly, "Legal Affairs gave us strict—"

"God damn it! I was flying the line before you were born. I don't need you to tell me what to talk about." DelVecchio turned to MacHenry. "On your honor, MacHenry. This goes nowhere. Agreed?"

"Yes, sir."

"It involved a 767 operated by Lauda Air. It went in over Thailand a few years back. Remember? Well, the thrust reverser cans deployed because the electronic lockout failed. The system used hydraulics and checkvalves to keep the reversers in trail. It was a hybrid system, one foot in the old ways and one in the new." DelVecchio looked at Kelly. "Correct me if I'm wrong."

Kelly stared, silent.

"You had some black box driving old-style hydraulic valves," DelVecchio continued. "A real plumber's nightmare stashed underneath an electrical mare's nest. The company that built the Thrust Management Computer, they were learning on the job, you understand?"

"What happened?" asked MacHenry.

"They made a mistake on one computer. One stinking black box. They caught it at the factory, and instead of throwing it out and starting over, they made a fix with a jumper wire and shipped it to us. We installed it. The wire vibrated loose and sent a bad signal to the hydraulics on a flight. A valve opened and the thrust reverser cans on one engine deployed while the ship was in a climb."

MacHenry could well imagine what would happen next. Climb thrust blasting into a reverser, one engine pulling for all it was worth, the other pushing. A spin would be impossible to avoid.

"Mr. MacHenry," said Kelly, "there are no runaround wires, no jumpers, nothing whatsoever of the sort, in the TMC module of the 7X7."

MacHenry stared up the new path. Did it neck down to a nugget of hard truth or stop at a blank wall? "Who builds these TMCs?"

Kelly answered. "Norton Aerodyne is the lead vendor on the Thrust Management Computer."

"Did Norton Aerodyne make the TMC with the problem? The one on that Lauda jet?"

"Yes," said Kelly.

"And they also made the chips for the TMC, or was that farmed out overseas?"

"That's hard to say. If they meet our specs, and they haven't tried to sneak a jumper wire by our QA process, then that's the end of the line."

And the man with the job of finding a problem like the one that downed the Lauda jet was none other than Lawson Wheelwright. "Okay," said MacHenry, "the TMC unit, who actually tests it before it goes onto an airplane?"

"Propulsion Engineering."

Lawson Wheelwright's division, thought MacHenry. Another

click, another piece in place. "Tell me about this TMC. What does it do exactly?"

Kelly was on safe ground again. "The TMC is the interface between the engines and the throttles in the cockpit. In effect, it translates the pilot's command into signals the engine can use. It's a major systems node on the AIMS. Lots of signals coming and going. Lots of connections to a lot of other modules. It takes in information from the primary flight computers, the FADEC units on each engine, the throttle control system. Basically, if it has anything to do with the engines, it's at least connected to the TMC box."

"Now I know why the crews call your system the Octopus," MacHenry said. "But this TMC, if you had to boil it down for me, what is its main purpose?"

"Well, generally, it calculates the maximum thrust for a given condition."

"You mentioned reverse thrust. Does it set the maximum for that, too?"

"No. When the pilot arms the thrust reversers, and the gear switches say there's weight on the wheels—in other words, the airplane is rolling on a runway—the engines are allowed to spool up to whatever value they can achieve. The pilot wants to stop, after all, and the ship's going about as slow as it ever will. He's already on the ground, so the mass flow through the engine is low. He can't hurt anything by overthrusting, and in an emergency, it helps him to get stopped quickly."

"The TMC does all of this automatically?"

"Yes. But I have to tell you we made substantial changes in the TMC unit from the old 767. The new one is not subject to the glitch that took down the Lauda plane. You will keep this confidential, won't you? Legal Affairs would have our hides if it came out."

MacHenry sailed right by that question and on to the one he really wanted to ask. "Propulsion Engineering must test them pretty thoroughly. Are there records?"

"I guess so. Why?"

"Can we see some of them?" said MacHenry.

"Test records are not in the public domain."

"Mr. Kelly," said DelVecchio, "I will stand right here while you

call Legal Affairs for an okay. How much more time do you want
to waste?"

Kelly thought about it, then the worry seemed to lift from his
face. "Okay. Hang on a second. Let me see if I can find something
to show you." Tom flipped open the laptop and tapped a few commands. "We're linked into one big network here at SIL. I can access
anything in archives, from any division. Even some that aren't involved with the 7X7. But some of it's classified B-2 stuff. I have to
make sure."

"Great," said DelVecchio. "Maybe you can find this Warelord
while you're at it."

"I doubt it. He'd be more careful than that." Kelly punched in
some more commands. "Here we are." Tom turned the screen so
they could see it. A series of dates scrolled down the left-hand side.
Numbers and initials filled the rest. "We don't run too many TMC
boxes through Seattle. There are only two on each airplane. So these
records go all the way back to last January with TMC—NA001–128.
The dash 128 was the first flight-certified software package we released
to the airlines. The one that gave us a problem on the 767 was an
even earlier version."

"You mean the TMCs are physically the same on the 767 and
the 7X7?"

"A box is a box. The smarts are all new, all improved," said Kelly.
"And no jumper wires no way, no how."

MacHenry watched as Kelly sped through the data. "Go slow
there, will you?" MacHenry saw that the numbers changed halfway
through the month of May. He asked Kelly about it.

"Software update," Kelly explained. "When the Beta testing in
the field showed up some minor problems, we went from the dash
128s to the dash–131 module."

"I see." MacHenry didn't need to be told that a minor problem
for a programmer might look altogether different, and more serious,
to a pilot. "Were all the old TMC computers switched at once?"

"Oh, no," said Kelly. "They'd wait for a time when the ship was
down for maintenance. Then they'd switch out the dash 128s for the
updated TMC."

"You said that to change the software, you would have to physically change the chips."

"That's right. The old ones get pulled and destroyed, the new ones plug right in."

"Can you tell how many 7X7s are still flying with the old version?"

"Sure. That's . . ." A little symbol was flashing at the upper right-hand corner. "Huh," Kelly said, and then looked at MacHenry. He seemed genuinely worried now. His Adam's apple bobbed. "Is someone else working with you on this?"

"No," said MacHenry. "Why?"

"There's another user on-line down at Central Archives. He's looking at the same page we are."

"Can you tell who it is?"

Tom knew the computer system at Boeing like DelVecchio knew a cockpit. An ID number appeared. He ran it through the employee files, then turned the screen so it faced them once more.

Sam Nakamoto. Japanese liaison office.

TMC. Norton Aerodyne. Lawson Wheelwright. Roger Case's belief that the Japanese were somehow involved. "You know this man?"

Tom Kelly nodded. "I've played racquetball with him." He moved a mouse and started clicking. "Most of the system's wired for video conferencing. I can bring up the station camera where Sam's working." He clicked again. The screen on his little laptop split into four. The upper-right quadrant displayed a face, a stiff-posed ID shot.

The screen brightened. Kelly cocked his head as though he hadn't heard properly, curious. "That's weird."

"What?" MacHenry walked around the desk and looked at the face. "What's the matter?"

"This user is running Sam's ID"—Tom looked up—"but that sure isn't Sam Nakamoto."

DelVecchio had had enough computer games. "Let's get down there fast." He looked at Kelly. "Call security and have them meet us. MacHenry?"

"I'm with you, Captain."

★   ★   ★

Shig was finally in the driver's seat. Up to now, the facts kept arriving in strange packages, like a carefully boxed muskmelon that, when opened, revealed a crab, its pincers up and ready. But here, at last, in the basement of a building in America, he was working on his own turf.

Shig Onishi might not be much of a policeman. Ozawa didn't seem to think so. Shig certainly didn't know anything about airliners. But he was a Waseda-trained accountant. Faced with a page of numbers, he could glance at them and find the mistake another person would need a calculator and a full day to uncover. It was a gift, like perfect pitch.

Looking through the May records, he began to feel unaccountably odd. His nose twitched. What was it? He passed his finger down the columns on the screen. There was something strange here. But what?

The page showed the acceptance records for some piece of hardware known as TMC-NA076–128. NA was a vendor code for Norton Aerodyne. The initials LW appeared next, followed by a test certification number: 007AB. It was this number that drew Shig's attention. It was familiar. Why? He'd seen it before. He pressed the page-up command button. Nothing. A second page. There it was again: 007AB.

He went back to May 1 and discovered fourteen entries bearing the same test code, and fourteen that were identical except their test numbers were different. Why? How could one test cover fourteen different items in one case, yet require fourteen separate tests in another? The inspector LW had certified every one with the 007AB code.

Abrams had said that logs were missing from Propulsion Engineering for the month of May. But there was no gap in the records for those lost numbers to fit in. Not one. Unless the mysterious 007AB was simply duplicated to cover up the holes. The records looked meticulous. Real gold has luster. Fake gold has shine. Something, something was . . . The sound of a shoe scuffing floor tile made him stop and look around. He expected Nakamoto with Abrams in tow. But once again his expectations were off base.

At the end of the long, narrow corridor, a security guard was walking fast in his direction. He stopped, spoke into a radio microphone pinned to his lapel, then plucked something from his belt.

Shig was a guest of Boeing. An investigator from the Economic Crimes Division of the National Police Agency. He had nothing to fear from a guard. That was what his brain was saying in careful, metered sentences. But something else said, *Run!*

The guard sensed it, too. "Stop!" he yelled, even though Shig hadn't moved a muscle. It must have been in his eyes.

He grabbed the stack of printout as the guard broke into an awkward trot. Wishing he had his Nikes on instead of leather-soled shoes, Shig took off in the opposite direction down the stacks, sliding as he rounded the end. He bounced off a concrete-block wall, registering the presence of a metal panel. He spun. Circuit breakers! He yanked open the cover and began slapping at the brightly colored switches.

The overhead lights began to go dark, row by row. Dimmer, dimmer, until they were all out. Only the faint glow from the computer terminals lit the blackness.

"Shit," someone said, altogether too close for comfort.

Shig began to ease away. He tried to remember the layout of the room, the one and only door to the outside. How many times had he turned? Which direction was it?

A click. A hot, stabbing beam of light.

"Freeze!" The guard pinned him.

Freeze? Oh, no, indeed. Shig knew that *freeze* was American for *I'm going to shoot you, slant-eye!* He bolted, ducking around a corner, letting his hand slap against the tape stacks as he ran. He counted two rows, then headed for the one and only door. He saw the guard's light flash beneath the tape stacks, hunting for him.

"Christ! MacHenry? Where the hell are you?"

He turned. Another man!

"He's here!" the guard shouted, splashing Shig's feet with light. "I see him!"

The light shifted away, then reappeared as the guard showed up at the end of the aisle. The bright beam dazzled Shig as he approached.

Shig was caught between two men. There was only one way out. He loosened himself, letting the energy flow to his limbs. The stack of computer paper dropped. Unneeded now. His feet splayed out, seeking purchase on the tiled floor. His weight was centered. Perfect.

The flashlight brightened to a nova. "Easy, easy," said the guard, speaking to him as though he were some kind of wild animal, and not the other way around. At least he didn't have a gun in his hand.

"Don't come any closer!" Shig shouted, but in a language the guard didn't understand. The security man blundered right through the circle of possibilities, the ring of danger, into the core zone of action. Shig let him, letting the force coil inside him. First one, then another fist came up, fingers cupped slightly, offset. The guard could see his eyes, not his hands.

Someone else yelled, *"Watch out!"* But it was too late. Shig screamed so loud the guard froze, paralyzed. The strike came in that open instant. One fist to the guard's solar plexus threw him back against the tape reels. The flashlight arced away like a meteor and went back with a tinny crack. The guard grabbed a stack of reels as he fell. They clattered to the floor and split open. The tape sprang free like a nest of angry adders, coiling around his legs as they unspooled.

The guard's arm came up. It was too dark to see. But Shig sensed it. He acted on pure instinct. The kick sent a black plastic box flying down the narrow aisle with a 120,000-volt shower of blue sparks. A stun gun! Completely illegal! He could file a complaint another day. He turned and ran straight into a broad chest and a pair of grappling arms.

MacHenry wrapped himself around the intruder with a bear hug and shouted for DelVecchio. An overhead light buzzed back on as somebody found the breaker box. MacHenry thought the young Japanese had given up when he suddenly went limp. "Okay. Just don't—" Suddenly, MacHenry was flying. He crashed into a stack of tape reels headfirst and the world dissolved into a zebra pattern of jagged lines and flashes. There was a sound, one he could not identify, a kind of clang a poor theater company might use to simulate thunder.

DelVecchio stood with the heavy tape canister in his hand, ready to deliver another blow. But the intruder was down. "MacHenry? Are you—"

"Stop that!"

Running feet made DelVecchio turn, ready to swing again. But it was Sam Nakamoto and Abrams from Legal Affairs. They slid to a stop and gazed wide-eyed at Shig's body.

"Jesus! What did you do?" said Abrams.

"Mr. Onishi is a policeman!" said Nakamoto.

DelVecchio screwed up his face. "A *what?*"

"He's a Japanese policeman!"

ELEVEN

"BA Ten heavy, taxi into position and hold. Be ready for an immediate departure. Traffic is inside the marker."

"Position and hold, BA Ten heavy."

The British Airways 7X7 swung out onto Kennedy's Runway 13 Right. Fourteen thousand five hundred feet of concrete lay dead ahead, ending in the marshes, Jamaica Bay, and finally the cold waters of the Atlantic. Two hundred and thirty-three passengers were on board, including a youth orchestra from a Manchester suburb returning after a U.S. tour.

"Pretakeoff checks and cross-checks," said the first officer. "Flaps and slats are set, amber lights are dark."

"EICAS?"

"Full display. Stabilizer set. Harness?"

The captain leaned forward against his straps. "Locked. Should be rather a long—"

"BA Ten heavy, cleared for takeoff."

"On the roll, BA Ten." The captain applied the brakes and gripped both throttle levers with his right hand. The first officer placed his left hand behind and over the captain's. It was a small intimacy designed to keep the throttles from rolling back should something unexpected take place, though with the Octopus driving the engines, there was very little risk of that.

Together, both pilots smoothly advanced them to the stops. The twin General Electric engines snarled as they dug in. The whole ship shuddered, nose low like a bull pawing the earth. A squeal announced the brakes beginning to slip.

"EPRs and temps are matched," said the first officer.

"Here we go." The captain brought his feet off the brakes and the packed jet began to roll.

"Airspeed's alive," called the first officer. "Forty knots."

The captain guided them down the runway centerline. A slight drift corrected. The steady rise of the airspeed, the sights and the sounds of great powers unleashed, but under his command. He did it all automatically. His brain concerned itself with a different question: buildings didn't have a thirteenth floor. It was still considered unlucky. Why a runway thirteen, and why have I not noticed that fact before?

The seams in the runway thumped faster and faster.

"V-r. Rotate."

At 152 knots, the captain brought the nose up, and the wheels left the earth. A black shadow fell away from them as they climbed into a pearl gray sky. The wheels rumbled up into their wells, the flaps crept in from their takeoff position, and the wings sliced the air clean as newly sharpened knives.

The angle-of-attack symbol on the captain's altitude display unit commanded a steeper climb. The captain obliged, following the complicated routing of the Kennedy Nine Departure as it vectored them first southeast, then east, then north. They punched through a milky undercast, and once more the shadow of the great jet lay projected below them, receding from a recognizable shape to nothing more than a dot surrounded by the full circle of an aviator's rainbow.

Finally, away from the dense New York traffic, the jet settled into a profile climb; well before the Nantucket beacon passed invisibly below, the 7X7 was five miles above the sea.

With a cabin full of passengers and fuel tanks heavy with a transatlantic load, the climb rate tapered off as they rose into ever-thinner air. The warm outside temperature—it was a balmy minus forty— didn't help. Thirty-three thousand. Thirty-three five.

"Tell Center we shall be in their way awhile longer."

As the copilot informed air traffic control, the captain pushed over on the yoke and allowed the big jet to accelerate. The mode selector on the EICAS screen changed from T/O to CRZ. "Engaging the autothrottles." The captain pulled both power levers back to the first detent. The letters *ATS* popped into view on the EICAS screen. The GE-90s automatically throttled back to cruise.

"Should get a bit more climb out of her when we burn some

fuel away," said the first officer. Higher was better. Higher was where they'd been told to find a hefty tailwind, and that meant a more profitable flight. "Did you see all the bloody boxes in the hold?"

"Musical instruments." The captain turned.

"What's our routing today?"

"The Octopus is still working it."

The shortest flight between New York and London is not a straight line. Instead, it is a family of lines, of possibilities, all of them changing with the season and even the hour.

Time represented money, a lot of it. And so the art of hunting for the best altitude, the best route, and the least objectionable wind was a blood sport among airline crews. Until a computer with enough raw processing power came along that was small enough to fit into a jet, it was the captain who drew what he hoped would be the quickest line between the continents. But those days were over. Now, in the Boeing 7X7, the Octopus handled the job.

"Looks like we'll miss Greenland entirely," said the first officer when the Octopus flashed its decision.

The Atlantic grew dark below the eastbound jet.

"A piece of trivia for you," said the first officer as he entered the necessary takeoff reports into the Aircraft Information Management System, the bookkeeping arm of the Octopus. The scratch-pad screen at his elbow queried *TRANSMIT*? He pressed *Y*. "That was our thousandth departure."

The captain held up an imaginary pint of ale. "To our thousandth arrival."

Greg Chiang was a deep disappointment to his parents. His father was a physicist/entrepreneur and his mother played cello in a regional orchestra. She believed Greg was born with his father's sense of beauty; his father sighed that young Greg possessed his mother's head for business. Worst of all, at twenty-eight, he was unmarried, a condition that Chiang, citing the motto of the British Foreign Service, was unwilling to apologize for or explain.

But he wasn't unmusical, and he had a very practical bent. What Greg loved most was composing, bringing something beautiful out of nothing. He also knew it paid poorly, so he became adept at computers by way of four years at MIT, then graduate studies at Cal Tech.

His parents' loss was the FBI's gain.

During the day, he worked at the Bureau's Washington Photographic Interpretation Center in the basement of the huge annex on Ninth and E streets. It was a poor relation to the National Photographic Interpretation Center. NPIC had the very latest, the very best gear. Of course, the spooks at NPIC were funded offbook. The FBI had to beg for every dollar in person.

Buried in his small, green-painted room, Chiang manipulated images through the keyboard of his Sun Microsystems workstation, bringing something out of the murky nothing of mug shots and bank security-camera photos. By night he listened to his old MacIntosh Quadra AV play the digital symphonies that lived inside his head.

Aaron Freeman, the agent in charge of the Wheelwright case, quietly entered Chiang's lab and stood behind the young man, watching as he worked on a bank robbery caught on tape. He knew better than to call ahead or knock.

Chiang had his suit jacket draped across the back of his government-issue swivel chair. His bow tie was neatly tied. His striped shirt pressed. His Sun machine had been state-of-the-art four years ago, an eon as far as computers went. Greg Chiang made do. He liked the challenge of finding things where the eye said nothing was there to find. Of putting a name on the fleeting face of a criminal certain he would remain nameless.

"Bank of America?" asked Freeman.

Chiang nodded. He'd seen Freeman walk in by looking at the reflection on his monitor. That was the kind of thing he was good at. "I think I'm about to find something."

On the screen, in the jerky stop-time motion common to cheap security films, two men in ski masks backed out of the bank's front door. Customers sprawled on the floor, and tellers crouched behind the counter. Both robbers were armed, one with a handgun and the other with a sawed-off shotgun. The one with the handgun held a black bag containing $26,000.

When they were outside, they broke and ran for the getaway

vehicle, a dark Ford van. Unfortunately, the security camera mounted out there had been bumped by the window cleaners and was staring uselessly into the sky. The one inside couldn't see the van's license plate, and though nearly twenty people out on the street gaped at the robbery, nobody could recall the plate. Of course, Freeman thought bitterly, the bank was in Berkeley, an enlightened municipality where crime was viewed as a problem of a felon's poor self-esteem, and robbery just another means of income redistribution. What was a criminal? Just another morally challenged victim.

"Watch." Chiang stopped the action on the screen. He maneuvered a white box over a bright glint reflecting from the bumper of a car parked directly behind the getaway van. He stepped up the magnification, and the glint became a large starburst of poorly focused light.

"You think there's something in there?" asked Freeman.

"There's always something in there." Chiang applied a custom-designed algorithm that enhanced signal while rejecting noise. Signal was the image he was hunting. Noise was everything else. The sun glint was digitally disassembled, analyzed, then slowly, bit by byte, put back together on the screen. Like a photo emerging from a developer tray, the image of the Ford van appeared on the bright, shiny chrome bumper. It was curved and reversed, but recognizable. Before it could wash out and overexpose, Chiang stopped the action, snapped another white box around the image, and blew up the scene again. It re-emerged larger and much the worse for wear, but the plate was no longer hidden.

"There." He pressed a button and saved the image. "California 3AA2592. With a '95 registration sticker."

"That's amazing," said Freeman, though he imagined the van was at the bottom of San Francisco Bay by now.

"I guess it is." Chiang turned. "Now what can I do for you, Agent Freeman?"

Freeman tossed Roger Case's videotape to him. "Take a look at this. Clean it up and tell me what you see."

"Is there a budget code?"

"Write it up under F as in favor. It's an amateur tape. Copy of a copy. The key parts are out of focus entirely. You probably won't see a damned thing."

Chiang smiled. He liked challenges. "I can take a look at it tonight after work."

"Just so I can say it's in the grinder."

"What's supposed to be on it?"

"It's the torch case out at Dulles. Lawson Wheelwright. Led me on a merry little chase for almost six months. Wanted for interstate flight for arson out in Seattle. And maybe here in the District the other night. He burned up the other morning in a fairly nasty way. I have a friend"—Freeman paused—"make that a professional acquaintance, who thinks it wasn't an accident."

"What do you think?"

"I think the guy was a firebug. Live by the match, die by the flame. But I have to play this one out. My friend's a major pain in the ass. It's worth keeping him quiet."

Chiang appraised the tape. "Cheap. Where's the master?"

"The networks own it. I can call, but . . ."

"Subpoena."

"Yeah. I know. See what you can find first."

"No promises."

"Thanks, Greg. I appreciate it." Freeman turned and left.

Greg pulled the Bank of America tape out and inserted the new one. He was already wondering what there would be to find, how he would find it, and whom did he know over at the television studio?

Shig recognized the conference room from yesterday; the same framed photos of Boeing planes, the same polished cherrywood table. The same computer screen. The plate glass framed another lowering gray sky, the Seattle skyline a wet fence of uneven stakes on the misty horizon.

Abrams closed the door after MacHenry, DelVecchio, and Nakamoto filed in. "All right, gentlemen," he said, "I want to know what the devil this is all about. Top to bottom."

Sam Nakamoto pulled out a chair, but before he sat, he bowed so deeply his chin nearly touched the conference table. "Please excuse the unpardonable behavior," he said to Shig. "They did not realize you were our guest."

Shig had to give the liaison credit. He certainly knew all the right words. But his head was speaking a very different language. What did that bald gaijin hit him with, anyway? A sledgehammer? He glared at DelVecchio, who returned the courtesy in spades. A mad monk, thought Shig. That's who this one is. A very mad monk. He rubbed his temple. "*Atama ga itaidesu.*"

"His head hurts," Nakamoto explained.

"Go fetch him some aspirin," said Abrams. The translator left.

Shig dipped a napkin into a pitcher of ice water, then put the cold cloth up to the laceration in his scalp. "My boss warned me that Americans were sneaky."

"Who the hell was sneaking around with a false ID?" DelVecchio shot back.

"What are you talking about? I was sitting there—"

"Gentlemen, please," said Abrams. "Mr. Onishi was not using a false identity. He is here as our guest."

"What about the guard?" said DelVecchio. "He just fell down?" He pointed at Shig in a rude fashion. "Your guest here knocked him around pretty good."

"That was a mistake," said Shig.

"Like Pearl Harbor?"

"Oof." Would they never stop blaming others? "I was born in 1965. All right? So please. No more Pearl Harbor."

Abrams looked like a responsible adult watching a schoolyard bookbag fight. "If you're both finished, I'd like a little information myself. First," he said to Shig, "this gentleman, and I use that term loosely, is Joe DelVecchio. He's in charge of Boeing's Flight-Test Office, though you wouldn't know it from his behavior downstairs. I'm afraid I can't introduce you to his friend."

"MacHenry. Brian MacHenry." He turned to Shig. "Mr. Onishi, I'm responsible for the error. Please accept my apologies." He held out a hand.

Shig warily took it, then dropped it. Maybe Americans bit.

MacHenry? Abrams noticed the guest pass pinned to his jacket. "Maybe you can tell me why you are here." Abrams had a bad feeling about this MacHenry.

"MacHenry's my old copilot," said DelVecchio.

"That gives him the right to run around Boeing attacking our guests?"

"Look, *I'm* the one who hit him," said DelVecchio.

"No, Joe," said MacHenry. "I take responsibility."

Shig listened closely to MacHenry. It was almost a Japanese approach. The younger person taking the blame for the older. Who was this MacHenry, anyway?

MacHenry took a deep breath, then spoke. "I'm working on an investigation that involves the 7X7. One that may shed some light on why two of them have gone down. I asked Joe, I mean, Captain DelVecchio, to take a look at what I found. He thought it was important enough to show Tom Kelly."

Abrams filed away each fact. "Our chief programmer?"

"Yes. We were demonstrating a software glitch to him when we saw someone else on the system, looking at the same data, and using Sam Nakamoto's ID number. But it wasn't Mr. Nakamoto. It was Mr. Onishi. That seemed odd enough to—"

"I told Kelly to call security while we went down to see who this person was," DelVecchio broke in. "So you can fry me, Abrams. I've been cooked before."

MacHenry shook his head. There was no reason for DelVecchio to suffer any retribution. "The whole thing really starts and ends with me. This is my investigation."

Alarms were ringing inside Abrams's head, loud. "Who are you working for, Mr. MacHenry? The FAA?"

"No, sir. Although I used to be with the agency. I was an airline-safety specialist." MacHenry took another deep breath. "Now I freelance accident investigations."

"I see," said Abrams. "For whom are you working?"

MacHenry knew what the next few words were likely to do. "I'm working for a Washington attorney named Roger—"

"Case?" Abrams broke in. "You're hauling water for *Roger Case*?" Abrams swung on DelVecchio, his words icy as the rain falling outside. "He's working for one of the most suit-happy attorneys in America, and *you* signed him in?"

"He's my, I mean, he was my copilot." DelVecchio looked glum. This was not going to be easy to explain.

"I'm not here to dig up dirt, Mr. Abrams," said MacHenry. "I—"

"Quiet!" Abrams slammed his hand onto the table. "You aren't here to help. You're here to make someone rich by tearing off a big strip from Boeing's hide. The bigger the better, and the truth be damned. That's the name of your game, isn't it?"

MacHenry leaned over the table. "No. You've lost two jets. Nobody knows how or why. That's the name of the game."

"They were sabotaged by bombs smuggled aboard." Abrams sat back.

"No, they were not," said MacHenry. The force of his own words surprised him. "No investigating agency has found evidence of a pre-crash explosion. Not the FAA. Not the FBI. Not the NTSB. And neither have you. What I don't understand is why you knew there was a potential problem in the electronics and never bothered to inform the FAA."

"What are you talking about?"

MacHenry was about to say Lauda Air. A jumper wire in a TMC. Thrust reversers deploying in flight. But he held it back.

"Your friend seems to have lost his voice." Abrams turned to DelVecchio.

So it's true, thought MacHenry. "Not at all. I'm willing to share everything I have with you. Right here, and right now. Everything on the table. If we can cooperate, then—"

"Cooperate?" said Abrams. "You aren't cooperating. You're fishing. You're looking for a chink, an opening your boss can develop into a nice fat lawsuit. And as for your allegations, I deny it, and if you choose to take it out into the world, I'll be at your throat in a flash, MacHenry. Both feet."

"Excuse me, but in Japan, we have a better way to solve a problem like this."

Abrams, DelVecchio, and MacHenry faced the young investigator.

"We try to discover what is at fault, not who. Perhaps we could try that." Shig addressed the gaijin he most nearly understood. "Mr. MacHenry, I am an investigator for the Japanese National Police

Agency. You and I seem to be standing on the same circle looking in. Like you, I am on an investigation that seems to involve Boeing, and the unfortunate events that have happened."

"The National Police?" said MacHenry.

"The Economic Crimes Section. We believe that members of an organized-crime syndicate might have had a hand in funding the Nippon Aerospace Consortium. As you know, they are planning to buy into this company."

"What is the connection, Mr. Onishi?" asked MacHenry.

"I'm sorry, but talk like this ends our ability to work with you." Abrams picked up the telephone on the table. "I'm calling security to have Mr. MacHenry shown the gate. Can I call you a cab?"

"Not yet." Shig reached over and did a very un-Japanese thing. He clicked the telephone off. He wished they would all leave, except for the quiet one. "Perhaps if we told each other what we have found, then this puzzle might be solved more quickly."

Abrams shook his head. "No thank you, Mr. Onishi." He scowled. "He's working for a lawyer who would make a mint if the company were successfully sued." He faced MacHenry. "And so would you. That's how you freelancers get paid, isn't it? Dig up some unlikely dirt, shop the venue to find some gullible jury, and convince them everything is our fault. You win big, and everyone here loses. Hell, it doesn't even have to be true. It just has to make a good story."

MacHenry's face flushed. "You don't know me. I don't make up stories and sell them to juries. I don't fabricate evidence or ignore clues that don't fit. I'm after the truth. I may have found some, too. And if you'll give me a chance, maybe I can prove it."

MacHenry retold the story of the Easter egg. He left out mention of the Lauda Air wreck.

Abrams listened. He picked up the telephone again and looked at Shig. "With your permission." He summoned Tom Kelly to the conference room.

"There are just too many dark corners in the programming," MacHenry concluded. "Kelly said it himself. The entire 7X7 lives and dies by its computers. But they're so complex, there was no way to test everything. I think someone used that fact to hide not just a little personal message, but something worse. A virus. One of your own inspectors thought so, too."

"Oh?" said Abrams. "Who is that?"

"Lawson Wheelwright."

Abrams registered a hit, but he smothered it. "You've spoken with him?"

"I didn't get the chance," said MacHenry. "He died yesterday in Washington."

"He . . . he's dead?"

MacHenry nodded. "He left a note at Roger Case's office about problems in the 7X7's TMC computer."

LW. Lawson Wheelwright, thought Shig. He was connected to those strange record entries, too. "Excuse me, but this man who died, his initials were on the test records I was looking at downstairs."

Nakamoto returned with the aspirin, but Shig paid no attention. He and MacHenry were very different, but also very much the same. It was a paradox. But then, in Japan, swordplay and flower arranging were both considered martial arts. Two roads seeking to cross one river. Could they meet in the middle?

Tom Kelly knocked at the conference room door.

Abrams looked away. "Come!"

"Wow," said the computer expert as he surveyed the men gathered at the table. An odd flicker of unease crossed his otherwise amiable expression. "What's going on?"

"Take a seat, Mr. Kelly," said Abrams. "For the record, you are the man in charge of computer programming on our 7X7."

"I spec the programs out. But I'm responsible for all the software meeting those specs."

"Now let me ask you one question. Did this outside investigator," Abrams said, meaning MacHenry, "bring anything to your attention that should cause us to lose any sleep?"

"Mr. MacHenry found a message hidden away by a programmer somewhere along the line. Hit three buttons together on the center stand on the 7X7, and the word *OUCH!* comes up on the EICAS screen."

"Hit six buttons and the son of a bitch's name came up," DelVecchio growled.

Abrams silenced him with an icy look. "Is this message, this Easter egg, a safety issue?"

"No, sir. It is not."

"Why not?"

"We wouldn't be so dumb as to leave any flight-critical software open to a real virus. You know, the FAA was worried about an airliner with pure fly-by-wire controls. Airbus Industrie lost some ships over bad code. The Swedes had a real kludge on their hands writing the flight laws for their new fly-by-wire fighter. The Gripen. And we had that little problem with the Lauda Air 767."

Abrams pointed his finger like a pistol right at MacHenry. "That doesn't go outside my office. You did not hear it."

"He knows already," said Kelly. "I thought it was okay to mention since Captain DelVecchio mentioned it."

Abrams swiveled a cold look at DelVecchio. "When?"

"He promised to keep it to himself, Abrams," said DelVecchio. "We can trust—"

"I'm sure he did." Abrams turned back to Kelly. "Go on. I might as well know how much damage we've inflicted on ourselves."

Kelly continued, "Anyway, with all these concerns over software security, the FAA told us to make the flight code laws absolutely unbreakable. That was my job."

"But you must know how to break the codes," said MacHenry.

Kelly glanced at Abrams. "I don't think that's the kind of thing we can discuss. But I can assure you, anything that's related to safety is protected by a real thick wall." Kelly chuckled. "A bunch of walls, a moat with alligators, and an electric fence. There's no way a virus could attack it. Take it from me. I designed it."

"Put it in writing." Abrams looked at MacHenry. "Sir, apparently you've accidentally learned of a matter that is still under negotiation between Boeing, Lauda Air, and one of our contractors. I will ask you not to use it or to reveal it. If you choose to anyway, I promise I can, and I will, make your life very expensive and unpleasant. Do we understand each other?"

"Yes, sir."

"Excuse me," said Shig. "I am very satisfied to hear the degree to which Boeing has made a secure system, but one small item still troubles me."

Everyone turned.

"The records I looked at downstairs? There was something odd about them."

"Odd?" said Kelly.

"In the month of May, the last month that LW appears on the system, twenty-eight items called TMCs were checked through his division. Fourteen had the same test code. Fourteen had individual test codes. I wondered, which is correct? Why is one set different? Perhaps there is a simple answer."

"There is," Tom Kelly answered. "You misread the file."

Misread? A Waseda-trained accountant? Shig was insulted. "That should be easy to prove," he said, glancing at the blank screen on the table. "Can you call them up from here?"

"Sure." Kelly looked at Abrams. The VP from Legal Affairs nodded. He tapped a command into the keyboard and the screen flashed bright. "Which records, Mr. Onishi?"

"May. The test numbers for . . ." He stopped. "A component called a TMC-NA076-128."

"That's an old dash-128 Thrust Management Computer," Kelly explained.

"You seem to have a head for numbers," said Abrams.

"Thank you."

Kelly entered the correct sequence of commands. He scrolled down until May came up, then swung the screen around to show Shig. "Here you go."

Shig moved close. There! "This unit was tested by LW."

"Lawson Wheelwright," MacHenry explained.

"His test was recorded as number 007AB." Shig moved the screen forward. There was another LW entry. But . . . "That's strange," said Shig. The test numbers were now completely consecutive. There was 008AB. And a few lines down, 009AB. All signed off by LW. "Something has changed."

"In Central Archives?" said Kelly. "I don't think so. It's read-only memory."

Shig slowly nodded. "You must be right. My sincere apologies. I have been pursuing ghosts after all."

"Maybe you have, but I haven't," said MacHenry. "The fleet needs to be grounded and checked for a virus."

"That's about enough out of you, sir," said Abrams. "You found something that our best man says is no big deal. An Easter egg. On the basis of this, you want Boeing to recommend grounding all eighty-two 7X7s that are flying? Don't be ridiculous." Abrams faced Shig. "And you. You would have us question a very valuable working relationship with the Nippon Aerospace Consortium. That's not going to happen, either. Do you understand? Both of you?"

Shig did indeed. Boeing was up to its ears in this mess. This was way beyond him. Way beyond even Ozawa. "Yes," he said. "I can understand you completely. I believe there is nothing more for me to discover here."

Finally, DelVecchio couldn't hold back. "Listen. How long would it take to check this TMC thing out, anyway?"

"This discussion is at an end." Abrams got up and left, only to reappear a moment later with two security guards. "These gentlemen will escort you all to the gate."

As the three were escorted to the front door, Abrams picked up the extension and called down to his own office.

"I want you to find a phone number," he said to his secretary. "In Washington, D.C. For Roger Case."

The copilot checked the fuel burn. The climb to thirty-seven thousand had consumed a lot of Jet-A. Now, they were light enough to climb higher and catch some of the promised tailwind. He tapped the EICAS screen as a reminder.

"Right," said the captain. "Tell Center we'll be climbing to four one oh." As the first officer complied, the captain grasped the throttle levers. They were still in the first detent. "Coming out of AUTO," he said as he moved them forward to the stops.

"Climb mode selected."

"Enable."

The EICAS screen display switched from CRZ to CLMB. The

exhaust-pressure-ratio displays showed the engines throttling up. A red line marked the maximum values calculated by the Thrust Management Computer.

"EPRs are matched. How much push can we expect?"

"That Virgin chap had a minus twenty westbound. Pretty good headwinds for them. Should be good for us."

"Want to bet we have a minus twenty eastbound, too?"

They both laughed as the engines spooled up tighter and tighter.

The altimeter rose through thirty-eight thousand feet.

Suddenly, the air traffic controller responsible for their sector boomed into their headsets.

"BA Ten heavy, Gander. We have a priority message for you. Ready to copy?"

"BA Ten, roger. Go ahead, Gander."

The altimeter climbed through thirty-nine thousand.

The frequency shrieked as another transmission blocked Gander's.

The pilot waited for the noise to settle, watching the needles move on the EICAS screen. They weren't real needles, of course. It was all computerized. Bits of information flowing through the 7X7's electronic pathways, all routed through and by the Octopus.

". . . to Kennedy. Break, break, did you copy that BA Ten?"

"Negative, Gander. You were blocked."

The needle on the altimeter display touched the forty-thousand-foot mark.

"Coming up on EPR limits," said the copilot as the needles rose.

"BA Ten heavy, Gander. Fly two five zero, vectors back to Kennedy. I say again, vectors back to JFK. They think there might be some unchecked baggage on board your flight."

"Unchecked what?"

"Captain! EPR alert on one."

"What was that?" asked the captain. What?

A distant *crack!* made the entire plane shake. Both pilots looked off to the left, seeking the source of the unnatural sound. The nose snapped to one side.

"Number . . . one! We're overthrusting!"

The captain rammed the yoke full right and stood on the right-hand rudder pedal, then shoved the leftmost throttle lever back one click, two. Three, all the way to flight idle. Nothing! Suddenly, two more cracks sounded, again from the left, as the thrust reverser cans broke off in the slipstream and fell like petals, tumbling over and over, eight miles to the sea.

"Mayday, Mayday, Mayday, this is BA Ten . . ."

"BA Ten, BA Ten! How do you read, Gander?"

There was no answer as a cold kerosene rain began to fall across the gray Atlantic rollers. It spread out into greasy rainbows and disappeared.

TWELVE

No one paid any attention to the couple parked in the employee lot across from the Systems Integration Lab. The area was patrolled by Boeing security, and they paused only long enough to determine that the smoke coming from the cracked-open driver's window was of the legal variety. Lots of Boeing employees went outside for a quick cigarette now that the Lab had gone nonsmoking. One of the guards sniffed, caught a whiff of perfume, said something to his partner, and they both laughed.

The woman behind the wheel and the young man next to her didn't draw further interest. Rain beaded up on the windshield, making it hard to see inside the Buick. But it wasn't hard at all to see out. The field of view in the Nikon's zoom was razor sharp.

A Boeing van pulled up to the SIL lobby doors. A security guard came out first. He opened the side door and waited. Next, a familiar face: MacHenry. He merited a photograph. Then DelVecchio. The Boeing pilot looked dejected as he stood to one side, not joining MacHenry inside the van. Another quick snapshot. They were followed by a stranger, a tall Asian man, a Japanese, and not nisei, but the real thing. Close-up, one, two shots for identification purposes. Then, the last man emerged from the lobby.

Her finger hesitated on the camera trigger. Not out of disinterest. But surprise. She overcame it and fired. One, two, three photos. The motor winder whined. A fourth. Despite her training, her heart began to beat faster. She waited. The van door slid closed. Tom Kelly stood under the projecting overhang at the lobby entrance with DelVecchio. He turned and walked back inside as the van drove away.

DelVecchio was not a concern. The Japanese was an unknown for now, though a name could—and would—be attached to his face quickly enough. But Tom Kelly and MacHenry had just spent some time together. Doing what?

She dropped the camera beneath the seat and switched the engine on. The windshield wipers began to slap. She backed out and headed for the main gate.

As she slowed, the Buick hit a speed bump. The man next to her slumped forward, his torso hanging at the limit of the seat belt's reel, chin pressed sideways against the dashboard, his face a toothy sneer. She shoved him upright and jammed her right arm across his waist to keep him there. The gate guard barely looked up. When she was far enough from the facility, she let him fall forward once more, then plugged a STU-III encrypted telephone into the cigarette lighter and placed a call to Washington.

The Gray Flamingo was a popular café for off-duty Boeing employees. Its logo was a tropical bird surrounded not by palm trees and beaches but by curtains of rain-heavy clouds. The bird held an umbrella with one wing, a coffee cup with the other. The rich, greasy aroma of frying onions and homemade hamburger patties could make a militant vegetarian salivate.

The tape of last weekend's football game played on a TV mounted above a shadowy alcove that contained a four-stool bar. Every stool was occupied. A lot of ex-Boeing people were around.

"I hope I haven't put your good friend into hot oil," said Shig.

"Hot water. No. Joe has a tough hide," said MacHenry. He sipped the coffee the waitress had placed in front of him without asking. "I don't think I made much of an impression on Abrams."

"There was very little chance you would."

MacHenry looked up from his coffee. "Why is that?"

"We have a saying in Japan. A scratching dog never has just one flea."

MacHenry shook his head. "I don't get it."

Shig wondered how well trained this American investigator could be. "Then I will try to explain. I started on this case when it was very small. I followed it, and every turn it got bigger and bigger. A gangster's payoff. A bad bank. A big industrial consortium that is not what it seems to be. A lot of money is on the line. Maybe more than just money, too. With so much at risk, Boeing has to be in on the crime."

"Oh?"

"It's obvious. The Consortium supplies them with critical parts. Japanese airlines are big customers for Boeing. If trouble comes with the Consortium, Boeing is between a stone and a hammer. Now do you see?"

"That's a rock and a hard place." MacHenry put down his cup. "I don't believe that Boeing is sabotaging its own aircraft."

"The facts speak the loudest."

"They speak for themselves. Or at least they're supposed to." MacHenry changed the subject. "Tell me something, Mr. Onishi. Why did you run when that guard showed up?"

Shig shook his head. "I don't know. I felt there was danger. I'm sorry I threw you down."

"Accepted. Where did you learn martial arts? Police training?"

Shig smiled. "In the Economic Crimes Section?" It was almost funny. "No. They train us to catch the little thieves, and to leave big ones alone. My father made sure I knew how to defend myself. We had to know these things."

"I thought Japan was safe."

"If you fit in."

"You don't?"

Once more, their talk hit a dead stop.

MacHenry tried a different approach. "Up in the conference room, you suggested we lay out the particulars to one another. Are you still willing?"

Shig looked away.

MacHenry was running low on patience. "Mr. Onishi, I don't think time is on our side. Two 7X7s have gone down. The first was one operated by your own countrymen. It will happen again if we can't figure out what is going on with this aircraft. I don't know why, but Boeing won't help. You seem to think they're involved."

"Why do you find it so difficult to imagine Boeing is at fault? Don't you know it was Boeing's mistakes that caused the very worst aviation accident in Japanese history? Or didn't they bother to put that on your news?"

That hit MacHenry where it hurt. He knew it was true. Boeing had made some bad repairs on a 747 aft pressure bulkhead. The metal ruptured, and the huge, packed plane went in when the controls to the tail were severed. "Americans have died, Mr. Onishi. Americans and Japanese both. Boeing made mistakes in the past, but they've always owned up to them. This is different and it goes completely beyond countries. It's about the truth." MacHenry watched Shig react.

"Americans believe in only one truth. But there's always more to it than that. When they are faced with something complex, what do you do? You blame everyone else for making things inconvenient. But really, it's just a matter of view."

"No. The truth is still the truth. When that JAL plane went down, people died. That's truth. When that United ship scattered itself across a hundred square miles of southern Utah, that's truth. I deal in facts. They may not be easy ones, but by God, when I have something in my hand, I know what it is."

"If only everything were so clear."

"Okay. Fine. I'm sorry you won't cooperate. I should go check in with my boss." MacHenry started to get up, but Shig motioned for him to sit back down.

"No. Wait a moment." Shig decided to tread the line between revealing all and nothing. "I came to Boeing because there were strong hints that black money went into forming the Nippon Aerospace Consortium. Usually, when gangsters are involved, threats are not far behind."

He'd heard this before. But at least it was a beginning. MacHenry sat back down. "What kind of threats?"

"Nippon Aerospace Consortium is using shadow money to buy shares in Boeing. Perhaps to exchange bad money for good. Perhaps for other reasons."

"Not just shares. They control the source of critical parts."

"That's just good business. And remember. Nothing is being bought that is not for sale. The Consortium builds better parts than Boeing. Even Boeing says so." Shig thought of the inspector going around with a coin, tapping on metal seams. It was medieval.

MacHenry scowled. "Go on."

"I came to find out if it stopped there or went deeper. Actually, I was ordered to come here. Today, I found enough evidence to suggest Boeing is also involved."

"How?"

"Someone changed the TMC test-record data in the time it took us to go from downstairs to the conference room. Someone at Boeing."

MacHenry paused, then said, "I find that difficult to accept."

"Why is it so easy to imagine that Japanese are lying and that Boeing is not?"

"Japanese business is played by Japanese rules. And rule number one is, I win. No matter what it takes. Maybe it includes murder."

"No. Not *I* will win. Japanese business works by the principle *we* will win. Not an individual. Not just one company. But all of Japan. That is the one rule we play by. And to be honest, it works better than your way. Otherwise, why do Japanese companies have so much capital and Americans are always begging?"

"Japan isn't doing so well these days."

"Boeing isn't trying to buy Mitsubishi, Mr. MacHenry."

"Not by blowing up an airliner full of innocent people it isn't."

Shig came back to that fact. It was a truth they shared. "No, you're right. That's why I am here." He took a sip of coffee and continued.

"Boeing is in deep financial trouble. Abrams said that meant no blackmailer would bother with it. I think it means just the opposite."

"That doesn't mean Boeing is a coconspirator."

Shig felt like reaching over and shaking this thick-headed gaijin. MacHenry was slow! "Then who changed the test records?" He sat back against the padded booth and waited for the truth to dawn on MacHenry.

"You said you misread the file."

Shig sighed. Maybe MacHenry wasn't so smart. "I do not misread files. I said what I said because nothing would come of pointing out the obvious. Those records were changed. So you see, Boeing has a few worms in it, too. American worms. Not Japanese. Obviously, they do not wish to cause any difficulty with this so-called Consortium. Boeing doesn't want to rock the cradle."

"Boat. Rock the boat." It sounded very much like what Roger Case had thought. A weakened Boeing vulnerable to any rescuer with enough cash in hand. Or terms. And the bugs in the basement, the worms boring through Boeing, wouldn't the company try to hide them until, as Case had said, the check clears? But was the company protecting a valuable partner, a simple error, or a deliberate flaw?

"Now," said Shig, "perhaps you can tell me your side of the story."

"I might as well. It begins with Lawson Wheelwright. He was a quality-control inspector. His initials were the ones you saw on those test records."

"LW. The disgruntled employee who disappeared."

"He reappeared in Washington." MacHenry told the story again. "I found out that TMC stands for Thrust Management Computer. There are two of them on every Boeing 7X7."

"Interesting. He claimed to have five samples with him?"

"Yes. And now he's dead."

Shig cocked his head. "A computer is not a small thing. How could he have five?"

"We'll never know."

But Shig was carrying the line of thought to a very different conclusion. "Maybe he didn't need the whole computer."

"What does that mean?"

"Perhaps he had five pieces, five . . . what is the word? Microchips. That's where a flaw in the program would be found, isn't it?"

"I suppose so. Yes." Why hadn't he realized that? Five chips would be easy to hide. And impossible to find. One step forward. Five back. "Wheelwright burned to death. The police say he was caught trying to set another fire. This time at Dulles airport." The awful scene replayed itself again. "He made a mistake and doused himself with solvent. He burned to death out on the airport ramp. In front of a hangar owned by the Smithsonian. Actually, the Air and Space Museum."

Shig drew in a sudden sharp breath.

"What is it?"

Shig had heard of the Smithsonian. But something else nagged at the back of his memory. A list. He'd seen a list with that name on it recently. A file. And a Waseda man did not misread files. Or forget them. "A hangar for historic airplanes?"

"Yes. Maybe the most famous of them all. Or infamous," Mac-

Henry added for Shig's benefit. "The *Enola Gay*." He didn't think it was necessary to mention what the old B-29 was so famous for.

The list! It was Ozawa's Red Sash file! The Hibakusha Foundation. One of the Foundation's projects was this very airplane, the *B-san* known as the *Enola Gay*. A small line item in an enormous annual budget. A hundred million yen or so. Shig looked back at MacHenry. "These samples he claimed to have. Assume they are chips. Perhaps they were left where Wheelwright was staying. Has anyone checked?"

"We haven't found where he was staying."

"The police have no idea?"

"Not when I left they didn't."

Shig emptied his coffee cup. "There isn't very much to your case, is there?"

"No. And now I don't think we'll get anything more out of Boeing. Washington is still thinking bombs. Unless we find those TMC samples Lawson Wheelwright was talking about in his note, I don't see how we can take the last step. Or stop it from happening again."

Shig took a deep breath. That was another hard truth, wasn't it? People had died. More would be killed if they didn't find a way to act. "And the only man who knows where these TMC units were hidden is dead."

"Ready to order, gentlemen?"

Shig sat back and looked up. The waitress was not young, not pretty, and not patient. She looked as if she might have been around when the Gray Flamingo opened. Her dyed-black hair was drawn back in a net. "The soup of the day is chicken noodle. Fire away."

Noodle? Shig wished he were back on familiar territory. Back at a little *soba* stand by the subway station. He looked up. "I will have chicken noodles."

"One soup. Anything else?"

"The same," said MacHenry. He wasn't really hungry. The waitress left. He checked his watch. The old Rolex Air King said that Roger Case was probably still at his office back in Washington. He should call. "What do you think, Mr. Onishi? I don't suppose you can suggest where a dead man might hide a handful of computer chips?"

"No. But I am very sure there is someone right here at Boeing who knows what is in them. He's the same one who changed the files in the time it took to go upstairs."

"You have a theory?"

"Who knew the records system better than anyone? Who helped to develop it? The same man who must be afraid of what I found. It's really very clear." What kind of investigator was this MacHenry, anyway?

MacHenry paused. "Kelly? The programmer?"

Americans required such endurance. "I am glad we are finally thinking alike."

The bowl of soup arrived, along with coffee refills.

Shig screwed up his face as he ran a fork through the bowl. There was plenty of water and precious few noodles. He looked around, his eyes settling on MacHenry's empty water glass. "Excuse me," he said, reaching over and taking it. He tipped the soup bowl onto its lip, pouring out the liquid into the glass, holding back the noodles with his fork.

MacHenry watched the performance. So did the diners in the next booth. "Why would Kelly cover up holes in those records?"

Shig slurped noodles into his mouth. They weren't bad, but there weren't very many. If his father had tried to serve such a dish, he'd get thrown out the door of the shop by irate customers. He dabbed his mouth with a napkin. "Kelly is protecting Boeing against outsiders."

"Maybe he's protecting himself."

"Himself?" This MacHenry would never make senior investigator. He had all the wrong instincts. "Very unlikely. Why would a Boeing man do something that risked his own company?"

"Maybe somebody made him a better offer."

That was never done in Japan. Firms competing for the same employee would put their heads together and decide who would get him, and for how much. "I don't understand what you are suggesting."

MacHenry wondered how good an investigator Onishi was. "It's obvious, isn't it?" He remembered Case's instructions: You want to get to the bottom of a mystery? Then follow the money. "Who stands to benefit from Boeing jets going down? Not Boeing."

"Other aircraft manufacturers?"

"Who's looking to buy in at the lowest possible price?"

"The Consortium? You think they hired Kelly to create a virus? To drive down the price?"

MacHenry nodded. "I am glad we're finally thinking alike, Mr. Onishi."

Suddenly, the loud chatter echoing off the café's walls died down to a whisper. It was as if someone had thrown a switch. A few lingering conversations here hushed to silence. The bartender got up onto a chair and switched the channels on the TV to CNN. He was rail thin, his dark hair plastered to his skull. A newscaster's grim face filled the screen, along with a map of the Atlantic Ocean. A large white square had been applied to the chart.

"What is it?" asked Shig.

They found out quickly enough. A graphic symbol of an airliner broken in two, surrounded by a halo of bomb blast, flashed onto the screen. Then the blue Boeing logo appeared.

The café was dead silent. The coffee urn rumbled against the swish of tires on a rainy street outside.

Abrams stood silently in the elevator as it came to a stop. He felt a curious mix of emotions. On the one hand, he'd just told Roger Case off but good. He'd nipped that problem in the bud. It was why Boeing paid him so well. But then the word came.

Boeing might be the biggest manufacturer of jets in the world, but it wasn't so big that something like this didn't hit each employee like a death in the family. *Another of our planes went down.* Not United or JAL. Not British Air. But *ours.* An airliner might fly for decades, wear the livery of a dozen different carriers, but it never stopped being a Boeing.

The doors opened. There was no reason to announce the new crash over the PA. Everyone knew. The corridors were hushed. The public affairs types were already cranking up to meet the inevitable crush of media requests. The 7X7 project office was in a state of shock. Tom Kelly's secretary was nowhere to be found. Abrams went straight to Kelly's door and knocked. When the chief programmer didn't answer, he pushed it open. "Tom?"

A laptop was open on the desk. Kelly was gone, though his suit jacket and pants hung neatly from a hanger on the back of the door. Where was he?

Call it gut instinct, but Abrams was uneasy. He walked up to Kelly's desk, admiring the marathon medals hanging in their wooden case. Kelly was quite an athlete. A real competitor. The framed photographs on the wall showed him leading a pack of runners to the finish line. His face was fierce, driven, even through the obvious pain.

Abrams stood behind Kelly's desk. He was tempted to open the drawer, but held back. The computer screen was dark. He touched a button, and the display lit up. Abrams peered at it. What was this all about?

The screen showed an air traffic controller's radar. Tiny dots representing airliners were converging from the edges toward the center. A message began to flash: *CONFLICT ALERT.*

Abrams watched as two dots drew closer, closer, then merged. *CRASH!*

The screen blanked, then another message appeared: *PLAY ANOTHER GAME Y/N?*

Abrams folded the screen down. The computer shut itself off. He walked to the window. Cold rain streamed down the glass. He could see the parking lot below. A bald head fringed with brown hair appeared. A runner, dressed in a light jacket, shorts, and Nikes.

Abrams cocked his head. A third plane bombed, and all of Boeing would shortly be in mourning. People grieved in their own ways, but what on earth was Kelly doing out running in the rain?

Kelly didn't even slow at the main gate. He ran straight by the guard booth, feeling the heat rise up from his muscles as they loosened. He jogged right, taking the empty sidewalk along East Marginal Way for himself. The rain seemed to evaporate the instant it fell on his hot skin. His motions became more fluid as he found his pace.

The Boeing buildings drifted by him like a diorama. Lights were on in the offices. He knew what the people inside would be talking about. He came to a landmark. One mile. He knew the route down to the second. Running wasn't exercise. It was an art. He was an artist, and time and distance were his materials.

Running shut out everything else. It closed up the brain against itself, isolating everything behind a heavy wall, permitting nothing to come between his legs and his will. It was like the armored center of the Octopus, impervious to attack. Only he knew where to look for the trapdoor.

The Federal Aviation Administration had thrown their best engineers against it to no avail. His walls had held. The Octopus could not be tampered with in any meaningful way. Not by anyone else. His feet seemed to fly, barely touching the wet pavement. The next landmark came into view. Two miles.

Only he knew the needle-thin pathway that went straight into the Octopus's brain. Only he knew how to make the Octopus a willing partner in its own destruction, how to make it hide the signals that would otherwise appear on the flight-data recorders. It was his right as creator. No more, no less. The end of the sidewalk appeared ahead. He checked his watch. Three seconds off. He quickened his pace. He would cross the street and run back for another two miles, then cross back for the final mile to the Systems Lab gate for a total of five. The rain was perfect, keeping him cool as his body radiated waves of heat. His stride fell into place.

The light turned yellow out ahead. Even though it was late morning, the cars all had their headlights on. Kelly knew it was a dumb, fifteen-second signal. He checked his watch. Perfect. He didn't even slow down when he came to the curb. The signal turned red as his Nikes hit the street. He crossed between rows of hot white headlights.

It was Boeing's own fault. What had they offered him after the 7X7? Nothing. They would never be able to afford to design a new jet. The world was changing and Boeing was a dinosaur bellowing from the tar pits. The world belonged to winners, not used-to-bes. Winners. Everything else was just tap-dancing.

Kelly felt the greasy street under his running shoes, the gutter running with cold rain. Then, the curb. Up, turn left, and run! He shivered as he pounded up the sidewalk. It went away as he warmed up again. Three miles.

The Systems Lab came into view across the street. He could see his office window. A little slot. How little they knew. His feet slapped the wet cement as he entered mile four. The final intersection appeared. A car was idling, parked at the far curb. Some slacker in a Buick killing time.

He arrived at the crossing just as the light turned in his favor. He hit the curb as the yellow light winked red. The little crossing symbol flashed its approval, not that he needed it. There was no traffic to dodge. He felt strong, his blood pumping hot. *Go for it!* He sprinted for the far side.

Halfway across, he registered the sound of a powerful engine revving high. The squeal of tires seeking a grip on wet pavement. Not braking. He turned his head in time to see the catfish mouth of the Buick's grill. A wet windshield. A flag of white steam pluming behind the accelerating car. A bumper with a little Boeing tag on it. He sucked in a breath of air involuntarily.

A thud, a crack of bone, flying, striking, the breath driven from him. He rolled, smashing hard against a curb. He tasted blood, gagged at the fragments of teeth in his throat. His leg was bleeding! A white, splintered stub protruded from the gash. That goddamned idiot! He heaved himself around in time to see the car veer in his direction, not slowing, speeding up. The Buick flashed its lights, four high-beam dazzles. In the center, an emblem, three little shields in a circle. The two front tires were slim, edge-on rectangles surrounded by halos of splashing water. Coming right at him.

What? Black rectangles, worn tread, raging engine, and then locked brakes, sliding, sliding. An instant before the car struck him, Kelly opened his mouth to scream.

The Buick ramped over the curb and onto the sidewalk, dragging the body beneath it. It came to rest against a chain-link fence. The engine died. The rain stiffened, washing a bright swipe of red off the sidewalk and into the gutter.

THIRTEEN

Maggie Atwood had ruled the office of Case, Rudge, McDivitt et al. for nearly twenty-five years. Office manager, executive secretary, marital counselor. She knew things that even some partners were not permitted to know, and what she did not know for certain she could usually sense. So when she saw Case sitting at his desk in the afternoon gloom, his bad leg propped on that disreputable old ottoman, the desk lamp off, she figured something was wrong. "You'll go blind, Mr. Case," she said as she switched on his light.

"What?" He looked up. "Oh. Thanks."

"Bad news?"

"It seems I may have been wrong about something."

She could guess what it was about. She'd put the call from Boeing through to him, after all. "You were talking with that man from Seattle for quite some time."

Case nodded. "Vice president for Legal Affairs, Walter A. Abrams. Apparently our Mr. MacHenry has been misbehaving."

"How?" That didn't seem possible. She'd met him and liked the accident investigator.

"Assault. Breaking into a secure area. Uttering terroristic threats . . ."

"Is it true?"

"It doesn't have to be true to be expensive. That mealymouthed son of a bitch threatened us with a lawsuit. He said he didn't even care if he won, just so long as it was, in his words, 'protracted and costly.' "

"Would he win?"

"How the hell do I know?" He snorted. "We don't have the time or the money to prove him wrong. Not anymore."

Maggie knew enough not to ask for the details. "Anything I can get for you?"

"Yeah. Arsenic."

"One finger or two?"

He cocked an eyebrow at her. She was a feisty fifty, glossy salt-and-pepper hair, big brown eyes, and damned well preserved. Not that he would let her know he noticed. "Three."

"Coming up." She started to leave.

"Wait. Do we have the number MacHenry left? Where he's staying?"

Atwood smiled indulgently. What a silly question. Her memory was at least as good as Case's, and his was all but photographic. "The airport Radisson. But I believe he had a friend out in Seattle he hoped to stay with."

"Call the hotel. Find out if he's there. If he is, tell him to get his ass back here. We'll cover his costs. Tell him to stop sticking pins into Boeing's hide. That we *won't* cover. If he isn't, call up his pal. What was the name?"

"DelVecchio."

"Right. Get to it."

She frowned. "Wouldn't you like to speak with him yourself?"

Case thought about it for a microsecond. "No."

"Are you avoiding Mr. MacHenry for some reason?"

"That's a hell of a question for a goddamned secretary to ask the senior managing partner."

"That's a hell of a way to answer a civil question," she replied sweetly.

"Ouch." He put on a grimace. "Just go yank MacHenry's leash before he costs us a million-dollar settlement." He paused when she didn't move. "Please."

She left. Almost at once, the telephone rang.

"Mr. Case? It's Mr. MacHenry on line two."

"I thought I told you I—"

"He called. I didn't. Shall I put him through or do you want me to tell him you're in hiding?"

Case sighed. "Go ahead. I might as well get this over with."

The line clicked, then clicked again.

"Hello?" A siren howled in the distance behind MacHenry's voice. "Mr. Case? MacHenry here. I'm—"

"I know where you are. I sent you there, remember? What's that I hear? Are the cops after you?"

The siren reached a crescendo, then fell away. "Looks like a police car. There was an accident, I guess. I don't know. But I think we found . . ." MacHenry paused. This was not a secure line. "I think I found part of what I came for."

"That's not the way it looks from here."

A second police cruiser screamed by, heading elsewhere fast. "What's that?"

"Listen to me, MacHenry. Listen well. I want you to stop whatever you're doing and hightail it back to Washington. Tonight would be great."

The transcontinental line popped and sizzled. The siren faded in the distance. MacHenry turned and saw flashing red lights at the far end of East Marginal Way. "What does that mean?"

"It means," said Case, "that you were right and I was wrong. It's not Boeing. It's not even the goddamned Japanese, much as I might like it to be. I got a call from my contact at the Bureau. He's the AIC, the agent in charge of the Wheelwright case. It was a good-news, bad-news kind of conversation."

"I'm listening."

"The good news, if you want to call it that, is they're pulling apart that videotape. The one we saw here in my office."

MacHenry nodded. The image of the fire flared inside him once again. "And the bad news?"

"You heard about the British jet or were you too busy raising hell at Boeing?"

"Yes. It just came over the TV. That's why we—"

"Well, you better sit down. Ready? Hanging on to something solid? Okay. It was a bomb, MacHenry. It looks like they all were bombs. Just like the FAA, the NTSB, and all the rest of that crooked alphabet soup said all along. Not a flaw. Not bugs in the timbers. A bomb."

"*What?*" A Boeing security car roared by. "Who says so?"

"The FBI. So does the VP for Legal Affairs at Boeing. I take it you two have met."

"You've spoken with Abrams?" How had that happened so fast?

"I got to listen to the son of a bitch. He said you entered a secure building, that you attacked an employee—"

"No! That's not—"

"—and when building security apprehended you, you uttered terroristic threats against Boeing. None of it has to be true to make it very, very costly. You steer clear of Boeing, and that's an order. Especially now."

"That's a load of nonsense." MacHenry felt the facts coming at him too fast to make sense of. None of this fit. None of it. "The BA crash. What did the FBI come up with?" And how did they do it so fast? he wondered.

"Plenty. For one, the guy who did it."

"Who do they have?"

"Officially, he's John Doe. Unofficially, his name is Badr Muhammad. He works for the Port Authority. Had a badge that got him in everywhere. The cops were running a sting on baggage handlers who steal luggage out at Kennedy. The cameras picked up this guy tossing a musical-instrument case onto the loading cart after the cart had cleared the bomb-detector gizmo. Apparently, there was some kind of orchestra on the flight."

"That's not—"

"Are you talking or listening? Anyway, the stakeout team noticed and wondered who the hell was this character? They called the Bureau, and the feds caught him as he was driving out of the employee parking lot. He said he found the instrument case where it fell off a baggage cart. Claimed he was trying to make sure it stayed with the owner on that jet. A model employee."

"But?"

"Well, it turns out he's associated with that sheikh down in Jersey City. The one that tried to blow up the Trade Center a few years back. They busted his apartment building and found a drum of something called ANFO—"

"*ANFO?*"

"Yeah. Does that make any sense to you? My contact wouldn't tell me what the hell it meant."

MacHenry closed his eyes. "Ammonium nitrate, diesel fuel, and nitrate emulsion. It's called blasting blend." ANFO was big and stupid and cheap. It was crude. It made a big bang, but it wasn't the kind of explosive you'd choose to down an airliner. Two pounds of plastique would do that job nicely. Not a drum of ANFO. "How do they know it's his? Was it in his apartment building or in his apartment?"

Case came up short and hard against that one. He didn't know. "What are you? Counsel for the defense? A bomb factory is a bomb factory. Anyway, there was a mix-up getting word to the jet. By the time they figured it out and called them on the radio, nobody answered. Heads are going to roll over that one, I promise you."

It had to be a macabre coincidence. It *had* to be. "Did the Port Authority guy confess?"

"How the hell would I know? He's an Arab from Jersey City with bomb-making materials in the basement. They taped him tossing some uncleared baggage onto a jet that went down. You think the feds need any more than that? Think again." Case breathed in deeply, then slowly let it out. "I'm sorry, MacHenry. We'll cover your costs. But it's over with. No more jousts with Boeing. You better come on home before Abrams has you thrown into the slammer."

MacHenry's head was spinning. The delicate ladder, the chain of evidence leading to the probable cause, was tilting, tilting, falling. An ambulance went by, lights flashing but siren off. "No," he said. "That's not right. I don't know what the FBI thinks it has. But it isn't right. It's too damned fast and it's not right."

"You're sounding awfully sure of yourself."

"There *is* a problem on that jet, and I think we may have found it. And in spite of what I thought, Boeing's at least partway involved. I don't know who this Port Authority man is, or what he may have done, but there *is* something wrong with the 7X7, and it has to be grounded until we find out exactly what it is. Right now. Tonight."

"On what basis? You say Boeing's involved? That's going to be an expensive allegation. Are you prepared to back it up? If so, with what? Go ahead. Tell me a story, MacHenry. I could use one right about now."

"I can . . ." What exactly did he know? That the 7X7 was a computerized jet, impossibly complex, with room for a computer virus to worm its way in. But what else did he really know? What else could he actually prove?

"Well?"

"I can reach a solid probable cause if I can find one last piece," MacHenry said at last. "I need those samples Wheelwright had."

"The bogus bolts?"

"They aren't bolts. I think they're chips. Computer chips. We need them and a computer specialist who can find out what's hidden inside them. Then, everything falls into place. I can nail them, Mr. Case. But I need those chips."

"Then, friend, you got nothing. They found Wheelwright's possessions. He was sleeping in a park. In a pump room. The Park Police found everything there. Clothes. A pad of paper that matches the one he used to leave his little notes on. A gun, too."

MacHenry listened. It was like an unforecast total eclipse of the sun. One moment it's bright, high noon. The next, not a cloud in the sky, it gets darker, darker. Where the hell was all *this* coming from? "Would they know to look for a computer chip?"

"I doubt it. But from here, I'd say it doesn't make a lot of difference. Face facts, sometimes the obvious answer is the right one. Heaven knows I didn't think there were some Japs in the woodpile. But this bomber ties up a lot of loose ends. Wheelwright was probably just what everyone said he was: a nut. Maybe he was a nut who got too annoying to somebody. You did your best. We tried to make the save. But after the ceremony, there ain't gonna be much worth saving."

"Ceremony?"

"Tomorrow at noon. The word around Washington is that CFIUS is coming down pro Nippon Aerospace. It'll be announced at the dedication of the *Enola Gay*. The CEO of Boeing is flying in for it, plus a bunch of Jap honchos. Bottom line is, we don't have a case. After tomorrow, it won't matter anyway."

"I think we do," said MacHenry. "And so did you a couple of nights back."

"So I made a good case out of a lousy bunch of facts. What do you want? I'm a lawyer. That's my job."

"You didn't believe what you were telling me?"

"I believe what I can prove. I can't prove any great conspiracy to sabotage Boeing airliners. From what you've told me, neither can you. Come on back and finish up that Arrow Air report. We're through. The deal is done. We lost."

MacHenry found his knuckles whitening as he gripped the telephone. He swallowed his anger, keeping to safe terrain. One step, one more jab from Case, and he'd explode. "Not if I can find those five chips."

"Chips. Bolts. They don't matter if the feds have their hands on the original mad bomber."

"I say they do. There's a problem with that aircraft. And if you don't have the sense, or the guts, to recognize it, then I'll go this alone."

"Good luck."

Maggie knocked once, then brought Case in his Jim Beam.

He snapped his fingers and pointed at a cleared space on his desktop. "I don't know, MacHenry. Maybe if you find a way to prove there's a problem with those what—chips? How do you know there is a problem anyway? Hell. How do you know they're *chips*?"

"Wheelwright said he had five TMCs. That stands for Thrust Management Computer. A TMC's too big for him to have five whole units. But inside it, where the program lives, are hundreds of microchips. What's on them, or in them, that's the problem. Lawson Wheelwright was the last man to see those TMC computers before they went out into production. I think he intercepted some questionable components and took them to Washington."

"Try this: maybe he let them go through and then had an attack of conscience."

"No."

"No? What's so unbelievable about that? People aren't like machines, MacHenry. We don't execute programs. We're complex and ornery, and we all have a vast, untapped potential for evil. Every one of us. Especially if there's money involved."

"That's your take on things, Mr. Case. In the meantime, I want those chips."

"Maybe they burned with him. Maybe they never existed. Maybe you should just come on home."

MacHenry shook his head. He refused to think that. "Wheelwright was smart enough to evade capture for months. He would be sure those chips were safe."

Case sipped his bourbon. Maggie stood there, watching and listening. "Maybe there's something to what you say. I don't know. Frankly, it sounds pretty shaky."

"I know what I know, Mr. Case. And I know that something's not right with that aircraft. I'll call when I get back to Washington." MacHenry hung up.

Maggie clapped slowly and unenthusiastically. "Did MacHenry convince you, or did you just let him think he did?"

Case started to chuckle as he slowly put the phone down. He looked at Atwood. "I'm not sure. I'm really not sure." An idea flashed into his head. "Maggs, better find out where they're holding that poor son of a bitch. See if they're willing to talk bail. If they've appointed counsel, I want his name."

"Which poor son of a bitch would that be?"

"Badr Muhammad. The Jersey City Bomber." Case spun his foot off the ottoman and took out a fresh pad of yellow paper. He noticed that Atwood was still there. "Christ, Maggs. An innocent man is entitled to a lawyer, ain't he? Get going!"

The waitress kept Shig's cup filled with coffee. He'd felt obliged to drink it. After all, in Tokyo, each cup was a thousand yen, and no free refills. So he drank. But it made him edgy, as though a motor were revving up to redline in ultralow gear. Lots of vibration and very little distance covered. Shig watched as MacHenry argued on the telephone. He winced when the tall gaijin hung up abruptly, rudely. When MacHenry came back to the café booth, Shig could see problems written all over his face. "Troubles?"

"Yes."

Shig involuntarily looked up at the blank TV screen over the bar.

"Apparently there's evidence, pretty good evidence, that the BA ship was bombed."

Shig's eyes widened. "Not a computer error?"

"The FBI has a suspect."

"That was very fast."

"Too damned fast." MacHenry drummed the Formica tabletop with his fingers. "Either I figure out where Lawson Wheelwright stashed those infected TMC chips, or we wait until another plane goes down. Then they'll have to listen."

Shig toyed with his spoon. "What about the thrust computers from the first two crashes?"

"JAL went down over water. I'm sure they're still sifting half of Utah for pieces of that United flight. I don't know if they have the TMC boxes or not. On the other hand, they have a bomber in custody. Who wants to reopen a case that's solved?" MacHenry shook his head. "Roger Case is right. I'd have to have some reasons that were a whole bunch better than any I have right now. But . . . Boeing has to ground those planes. They have to."

Shig sipped his coffee. Do I tell him that the man who left the note, the man who was burned to death, was killed in front of a facility financed by the Hibakusha Foundation? The same foundation that provided the bulk of the funds to organize the Nippon Aerospace Consortium? Do I tell him that Japanese are sneaky, untrustworthy, that everything he probably thinks about us is justified? "And if Boeing won't voluntarily ground them?"

MacHenry shrugged. "Then I have to try and interest the NTSB in this thing. At least talk with the Go Team that's investigating. But if they know Roger Case hired me, they might figure me to be just another conspiracy nut." He glanced up. "What about you? What will you do?"

Shig checked his watch and did the required conversion. It was just after one in the afternoon, Seattle time. "It's still too early to call Tokyo. Another two hours and I can call my supervisor and tell him there is a strong possibility that Boeing has been compromised. From there, it's out of my arms."

"Hands. Out of your hands. But what about the crashes? *Three* of them now. That must count for something, doesn't it?"

"I work for the NPA's Economic Crimes Section, Mr. MacHenry. Not the Transport Ministry."

"You mean you're giving up? So long as a Japanese company wins, it doesn't matter if they committed murder. Is that it?"

"I have told you more than you knew. How is this giving up?"

"You put together the pieces and then turn your back. Why, Mr. Onishi? Because it might implicate a big Japanese business? Because you and your government don't want to *offend* these criminals? Why not *do* something and throw them into jail for what they've done?" MacHenry's face was flushed. Even as he spoke, he knew he was taking out his beef with Roger Case on the nearest available set of ears.

Shig ignored that remark. "I'll call Tokyo in another few hours. It's already tomorrow there. If they wish me to continue, then I will." Leave the truth for this MacHenry. He doesn't have to worry about getting moved to a desk by the window. "I am sure you will meet with greater success in the future."

"That's a hell of a thing for a policeman to say," MacHenry all but snarled. "Don't you care if the people behind this get caught?"

Shig did. Why couldn't he say so?

"Well, I'm very sorry." MacHenry checked the time himself. "Joe DelVecchio said he'd call his friend to give me a lift. She should be here any minute."

"You'll fly to Washington tonight?"

MacHenry got up and tossed some money onto the table. "Good luck, Mr. Onishi."

The red Lexus coupe glided up to the front door of the Gray Flamingo, Dyonna at the wheel. She honked.

MacHenry grabbed his battered leather flight bag and left without another word.

Shig watched as the tall gaijin got into the waiting car. The Lexus pulled away. A second car slowly cruised by the restaurant. A woman in dark green sunglasses looked in, then pulled away after the first.

Sunglasses? There wasn't a hint of sun in the sky. The world was full of mysteries. Perhaps when he called Tokyo and spoke with Ozawa, Shig could unload the heaviness he felt in his heart at seeing this mystery rise to the surface like a crab on a trap, only to watch it scuttle off and fall back down into the depths of a dark green sea.

FOURTEEN

"Very impressive," said Shintaro Ishii as he followed Bridger through the vaulted hangar. Spotlights played across the brilliant aluminum skin of the *Enola Gay*. Yoshi the bodyguard trailed at a respectful distance. Behind him, two American men, Bridger's, chatted and ambled like tourists on holiday. "You've done well. For my father's sake, I am glad it did not go up in smoke the other morning."

"I know it was important to him," said Bridger, "but doing my job is what you pay me for. And as for the arsonist"—he turned and indicated the two security men at the back—"you should thank them for yourself."

Ishii turned. These two certainly didn't look competent. The tall one wore his hair in a gangster's ponytail; the short one looked more like a wrestler. Thick and stupid. Yet they'd stopped that crazy man in the act of setting the hangar on fire. "I will see that they are rewarded," Ishii told the Hibakusha Foundation's chief Washington lobbyist. "Is everything ready for tomorrow?"

Bridger crossed his fingers. "The dedication's very important to us. It's a stamp of approval official Washington will place not only on this project, but on you and Japan as well. A political coming of age, if you will. Everything has to be right."

"Tell me the schedule."

"First and foremost, the photo session," said Bridger, ticking off the milestones, and the dollars, in his head. Tomorrow would be an expensive day for the Hibakusha Foundation, and a remunerative one for Bridger. "You, Amory Tasker from Boeing, Regano from Treasury, and—"

"You of course."

"Yes. The image here is partnership. Japanese and Americans working together to bring back this historic aircraft sets the stage for

Japanese and Americans working together to bring back Boeing to its old preeminence."

Ishii nodded. It was a remarkable feat of political engineering. Every bit as amazing as the work that went into restoring the *Enola Gay*. No, he thought. Far more. "And after the photo session?"

"The dedication at noon." Bridger paused and gave an in-the-know sort of smile. "There may be some very significant surprises."

"Surprises?" Ishii looked alarmed. He didn't like surprises in any flavor, not in Japanese, and surely not in American.

"Yes," said Bridger slowly, savoring the word, massaging it into at least two, and maybe three, syllables. "Quite possibly the next president of the United States will join us for a quick speech after the dedication ceremony."

Ishii stopped. "Is this a joke, Mr. Bridger?" Maybe old Kazuo Ibuki was right. If Bridger had that much influence, if he was able to draw that irascible Republican from Kansas, an avowed Japan basher, then he was worth whatever they paid him.

"But Regano is a member of the administration. This will not anger Mr. Clinton?"

"Bill Clinton is history and everyone in town knows it. Including Regano. He's looking to the future."

Ishii could see his reflection in the aluminum skin of the *Enola Gay*. It was another way the two countries were different, one respectful of the past, the other disdainful. If you really wanted to insult someone here in the States, you say he was history. It explained a lot. Ishii turned back to Bridger. "I appreciate your diligent efforts, and the way you have turned a potential liability to our benefit."

Bridger gave another fleeting smile. "My pleasure."

Yoshi listened and frowned. He didn't like this American. He didn't like the way he spoke to young Ishii. Bridger was all parry and feint, but no thrust, no sword exposed to the eye. He didn't like the way his words flew in one direction but his body, his facial expressions, went another. He was a liar. But Yoshi still didn't know what he was lying about.

Shintaro admired the old warplane. "I still can't believe the American government really was going to allow it to fall into pieces before my father rescued it."

"There was no constituency for it except a bunch of old geezers from the Second World War," said Bridger. "And they're dying out."

"And what about the original crew members?"

"They're still around. Most of them, anyway. But they're a tough bunch. They were pretty adamant about not coming if . . ." Bridger stopped.

"If any Japanese are here," Shintaro finished. "I suppose history has different meanings to them."

Bridger shrugged.

"How did you manage to convince Dole to come?"

Bridger explained. The senator from Kansas looked like a shoo-in for the presidency in the next election. His team thought that the B-29 would make a great background for a quick stump speech that would launch one of next year's major themes: the New Partnership.

The great ship would be wheeled outside and its four big Pratt and Whitney engines run for the waiting cameras. The wind would whip a brace of American and Japanese flags, and the senator would speak, not of ancient enemies, but of new partnerships, or as the electioneers preferred, New Partnerships.

The *Enola Gay* would be spun not as war booty going to the new victors, the Japanese, but as a piece of history given back to America by Bridger's client, the Hibakusha Foundation. With him would be the other members of the New Partnership: the leader of the Machinists Union, representatives from the Aerospace Workers, and the president of Boeing Commercial Aircraft. The old Democratic alliance with labor could be shattered for good. Who created the jobs? Who stamped the paychecks? That was all that mattered. Not whether the capital had its origins in New York, Tokyo, or Timbuktu.

Bridger reached over and clapped Ishii on the shoulder, making Yoshi step closer behind them.

"Your little whirlwind tour of the District really helped nudge some fence-sitters into our column," said Bridger. "Regano at Treasury is on board."

"It's all right," Shintaro told his bodyguard.

"I think they're willing to give you the benefit of the doubt. After all, it's not like you can pack up Boeing and take it to Japan, right? We're talking jobs. American jobs."

"Yes."

"I like that. Give the Japan bashers the low ground. We'll stick to a positive message: 'The New Partnership means jobs.' "

"Kazuo Ibuki is coming," said Ishii suddenly.

"I know." Bridger pulled up a cuff and checked his watch. He let the gray flannel fall back into place. "His flight arrives out at BWI this evening."

Shintaro was surprised. "You knew?"

"Sure. His office called a couple of days ago to set things up."

"A couple of *days*?" That was *before* he'd told Ishii!

"It takes time to put together a proper celebration in honor of the Boeing deal going through."

"It's a bit early to celebrate."

"With Regano on our side, and the next president of the United States dropping by to sprinkle us with holy water, I'd say it's all over except for the shouting. Trust me."

Shig placed the call to Tokyo from his room at the Double Tree. It took so much effort to use a telephone here in America. You had to talk to half a dozen different operators before the call could go through. And the pay phones were even worse. You needed a kilo of coins to make even a short call. They didn't take the ubiquitous charge cards everyone used in Japan. And the phones here were too dumb to make change; they wouldn't give you any money back even if your call was short. The phone buzzed, clicked, then it began to ring. It clicked again, and the voice of the office *bucho* at Economic Crimes came on, unmistakable.

"Moshi moshi!"

"Junior Investigator Onishi here. I'm calling from America. Let me speak with Section Chief Ozawa if you please."

"Onishi-san! Hai!"

Shig's eyebrows raised. That was certainly odd. The *bucho* was Ozawa's underling, but he still lorded it over the office, making everyone, Shig especially, feel like so much dirt swept up into a conspicuous pile. But now he sounded positively respectful. Very, very strange.

"Hello? Is that our star investigator? Onishi? Can you hear me?"

Shig involuntarily came to attention as he sat on the bed. "Mr. Section Chief!"

"My dear boy! How good it is to hear from you! Everyone is talking about you here."

Onishi's mouth dropped. He didn't say anything.

"You have really hit a home run this time!" Ozawa went on. "And to think we almost had to let you go. What a tragedy that would have been! But I thought you could pull it off, Senior Investigator! I always knew you had it in you!"

"Thank you, sir, but . . ." Shig stopped. *Senior* Investigator? Since when? "I . . . ," Shig stammered, "I'm afraid I don't understand."

"Then let me be the very first to congratulate you! You cracked the case wide open with your diligent work. You ferreted out some very big names."

"Sir, I wasn't . . ."

"Now, don't be modest. You are a credit to this entire section, and to our university. Your promotion to senior investigator took far too long. You have my sincere apologies. A Waseda man always rises to the top."

Cracked the case? Hardly. He thought of the business at Boeing, the covered-up files. The fact that Nippon Aerospace had wormed its way so deeply into the giant American company that now, to pull it out would kill Boeing. He thought of MacHenry leaving for Washington with failure and anger written in equal parts on his face. How had he cracked anything?

"This must come as a surprise," said Ozawa.

"Yes, absolutely."

"Then let me explain. Remember your first report, the one that opened up the nasty business at Manufacturers Credit? You uncovered a list of contributors to the *sokaiya* gangsters. That was the key."

"Sir?" Gangsters? No. That wasn't right. The names of the political heavyweights he'd found weren't connected to the *sokaiya*. They were connected with the fund that launched the Nippon Aerospace Consortium!

"Well, I took the liberty of meeting in private with the finance minister himself. We worked out a fast solution based on your facts. Everyone here already knows, but by this time tomorrow, Rondon-Nomura will be front-page headlines! Congratulations!"

Rondon-Nomura? That was the very *least* of what Shig had found! This wasn't at all . . .

"Corruption has been dealt a severe blow because of you. The papers will lead with that story in the morning. Your name will appear as chief investigator. I admit, we had our differences, but now our hearts understand each other, eh, Onishi? We're on the same winning team. So when do you come back?"

"I . . . The Rondon-Nomura matter was not that important. It was—"

"I insist you take credit where credit is due!"

"I'm not trying to be modest, sir. The *sokaiya* money came from the same source as the funds that founded Nippon Aerospace. They're deeply involved in trying to extort their way into—"

"No. All of this is neatly wrapped up now, thanks to you. Mr. Finance Minister arranged a meeting of banks. What would the world think if it found out that gangsters had penetrated one of our most prestigious institutions? The market would overreact and it would cost everyone billions. So they've put together a pool of funds to shore up Manufacturers Credit. The names you uncovered are going to be in a real hot seat after the investigations!" Ozawa shouted as though he could get his message across by sheer volume. "No, Senior Investigator, you must not be so modest. It's a new Japan, after all. You can stand out and receive the rewards that you have so richly earned." Ozawa cleared his throat. "Now, when can you get back here to work?"

Shig didn't need a diagram to understand what had happened. They'd picked the smallest of the transgressions he'd uncovered and used them as leverage against the heavy hitters who were up to their chins in far dirtier matters. Information like this was useful to the new government, obviously. And to the National Police Agency as well. What had been the price of silence, the price of his promotion to senior investigator? How many people had died on those jets?

"Onishi? Are you there?"

"Yes. I'll look into flights immediately, sir."

"Excellent. Get back fast, Onishi. Don't let anything deter you. Not one thing. Remember! Teamwork!"

Now that was an even clearer warning, thought Shig. "Understood!"

The line clicked dead.

He sat there on the bed, the lights off, the room lit with the wet, gray light of a Seattle autumn afternoon. Senior investigator. The solver of Rondon-Nomura. No more fear of joining the tribe of the window sitters. He'd have a certain amount of prestige, even. He could stop taking money from his hardworking father. Maybe the old man could sell out to Kentucky Fried Chicken and retire. Who knew? It should be more than enough, even for a Waseda man. Finding out *what* was wrong was the important thing. Not *who*. And he had done his job. His superiors had the case well in hand. They knew what he did not know. It should be enough.

Then why wasn't it?

Shig sat there, wondering how a simple straight line, an investigation, a life, could suddenly veer so far from its neatly established course. He wondered how many flights would leave Seattle for Washington, D.C. And which one MacHenry would be on.

It was already Friday in Tokyo. The morning rush was over, and he was cutting up meat and vegetables for the early-lunch crowd, tossing handfuls into a fry pan, when they walked in. Punch perm hair greased back and then up into insolent little spikes. Loafers with oversize tassels. Suits made from some shiny fabric. *Yakuza.* Gangsters. And low on the pecking order. He looked them over, then went back to his work. The cleaver chopped and banged against the scarred cutting board as the fry pan sizzled and spat. "Closed," he said, his hand tight around the old cleaver's handle. "Come back later."

"He wants us to come back later," said one.

"He certainly does," said the other.

He could smell trouble coming. It was like a greasy odor wafting across the train tracks from the Kentucky Fried Chicken shop. "Closed!" he said again, and looked down to his onions and his gingerroot.

They didn't bother telling him who they were or why they were here. With a crash of overturned tables and stools, the two *yakuza* went about the job of wrecking the little noodle stand with an almost disinterested professionalism, taking care to sweep the counter of soy bottles and sake cups as an afterthought.

"Stop that! Police!"

"They're all someplace else, papa," said one of them with a laugh. He yanked the banners down from the entryway and kicked them into a corner. "You should be, too."

He flipped the heavy cleaver in his grip so that the blade faced backward, the thick pounding edge forward. He didn't want to kill them. Just bang them up enough to teach them whom they could intimidate and whom they could not. "I won't pay!" he shouted, thinking they were here to encourage him to hand over protection money.

"Don't worry. This is free. Isn't it?"

"Certainly is," said his friend.

Shig's father leaped over the counter and charged them, silver cleaver flashing in the lights. He was fast. Much faster than they expected. He swung it, bringing it down hard onto the shoulder of one of those shiny suits. The thug went down with a surprised squall of pain. Shig's father leaped in the air and spun, ready to teach the other one the same lesson.

There was a pop, another. Impossibly small. He raised his arm to strike again, but it refused to obey. Two red holes had somehow appeared just above the right nipple, staining his greasy white cook's outfit. He sagged down to the tiles as the second thug walked over, kicked him flat, and put a third .22 into his head. A fan of red sprayed across the clean white tile floor.

The one he'd hit with the blade cursed as he staggered over to the fry pan and turned the gas flame up to a full blowtorch. The food went from sizzle to char. The metal gave off a strange, pungent smell. He took a wad of paper napkins and tossed them on. They went up in flames immediately.

As the two left, one reached into his pocket and flipped a little white card into the air. It fell, looping over and over like a leaf. It came to rest upside down, still bent in the shape Shig had left it when he'd used it to blind the security camera's eye at the NAC building. It was a tiny arching bridge over a flowing red river of his father's blood.

Joe DelVecchio had had enough discussion. MacHenry had shown him something strange, and even if Tom Kelly said no big deal, it gnawed at him. *OUCH! . . . the Warelord!* Who knew what else lived in the circuitry of the Boeing 7X7? No more jumper wires like the ones on the Lauda Air jet, but something. Something. What?

He caught the interplant shuttle and made straight for his own domain at Boeing Flight Test. In between his departure from the SIL Lab and his arrival there, word had arrived that another ship, another Boeing 7X7, was down. He could see it in the faces at the office. Nobody needed to say a word. He walked up to Melanie, the young woman who sat in the same chair his dear Dyonna had once occupied, and said one word: "Who?"

"British Air. It was bombed."

"Jesus. For sure?"

She nodded.

The entire crew at Flight Test reacted in a decidedly mixed way. A loss was a loss, and everyone felt it. But when the news flashed that a man had been caught planting a bomb on board, a wave of unmistakable relief flooded everyone's ragged nerves. *It's not us,* was the clear message. *We haven't screwed up.* Now it was time to put it all behind and get on with the business of being the world's largest, and best, builder of jet aircraft. Everyone felt the weight of the unknown lift from their shoulders.

Everyone except Joe DelVecchio. He hustled out to the aircraft ramp and spoke to one of the maintenance techs on duty. The long, smooth wing of a brand-new Boeing 7X7 spanned high above their heads. It was a green ship, unpainted except for the chemical preservative Boeing used to corrosion-proof its transports. A rolling workstand was shoved up against the number-two Pratt and Whitney turbofan. Fifteen minutes later, DelVecchio was trotting toward the Flight Test locker room with a metal object in his hands. It was black and longer than it was wide, a flattened shoebox.

"We're standing down," he said as he marched in. "No more

flying today." DelVecchio caught up with the pilot scheduled to fly the day's next test hop. The young engineer had just slammed the locker shut and spun the dial.

"Why not?" he said. "I'm supposed to—"

"Because I say so." Joe DelVecchio was not a man to be questioned. Not ever, and most especially not by some wet-behind-the-ears flight-test jockey in a blue sack suit. "Besides. Your ship is down for maintenance."

The flight-test pilot checked his clipboard. Hull number eighty-nine was just out of final production inspection. There wasn't a damned thing wrong with it. "Not according to my logs, sir."

"Your logs have just been superseded." Joe DelVecchio hefted the black box. Each end was studded with cannon-plug connector pins. A serial number was silk-screened onto the top, along with the logo of Norton Aerodyne. "She'll fly all day without a pilot at the wheel, but she won't fart without this."

He caught the next shuttle headed for headquarters on East Marginal Way. If that forked-tongued lawyer at Legal Affairs wouldn't act sensibly, then Tom Kelly would. Together, they'd plug this thing into the Iron Bird and go through it, circuit by circuit if need be.

But when he got to Kelly's office in the Systems Integration Lab, he saw he would have to take a number. The chief programmer's outer office was full of people, including two uniformed officers of the Seattle police. What had happened? Kelly's secretary was sobbing. And there was Walter Abrams looking even more worried than usual.

"What gives?" DelVecchio asked the secretary.

Red-rimmed eyes, puffy cheeks, and Kleenex in hand, she tried to answer, but she couldn't stop crying.

Abrams came over.

"What's with the convention?" asked DelVecchio. "Where's Kelly?"

Abrams peered at DelVecchio closely, as though trying to see inside his head for an answer. "Tom Kelly's dead."

FIFTEEN

Where is he? thought Shig as he headed away from the Northwest Airlines gates. Where is MacHenry? He hadn't booked on Northwest. That narrowed his search, but not by much. He checked the ceiling clock. He'd memorized the next dozen departures for Washington, D.C. He had fifteen minutes to go if he was going to tell MacHenry that Lawson Wheelwright had died in front of a building owned and financed by the Hibakusha Foundation.

Shig trotted down the corridor to catch the underground shuttle to the United gates. SeaTac was busy with late-afternoon departures, perhaps the busiest hour of operations except for holidays. But it was nothing compared with the Tokyo subway. To Shig, it seemed strangely empty. He darted as the doors began to close and leaped through at the last possible instant. Absolutely impermissible behavior back home, where "packers" stood by each open door to force the late arrivals into a semi-solid mass of flesh. But here in America, a person had a lot more options. Was that why he was going against Ozawa's edict? Had he become infected with the American disease of rebellion?

He quickly found a seat, another rare commodity in Japan. A warning bell sounded and the train slowly, ever so slowly, began to roll. No. He'd caught the rebellion bug very early, and all by himself on his first pilgrimage to Fuji.

To a Japanese, climbing Fuji was like an American's visit to Disneyland blended with a Muslim's hajj to Mecca. Every Japanese did it at some time or another, and many did it again and again. The sere slope of that perfect volcano had a trail hammered into it by the tread of a million pilgrims; some wore hiking boots, some dress shoes, and some—Shig had seen it—high heels. Despite the well-worn trail, it was a long and arduous climb to Fuji's 3,800-meter peak.

The real prize was arriving at the top just before the rising sun burst from the horizon. Shig had planned his ascent accordingly, staying at one of the overnight inns perched on Fuji's flanks in order to get an early start.

The trail leading up was as busy as a Tokyo sidewalk at rush hour. The unheated inn turned out to be one room with tatami mats spread from wall to wall. By nightfall it was so stuffed with humanity that despite the bitter cold outside, the room was hot and steamy as a jungle.

The next morning, with the room still resounding to snores, he rose from his mat, dressed, and began his final climb to the top. It wasn't even four A.M., but the trail was already crowded. Hawkers selling souvenirs were up and busy. Tea stalls billowed fragrant clouds of steam in the cold night air. Everyone had a wooden walking stick. It was the thing to do, an unspoken essential. It would have seemed strange to ask why everyone was carrying one.

Little braziers glowed cherry red in the predawn dark as they heated up branding irons meant to inscribe the altitude onto the sticks: 1,000 meters, 2,000 meters, 3,000. Collect each one! All the way to the top. The higher you got, the more expensive the brands became, but who could go home without the ultimate mark burned onto his stick?

As the east turned milky white with the coming day, Shig was still a hundred meters from the peak. It was windy and cold, and the stars burned down bright as nails hammered through the velvet dark bowl of sky. Up ahead, a snaking line of flashlight-wielding humanity blocked the trail, winding between what at first looked like boulders, but as the sunrise neared, Shig saw were souvenir booths. People stopped and bought some trinket, then moved on. The line inched upward. There was no way he was going to make it in time. A cloud burst into flame.

He was going to miss the sun. He didn't need his walking stick branded. He didn't have one. And he wasn't interested in the little mementos being sold in the booths. He wanted to get to the top in time. But you couldn't barge through the solid line. It would be un-Japanese. Shig turned and saw the white in the east turn red. He made up his mind that after all this effort he was not going to be caught so near the goal and come home empty-handed. Not without a fight.

The trail was marked off by cables. The climbers were shoulder to shoulder from one side to the other, herded into a tight, upward-oozing stream. As the new day began to break, Shig ducked under the steel ropes, out of the line, onto the rugged lava stones and shattered basalt, the rotten snow left from winter, and ran for the top.

Some watched in horror. The younger climbers yelled. Children pointed. More than one outraged citizen poked a walking stick out to trip him. Rude man! Uncivilized elder brother! And worse. He closed his ears to the insults, dodged the obstacles, slipped in the crusty snow, but Shig hit the crest just as the first red incandescent sliver ignited the east. A great *OOOOH!* went up from the crowd, and he was instantly forgotten.

No. He didn't catch the rebellion disease here in America. He'd been infected by it long ago. But here, where doing things your own way seemed perfectly natural, the virus had flourished.

The little train slowed and stopped. The sliding doors opened. Shig bolted through and headed for the scanner booth that barred the way to the departure gates. He had nothing with him, but his wild-eyed pace scared the security guard enough for her to make him stop and go back through again.

Shig ran for the United lounge, dodging the ambling passengers. Unlike the lines at Fuji, nobody seemed to care who got where, or when. He skidded around a corner as the PA system came on.

"United 311, service to Washington, D.C., will be boarding at Gate . . ."

He ran.

". . . those needing help or traveling with small children . . ."

There! A line of suited businessmen waited patiently for the board-ing to begin. Some sprawled in their hard plastic chairs, not bothering to stand in line. Was that . . . ? No. Over there!

His heart sank. MacHenry wasn't here.

Shig checked his watch. Continental would be leaving in twelve minutes. It was another shuttle-train ride away. He gathered himself up and ran.

★   ★   ★

DelVecchio used Tom Kelly's office phone and called his own car number. He kept the TMC module in sight on the desk. The telephone trilled, then clicked. Road noise flooded into his ear. "Dyonna?"

"Joe? What's wrong?"

How does she know? he wondered. "Where's MacHenry? Put him on."

"I just dropped him off. He's catching a flight back to Washington."

"Damn. Which one?"

"American. What happened? I thought he was staying with us again tonight. I liked him."

"Me, too. Look. A lot has happened. I may need the car. How fast can you get back here to the lab?" Even before she answered, DelVecchio could hear the powerful engine rev up. Good gal, he thought.

"I'm on I-5, just coming up on Skyway. I'll be there as fast as I can."

He hung up. Abrams was standing near, holding up a framed photo of Tom Kelly, his wife, and his daughter. Kelly was in running attire, shorts, cutaway T-shirt, and a race number. He was doubled over in pain, his face drawn, but the finish tape hung from his shoulders. "Where did it happen?" DelVecchio asked.

Abrams placed the photo back down. "Out on the road. The driver had a heart attack and Tom got in the way."

"The driver okay?"

"No. The EMTs couldn't revive him. He worked here at the SIL. A young guy, too. Real young for a heart attack."

"Somebody see it happen?"

"I don't know. I don't think so."

DelVecchio glanced at the photo, then through the open door to Kelly's office. The afternoon light was fading in the plate-glass window. Idiot goes out and runs on a wet, dark afternoon, he's looking to get run over. He was asking for it.

Suicide? He looked at the family portrait. Kelly was a driven man, but could he have done such a thing? Would he have jumped in front of a car, all because of a little fudged computer data? All because MacHenry had discovered an Easter egg tucked away in his program? He picked the photo up. Cute wife. Pretty kid. He set it back down. No way. Not unless there was a hell of a lot more behind the little *OUCH!* glitch the Warelord had inserted into the 7X7's flight computer. A lot more. His eyes went back to the TMC box.

"What's that you have?" asked Abrams.

"This?" DelVecchio picked up the TMC unit. There would be no testing it down on the Iron Bird now. There was no one who could pull it apart and look at the pieces like Tom Kelly. But there was someone else who might know who could do it and how. "This is homework," he said. He turned to leave. His Lexus had the biggest engine available from the builder. Dyonna would roar up to the front gate any minute. "I have to go. Sorry about today. MacHenry will keep quiet about the Lauda deal."

Abrams didn't answer. He watched the chief of Boeing Flight Test hurry out with what could only be an airplane part under his arm. A black box with the NA logo of Norton Aerodyne on it. That was what MacHenry was raving about just a few hours back, wasn't it?

"Sir?" asked a policeman from inside Kelly's office. "Could I ask you to step inside? We have a few more boxes to fill in and then we're done."

Abrams turned. "Sure." DelVecchio was gone. Abrams realized he might have a few more boxes to fill in himself.

MacHenry wasn't at the Continental gate. It had to be American. The departure-information screen played in Shig's head as he left the underground shuttle train behind once more. Gate 12A. A four-fifteen flight, and it was already after four. Shig slowed down to a deliberate pace as he approached the security checkpoint at the head of the long corridor that held American's departure gates.

". . . American . . . Flight 121, nonstop service to Washington, D.C., is now ready for boarding, Gate . . ."

No! He sprinted now. Gate 5. Gate 6. Gate 6A. He wasn't going to make it! He nearly knocked over a burly black man in an airline uniform as he dodged back and forth down the corridor, caroming off people like a pachinko ball on its way down a maze.

"We'll begin our boarding process with passengers assigned to seats in rows twenty to . . ."

He rounded the last corner and came to a circular, vaulted room with boarding gates radiating in all directions. He found 12A and saw a line already moving by the gate agent. Where was MacHenry? What if he had already passed the agent by? He ran by the line of passengers holding tickets and carry-on luggage. The gate agent ripped a ticket stub and handed it back to a man at the head of the line. She smiled wearily. The line inched forward. Where was MacHenry? He wasn't in the lounge. He wasn't in the line. Could he already be on board?

"Young man! The line starts back there," said a combative-looking old woman clutching a plastic shopping bag.

He ignored her and walked on.

"Hey! Naranderu yo!"

Shig nearly fell as he swung to see who had addressed him so in Japanese. We're lining up! someone had yelled pointedly. But he didn't see anyone who looked remotely Japanese. He went on to the front of the line, straight to the gate agent. "Excuse me!" he said, his voice harsh, his breath coming in gasps.

She tore off a ticket stub and looked up. Her eyes darted to find the nearest guard. There was one nearby, thank goodness.

"I need to know if someone is on this airplane." As he said this, he saw, way down the boarding tunnel, beyond a sea of legs and baggage and overcoats draped over arms, a familiar-looking piece of luggage. It looked a lot like MacHenry's battered leather flight bag. "Mr. MacHenry!" he shouted.

Oh-oh. "Sir!" The agent moved to block the gate-crasher. "We're boarding. You can check the passenger list down at . . ."

But Shig had made up his mind. It wasn't a Japanese thing to do. It wasn't even an American thing to do. He shoved the agent aside and ran for that receding piece of luggage. "MacHenry!"

The gate agent tripped and fell. The miffed lady in line yelled, *"Police!"*

"MacHenry!"

A uniformed guard appeared.

"He's got a gun!"

Someone screamed and everybody dived for shelter. Americans might not know how to build cars, thought Shig as he ran, but they sure are well versed in combat tactics. The flow of passengers parted as he ran down the narrow tunnel. The floor flexed underneath his pounding shoes.

"Hey, you!" yelled the security guard. "Stop!"

Shig pushed aside one man, then another. And there he was.

"Mr. MacHenry!"

"Onishi?" MacHenry stood there. "What the devil . . . what are you trying to do?"

"Freeze!" The airport guard stopped. He was fully accessorized with radio, key chains, nightstick, and other appendages hanging from handy little loops and buckles. But he didn't have a gun. He wasn't about to charge up against someone who might. He fumbled for a can of pepper spray that remained stubbornly attached to his belt.

He didn't have to rush. Shig wasn't going anywhere. "Mr. MacHenry. I apologize for this intrusion. But there is something we must discuss."

"My flight's just about to—"

"No. There's another one in an hour. We have to talk."

The guard came up slowly. "What's going on?" he demanded, the pepper spray held out in a two-handed grip like a .357 magnum.

MacHenry held up a hand, indicating that the guard should calm down. "It's okay, Officer. Mr. Onishi is a policeman."

"Police?" The guard eyed Shig. "Yeah? From where?"

Shig reached into his jacket pocket. The guard froze in terror. Maybe this guy was packing . . . Someone screamed again as he took out a small white packet.

"No! No gun. See?" Shig held out a card. "Shig Onishi. Economic Crimes Section of the National Police Agency. I am from Japan."

★ ★ ★

She read a magazine, or appeared to, as she sat at a passenger lounge two removed from 12A and watched as MacHenry and the one she'd seen before at the Boeing building put their heads together. The Japanese man had appeared very suddenly. She was in line herself and had confirmed his nationality with a quick burst of an appropriate phrase. She'd been right back when she first saw him at Boeing. Japanese. She'd heard MacHenry deflect the guard with something about him being with the police. This Japanese policeman was far from his beat. That was all for the good.

Kazuo Ibuki arrived at the Smithsonian hangar accompanied by his bodyguard. No Japanese businessman of any rank traveled to America these days without one. Ibuki's man was slim and elegantly attired in Armani. The effect was diminished by the big white button in his lapel. It read *Wow Wow*, the name of Japan's biggest satellite TV network.

"*Konban wa*," said Shintaro Ishii as he bowed to Ibuki. "I trust your flight was not too difficult."

Ibuki returned the bow ever so abruptly. Only a Japanese would recognize it for the insult it was. "I'm here. Where is Bridger?"

"Bridger is taking a telephone call. I have interesting news about tomorrow. It seems that a presidential—"

"All that can come later. First I must see Bridger."

Yoshi caught Wow Wow's eye and nodded. It felt good for there to be at least one other professional around. He certainly had no respect for the two men Bridger kept. They'd spent the last half hour ostentatiously cleaning their little pistols, chatting and laughing like two crows.

"Bridger-san?" Ishii was taken aback. "He's been gone only a few—"

"Get him," said Ibuki. "I have no time to waste and neither do you."

Ishii's face burned in embarrassment. He nodded for Yoshi to do the job.

"*Hai!*" The bodyguard stiffened to attention, bowed, and raced off to where he knew Bridger could be found. But Bridger was coming out even as Yoshi reached for the door. The American brushed by and made straight for Ibuki.

"Kazuo," said Bridger. "Welcome to Washington."

"Ah, Mr. Bridger." Ibuki's leathery face deepened into a spider-web of wrinkles. "I hope you have good news for me."

"Yes and no. Perhaps we could talk in private for a few moments," said Bridger, pointedly excluding Shintaro. "I want to bring you in on something that needs taking care of. It's not necessarily good news. But I think we have it under control."

Ibuki understood. "Of course." He looked at Shintaro. "You wait. We will be back in a moment."

SIXTEEN

MacHenry closed his yellow pad. "If I understand you correctly, Mr. Onishi, you've established a trail that connects this organized crime group with the Nippon Aerospace Consortium through the workings of a charitable group. The Hibakusha Foundation."

Onishi bowed his head. "Thank you. I have done my best."

"Even if it were true, you haven't helped me find those missing computer chips."

"Excuse me, but there is no plausible way that Lawson Wheelwright could have known about the Hibakusha connection. He did not go seeking *them*. That means *they* found *him*."

"And brought him to that hangar." It did clear up the question of how Wheelwright could have left a note at Roger Case's office and found his way out to Dulles. Not as a seeker. But as a prisoner. "If they found him, they probably found the computer chips, too. They're good as gone."

"I think not." Shig shook his head. "You must understand. If Wheelwright was captured, it was most likely by people working for the crime syndicate. Local employees. After all, you don't have *yakuza* running around America. Too obvious. They would hire Americans."

"So?"

"Americans would not have the authority to destroy those chips. They would be told to wait until someone from Japan came to deal with them. To do otherwise would be to take more authority than anyone in Japan would have given them."

"Meaning they still have them someplace, waiting on the word from Tokyo?"

"Not word. More likely someone would come and pick them up personally. They wouldn't trust . . ." Shig stopped. "They would want to be sure for themselves."

What had Roger Case said? That some Japanese honchos were showing up for the dedication of the *Enola Gay*? That was tomorrow! "Who are these Hibakusha people anyway?"

Shig paused. MacHenry was a foreigner, and these were delicate matters concerning the innermost workings of Japanese society, Japanese commerce. But this was his chance, maybe his last chance, to see the case solved. Really solved. Not buried. MacHenry was his partner. MacHenry was on the inside. Not the outside. He took a deep breath and began.

"The Hibakusha Foundation is an organization of atom-bomb survivors. It is a legitimate group, but they are involved with the Inagawakai through a man named Ishii. He was the Foundation's main source of funding for many years."

"Was?"

Shig nodded. "He died in 1994. His son is now CEO of Nippon Aerospace. There is another man. The Ishiis' legal adviser. Kazuo Ibuki. He is very powerful. I believe that is why this case will not be allowed to proceed and why I have been recalled." And promoted. Teamwork!

Was it Roger Case's nagging voice, or was this Japanese policeman making sense? He jotted down a few more notes, then paused. "The *Enola Gay* is being dedicated tomorrow morning. My boss says there's a whole bunch of bigwigs due in from Japan for it."

"If only Mr. Wheelwright had told you where he put those chips, then we would not have to guess."

We? thought MacHenry. "If only." MacHenry thought of the videotape Roger Case had shown him, the one the FBI lab had taken apart. He wished he could get rid of it, banish it from his memory. But he could still see the fire-wreathed figure standing in front of the open hangar doors.

"Something is the matter, Mr. MacHenry?"

"Watch my things for a moment. I'll be right back."

MacHenry found the first bank of rest rooms closed off for cleaning. A woman was mopping the tiled floor on the women's side. He walked down the long corridor. Could those chips be sitting, waiting for the chief honcho to show up and personally take them back? He tried the handle on the next rest room he came to. It was open.

★ ★ ★

Shintaro Ishii watched the Virginia countryside go by. It was fully dark by the time the hushed limo rolled by the Fairfax exit eastbound.

Ibuki, Bridger, and Shintaro Ishii were all in one car, a black Chrysler. Yoshi and Wow Wow followed in a nondescript Ford. His father would have put Ibuki in his place. Shintaro was the head of the Foundation! The man in charge. Ibuki seemed to have forgotten that.

The big Chrysler took the Annandale off-ramp and dove into rolling horse country. Long winding drives ambled away from the two-lane road, their entries guarded by iron gates. Flickering through the trees, the bright lights of the secluded estates swept by like distant galaxies.

Shintaro leaned over from the jumpseat. "Mr. Bridger hasn't told me what he's prepared for us tonight."

Bridger began to answer, but Ibuki spoke first. "A club. A very special kind of club." His face was tinted green by the instrument-panel lights. "A place where we can experience the real America."

Shintaro's stomach growled. He hoped the real America included dinner.

The car barely slowed as it took a turn onto what seemed a deserted one-lane drive. They flashed through a stone archway. There were no gates.

"Here we are." Bridger sat back in the plush seat as they came to the main house, slowing to a stop in front of a set of wide stone stairs. Carriage lamps glowed softly to either side of the doorway. Both cars stopped and a uniformed attendant bowed as he opened the door for them.

Ibuki, Bridger, and Shintaro got out. The two bodyguards in the other car did the same. Breath flagged white in the chill night air. Above the wooden door, carved into a heavy oak beam, were the letters *AHC*.

Inside the entry, a tall woman with long, auburn hair met them. Her hair shimmered like some precious, exotic wood. She wore an immaculate velvet tuxedo. The wood floors glowed a warm chestnut brown. Huge oriental rugs were scattered haphazardly across them. The walls were decorated with hunt scenes and mounted game. "Mr. Bridger," she said with a long bow. "Welcome to the Hunt Club.

The dining room you reserved will be ready in an hour." She glanced at the bodyguards. "Your staff will be taken care of, too."

"Good!" Ibuki clapped excitedly. "That gives us time!"

For what? Shintaro wondered.

"Gentlemen? Please follow me."

Both bodyguards trailed behind their charges. When the doors opened, Yoshi tensed. The Ishii family guard didn't like what he was hearing. The sound of distant, muffled gunfire came from the room beyond. Thump! Crack! Thump! Crack! Every now and then an enormous *boom!* silenced the others. Was it a movie? He shot a questioning look at Ibuki's guard. Wow Wow shook his head. He had no idea, either.

"Here you are," the hostess said. "Please enjoy your evening."

"What is this place?" asked Shintaro as he followed the other two into a large room lined with glass gun cabinets. A smiling man stood behind a counter, looking for all the world like a jeweler displaying his precious wares to a likely bunch of customers.

"Something we cannot reproduce, even in Japan," said Ibuki with a childlike glee. "This is what sets America apart from the world. It's last area of distinction." He chuckled. "A cultural park, if you will. But one that's far too dangerous to have back home."

"Welcome, gents," said the man behind the counter. "I'm the rangemaster tonight. What can I interest you in? We have it all."

Shintaro's eyes widened. There was everything from one-shot target pistols to fully automatic assault rifles. HKs, Kalashnikovs. M16s. Even the street guns were there, the Uzis, the Tecs, the Bull Pups, all the ugly pieces of metal and plastic that had turned American streets into combat zones.

"Ah, like 007!" Ibuki chose a slim Walther PPK, a very concealable weapon. Bridger opted for a lever-action Winchester with a decided antique look.

The rangemaster motioned Shintaro to the cabinet. "What about you, sir? What's your pleasure? Ever fire a machine gun? We have a drum-fed Thompson I think you'll enjoy."

"No. Thank you. I, I will just watch."

"Your selections have been registered," said the rangemaster. "Your weapons will be ready in the firing room. Enjoy your stay."

He pressed a button and a bell silenced the firefight on the indoor range. He picked up a microphone and spoke. "Five minutes, five minutes cease-fire. All shooters please step behind the red line."

"Shall we?" said Bridger.

Ibuki nodded. "I wouldn't miss it for all the world."

The cleaning lady looked up when Oka walked in. She eyed the young woman's clothes, tight black sweater with a single strand of pearls. A leather miniskirt the color of gunmetal, the long, dark legs, heels that clicked with a determined, almost insolent beat on the tiled floor.

The cleaning woman stared. She would never have these things, never look this way. But, she thought, she did have a certain power. "Room's closed for cleanup," she said brusquely. "There's another one down the hall."

"I won't be needing it." Oka closed the door behind her and threw the slide bolt shut. The snap made the cleaning woman stop mopping and stare.

"What . . . ?"

Oka snatched the wood-handled mop out of the cleaning woman's hands. She held it in a two-fisted kendo grip and brought the rounded end up hard against the woman's head. She could feel the blow connect, a sharp, electric sensation that traveled up Oka's elbow.

The cleaning woman toppled in a heap of dirty clothes and spilled Pine Sol. There wasn't time to wonder. Time to wait to see what might, or might not, happen. Minutes counted. She dragged the woman into a toilet stall and placed her head across the bowl. She brought the heel of her hand down onto the back of her neck and heard bone crunch, then crackle against porcelain.

A minute later, the door opened again. Oka wheeled the mop bucket out, turned, and locked the door using the keys she'd taken. Her beautiful clothes shed like a molted snakeskin, she was in stained tatters and old flat tennis shoes. Mop in hand, she headed for the next bank of toilets.

"You want me to wait, Joe?" asked Dyonna as she pulled up to the terminal.

He opened the door before the red Lexus even stopped. He

jumped out, the TMC box under his arm. He leaned back in. "Put it in short term and meet me at American." He slammed the door shut.

He had no trouble negotiating the airport corridors and trams until he came to the security booth that blocked the wing leading to the American gates. He walked through without thinking, and the alarm rang so loud even he looked around to see who had tripped it.

"Sir, would you mind putting that piece of luggage through on the belt?"

"Luggage?" He looked to see what the nutty woman was talking about. "This?" He held up the TMC module. "This isn't luggage. It's a computer," he said impatiently. He hoped MacHenry was still around. He should have called ahead. What if he had made an early . . .

"I'm sorry to delay you." A furrow of worry spread over her face. This was a strange-looking thing indeed. What with a bomb bringing down that flight back east, she wasn't about to let this thing through *her* belt. "Can I see it operate?" If it whirred and buzzed and a screen popped out, well and good. If Super Mario appeared, even better.

"No, you can't. It isn't a complete unit. Just a part."

"Then I'm afraid you'll have to check it in at the airline desk, sir. Right behind you."

DelVecchio could read the tea leaves. "Look. Can you page a passenger?"

"The phone's right over there," she said, nodding at a white wall unit. "I'll watch your article for you in the meantime."

DelVecchio gritted his teeth and jogged over to the phone. Damn! he seethed. "Hello? I want a passenger paged immediately. It's an emergency. . . . Yes. His name's MacHenry. I'm at the scanner at the end of the American gates. . . . Yes. You have a nice day, too." He slammed the phone back down.

MacHenry ran the water until it was ice-cold, then washed his face. He was exhausted and jet-lag scrambled. Onishi thought the chips were still there to be found. How could he get into that hangar? It must be guarded. How would the dedication ceremony tomorrow be run? Could it . . .

The sound of a door softly closing made him stop and turn. It was the cleaning woman. "I'll be finished in a second," he said.

Oka rolled the bucket forward, then turned and threw the bolt shut. "Why wait?"

MacHenry dried his face. What had she just said? He looked up as Oka advanced, the wood-handled mop once more in a cross-chest grip. Blond hair, dark eyes. He'd seen them before. Where? Wasn't it . . . Then he knew. "Maria? What are . . . ?" He staggered backward an instant before the wooden handle swished through the air an inch from his eyes. He could feel the wind of its passing on his wet skin.

What's keeping him? Shig wondered. He looked at the bank of toilets down the corridor. Wait. That plastic sign wasn't there before, was it? It was in front of the door to the men's room.

The PA system crackled to life. "Paging passenger MacHenry, passenger MacHenry, please meet your party at the American Airlines desk. Paging . . ."

Party? What party? Shig got to his feet. He grabbed the flight bag MacHenry had entrusted to his keeping. Where was MacHenry?

He backpedaled until he struck a toilet partition. That was as far as he was going. Oka swung the wood-handled mop through the air in an elegant, almost ceremonial motion and moved in.

"Why are you doing this? Why did you follow me?"

His answer came in a blow to his midsection that materialized out of nowhere. It blew the air from his lungs in one explosive gasp. He toppled like a landed fish to the white tiles. She stood over him and raised the wood handle again. He rolled away as it came down in a killing-hard blow that snapped it in two. The pieces rattled and bounced where Oka tossed them.

"MacHenry?" A faint sound came from the other side of the locked door. "Mr. MacHenry? Are you in here?"

Oka hissed like an angry adder. She saw MacHenry divert his eyes from her and threw a kick that caught the side of his jaw, snapping his head back, exposing the neck. One more kick would collapse the windpipe and . . .

"Mr. MacHenry!" The door pounded.

She twirled and jumped to the door. Oka yanked the bolt free and pulled.

Shig Onishi toppled inside. MacHenry's leather flight bag skittered under the sinks. His surprise was so complete he didn't react in time to keep her from sliding the bolt back shut. The power, the incredible, almost sexual tension that lived in her thigh, the blow she had not released against MacHenry, she aimed instead at Shig. She gave a full-swivel kick that sent him flying back against the sinks. He was open to a killing blow now. She moved in confidently once again. The power building up once more in her leg, muscle to steel cable, steel cable to lightning.

Shig dodged the kick his senses knew was coming. He heard her foot connect with the edge of the sink, heard the snap of bone, a tiny, quick gasp of pain. He scrambled to his feet as Oka advanced, no emotion at all showing on her smooth face, her hands waving, sinuously, hypnotically in front of her. His feet fell beneath him, his weight lowered, steady. His hands came up into two defensive fists.

Oka shouted, but it didn't paralyze Shig the way she'd expected. He moved, and her wedge-hard hand slashed the collar of his shirt instead of his neck.

Shig took one step in the direction of the door to draw Oka off her balance. He swung around abruptly and drove his elbow into her stomach. It felt hard as a granite slab. He raised an arm to ward off her return, and when it came, it left his forearm ringing, then numb. A second blow caught him in the side, but whether it was delivered by hand or foot, he couldn't tell. It was too fast.

Shig straightened up, sucking on air. She was good. Better than he by far! Oka came at him again. He dodged left and aimed a reverse kick that swept through the billows of her skirt. He tried the same thing again, this time leading her in anticipation, but his foot was deflected away. He staggered off-balance, Oka following, moving in like a stalking cat on wounded prey. The only sounds in the room came from two people breathing. Heavy, rhythmic.

She swung a kick at him, almost lazily, testing his defenses. He avoided it, but slowly, painfully. She moved in, sure now of . . .

Shig sprang at her and slammed a balled fist into her solar plexus. She staggered back, still no sound escaping from her lips. Her eyes seemed to burn. Her nostrils flared. Shig kept his distance as she reached into the top of her blouse and pulled out a tiny black blade. She came at him again, one step, two, three, faster, faster, then a running leap that caught him and sent him sprawling down to the tiles. She brought the blade up.

"Help . . ." MacHenry began to come to. He rolled onto his side and saw the two locked together on the floor. "Help!" he said louder now. "Help!"

Shig twisted away. There was a tap as the blade's needle tip struck the tile floor. Shig brought the heel of his hand up under her nose and felt the cartilage break. A gusher of hot blood sprayed across him. He swiped at his eyes to clear them.

"Help!"

Oka jumped to her feet, staggering when she landed on the broken toe, and hopped to the door. She threw the bolt and swung the door open, shutting it behind with another click, this time from the outside doorlock.

Where is he? DelVecchio steamed. He turned to the ticket agent. "Look, will you hold on to this thing for a minute? It's extremely valuable."

She looked at the box as though it had a sparking fuse coming out one end.

"I know, I know," he said. "But it's safe. It's a piece of an airliner. I'm with Boeing. Look. I'll show you my ID, okay?" He fished out his wallet and held up the Boeing picture identity card. "Hell," he said, offering her the wallet, too. "Hang on to this if you want. I have to go find this guy before he takes off." He tossed the wallet at her and left for the scanner gate. Without the TMC box, he walked though.

He was halfway down the line of gates when four bell tones sounded over the PA. A security guard ran by him. Then another. A third. They were gathered in front of a rest-room door, helping someone out. He didn't recognize the first man, not immediately. There was too much blood over his face. But the next one he knew.

"MacHenry!" He broke into a run as the guards helped his old copilot out, one to each side, steadying him on his feet.

MacHenry breathed heavily, his eyes fighting for focus, as DelVecchio ran up.

"What the hell happened!"

"Cleaning woman snapped out!" said someone. "She went nuts!"

Another shout made everyone turn. A guard was standing by the rest rooms up the corridor. He was talking to a woman who had been rudely shoved aside by the cleaning lady. He tried the door. It was locked from inside.

"She's in here!"

DelVecchio took hold of MacHenry and helped him to sag down to the carpet, his back against the wall. A hand on his shoulder made him jump.

"Is he all right?" asked Shig. He'd wiped most of the blood away from his face with a paper towel. But there was still enough left to frighten the daylights out of DelVecchio.

"You! What happened in there?"

The guards gathered by the ladies' room door. Keys came out.

"Joe?" said MacHenry, as though he'd only just now seen him.

"Jesus, MacHenry." DelVecchio turned to look at Shig. "Who did this?"

MacHenry sat up straighter. "Not . . . him." He shook his head. His neck muscles felt stretched to the point of rubber. "Why . . . why are you . . ."

"It's Tom Kelly."

"The programmer?" asked Shig.

"He was killed this afternoon."

Shig sucked in a short, sharp hiss of breath. "How?"

"Hit by a car. Up to now, I figured it was an accident."

MacHenry glanced at Shig, the same idea flashing across the narrow space between them. Shig was right, thought MacHenry. His breath was coming back to him. "Do . . . do they have the driver?"

"Yep, they do," said DelVecchio. "Only thing is, he's dead, too. A young guy. Not the kind you'd figure to have a bad heart."

MacHenry closed his eyes.

"Listen, partner. I don't know about computer viruses or bombs. What am I? A dumb-ass pilot. But I know trouble, and you've been drawing it like a lightning rod." DelVecchio turned to look at Shig.

"I agree completely," said the Japanese. He watched as the guards unlocked the ladies' room. He had a very bad feeling they didn't know what they were in for. "Mr. MacHenry, I think I should tell them . . ."

"Go," whispered MacHenry. "Hurry."

Shig sprang for the guards to warn them, but it was too late. The two uniformed security men were inside. They emerged a moment later.

"She's in there," said one of the guards.

Shig drew back, ready to defend himself again. "Be careful! She's very dangerous!"

The guard just shook his head. "Not anymore she ain't."

Shig pushed by them and went inside. A pile of bloody clothes lay where they'd been thrown. The door to one of the toilet stalls was open. Sitting upright, stripped to her torn underwear, was the cleaning woman. A bruise darkened one of her temples. Her head lolled to the left at an impossible angle. Impossible, that is, for the living. Shig turned and walked out, scanning the crowd that had gathered to witness the excitement.

The guards were wrong. She was out there all right. And Shig had not the slightest doubt that she was dangerous indeed.

SEVENTEEN

The sharp tang of gunpowder was everywhere. The oak-paneled walls exuded it. It was impossible to wash it off your hands. It penetrated your clothes. It was a thick perfume so strong that Kazuo Ibuki's cigar fought it and lost. A curl of tobacco smoke rose and mingled with the trophy heads mounted on the dining room walls: stags with enormous spreading antlers. Mountain lion. Bear. Antique rugs covered the floor. The table sparkled with white china and Waterford crystal, all bearing the Hunt Club crest.

Shintaro Ishii picked at his food, sipped his wine, while Ibuki puffed and Bridger spoke of the next day.

"I'd say we're on rails," said Bridger, summing up. "After tomorrow, I don't foresee any difficulties. The photo op will seal the deal. You," he said with a perfunctory nod to Shintaro, "Amory Tasker from Boeing, and Bill Regano from Treasury. When that image goes out over the wires, the entire nature of the debate, Japan, America, our jobs, your economy, all of that will change. The New Partnership will be born."

Ibuki tapped the ash off the end of his cigar and put it down. "You have served us well," he said as he sliced off a thin wedge of Kobe beef. He popped it into his mouth and let the fat melt. Like the very richest underbelly strip of the very best tuna, it didn't need chewing. It simply burst forth in a final display of taste and texture, then dissolved like fireworks against a night sky.

· "Thank you," said Bridger. "With Regano weighing in behind us, the Select Committee will vote it up next week. NAC's buyout will be impossible to stop."

"We will show America how Japanese business really runs, and why it is so much better," said Ibuki. "The car makers built the bridge that we, and Boeing, shall cross together."

"I like that," said Bridger.

"Still, I worry over the loose threads. But your associate seems very capable. When will we hear news?"

Associate? wondered Shintaro. What threads?

"Confirmation should come before the end of the evening."

"That would be a very welcome relief." Ibuki took another bite of rich steak.

"Either way, I think . . ." The waiter came over and whispered something into Bridger's ear.

"Confirmation?" asked the old lawyer.

Bridger pushed away from the table. "Excuse me, I'll need to take this call." With that, he quickly left.

"What is that about?" asked Shintaro.

"Sometimes I wonder why the gods play such games with us, Shintaro. I tell you, tomorrow morning may be a great victory, but it comes when we are a whisker away from an equally great defeat. Japan made itself rich by turning hard as steel. Some would say we must become soft. We must bend like America has bent. There are lessons for America, but also for us."

"My father was not soft."

"No. He was not." Ibuki looked at the pale reflection of the father. This shell-less creature, so vulnerable, so moldable. And in the end, so contemptible. A son so unworthy of the Ishii name. "It's a shame your father isn't with us tonight. He'd enjoy this club, don't you think?"

"I never knew him to be interested in guns."

Ibuki found that funny. "No? Your father was interested in many things."

"You knew him better than I."

"True." The old lawyer nodded. "We shared everything back in the early days. Back when there was little enough to share. Food. Money. Even girls. Why . . ." He was going to say, you could be my son, not his, but he stopped himself. What a distasteful notion! "We were like good steel, your father and I. Tempered by fire and sharpened by struggle. It is something your generation never had to learn. A shame." He gazed directly at Shintaro. "It is easy to get rich. Anyone can do it. But it is hard to stay rich."

Was that a warning? Ibuki made it sound that way. Shintaro decided to change the subject. "I'm very curious," he pressed. "My father never mentioned why he was so generous over the years with the Hibakusha. Was it guilt?"

Ibuki paused, considering. Why not? "It's an old story, really." Ibuki took a sip of the deep red wine, then put the glass down. A uniformed waiter refilled it. "His father was killed early in the war, you know. He was brought up in a house of women. It gave him a certain sentimentality."

"I often wondered what his mother and sisters were like. No photographs survived the war."

Ibuki's eyes glistened in memory. "What did he tell you about his mother? Your *obasan*?"

"My grandmother? Not much. Only that she disapproved of him and his way of life. He ran away and lived apart from them. She died near the end of the war in a bombing raid on Nagoya. The entire district was burned off the face of the earth. Nothing was left. No one could say where or how she was killed. There is no marker. No shrine. There was a great deal of confusion then. He used to say how he wished he knew where she'd died so that he could visit the place again and raise a shrine."

"Really? He told you that?"

"Often. Why? It's true, isn't it?"

Ibuki chuckled. "Some of it." He took another bite of marbled beef. "Your father's mother was killed in a bombing raid all right. But it was not Nagoya. In fact, she was killed by the very airplane we saw tonight. The *Enola Gay*."

"But that was Hiroshima."

"Just so. Your father was a liar. But a survivor, too. He knew how to survive even then, during the worst part of the war. He stole food and brought it home so that his mother and sisters could eat. It must have shamed her deeply to be the one family with fat on their bones while everyone starved. There was a fight, and she threw him out one week before the bomb fell. Imagine. Throwing a son out into the streets. It wasn't done. But she did it. After they dropped the bomb, it was too late to make amends, to go back to the way it was before. But your father was stubborn. He did go back. He couldn't make himself believe she was gone."

"He went back to Hiroshima after the bomb exploded?"

"He went through the ruins of the city while the ashes were still hot, looking for her. He stayed in those ashes a little too long, I'm afraid."

"Then his cancer . . ." Shintaro put down his fork.

"Some people wear tattoos on their skin to tell the world who they are. Your father was tattooed here." Ibuki pointed at his chest. "The bomb burned its name into his very bones."

"A *hibakusha*? My father?"

"One name. Another. What difference does it make now?" Ibuki balled his hand into a tight fist and slowly, slowly brought it down to the polished table. "He was a survivor, Shintaro. We all were. He joined a gang of scruffy boys, all of them survivors. They stole from the occupiers and kept most of it for themselves. Food. Bicycles. Medical supplies. Even heavy equipment." He laughed. "Some of Japan's biggest contruction companies started out with a stolen American bulldozer in 1946. But your father realized that the real money was not in supplying poor Japanese with American goods. But supplying rich Americans with the things they missed most." Ibuki nodded. "He built an empire from that one idea."

"Then he knew where his mother and sisters died. He knew all along. Why didn't he tell me?"

Ibuki blinked. "The Foundation was a way of honoring them without pulling their names into the dirt. And as for a shrine to his mother," he said, "I can hardly think of a better one than the one your father has finally arranged."

"What do you mean?"

"First, the *Enola Gay*, of course. He paid for its restoration in her honor. To close a very old wound. Remember, it's leaving here for Japan after the dedication ceremony tomorrow."

"To the War Museum."

"Just so." Ibuki took another bite of steak. "But there is another shrine he meant for his dead family. A far bigger one." He paused. "After tomorrow, we will have our foot on the throat of the company that built the *Enola Gay*, and that, Shintaro, is the real prize. A memorial, yes. But one that doesn't just recall the past. It will open up the future."

Shintaro looked puzzled.

"We are an island nation, Shintaro. Small and vulnerable. Where is our coal, our oil, our uranium? Where does our food grow? You see? We rely upon transport as no other nation in the world. The world is knitted together by air. Soon we may have need to defend ourselves against other nations far more blessed with natural resources. After tomorrow, we shall no longer have to worry about isolation. About being cut off by boycott or stupid politicians. We shall control our own destiny once again. We will own the air."

Shintaro never suspected his father of such sentiment. Were these his words, or Ibuki's? "He never told me any of this."

"He wasn't given to talk. And when he did, well, sometimes it was true. Other times, he only wished it to be true. You can forgive him that, can't you?"

Then it all came together for Shintaro. His father. His hidden family history. This man he had grown up to think of as uncle, now surrogate father. "You knew him back then. You were . . ."

"Yes," Ibuki said with a smile. "We were a flock of wild pigeons. We went where we wanted to go, took what we wished to take. And in spite of what you see today, the gray hair, the eyes that do not see sharply, my fancy clothes, my lawyer's camouflage"—he leaned over and whispered—"I still am a survivor. Do not forget this. Not ever."

Bridger walked back in with a worried look on his face.

"Ah," said Ibuki. "The confirmation came as you expected?"

Bridger looked at Shintaro. "Not exactly. There's been a complication."

Ibuki frowned. "America seems to be very complicated lately."

"This complication isn't American. It's Japanese. A man named Onishi."

"Onishi?" Ibuki picked up the smoldering cigar and puffed it, his eyes on Bridger the entire time. "Whoever he is, we know his superior. And *his* superior."

Bridger didn't look satisfied. "Is the Foundation's jet available tonight?"

"Tonight?" said Shintaro, though Bridger had not posed the question to him.

"Is it necessary?" asked Ibuki.

"Yes."

The old lawyer put his cigar down, then looked at Shintaro. "Perhaps you would enjoy a walk to settle the stomach. Don't be too long."

They parked the Ford Escort at the curb marked for those meeting arriving flights. Sturgis switched on the flashers and they both got out. Once inside the terminal, they separated, then coming from opposite directions, they went through a little charade, of one man meeting an arriving friend at the airport.

Together, they walked out to the short-term parking lot at Dulles. The short one carried a soft-sided piece of carry-on luggage, his eyes scouring the rows of parked cars while Ramón took in the scene as a whole. He was the one to spot the security camera on a pole. "Eyes up."

Sturgis nodded. "How many?"

"Four corners and two in the middle. Where's the vehicle?"

"Right where he left it." He nodded at an elderly Jeep Wagoneer.

Ramón fished a small laser designator from his pocket. It was no bigger than a box of matches, but it was powerful enough for the job at hand. He picked the camera that gazed down on MacHenry's car and placed a tiny but brilliant red dot onto its lens. Keeping the light square in the center of the camera's eye, they ambled up to the Wagoneer and stopped.

Sturgis put his bag down and unzipped it. "Car this old, probably need a jump to get him going, you think?" He withdrew a small, sensuously shaped piece of molded fiberglass. It looked like an oversize bar of olive drab soap, curved to fit a giant's hand. Across the convex face were the words FRONT TOWARD ENEMY. It was a cheap Chinese knockoff of the ubiquitous M-18 claymore mine, modified with a small, neoprene-rubber pressure plate and a wire safing pin. Inside it, hundreds of steel ball bearings were mixed in with the explosive, turning it into a short-range, omnidirectional shotgun.

Sturgis checked the driver's door for telltales, found none, and gave the handle an experimental tug. The door squealed open. "Fucker didn't even lock up."

Ramón shook his head sadly. "You got to feel sorry."

Sturgis got to his knees and placed the antipersonnel mine directly beneath the driver's seat, wedging it so that the cushion's steel frame rested lightly on the rubber pressure plate. The plate covered a wide, round button that would depress with the slightest movement. He gently tugged the little wire safing pin out. "Now on the other hand, what we got here is the world's most perfect soldier."

Ramón kept the laser light dazzling the camera. "How's that?"

"It don't eat, it don't bitch, it's patient." Sturgis stood up and brushed his knees off. He eased the door closed again, very carefully. "And it don't ever miss."

MacHenry watched as the three uniformed police walked off. I hope I did the right thing, he said to himself. What were the options? Tell the truth, say that the body they recovered was another victim and not the murderer, and chance getting stuck in Seattle for weeks? Or lie and play into their suspicions and make it to Washington in time to stop an even greater crime from taking place?

"When's your flight?" asked DelVecchio.

"If I make it on board this time, the red-eye for D.C. leaves in one hour," said MacHenry.

"Forty-five minutes," Shig corrected. "Arriving at Washington at five-ten in the morning. But what about her?"

MacHenry involuntarily looked at the crowd passing them in the terminal. What about her? What about the woman who had tracked him from Washington, followed him here, and tried to smash his skull with a broom handle not a half hour back? He turned to DelVecchio. "I arrive at BWI," he said, meaning the D.C. area's other large airport, Baltimore-Washington International. "My car's way out at Dulles. I'll have to call my boss when we get in and get a ride. Unless . . ."

"You have his number?" asked his old captain. "I'll call for you."

"Done." Now, wondered MacHenry, how am I going to get inside that hangar to look for Wheelwright's evidence?

"Before you go," said DelVecchio, "I have something for you. Follow me."

They made their way straight to the American Airlines ticket counter. The agent handed DelVecchio's wallet back, then the TMC module. She looked glad to see it gone.

"May I see it, please?" asked Shig. His face was washed clean of blood, though there were still wet places on his shirt from where he'd scrubbed. He took some satisfaction that not a single drop of it was his.

Shig took the TMC box and flipped it over to read the serial number. "Too bad. It's a new one."

"How do you know that?" asked DelVecchio.

"It's a dash 131. Not the original dash-128 version." Shig gave it to MacHenry.

"Damn if he isn't right. I took it off a ship right out of final inspection. You have a head for numbers, mister," said DelVecchio.

"Thank you, Captain."

"He's not bad with his hands, either," said MacHenry.

Shig kept quiet. He'd seen the poor woman propped up in the toilet stall, neck snapped. He knew why they'd kept the truth to themselves, but it nevertheless offended his sense of professionalism. It wouldn't get by a junior officer in the traffic police back in Tokyo. Here, it seemed, they expected people to go crazy, strip to their underwear, and then break their own necks on a toilet bowl.

"Well," said DelVecchio, "all I can say is, it's yours to take to the feds. The FAA. The Safety Board. There must be someone who can pull it apart and find out if there's a bug. Just be damned careful with it. It's probably worth a hundred thousand bucks. Problem is, they'll make you check it through. They won't let it pass through the scanners."

MacHenry hefted the computer module. It weighed only a few pounds, no more than five. He checked his watch. What time was it in Hawaii? Could he call Julia and have a hope of getting her out of her conference? "I need to make a call," he told them. "I have a friend who's flying home and I want to be sure it isn't on a 7X7." He gave DelVecchio the TMC. "I don't need the whole box, Joe. But it sure would be great to know what the insides look like."

"Perhaps I can help?" Shig had out his multifunction knife.

"What the hell is that?" asked DelVecchio.

"A Japanese Army knife."

"You mean a Swiss Army knife."

"Oh, no," said Shig as he selected a small wrench from it and tested it against the fasteners securing the TMC case. "This is the original."

MacHenry found a free phone booth and dug out the number from his pocket. It was a crumpled piece of paper. He punched in his code, the number, and waited.

"Hello, Kona Waikaloa, may I help you?"

"Dr. Hines, please. Dr. Julia Hines."

A few clicks ended in a ring, another, a third.

Damn! She was probably still at the conference. She . . .

"Hello?"

"Julia! This is—"

"Brian? Where are you? I've been calling and leaving messages on the machine but—"

"I'm in Seattle."

The line went quiet. Was it a gap created by voices traveling great distances, or something wider and deeper? Finally, Julia spoke. "Boeing?"

He waited to be sure she was finished speaking. "Boeing."

"I heard about the bomb on that British jet. They say someone at the airport did it. Is it true?"

"I don't know. Not yet." Pause. "I'm still working on it."

"The conference went well. Lots of work and new ideas."

"Great."

"I met someone who's doing some really interesting research up on the Greenland ice cap. It's ironic, don't you think?"

Cold seawater flowed through MacHenry's heart. He swallowed. "I'm not surprised."

Another pause. "I was. Can you imagine global-warming data coming from the ice record? I may collaborate with them next summer." She'd already been asked.

That would make for a convenient break, a logical end to a faltering romance. Is that what he wanted? "Listen. This is really important. I called for a reason. What airline are you taking home?"

"Continental. They were the best deal. Why?"

He sighed with relief. They didn't fly the Boeing 7X7. "Good. Continental's just fine. When do you get in?"

"Tomorrow late. At Dulles. Look. I've been thinking a lot."

"About Greenland?"

"About things . . ." Her voice trailed off. "Maybe we should talk."

Another tide of ice flowed through him. "I'm sorry, Julia. But things will have to wait. I'll pick you up at Dulles. We can talk there. I'm parked in short term in case . . ."

"In case what?"

"In case you get there and I'm not." He looked up and saw Shig pry the TMC box into two parts. "I've got to go and catch a flight. I'll see you at Dulles, okay?" He didn't wait for the answer before he put the receiver back on the hook and rejoined Shig and DelVecchio. They'd removed the dozens of little machine screws that fastened the top of the TMC case to the bottom. A heavy red silicone-rubber gasket sealed the gap. A clear plastic wrap provided another layer of defense that the white-handled knife quickly breached. With the top off and the wrap shredded, dozens of green circuit boards were open to view.

MacHenry took the split-open module. It was like looking at a city while flying high overhead. Black, rectangular chips covered the entire surface of each board. The squares were connected to one another by silver thoroughfares of etched conductor paths. The electronic streets converged into highways, gathering, turning sharp corners, and finally ending up at pins that shone bright with gold. And that was just the topmost board. They were stacked five deep. There was not one wire in sight. Everything looked solid enough to throw against a brick wall and survive, which, in fact, it was. "Are we looking for a whole circuit board, a chip, or something else? I still don't know."

"I suggest these are what we are looking for, Mr. MacHenry," said Shig, pointing at one of the black rectangles mounted on the board. "These are the ROM chips. Where the program lives." He unfolded a flat blade from his knife and slipped it under a chip, one of the larger ones. It was nearly an inch square. It wouldn't budge. He tried a little harder. It finally gave with a snap of cracked silver solder.

"That's an expensive sound, Mr. Onishi," said DelVecchio, wondering how he was going to explain this back at Boeing.

With its dozens of conductor pins dangling, the chip looked like a prize specimen of some exotic insect. Shig gave it to MacHenry.

"This little thing," said MacHenry. He didn't need to add, has been the death of nearly a thousand people. It's driven the market value of a vast American company down to the point where gangsters dreamed of snatching it away. It had a number and a name printed on it. "It's Korean."

Cirrus Logic
CL-SH-271-14QC-B
00408-79AC
9046 E
Korea-B

MacHenry pulled out his handkerchief and carefully wrapped it, then stuffed it into his pocket. Five of these. Lawson Wheelwright had them. They could be absolutely anywhere.

DelVecchio looked at MacHenry closely. "You feeling okay? You look like hell."

"It's been a long couple of days."

"Sure." DelVecchio didn't buy it, even though he knew it was true. There was something else. "You better get going. Take care of yourself. I'll do what I can from my end, but you'll have to carry the ball."

MacHenry thought of the tiny chip. It was impossible. Impossible. "I'll take what we've developed to the NTSB," he said, automatically reaching for a fallback in case his hunt for Wheelwright's evidence came up empty.

DelVecchio looked into his old friend's eyes. "Put a stop to it, MacHenry. You've got to. If there's something there, find it and stop it."

"We will," said Shig.

"We?" said MacHenry. "I thought you said your boss ordered you back to Tokyo."

"Section Chief Ozawa told me to return as soon as I could. But he didn't mention which direction I should travel. I believe there are flights connecting Washington to Tokyo."

"You're becoming very devious, Mr. Onishi," said MacHenry.

"My boss warned me Americans were like that. It rubs off."

It was midnight Thursday, and Gregory Chiang was still at his desk, facing a glowing monitor, long after the FBI Annex ended its normal workday. Only a few investigative teams were still around on time-urgent matters. More routine affairs were handled by the night-duty desk, an uncoveted position awarded the most junior agent in the District.

But for Chiang, the hours from five in the afternoon to midnight were his most productive. Working in the digital world was above all else a matter of detail and concentration. Its practitioners were by nature a solitary group.

He settled himself at the keyboard of the image-processing gear. A cup of pungent green tea steamed on a little electric warmer. He'd managed to convince the TV studio to send a better copy of the video Agent Freeman had handed him. It was all very unofficial, and the truth be told, if the FBI knew who his contact was over at the station, Chiang would most likely find himself out on the street. Hoover was long dead, but his intolerant ghost still roamed the hallways.

The tape they'd sent over still wasn't the original, but it hadn't been edited either, so it ran a lot longer. Chiang toned down the spurious signals, the random bits of data, the camera flaws, but so far, he hadn't applied any real muscle to wring the hidden data from it. For now, all he had was a tape worth looking at.

He played the sequence through to the end, watching the image go from soft to sharp focus and back on the monitor. The videocam that made the tape had a problem with its autofocus circuitry. It would probably fail altogether in the next few operating hours. But that was the way Chiang liked it. If the tape was crystal clear, who needed him?

He played the digitized image out on his screen, letting the computer discover the missing focus algorithm, letting it do for the tape what the camera could not do for itself.

The screen showed a dark runway crossing the field from left to right. Beyond it, a brightly lit building. A hangar from the looks of the big doors. They were cracked open a bit, probably not more than a few feet or so. Just enough for a man to squeeze through shoulder to shoulder. It made the hangar into something of a Fabergé egg: a tough metal shell enclosing a hidden world, with only a tiny slot to look through.

He ran the magnification up until the opening in the doors was a wide gray stripe running vertically down his screen. He could actually see patterns of light and dark in there. He zoomed back out and let the tape play on.

A passenger jet taxied by, its tail eclipsing the lighted hangar. When the wall appeared again, a tiny red dot had blossomed from within the opened doors. He didn't need spectrographics to know it was fire. And more, the lights in the hangar, the ones that had allowed him to peek through that narrow slot, were out. He stopped the action and increased the magnification again. Now the crack in the hangar's facade was a black sky against which Lawson Wheelwright's body burned bright as a nova.

Chiang allowed the awful scene to march forward. The red dot moved jerkily now. The image shifted as the handheld camera wavered off, then back onto the subject. The camera zoomed, turning the red dot to a fuzzy orange ball. Glints of reflected firelight played across the hangar doors, but there was a bounce from within the open doors, too.

He clicked his mouse to freeze the scan, then snapped a white rectangle around the orange ball. He ran an image-cleaning program. The orange ball shrank to a lemon shape, taller than it was wide. Another keystroke and the lemon became a fiery cocoon with a dark, irregular shape at its heart. He ran the cleaned-up image back to tape, then played the whole thing through once again.

Red dot zooms to orange fireball with man inside. The image evoked a memory, a photo from a history book, of a Vietnamese monk sitting inside saffron sheets of fire, swaying, swaying, tumbling to the street.

He stopped the action once more, this time paying attention to the glints of reflected light around the burning man. Reflections showed up on the hangar doors, but also from something inside the hangar. Something specular, shiny. A mirror? No. Maybe an airplane.

They had shiny skin, didn't they? The reflection came and went, ghosting in and out of view as though something, or someone, was moving in front of it, blocking, then exposing a shiny surface.

Let's see, he thought. He snapped a white box over this area, letting the computer analyze the missing pieces of data. His fingers flew across the keyboard. He was oblivious to each stroke, each command. If you stopped to ask whether he typed by eye or by feel, he could not have answered. Finally, satisfied, he reversed the image, dark for light, light for dark. Now, the object eclipsing the light showed up as solid.

A ghostly image of a man appeared between the burning black pyre that was Lawson Wheelwright and the airplane inside the hangar. A vaguely human shape.

So, thought Chiang. Wheelwright had not died alone. Of course he knew that someone had sprayed him with the fire extinguisher. But the ghost was there much earlier. Why had he waited so long to use the extinguisher? And why had he doused the hangar lights at the first sign of flames?

He rewound the tape to the beginning. The jetliner taxied backward, right to left. There was the hangar. The opened doors, illuminated from within again. He commanded the computer to dive through that distant, narrow slot. Into the Fabergé-egg world.

Click. Magnification times ten. Another click. Times twenty. Fifty. Each time the information on the screen became more and more diffuse, a gas expanding outward until individual pixels glowed like stars on a dark night. He was staring into the hangar now in the minutes before Wheelwright had caught fire. A tiny, thin wedge into a lost world.

He could see, under maximum magnification, that the shiny object that had glinted in the fire was indeed a window. In fact, several windows. Airplane cockpits had them. Was that what they were? He directed the computer to curve-match, to draw a shape that would accommodate the separate points of reflected light. Sure enough, a crude cylinder appeared, its front closed in with panes of flat glass. It *was* an airplane!

This was hardly groundbreaking stuff. It was perfectly natural for an airplane to be inside a hangar. But he still felt proud. He'd brought it out, summoned the data from the murk of chaos. How far back could he stare into the illuminated crack? How long before the lights went out and Wheelwright's body boiled up in flames could he see? Wouldn't it be interesting to see if he could pull something, anything, from the view he had of the hangar interior? But Agent Freeman wasn't interested in that. He wanted the fire sequence cleaned up. He decided to come back to that and to concentrate on events after that terrible red dot first appeared.

Chiang replayed it again, this time massaging the original red dot until it was the size of a half-dollar. He went back, scan by scan, until the circle of firelight winked out. Jump. Jump. The lights inside the hangar went out. Another scan. One more. Stop!

A tiny movement caught his attention. A little white spark. He froze it, rewound, and went forward again. It started at the figure he had reconstructed out of the shadows. It ended at the place where Lawson Wheelwright would, in a few scans, a few inches of magnetic tape, begin his final agonies. What was it? A reflection of something moving, like a flashlight? A sudden chill cascaded down his spine.

He watched the tiny spark of light arc through the gray background. Illuminating pixel by pixel as it made its way inevitably to the place Wheelwright was standing. He let the tape run through at normal speed. Flash. Fireball. Lawson Wheelwright fell, rose up, his body sheeted in fire, then collapsed again. The billow of a fire extinguisher's discharge blotted the scene in white fog.

Indeed. They'd waited a long time before dousing him. He checked the real-time counter. Almost forty-seven seconds. A long time to die. He rewound, then played forward again. The spark, enhanced artificially, made a perfect Newtonian curve. It was obeying gravity. It was not something in the hands of a person moving or gesturing. It was something thrown at Lawson Wheelwright. And his arm. What was Lawson Wheelwright pointing at? Was it instinct, agony, or was he pointing back at something, or someone? His murderer? Chiang thought of that tiny spark of light.

He went back to the mysterious goings-on in the illuminated slit. The image, blown up and poor to start with, was not really a picture at all. It was a connect-the-dots puzzle. He allowed the computer to play with the data, building solid bands of light from the tiny, distinct pixels the videocam had collected. Slowly, the nose of an airplane revealed itself in false colors. The shiny windows were bright red, the aluminum body of the plane a pale pink. Dull objects showed up blue. As he watched, jumping one scan at a time, letting the big computer redraw the artificial image again and again, he watched as one dull blue shape merged itself with the underside of the airplane's nose. A man climbing inside? It had to be. What else moved like that?

Then another blue shape. Then a third.

Three men had climbed up into the airplane in the minutes before Lawson Wheelwright burned. One shifting amoeba of blue reappeared seconds before the interior lights blinked out and all data was lost. Seconds after that, a spark flew across the darkness. An instant later, Wheelwright was on fire.

He let the images sink into him. What did he know? Wheelwright had not died alone. Three men had climbed up into the airplane, one, then two and three. Was he one of them, or were there four people present? He couldn't say. One showed up again an instant before the lights went out and the red dot blossomed. One man had stood by as he'd burned. Then the watcher had waited more than half a minute before using a fire extinguisher.

He took a sip of tea and considered. It was like watching opera through a soda straw. One tiny piece. Another. How did it all add up? He pulled the tape. Call Freeman tonight or wait? He checked his watch. It was Friday now. The spark of white light. The ghostly shape. Tonight, he decided.

He reached for the phone. Some things could wait. But murder was not one of them.

EIGHTEEN

"Not an accident?" Freeman snapped the bedside lamp on. He eyed the clock. It was just after one in the morning. Not a time an agent of the Federal Bureau of Investigation expected to hear good news. "How can you be sure?"

"Nothing's certain. You better come in and take a look yourself," Greg Chiang replied. "The station sent a full-length copy, and it's as good as I can make it without seeing the original."

Freeman knew they needed the original tape. That was where the secrets usually lurked. What were the chances of cranking out a subpoena before breakfast? About the same as his chances of making director by lunch. "Before we do that, maybe you can tell me exactly what you found out."

"For one, Wheelwright wasn't alone. There were at least two, maybe three others with him."

"Old news. We interviewed two rent-a-cops who caught him trying to torch the hangar. One of them tried to save him with a fire extinguisher. So?"

"He didn't try very hard."

"Not a federal offense. Next?"

"I was able to construct a figure out of the background. He was there very early in the sequence. Not moving around, not looking for an extinguisher. Just standing by watching. He watched a long, long time. Maybe forty, fifty seconds."

"For this you woke me up? Maybe rent-a-cop A was getting the extinguisher. He finds it, runs back, rent-a-cop B takes it and hits Wheelwright with the foam. That could take a while. This better get better, Gregory."

"It does. There's an anomaly very early in the tape."

Freeman paused. "Like what kind of an anomaly?"

"Before the first flames appear, there's a small burning object that appears coincident with the security guard and ends at Wheelwright. It's not a reflection or a bug in the tape. It follows a parabolic trajectory that—"

"Greg. Cut the crap. You're saying one of the goons tossed a match at him?"

"It looks like it. By the way, what kind of airplane is inside the hangar?"

This was not going to be a night meant for sleeping. "Why?" he asked irritably.

"Because I was able to work up some sequences in the minutes before the fire broke out."

"Before? How the hell could you do that?"

"The copy you brought was cut and edited to fit the station's format. But the tape I have here goes back almost two minutes before the fire. Apparently, the camera operator was sweeping the scene for quite some time. It shows that prefire, the hangar doors were open a couple of feet and the interior lights were on. I watched one, then two other people go into the airplane. I was just curious what they were doing."

"I don't have a clue. You really think this match thing will stand up?"

"Get the original tape and we'll run it through spectrographics. But I bet it'll show sulfur, phosphorus, and potassium chloride."

"A match." Breaks in cases were like babies. They never happened during business hours. "Can you ID the one you *think* tossed it at Wheelwright?"

"Not exactly. The best I could do is pull out a shape."

"Gregory, we can't arrest a shape."

"That's why I think we should get the original."

Freeman sighed. "Call up to the duty desk and see who we have on subpoena standby. If we can get it today, can you work on it?"

"Yes, sir. What about the security guards? You said there were two. Maybe somebody should go pick them up and see what they say. We know enough to catch them in a lie."

A shape. Could he bluff a confession out of those guards? Freeman thought about that. One short and built like a bulldog. The other taller and Latino. Both had the hard–edged look of soldiers, the direct eye contact that said fuck you while their mouths said yes, sir. "Maybe. Let me think on it. They're employees of some foundation. Japanese, I think. Christ, that's all we need." Wasn't the hangar going to be the site of a ceremony today? He wondered about the guest list, and how far up the pecking order it might go. Clinton was not going to show. He was in California. But Dole was in town and so was Cheney. For that matter, Powell was due back from Paris, too . . .

"Sir?"

"What? I'm still thinking."

"I can show you what we have if you want."

"Nah. I trust you. Call the duty desk and get the subpoena gears turning." There was no way around it. Freeman swung his legs out and stood. He looked down at the bedside holster with his FBI–issued Smith & Wesson 10mm. He decided to leave it. He hated the thing, anyway. "You make the coffee. I'm coming in."

Section Chief Ozawa fingered the report on his desk. He read it once again, then put it aside. He picked up a large manila evidence envelope and tapped it. Out popped ash, then a charred piece of paper. The remains of a business card. The fire at the noodle stall had been intense enough to shut down the commuter train line into Kabuto-cho for nearly an hour with smoke and fumes. But enough of the calling card had survived for him to make out the characters for *Onishi* and *Economic Crimes Sec* . . .

He sighed and reached for a Mild Seven. As he got it lit, he hoped Shig Onishi heard his warning well and was on his way home. Some cases were like cancers. Too invasive, too entwined and intermingled with the flesh to separate and excise. He scooped up the remains of Shig's business card and carefully put it back into the evidence envelope.

Sometimes, you had to leave such matters for the gods to cure.

There wasn't the least hint of sunrise, but Roger Case was already wide awake.

He was just about to leave home for Baltimore-Washington International when the phone rang. He debated whether to answer it or not. MacHenry was due in within the hour. He was impatient, but he was curious, too. He picked up the receiver. "Roger Case speaking."

"You're up early, Counselor."

"Aaron?" Case sat down.

"Who else?" Freeman was sitting next to Greg Chiang in the Image Analysis lab. He'd seen everything Chiang had put together. It was enough to move on. "I figured, if I'm working the morning shift, Roger Case can join me."

"I was just headed out to BWI. What's up?"

"Plenty. That tape you sent over was useless—"

"Useless or was it just too inconvenient for you to bother looking at?"

"—so we got our own from the station. That one wasn't useless. In fact, it was interesting. As in, very interesting."

"I'm listening."

"Number one, it looks a lot less like accidental death. Nothing's provable yet, but there's enough to make the overworked and underpaid reasonable man wonder. It looks like somebody tossed a match at Lawson Wheelwright. Satisfied?"

"Bingo," said Case softly. "Who's this somebody with the match?"

"Shape A for now. We got a Shape B, and a Shape C, and a possible Shape D, too, but that's unconfirmed. We're going to try to get the original tape from the network. They won't do it until the nine-o'clock suits show up for work, even with a subpoena. Can you believe it? There's your law and order for you."

"I wouldn't hand over original source material either. But the tape you looked at. What else does it show?"

"Like I said, three people, maybe four. All unidentified. One of them turns into Lawson Wheelwright. One of them tossed what my guy here called a small burning object at him, one that moves along a parabolic trajectory in accordance with Newton's many and, as far as I know, unbroken laws. And there was some kind of hanky-panky going on in the minutes before the fire, too."

"Like what kind of hanky-panky?"

"Three of those shapes were screwing around with that old airplane. Any idea why?"

"The *Enola Gay*?"

"Yeah. Shape A climbs into it, then B, then C. A couple of minutes later, the lights go out and Wheelwright burns. Before he collapses, he turns around and points back inside the building. At the guy who just torched him probably."

"You could *see* this?"

Freeman patted Chiang on the shoulder. "Hey, sleep well, Counselor. Your Bureau is wide-awake. So. Any motives you'd like to share? It looks like this could be a long day thanks to you."

Case thought of MacHenry. How he sounded so sure that something was rotten at Boeing, how he could nail the case shut with those five samples Wheelwright said he had. "Yes. Wheelwright may have had something they wanted. They wanted it badly. When they got it, they didn't want Wheelwright around anymore."

"Like what kind of something?"

"You still think this guy up in Jersey City is responsible for bombing those three planes?"

"Roger, I've been up since midnight. What kind of something did Wheelwright have?"

"The note he left here the night before he died said he had proof those Boeings were going down because of some bad parts getting installed at the factory. Like a bad bolt, you know what I'm saying?"

"Not this again. Please. I know you hate the Japanese. But they aren't under this bed. They ain't in this closet. It just so happens we got ourselves a real live mad bomber up in New Jersey."

"I don't think you do. I think Wheelwright had the answer, the *real* answer, with him. I've got a very experienced man on this and he thinks so, too."

"Badr Muhammad had the access. He had the big bad drum of chemicals that go boom. He was seen on a security tape tossing uncleared baggage onto that bombed jet. You want more?"

"Is there any?"

"We're still working on him. I expect a confession today. He cops a plea on the BA crash, we know what happened to the other two."

"You're offering immunity on the other wrecks to nail down this one?"

"I might. That's not saying everybody would," Freeman said with a sly intonation. "Lots of other charges he could be hung with. You know what I mean? But we don't tell him that until he comes to Jesus. Or Allah."

Deal on the BA crash, and then connect him to the others later on in a different venue. So that was their strategy, Case thought with a smile. Good. "My man says ANFO is not the kind of stuff he'd use to bomb a jet."

"He's such an expert, maybe he should offer courses."

"Look. I'd like you to meet him and review what he's put together. Will you do that much?"

"Monday, maybe. Today I'm going to arm-wrestle some network over a tape, then I'm going to pay a little visit to those shapes out at Dulles. There's some kind of ceremony going on and we can't have some suspected match-tosser hobnobbing with the rich and the famous. It's supposed to be a real who's who. Regano. Bunch of labor types. A CEO or two. A gaggle of Japanese executives. I hear even Dole and Cheney might—"

"I know." Japanese executives and CFIUS. He's going to hand the keys over. Case's eyes went to the ceiling, then back. "Okay. We'll meet you there. At Dulles."

"Roger, about this bomb thing? You helped us with Wheelwright. I was wrong. You were right. Quit while you're ahead. Badr's the bomber. No shit. It's going to stick."

"I'll quit when we're done," Case snapped. "And as far as Badr Muhammad goes, he won't be any pushover. Take it from me."

"Yeah? How do you know so much?"

"I'm his lawyer." Case let that sink in. "I'll see you at Dulles. At the parking lot behind the Smithsonian hangar?"

"Jesus! You mean—"

"We'll be there at nine. Good work, Aaron. You give me hope for the future. How's your mother? Still baking those poppy-seed cakes?"

"Roger, has anybody told you you're a sneaky, manipulative old man?"

"What do you mean, old?" Case hung up.

"You didn't have to come along," said Julia as the long, angry line she was in moved forward.

"I wanted to lobby you," said Dr. Camillo Ortiz, a climatologist from the University of Maryland. "I want you to go home thinking about what a great time you could have on the Greenland team next summer. We could really get a lot of work done on the cap."

Julia eyed him with a suspicious look. Ortiz was good-looking. Younger than she was by a year or two. They'd gone swimming, and he had a nice body, hairy and a bit flabby, his winter fat he'd said, but nice. He was doing good work on global warming up in Greenland. His ice-core samples were changing the way people looked at climate change. Her field. Why wasn't she interested? "Maybe."

"That's closer to yes than no. Think it over, okay? The university needs to budget the trip in the next couple of weeks. I'd like to fit you in."

"I'll call when I get back to Washington."

"Deal, Dr. Hines." Ortiz grinned, gave her the thumbs-up, and bounced away, sure he'd made progress.

She moved forward one more step. Was it her mood or was the departure lounge at Honolulu International an unhappy place? Both. The warm evening air was scented by exotic flowers. Water splashed into koi-stocked pools. And the beautiful smiling faces of the people who did not have to leave paradise were all around. In this Edenic setting, a sullen army of vacationers heading home to gray and slush and howling winds bawled and shoved like cattle inching up a ramp to the packing plant.

Something was wrong with her flight. On the overhead monitors, it kept moving, hopping down the list of scheduled departures. Now the monitor simply carried it as DELAYED.

"Can you read my ticket or what? Newark. N-E-W-A-R-K. Not Salt Lake City. Not Denver. *Newark.* So what's the deal?"

"Yes, sir, I know," the Continental agent replied as sweetly as she could. She went on to explain for the hundredth time that a mechanical problem would keep them on Oahu just a little bit longer.

Julia watched the ugly performance. What's the rush? She wore a pair of faded, comfortable jeans and a T-shirt cut to reveal a white shell necklace, but in her bag was a down sweater for later. Her arms were peeling, so was her nose. Who could resist that lure of a hot sun, a beach, and sparkling surf the temperature of a warm bath? Her bikini had gotten a very thorough workout. There was still a little golden sand in her ears, between her toes. She'd taken one last swim at Kona before catching the interisland flight.

She wouldn't mind getting marooned on the Big Island another day, but here she was in Honolulu, and Waikiki was not her style. When she made it to the front of the line, she handed her ticket across the counter. The frazzled ticket agent braced for another volley from the tall, brown-haired woman.

"Problems?" asked Julia as she put her leather carry-on bag down. She was conscious of her winter boots, so strange here in Honolulu. They felt so hot and sticky, but they'd be welcome once she landed back home in Washington. *If* she made it to Dulles.

"I'm sorry, but your flight to the mainland will be delayed," said the agent warily. "A part has to be flown in from Los Angeles, and it won't arrive until later tonight. You can wait for your flight, we can put you on a different Continental flight tomorrow morning, or try to find space with another carrier tonight."

Which would she prefer? She wouldn't get another day at the beach. Just a bus ride into town, a search for an overpriced room. "These other flights tonight. There's nothing direct, is there?"

The ticket agent brightened. Here was someone asking questions instead of shouting. "There's a United flight leaving for Washington with one stop in Chicago. Do you want to see if there's room?"

That was a better flight than the one she held a ticket on. It would probably get to Dulles earlier. An advantage, if leaving Hawaii was the idea. She thought of staying. Of going. Of seeing MacHenry. Would he care if she showed up at all?

As the ticket agent tapped on her keyboard, biting her lower lip, Julia thought of all the loose ends that were gathered together, waiting for her in Washington. There was her work at NOAA, the National Oceanographic and Atmospheric Administration. She was on track to take over the Mathematical Modeling Section if she could just hold out and survive the bureaucratic nonsense. But most of the open ends, the frayed threads, had something to do with one Brian MacHenry. They shared a farmhouse in the Virginia countryside. They sometimes shared a life. Some days she couldn't believe her luck in finding him. Other days, she couldn't imagine spending another hour in his company. There were more days of the last sort lately. Far too many.

"I can put you on that flight," the agent said. "It leaves here in an hour, stopping at Chicago O'Hare, then leaves for Washington Dulles."

"The same plane?"

"Yes, ma'am. It's a new one."

"What kind?" Julia asked, thinking this was the sort of question Brian might ask.

"A 7X7."

He wasn't hard to find. Case saw MacHenry sitting alone over a steaming cup of coffee at the only café open so early in the morning at Baltimore-Washington International. MacHenry looked bleary-eyed and exhausted. The only color in his face came from a bruise on his unshaven cheek, purple as an eggplant. MacHenry was sitting with his back to the wall, scanning the corridor as though he expected trouble. "Mr. Case," he said, though his eyes went beyond, searching, searching.

"Well. You made it back to civilization without costing me a lawsuit," said Case as his cane tapped the linoleum floor. MacHenry started to rise, but Case shook his head. "At ease. I have good news. Very good news." He pulled out a chair and eased himself down. "Who tapped you?" he asked, eyeing the bruise.

"It's a long story, Mr. Case. Let's just say I got lucky."

"So it's Boeing."

MacHenry shook his head. "No. I think there's good reason to suspect one person who worked there, though."

"Worked? Who is he?"

"A programmer named Tom Kelly. He was responsible for developing the flight software for the 7X7, and for making sure nobody could break into it with a bug. A virus."

"Where is he now?"

The words came out without emotion, tasting like sawdust. "Tom Kelly was killed yesterday."

Case waited to see whether MacHenry was serious. He was. "Jesus, don't make me pull it out! Where does he fit in? Come on. Snap to. We've got work to do. We're on a tight schedule."

"Sorry, Mr. Case. I'm tired. We alternated staying up on the flight back—"

"We? Who's we?"

Shig saw Case sitting with MacHenry and hurried over with his own cup of coffee. "Everything all right?"

Case turned and saw a very Japanese face staring down at him. His eyes went wide. He grabbed his cane.

"No! It's okay!" said MacHenry. "This is—"

"Senior Investigator Onishi," said Shig with a bow. He kept his eyes down, even though the old gaijin looked ready to crown him with that cane. "I am with the Economic Crimes Section of the Japanese National Police Agency." He looked up into Case's astonished face. "Mr. MacHenry and I are partners on this case."

It wasn't every day that Roger Case found himself at a loss for words. Finally, after one swallow, another, he said, "You're *what?*"

"Partners," Shig repeated. "We are working together on this matter. I have heard much about you and am happy to meet you in person."

Case swung to face MacHenry.

"Remember what you told me, Mr. Case?" said MacHenry. "If you want to know the truth, follow the—"

"God damn it!" Case smashed his cane flat to the Formica tabletop. "Don't you lecture me, MacHenry. What is this, a game? You know who this character is?"

"Shig Onishi. From—"

"He's one of them!"

The quiet was all the more pronounced as the scattering of patrons in the small café stopped and gawked.

"Mr. Case," said MacHenry, "if by 'one of them' you mean he's Japanese, then yes. He's one of them. If you mean that makes him involved with the sabotage of Boeing jets, or covering up a lot of shady deals between the underworld and big business, then no, he's not one of them. He's one of us."

"The hell you say." Case turned to Shig. "So what's your angle? Who pays your salary, Charlie?"

"Shig," Onishi corrected. He'd just told him he was with Economic Crimes. Didn't he listen? "I am tracing an arrangement between the second-largest organized crime syndicate in Japan and a group of manufacturers called the Nippon Aerospace Consortium."

I just bet you are, thought Case. "I suppose you can prove you are who you say you are?" he said, getting his voice back beneath his brain once more.

Shig fingered a business card printed in Japanese on one side, English on the other.

Case examined it, then tossed it rudely to the table. "So what? A card."

"I believe him."

"You're too gullible for words, MacHenry. You've been living off in that little farmhouse too long if you think you can trust one of them to work against his own damned ant heap of a country. They're all in it together. Shoulders to the wheel."

"So what if he's from Japan? The woman who did this"— MacHenry touched his bruise—"was a blonde. She followed me all the way from Washington. She sat *next* to me." The thought made him shiver. "She said she was German. So what if Mr. Onishi is Japanese?"

Case was about to speak, but Shig cut in first. "Mr. Case, since this matter, as you say, leads to Japan"—he gave another respectful bow—"then perhaps I can bring special knowledge to the case. I can be of assistance in establishing the facts."

"Assistance? What kind of assistance? So you can report back to your boss in Tokyo? So they can look over our shoulders and screw us just when we've got you dead to rights? No thanks, Mr. Senior Investigator. No thanks. That kind of help we do not need. And by the way," he said with a cold smile, "your card says *junior* investigator."

"I was recently promoted."

"Mr. Case," said MacHenry. "Shig has been working on this longer than I have. Now I understand you have reasons for your feelings—"

"Goddamned right I do." He raised his right pant leg to expose the twisted knot of scar where his kneecap used to be. "Your buddies gave me this, once upon a time. I saw what they did to their own soldiers. They made them jump off a cliff instead of surrendering to us. I saw what they did to captured Americans, too. It made jumping off a cliff look like a pretty good deal."

"Mr. Case, I was not born—"

"Nothing has changed over there. It's still a war. Now, instead of battleships and Zeros, you use yen and dirty dealing. But a war's a war, and that's what your country is up to." He let his pant leg fall and turned to MacHenry. "And if you had any sense, you'd know all these guys are in bed with one another. The police. The criminals. The politicians. All of them. And you invited him to help? Spare me."

That part's true, thought Shig. Every word except *all*. In a land of conformity, he'd been an exception before. He was one again. "Mr. Case makes many good points," he said delicately.

"Hold off," said MacHenry. "You have nothing to apologize for." He took the final swallow of coffee. It tasted bitter as bile. "Mr. Case, I understand why you feel the way you do. I don't agree. Shig and I are working on this together. Period. In fact, without his information, I don't think you have a ghost of a chance of doing anything except working this problem at the margins. He's on the team. Our team. Hear him out."

"*I* say who's on my team, MacHenry." Case sat back, one fist tight around the hilt of his cane. "But I'm willing to listen. That's it. Just listen."

Shig put it out as completely as he could. The original *yakuza* extortion. The Ishii money filtering through a weak bank, and then, under the guidance of Kazuo Ibuki and his industrialist friends, into the Nippon Aerospace Consortium. Finally, he summed up by describing how the giant money-laundering scheme would work, who would benefit, and why he'd been recalled to Tokyo just when he started to get close to the truth. How the last piece of evidence that would link it all together, the missing ROM chips, would probably wait for someone from Tokyo to come and collect them. Someone like Kazuo Ibuki or young Shintaro Ishii.

Case sat there, silent. He wasn't angry. He was stunned. Not because it was unlikely. But because it matched what he had secretly thought and worse, it was coming from *one of them*.

MacHenry was next with his story of the Easter egg, his old

captain Joe DelVecchio, their confronting Tom Kelly and Abrams, the Lauda Air 767 accident nobody wanted to talk about at Boeing.

"So it's happened before," said Case, almost in spite of himself.

"The TMC unit is a logical place to hide a computer virus," said Shig. "It would attract the attentions of an accident investigator looking for similarities to the Lauda Air crash. In this case, a jumper wire used to fix a manufacturing defect. But there is no such wire on the 7X7. The TMC unit would receive a clean sheet of health. The person who planted the virus was very skilled."

"Bill of health," said MacHenry. "A clean bill of health."

"None of this is clean," Case growled. "You have a group of big Jap industrial concerns hiding behind the skirts of a mobster, watching while a dump truck of dirty money gets laundered into clean Boeing stock. What do they get?"

"One-third interest in Boeing Aircraft," said Shig. "But more important, they are buying into a market they, I mean *we* in Japan, have never been able to crack. Now, with Russia gone, America has a monopoly on aerospace and monopolies are something the Japanese understand."

"Yeah." Case didn't like agreeing with Shig on anything. He didn't like having this Jap cop around. He could have set the whole thing up just to ingratiate himself with MacHenry, to weasel his way into, and defuse, Roger Case's own deep suspicions. MacHenry and Onishi. A team. Maybe Onishi was for real. He was thinking straight, which was a hell of a lot more than Roger Case could say about the FBI with their bombs and Arabs.

"I have a good idea what kind of technical flaw we're looking for," MacHenry concluded. "We need those TMC chips and a computer analyst to go in and see exactly what's in there."

"I know the best guy in town when it comes to computers," said Case. "He's ex-NSA. A real whiz."

"Good. Then we can present to the FAA and the Safety Board. Boeing, too, for that matter. We need an emergency grounding order to check all the TMC modules in the 7X7 fleet."

"All I have to do is sign on to working with some Japanese who thinks I'm going to—"

"Think what you want to," said MacHenry. "But it comes down to this. You can work with us or on your own." MacHenry reached into his pocket. "Now, in a couple of minutes, Mr. Onishi and I are going to Dulles, to the Smithsonian hangar."

"Where the Hibakusha Foundation funded the restoration of the *Enola Gay*," added Shig. "The plane that—"

"I'm familiar with the *Enola Gay*, sonny. I visited a little island called Iwo Jima and not as a goddamned tourist with a camera. Who knows? Maybe your father and I knew one another."

"My father was too young for the war. He owns a small restaurant in Tokyo. A noodle shop."

"Forget it." Case looked back to MacHenry. "So? You're going to this hangar. Then?"

"Then we do our best to find something that looks like this." MacHenry showed Case the ROM chip Shig had pried up from DelVecchio's TMC module.

Case looked at it, then looked at MacHenry. "That's all?"

"That's all it takes."

Case picked up the ROM chip. It even *looked* like a bug.

"Almost certainly Lawson Wheelwright was killed, probably by Americans working for the Inagawakai organization," said Shig. "But they would not have the authority to dispose of any recovered evidence." He looked at the black ROM chip. "That is why it might still be there to be found."

Case jabbed his thumb in Shig's direction. "How come he knows all this and the FBI doesn't?"

"Teamwork," said Shig.

"Well?" said MacHenry. "Is there anything you can add, Mr. Case?"

"All right. On the videotape the Bureau picked apart? There was some strange activity just before Wheelwright burned. Apparently the hangar doors were cracked open enough so they could peek in and see some motion."

"Motion?" asked Shig.

Case scowled, then thought better of it. "Yeah. Motion. You know? People moving around. First one, then another, then a third person were seen going into the *Enola Gay*. Then the lights go out. After the match was lit and Wheelwright is almost dead, he points back into the hangar at something. They could see this."

"Points? At what?" asked MacHenry.

"The FBI says he died pointing at that old B-29." Case looked at Shig. "You're so smart. Care to take a guess what it might mean?"

All three men looked at the black ROM chip.

The 7X7 leveled off at thirty-three thousand feet eastbound, its twin engines pushing them at eight-tenths the speed of sound into the night. The humid, flower-scented air of Hawaii was long gone. Outside the cockpit, the air was razor thin, icy, and lethal. The stars burned down with an unnatural brightness.

"Full house," said the captain. It was his leg to fly, and his hands rested lightly on the yoke. The machmeter crept up as they accelerated.

"We took on a whole bunch of refugees from that Continental flight," replied the first officer as he busied himself with postdeparture bookkeeping. "Glad we don't work for them."

The speed stabilized and the captain engaged the autothrottles. The letters *ATS* appeared on the EICAS screen.

The first officer sat there, silent, his face tinted by the warm glow of the cathode-ray tubes. He thought of the three ships, all 7X7s, that crazy Arab had bombed. He shivered despite the warm air gently flowing from the vents, shivered as though the air came straight from the blackness outside his window and flowed down his spine.

"Feeling okay?"

The first officer turned. "Sure. Perfect."

NINETEEN

The spotlighted terminal building at Dulles showed up like an alien spacecraft caught while landing in the dark Virginia countryside. The sun wouldn't put in an appearance for another forty-five minutes, and a quarter moon was riding high, surrounded by an eerie halo of ice crystals.

Case drove along a ring road that left the terminal area behind. Prefab metal buildings stood behind fences to either side. They were old, rusty-looking shops with the names of import/export operations on them, as well as shipping companies and the occasional aircraft-maintenance shed. Stunted, leafless tree branches shivered just beyond the reach of the headlights.

Case braked, slowing down as his high beams illuminated a gate barring any further passage. "The hangar's through that gate. It appears to be the end of the road, gentlemen."

"Park over there," said MacHenry. The fence was topped with coils of razor wire.

Case pulled off into an employee parking area. Suddenly, new headlights appeared from behind them. Case doused his own and switched off the engine. The headlights grew brighter. Just what we need, he thought. A rent-a-cop. "Now what?"

"Climb the fence?" suggested Shig.

It wasn't a police car. Instead, a UPS truck rolled to a stop. Its driver leaned out of the cab and entered a code into a small box mounted on a low pole at the curb. A beeping sound announced the opening of the rolling gate.

"Maybe we can . . . ," Case began, but he didn't get to finish the sentence.

Shig and MacHenry went for the door handles at the same instant.

"Hey!" Case yelled, but by then MacHenry was out. Shig was

nearly so when Case rammed his cane in front of him, barring the way. "If something happens to MacHenry, I know who saw him last. Do we understand one another?"

"Perfectly, but I should—"

"Come on!" MacHenry urged.

"Remember! You only have until noon!" But they were already gone.

The UPS truck made a cloud of foggy exhaust as it idled, waiting for the security gate to open wide. It was cold out, cold and wet with the feel of an impending snow. Keeping low, running in a half crouch, MacHenry and Shig stole up behind the brown van and eased up onto its rear bumper, holding on to the flat metal rails meant for the delivery driver to use as handholds.

The engine growled as the driver moved through the gateway, then he stopped to let it slide shut behind. Had he felt them climb on? Shig and MacHenry both watched the gate glide along its track, and when the *clanch* of the gate striking the lock sounded, they looked at each other.

"I hope we're doing the right thing," MacHenry whispered.

Shig nodded, his teeth chattering in the cold. The Yomiuri Giants baseball jacket was poor insulation against the cold. "I don't think your boss likes me."

"Don't take it personally. He treats everybody that way."

The UPS van accelerated. The two held on, their hands becoming stiff, unfeeling claws in the cold air. More metal buildings passed by to each side. They were newer looking than the others. All built within the last several years. Overhead, the crescent moon wore a fuzzy halo as a high, thin cloud deck moved in from the west. The buildings glowed in the pale moonlight. None of them seemed occupied. A postindustrial ghost town.

"Which one is it?" Shig whispered.

The truck began to slow.

"We'll find it." MacHenry dropped off the back of the truck. Shig did the same a few feet later and far more gracefully. They stood in a dissipating cloud of cold, oily fumes. The red taillights of the UPS truck receded, then turned off at the very next building.

"Look," said Shig, nodding at the nearest metal hangar.

A single car was parked in the paved lot, a small Ford of some description. A sign above the door could be made out in the moonlight.

Smithsonian Air and Space Museum Hangar 10
A Gift of the Hibakusha Foundation

MacHenry started to walk toward the door.

"Wait! There's a light fixture over it. It might be on a motion sensor."

"Or an alarm." MacHenry felt foolish.

"We are thinking alike, Mr. MacHenry."

From a distance, they could see only one door in the otherwise unbroken facade. There were no windows anywhere. Not even a vent or a grill. The wall was made up of metal panels, corrugated and bolted onto the steel framework. A solid line of buildings stood shoulder to shoulder. There were no breaks, no alleyways. They allowed for no passage to the runway ramp on the other side.

"It looks like a very new building," said Shig. "That may be helpful."

Why? MacHenry wondered. An old building would have windows and doors and offer more ways to gain entry. This wall was as blank as the face of a dam. But he didn't ask. He followed Shig as he walked far enough away from the one door to be out of the eye of any motion detector. MacHenry ran his hand down the row of fasteners that bolted the wall panels to the frame. The wall was warm. He snatched his hand away, thinking not only of the *Enola Gay* inside, but also of the people who owned the car parked right behind them.

He looked up. The bolts went up the side of the building to the roof. There would be skylights up there someplace, but how do you get to them? The bolt heads were too small to be climbed, and it would take a human fly to do that anyway. "Any ideas, Mr. Onishi?"

"There would seem to be no easy way." Shig stepped up and ran his hand down the corrugated metal wall. His finger stopped at a bolt, then moved on. Another. A third. They were spaced every six inches. The corrugated panels were eight feet tall except for a shorter row at the very bottom. Apparently the hangar was not an even multiple of eight feet, for the final sections bolted to the slab were less than two feet high and four wide. They were painted a darker color, though in the moonlight it was impossible to say which color it might be. The stripe went clear across the hangar wall.

MacHenry stared up the sheer cliff of metal. "No hard way, either."

"Perhaps." Shig reached deep into his pocket and pulled out the little white pocket knife, the one with the Rising Sun flag on it where the more familiar Swiss Cross might otherwise be.

"You can't cut our way in," said MacHenry.

"You are right." Shig selected the clever little pair of steel jaws that had an odd, polygonal opening at the end. It made it a kind of adjustable wrench. "Just like solving a case, a mystery, Mr. Mac-Henry," he said as he applied it to the first wall bolt. It was barely large enough, requiring Shig to tap it until it seated against the head. "Sometimes everything just falls into your hands. But sometimes we must take it apart one piece at a time. When my father says *gamman,* this is what he means."

"Gamman?"

"It means we must endure." Shig gave the little tool a short, sharp push. It bent, but with a crack the bolt began to turn.

That's one, thought MacHenry. And forty more to go. He looked at the car parked nearby. "What about the guard?"

"Tomorrow's wind blows tomorrow."

"Is that another Japanese saying?"

Shig turned. "I thought it was American."

In ten minutes, he had a vertical row of bolts hanging by their final threads. Not out, but finger loose. His hands were numb with cold. He came to the top of the dark stripe, the break in the wall panel, and began working across on the horizontal row. Four feet divided into six-inch intervals. Eight bolts.

Just then, another pair of headlights appeared out on the road. "Watch it!"

They froze as another UPS truck rumbled by.

Shig was tiring, but he hadn't come across a frozen bolt yet. Eight minutes later, another row was loose. He attacked the last ones across the bottom. The work complete, Shig pulled them all loose. He made a neat row of them on the ground. "Now we must be very careful, very quiet. The guards could be awake."

"What if they're sitting right on the other side of the damned wall?"

The last bolt came out in his fingers. Shig folded the wrench closed and pulled out a blade. Chrome steel flashed in the moonlight.

"I can't budge it," said MacHenry as he dug his fingernails behind the sharp metal edge. "There seems to be some kind of insulation behind that's holding it."

"Please." Shig inserted the knife blade and cut the fiberglass mat away from the metal. He worked his way around, slowly, methodically, silently. When he was finished, he gently, carefully twisted the blade to pry up an edge. "Special high-strength steel," he said in answer to MacHenry's doubtful look. "Very tough, but also very flexible."

With a crack, the blade snapped in half.

Shig pulled it out and ran his finger along the jagged edge. "It never did that before."

Just then, a rooftop heater began to whir, pressurizing the hangar's interior. With a puff of warm air, a wall panel two feet by four wide fell free. Both of them froze as it thumped to the ground. They waited for the alarm. It didn't come. The opening let a rectangle of pale gold light flood out from the interior. The air that spilled by their feet was warm and smelled of oil and hydraulics. It smelled like old airplanes.

MacHenry crouched down and looked. A small room ended at a frosted-glass door. Tools hung from the walls. A drum sat on a wheeled cradle. "It's a storeroom," he whispered. He stuck one leg through, worked his shoulders in, then pulled his other leg in last. Shig got on his hands and knees and followed.

"United 11, contact Oakland Center now. Good evening and aloha."

"Mahalo. We'll see ya later. United 11."

The first officer had already punched in the new frequency. This was the break between Honolulu Departure and Oakland control sectors, not that it was anything more identifiable than a dotted blue line on the chart. They were expecting a higher assigned altitude, and they were anxious to step it up. On an eastbound leg, higher nearly always saved them time. United was an employee-owned operation now, and the sloshing fuel in the tanks didn't arrive as rows of numbers and disembodied orders from on high. It came out of their hides.

The captain pressed the push-to-talk button. "Oakland, United 11 is checking in, three three zero direct Cape Mendocino."

The reply was immediate. The traffic between the island and the mainland was light at this hour. "United 11, roger. Did you copy the route change from Honolulu?"

Damn, thought the pilot. They were always playing games, introducing changes that inevitably caused delays. "Negative. What's the reason for the deviation?"

"To tell you the truth, I don't know. It just came up over the computer that way. It'll take you over the coast at Arcata heading zero eight five."

The pilot shrugged. The winds wouldn't help or hurt them much either way and the night was fine. "We're left to zero eight five, direct Arcata."

"And United 11, climb and maintain flight level three niner zero. Report reaching."

"Direct Arcata and up to three niner zero. United 11." He banked the great ship to the left so gently, so gradually, nobody in the back could possibly tell. It was the sign of a professional. Not like those yank-and-bank Air Force retreads who didn't seem to care. The stars shifted ever so slightly, then leveled once again. The copilot tapped the mode selector from CRZ to CLMB. The EICAS screen showed ready. The twin Pratt and Whitneys had a lot more thrust in them tonight. Sweet engines.

"Enable."

The ship began ramping up, not even slowing as it climbed. The EPR displays began to change.

"Great engines on this beast," the copilot remarked.

The captain answered by patting the glareshield. He knew the manuals said you could fly the 7X7 on one. The engineers had placed their stamp of approval on it. Well, where were those engineers tonight? Safe in bed. Good as they were, with so much riding on their flawless operation, the pilot knew you didn't fly your engines. You gambled with them.

MacHenry put his ear to the glass panel and listened to sounds coming from the hangar space beyond. There was a hum from some heating fans, but nothing else. Who owned that car parked outside? And where would they be? He put his hand on the doorknob and turned it ever so slightly, feeling the pressure on the mechanism build as the slack was taken up.

"Wait," said Shig. He found a piece of cardboard and slipped it into the crack in the doorframe at the latch. It would deaden the sound of it retracting. He nodded.

MacHenry twisted the metal knob, more, more. There was a faint click. The door was free. He pulled it in an inch and peered out through the crack as another gust of warm air went by.

The tail turret of the *Enola Gay* was not five feet away, the twin fifty-caliber machine guns angled up toward the rafters. The door into the gunner's cabin was wide open. The rounded tail soared high overhead. In the distance, at the far end of the hangar space, MacHenry could see the cockpit ladder under the belly, just behind the nosewheel.

He pulled the door open a bit wider. Mechanics' workstands and rolling tool chests were arrayed around the fuselage. Velvet rope draped from chrome stanchions all around the perimeter of the bomber.

A row of flags hung from white poles in front of the B-29, four in front of each wing, the Stars and Stripes to the left, the red sun of Japan to the right. MacHenry's eye returned to those rolling tool chests. They offered some cover. As he turned to see what Shig was doing, he heard the loud clack of an opening door and the scuff of boots on concrete.

". . . end of the line. Be fucking glad of it, too."

The sound of a door opening, then closing, echoed through the cavernous space. Then silence. The hum of fans. The cascade of warm air seeking to flow through the hole they'd made in the building's skin behind them.

"No motion alarms," said Shig.

MacHenry nodded. If there had been, the two men he'd just heard would have set them off. But where did they go? And when would they come back?

MacHenry opened the door again. His eye kept returning to the door to the tail gunner's compartment. He tried to reconstruct what he knew about the interior layout of a B-29.

The tail gunner lived in a tiny pressurized capsule at the very back of the plane. Was there some way to crawl from it to the main fuselage? He knew that somewhere out ahead of the tail gunner's perch was a big central cabin for the other crew members, gunners mostly. And at the far tip, almost touching the hangar doors, there was the cockpit. The place he'd find most familiar. He remembered a tunnel that connected the cockpit with the central cabin. It ran atop the unpressurized bomb bays like a hollow spinal cord.

Shig peered over his shoulder. "There's a door open," he said, meaning the tail gunner's access hatch.

MacHenry shook his head. "I don't think that's where we want to go." To get into the bomber, the place the FBI tape had shown some strange activity in the moments before Wheelwright burned, to get in they'd have to sprint to the front of the hangar and climb up into the cockpit. What were the chances of doing it without getting spotted? Each of the rolling tool chests stood five feet high. One to the next. They could use them to work their way to that ladder. It wasn't much of a plan.

"However you think best, Mr. MacHenry. But I think now would be a good time to try."

"Okay." MacHenry took a deep breath, then eased out through the door. He made it to the first tool chest, then motioned for Shig to follow. Leapfrogging their way forward, MacHenry came to realize what a big plane the B-29 truly was. The fuselage was slender, whippet lean, but it was a good hundred feet long. He ran to the next work-stand and looked up at the polished belly skin. Who knew where Lawson Wheelwright might have stashed those chips? Or if he did. Sixty feet of dodging and hiding brought him under the wing root and just ahead, the doors to the bomb bay. He turned. Shig was right behind. Forty feet to the cockpit ladder. He eyed the distance. There were no more tool chests ahead. They would be out in the open. There was no other way.

Keeping tight to the underside, his head brushing the polished aluminum, MacHenry ran for the boarding ladder at the nose. He was focused on it. So much so that he didn't notice the access panel on the ground, or the little white Styrofoam cup of hardware that stood next to it. He kicked both with an impossibly loud clatter of thin metal and a hailstorm of flying screws. Shig drew in a sharp hiss of breath.

MacHenry stopped, but Shig pushed him on.

"Hurry!"

MacHenry took the boarding-ladder rungs two at a time. He swarmed up into the cockpit with Shig right behind. Shig paused for a second at the lip of the hatch, trying to see how to make the final jump from the top of the ladder to the deck. MacHenry reached down and hauled him up like a landed fish.

A noise made both of them freeze as they stood there in the pale yellow light coming in through the cockpit glass.

". . . hell was that?"

"Don't know, 'mano. Like something fell."

MacHenry felt his heart hammering in his chest. He turned his head to see out the *Enola Gay*'s glassed-in nose. He had a fine view of the hangar doors. But not the two men. Where were they? Would they see the scattered screws, the panel? And if they did, then what?

"Spooky shit, bro."

"Let's check the perimeter."

They both heard each other's breathing, then the sound of a door closing out in the hangar.

"Mr. MacHenry," Shig whispered. "I'm afraid they will find the hole I made."

"Me, too." How long did they have? Something between seconds and minutes. Then they'd have to work their way back out through a gap the two guards could not help but find.

Ahead, the two pilot's seats were mounted behind freestanding instrument panels. Between them, a center control stand ended with a seat mounted low to the floor. The bombardier's perch. Behind them, in the darkness, a blizzard of dials and switches curved over the flight engineer's station.

MacHenry reached up and touched the quilted padding that covered the cabin roof. Every detail was exact. Correct. Perfect. He wondered: Did it look this good brand-new? MacHenry breathed in deeply. He could detect the unmistakable aroma of gasoline, hot insulation, hydraulic fluid, and leather. The smell exuded by a *real* airplane. Not some computerized kerosene-burner equipped with every conceivable feature except for one: a soul. He had no doubt the *Enola Gay* had one. It filled the cockpit like a fog.

Shig touched his shoulder and MacHenry jumped. "Perhaps we should use the time we have?"

"Sorry." MacHenry made his way to the nose, checking the nooks and crannies where five ROM chips might be hidden. Flying the B-29 took real teamwork. *Pilot and copilot,* MacHenry ticked off silently. He searched under the seats. Nothing.

He moved forward again. The deck stopped abruptly beyond the center console. Bombardier. His feet would have dangled into space up there surrounded by nothing but glass and a spiderwork of thin metal framing. MacHenry looked down at the two red bomb-release handles. The nose was clean.

He turned around and headed aft. He came to a fourth seat. Flight engineer's station. It was mounted beneath a curving wall of gauges and switches. Control levers sprouted from his panel. Throttles. Mixtures. Props. Oil doors. Cowl flaps. His hands hunted every recess, every edge. There were no chips stashed here.

Beyond the engineer's station, lit from above by light coming in through the navigator's astrodome, a small cabin contained two additional seats. To the left, a rack of ancient communications gear stood above a table. Radioman. To the right, a chart table and map cabinet for the navigator. He unhooked the map-cabinet doors. A brass sextant was nestled in its padded rack. The cupboard was bare.

He took the final three steps to the aft bulkhead. A metal wall sealed off the pressurized cockpit from the rest of the plane. It was breached by two openings. One was a low hatch that opened into the bomb bay. The other was a tunnel that hung from the bomber's backbone, allowing the crew in the front access to the gunnery crew in back without the bother of donning oxygen masks. The navigator's glass dome was set into the roof of the tunnel like an overhead light fixture.

MacHenry noticed a cabinet with an antique flashlight and what had to be an original thermos coffee flask. A crash ax was secured nearby. He took the old flashlight from its mount and covered the lens with his hands. He snapped the switch. He felt a chill run up his neck. It worked.

"Is that safe?" asked Shig.

"No," said MacHenry. None of this was safe. But if he was going to search the guts of this old bomber, he couldn't do it in the dark. The B-29 seemed designed to maximize the places a person could hide computer chips and minimize the chances of anyone ever finding it. He reached down and unlocked the pressure hatch leading to the bomb bay. It swung open, surprisingly light. "I'll check through the belly. There should be a second hatch at the back of the bomb bay. Meet me there. Keep your eyes wide open and try not to make a sound. If we can, we'll see if we can get out through the gunner's door in the back."

"What about the guards?"

"Tomorrow's wind blows tomorrow," said MacHenry with a smile. He locked two hands together, making a foothold for Shig. "Up you go."

Shig peered down the long tunnel leading aft. It looked disconcertingly like staring into the barrel of a very large gun. He let MacHenry boost him up and in. Gun. Bullet. Who, he wondered, was holding on to the trigger?

The east was white with sunrise as Agent Freeman came to a stop at the gate. Now what? he thought, wondering how he would get in. It wasn't as though he could show his ID to somebody. The little coding device wouldn't care if he waved his credentials at it all morning. He could always check in with the airport cops, but that meant driving way the hell back to their little office in the terminal basement. He looked out ahead, hoping someone might be coming the other way. A sign just beyond the gate warned that trespassers would be prosecuted, that it was a federal offense to tamper with an aircraft, and that the FBI would be notified. What a joke. He checked the time. It was already after seven. A truck appeared in his rearview mirror. It slowed to a stop. Freeman got out.

The driver rolled his door back and leaned down. "You can't get in there. It's a secure area."

Freeman reached into his jacket pocket and pulled out his FBI identity card.

The driver looked up, matching the man, the drab government-issue car, and the ID. "Then again, maybe you can."

A dozen bolts sat in an orderly row at the foot of the perimeter wall. "My, my, what have we here?" said Sturgis. "I'm thinking mice?" He got down on a knee. "You wait here. I'll go check around inside. Maybe I can flush them back the way they got in. You carrying?"

The tall Latino reached into his waistband and pulled out a Sig Sauer P226. The 9mm weapon carried fifteen rounds. "Armed and *mucho peligroso*. You?"

Sturgis tapped his waistband where the slightest bulge betrayed the little Walther TPH. A scaled-down version of the famously conceal-able PPK, it made an ideal backup weapon. "I never leave home without it. Keep your eyes wide." With that, Sturgis went inside, the slim black pistol in his hand.

Freeman knew the place. He'd been here once before. He pulled the government-issue Chevrolet into the small parking area behind the Smithsonian hangar. He saw the little Ford Escort he'd seen that other morning. One of those rent-a-cops, those Ollie North wanna-bes, was around. For the first time, he wondered whether it had been so smart to come out alone, and without the 10mm hand cannon he'd left by his bedside.

He parked next to the Ford and got out. He sniffed the air. It was either the world's most potent aftershave or some night-bloom-ing plant was nearby. The faces of the two guards came back to him. One short, the other tall. One blond, the other dark. He stood there as his Chevrolet ticked cooler, cooler. He put his hand on the hood of the Escort. Dead cold. Its owner hadn't used it lately. He was most probably inside. It was getting bright with the new day. Freeman walked over and tried the knob. Luck was running with him. It was open.

MacHenry let his light probe the dark corners of the B-29's bomb bay as he crept along a narrow ledge above the two belly doors. A red sign warned against walking on them.

Carefully, cautiously, he kept to the ledge, using the exposed girders and beams as handholds. Fuel hoses thick as his wrist ran along the sidewalls. He sniffed. There was a strong gasoline smell. Were they actually planning to *fly* the *Enola Gay* someplace?

He looked down at the pale crack that came from where the bomb doors didn't quite meet. It let in a faint light, not enough to search with, maybe just enough to see by. Feeling everything, his fingers moved through the dark spaces, the hidden places. One hand at a time, he inched his way along the ledge.

If the cockpit seemed like an attic crammed with forgotten treasures, the bomb bay was positively haunted. It was the dark cellar of atomic secrets. A place where the curtain between earth and hell had been raised that long-ago August.

Ten feet along, he was forced to duck under a yellow trapeze of tubular steel; these were the sway bars that had once kept Little Boy, the first atomic bomb, in its place. A massive hook dangled from overhead on a thick braided cable. He touched the heavy shackle. A surprisingly thin wire coiled down its length to a spring-driven latch. The surface of the hook was crudely fashioned. Rough edged, with none of the technical elegances of modern weaponry. It looked hand-cast, then hammered into shape by bare-chested men with sweat dripping onto a roaring forge.

He ran his finger through the opening of the electrically operated jaw. The last time it had snapped open, a ten-foot cylinder had dropped free. Nine thousand pounds of steel and alloy with two small lumps of uranium 235 nestled at opposite ends of a sawed-off howitzer barrel. Male and female, machined to fit together like no two human lovers ever could. Separated. Pending. Weightless. Falling. And then, reunion. A flash. Hiroshima.

He heard a sound, a scraping, and not from the tail where he knew Shig had crawled. But from behind in the nose. He snapped the light off and twisted around. The motion was enough to cause one foot to slip off the narrow edge. As he lurched out over the dark void, his head struck the heavy bomb shackle. He grabbed one of the yellow sway bars, hanging. Had they heard him? He hauled himself upright. As he did, his hand dislodged something. It fell with a muffled thump to the belly of the plane. As he was reaching down to see what it was, a sound made him freeze.

"Hello?"

MacHenry's heart leaped.

"Anybody here?" MacHenry heard a scrape from the cockpit area again, then a thump as someone crawled down the cockpit ladder to the floor. He sucked in a breath. They'd been right behind him, not fifteen feet away! The thought made him dizzy with fear.

"Yeah, I'm here," said Sturgis as he dropped to the floor of the hangar. He looked under the belly of the plane and saw dark slacks and wing tips. He checked the pistol to be sure there was a round chambered. The magazine was stuffed with little .22s, but of a uniquely deadly design. The Stinger rounds expanded explosively in flesh. He'd coated them with Teflon himself, just in case the target might be wearing body armor. "Who's asking?"

"My name's Freeman. We met a couple of days back. Remember?"

"Freeman?" Sturgis remembered. A fed. "How'd you get in here?"

"Door was open. Where are you? Can we talk?"

"About what?" Sturgis walked around the nose of the plane, brushing his left shoulder against the hangar door and his right against the glassed-in nose of the B-29. He emerged on the other side with the little Walther in plain sight.

Freeman stood under the row of eight Japanese flags. They hung listlessly, moving in the wind stirred by the paddle fans. Freeman saw the TPH at once. "That isn't necessary. I just want to talk about the other morning. About what happened."

"I'll be the judge of what's necessary. Right now, you're trespassing. What do you want to talk about, Freebie?"

"Freeman. Agent Freeman. The FBI, remember?" He reached into the jacket of his coat to pull out his ID.

"Don't—"

Suddenly, Freeman spun in a wild pirouette and fell. The heavy boom of the Sig Sauer came like a cannon shot from the other side of the room.

"Shit!" Sturgis screamed as he ran up to the fallen FBI agent. He held the TPH in a combat grip, swinging it back and forth to pick out the next target. It wasn't necessary.

Freeman was writhing on the floor, holding his stomach.

Sturgis raised the pistol as Ramón ran up from the shadows. "You gut-shot him, asshole!"

"He was goin' for it!" the tall Latino said, holding the weapon out in front of him. "He was makin' a fuckin' move!"

Freeman rolled to his side, his eyes white with shock and pain. The bullet had entered near his spine and blasted through a tangle of flesh and nerve and organ. He moaned. The yellow sodium lights turned the spreading pool of his blood black.

Sturgis looked up. "You stupid shit."

MacHenry heard the shot, the two voices. Not three anymore. They were right beyond a thin skin of aluminum. Five, maybe ten feet away. He sagged to his knees, soundless, his heart beating loud in his ears, reaching down in the darkness to pick up the shape, the soft thing his hand had found. There it was. A bag? His eyes were growing accustomed to the dark.

"Now fucking what? The colonel's gonna have your sorry taco ass, bro. I guaran-fucking-tee it."

"Shit, I thought—"

"Shut up," snapped Sturgis.

"We gotta move him, man. We gotta get him outta here. People are due. You know what I'm saying? Like any minute."

"Is he the one who made the hole in the wall?"

"Shit, I don't know. I tailed him in here real quiet. He reaches for his weapon, man, I take him down."

"These assholes never work alone," Sturgis replied evenly, as though the object at his feet were a dog hit by a car and not a man.

"We gotta dump his ass."

A pause. "Where?"

Another pause. "Come on," said Sturgis. "Help me pick this sack of shit up. And quit waving your weapon around."

"He's pumpin', man. He's still pumpin'."

MacHenry listened. There was an excruciating silence that ended with a short, sharp pop.

"Now he ain't. Come on."

MacHenry heard them grunt under a lifted weight, the scrape of something being dragged off. He listened. A door opened. He felt the little cloth sack in his hand. There was something in it. No, several somethings.

MacHenry shoved the little bag deep into his pocket.

The aft pressure hatch swung open. MacHenry didn't dare switch his light on to see. He worked his way back along the ledge. The bomb bay seemed to close around him. Jonah in the whale. TMC chips. Three Boeing 7X7s crashed. Two killers right outside. When he was no more than a few feet away, he saw Shig's frightened face framed in the round hatch.

Shig reached down, offering a hand up. "They killed someone," he whispered.

MacHenry reached into his pocket. He brought out the small cloth sack. Its neck was sewn shut. With a quick pull, he ripped the threads loose and shook the contents out into his palm. Five black squares studded with gold and silver connector pins tumbled out.

"Now what?" whispered Shig.

MacHenry shook his head. *"Gamman,"* he whispered. Endure.

"This as high as we're going?" asked the first officer as the big jet crossed over land just north of Arcata.

"Beats me. I quit trying to figure ATC long ago. They're devious."

On cue, the controller popped back into their headsets. It was a different voice. "Good morning, United 11. Oakland Center. Climb and maintain four one zero."

The captain looked to his right with a raised eyebrow as if to say, See? What did I just say? He commanded the Octopus to begin the climb.

The altimeter display began to rise. Thirty-nine thousand five hundred. Forty thousand feet.

"You know something, when we roll out at ORD," said the first officer, meaning Chicago, "that will be one thousand landings on this old bird."

The dark continent below was measled with a few lights. "Just broken in," said the captain as the jet burned eastbound.

TWENTY

Yoshi always rose well before his lord in order to prepare for the day. The Ishii family bodyguard had done it for old Susumu for years. He had served the father well. Now he did it for himself as much as for Susumu's infinitely lesser son.

Yoshi got out of bed and began his stretching exercises, following them with a short tai chi routine that gave him his balance and pumped energy through his body so strongly he could feel each and every blood vessel grow wide and full. When he was finished, he headed for the bathroom and slapped the wall switch on. The cold fluorescent lights buzzed. He made his way to the mirror to make ready his death face.

The death face. Yoshi was concerned with how the world would see him in death. To imagine yourself staring up from a casket was remarkably simplifying. It made a lot of other decisions easier.

He stroked the smooth skin of his cheek, tracing the old scar that ran down from his right ear to beneath the strong line of his chin. It was an imperfection, but it was also a mark of distinction, a tattoo of his trade. Just like the dark dragons that twisted their way from his left shoulder down to his forearm. Anybody could wear a tattoo. There was no lesson in it. The scar was different.

He reached down into the neck of his T-shirt and pulled out a long leather amulet. From it, he withdrew a wickedly sharp stiletto, the very blade that had given him the scar. He'd taken it from the young hoodlum who thought a piece of steel could make him a warrior.

Yoshi had been ambushed, and the blade had come within a milli-meter of nicking the fat arteries that roped his neck. He'd ended the fight by burying it into the heart of a man he'd considered a friend. Now it belonged to Yoshi, and he used it every day to shave his face and to remind himself that chance was the god of this world, and that chance could be delayed by skill, by luck, but not avoided forever. It reminded him to never walk into a dark alley with a friend protecting his back, for in a dark alley, allegiances changed in unpredictable ways.

He used the razor-sharp edge slowly, methodically, maneuvering it around the puckered scar tissue. When he was finished, he ran the water full hot. The mirror fogged as he washed. He looked up, his old, battered face set against clouds of rising steam. Yoshi would never be mistaken for handsome. Fifteen years in the back-alley warrens of Osaka and Tokyo, his years rising in the ranks of the Inagawakai syndicate, then, at the pinnacle, Susumu Ishii's personal warrior and guard. All of these had left their marks, just like this blade, but less obviously.

He was still young as a man, but old for a warrior. At forty-four, his eyes came to a slightly less sharp focus. His muscles moved a fraction of an instant slower. It took a little longer each year to stretch, to prepare. It took a little less imagination to see the face that stared back at him in the bright mirror as that of a corpse. Yet despite a lifetime in organized crime, it was an honest face. There was nothing hidden, nothing veiled. He was not a *bunraku* puppet master pulling on the strings to make others dance. He thought of Kazuo Ibuki, and of Ibuki's young, foolish puppet. A mannequin so innocent that when he felt the tug of the string, he imagined it to be his own free will.

He twisted off the tap and toweled his face dry. His skin gleamed like some rare polished wood. Now, whatever else happened, he would not be ashamed to die. How better for a warrior to begin a day?

They stood close together on the narrow bomb-bay catwalk. The sounds of cleanup, the swish of a wet mop, of bloody water sloshing into a bucket, were perfectly plain.

"We are trapped," Shig whispered. "Perhaps two of us could defeat—"

"He's got a gun. When did Case say the ceremony was supposed to start?"

"Noon."

MacHenry checked the glowing green stars of his watch. Four and a half hours.

The sound of powerful jet engines roared from outside the Smithsonian hangar. MacHenry got down on his knees, putting his ear close to the crack in the bomb-bay doors to listen.

The engines swelled to a hard roar, loud and close. Someone was parking a jet right outside. Was it an arriving official? A dignitary? Could they get out of this aluminum trap sooner than he thought?

"Fuck!" came the voice of the man with the mop.

They heard the squeak of the bucket getting wheeled away.

MacHenry took Shig by the shoulder. "Follow me. Be very quiet."

"Where are we going?"

"Out." The sounds of the jet engines would mask their footfall. They made it under the swinging bomb shackle to the forward bulkhead door. MacHenry went through first, climbing into the relatively bright radio room in the rear of the cockpit. As Shig crawled through after him, the jet engines outside fell away to a whine, then a rattle. Shig oozed the rest of the way through and got to his feet.

MacHenry eased up into the tunnel. The metal creaked as he shifted his weight. How was the metal tube held to the spine of the bomber? Rivets? Steel strapping half a century old? If it came crashing down . . . he stopped himself. If that happened, it would all be over. It would all come to nothing. It would not happen because it could not.

He got to his knees and put his head up into the astrodome. From his high perch, he could see all four walls of the hangar, but not directly down. It was enough to see a man in a stained white T-shirt and dark pants jogging quickly toward the front. He didn't recognize him. He looked short, but all muscle and no fat. A bulldog. With a rattle of locks and chains, he unfastened the door and went out to greet whoever had just arrived.

"Who is out there?"

MacHenry motioned for him to remain silent. The hangar door stayed open. Was there enough time? Should he slam that door shut and lock it or just run for the storeroom with the little hole in its wall? Which? Think! He got down from the tunnel and padded forward to the floor hatch. Shig was right behind. It was time to get out of here.

One way or the other. It was time. He put his foot down the hatch, feeling for the ladder. A few feet of space separated the deck and the topmost rung.

". . . happened to your foot?"

Shig grabbed him by the coat and yanked him back up.

"I broke it. It's nothing."

She'd wrapped her broken toe tight to an undamaged one, but the foot had swollen. She walked unevenly in her stocking feet, a pair of dark sweat pants looking strange matched with her elegant silk top. She noticed the red stains on Sturgis's white shirt. "What happened here?"

"We had an accident," said Sturgis.

"Where's Ramón?"

"He's doing a little disposal job."

Sturgis pulled the door closed behind. Once more, the chains rattled as they were fed through the lockbar. The hasp snapped shut.

MacHenry peered over the cockpit windowsill. He swore softly at what he saw.

"What is it?" asked Shig.

It was Oka.

Sturgis filled her in. She walked straight to the red-tinged area by the bomber's wing. A heater started up, and the row of white flags with their red centers trembled.

"Did you check the hangar completely?"

Sturgis paused. "Everyplace but inside that thing. I was just gettin' around to it when the fed showed. Asshole shoulda slept late."

They both turned and looked at the *Enola Gay.*

"Who's been told?"

"Nobody yet. The colonel's due here any minute."

"Finish cleaning this up. Go through the plane, then get cleaned up yourself. You look like a *bukaronin.*"

"A what?"

"A butcher."

MacHenry sagged to his knees, his face pale white even under the yellow light coming in through the portholes. He'd felt her eyes lock with his. Felt her look straight through him. "We've got to get out of here."

"If we each took some of the chips and ran, they might not get us both," said Shig.

"They locked the front door. We'd have to pass them on the way out the back."

Shig bit his lower lip. "A diversion?"

"I'm fresh out." Think! The engineer's desk sprouted control levers controlling the bomber's four engines, throttles on the left, mixture on the right. MacHenry let his hand fall to the power controls. They felt comfortable, natural.

"What are you thinking?" asked Shig.

"Nothing worthwhile." MacHenry brushed his hand along the rows of silver toggle switches. Oil-cooler controls. Starters. Battery master switches. Fuel-valve controllers. Fuel. He stopped and sniffed. There was fuel in the air, no question. High-octane aviation fuel. How much? he wondered. Enough for a diversion? He studied the panel more closely. He heard a sound, a thump, and looked up.

Shig reappeared from the aft cockpit cabin carrying the big yellow crash ax that had been secured to the bulkhead. "Then we will fight," he whispered. "If he comes back to search the airplane, he will be a *yakuza* with a very big head pain." He held up the ax.

"Put that thing down. And it's head*ache*. Not *pain*." MacHenry shivered again. Sturgis had been right behind him before the FBI agent showed up and diverted him. His hand returned to the engineer's panel.

At the far right edge a toggle switch was marked BATT. Next to it were two identical controls, these labeled GEN 1 and GEN 2. He touched the battery master switch. He thought long and hard. Throw it, and what might happen? He'd discover the batteries were dead. He'd discover they held a charge. He might discover that someone, sometime, had left another switch on, a light, a rotating anticollision beacon, and when he threw the master to ON, the whole world would know someone was inside the *Enola Gay*, fooling with the controls. That would be the end right there. But what if . . .

Shig was standing by the floor hatch with the ax in his hand. Not likely odds, those. Sturgis might come up any second now. What was there to lose? He took hold of the battery toggle and turned it to the ON position.

A cascade of relays flipped from OFF to ON. It sounded like a cricket convention. A few lights glowed on the engineer's panel. A dozen dials leaped to life. The batteries were at full charge! He quickly found the fuel and oil quantity gauges. There was just one dial for all the many fuel tanks the designers had squirreled away in the bomber's airframe. The needle on the dial read zero. He twisted the tank-selector control one turn. The needle didn't budge. Another. The same. Why had he smelled gasoline? There wasn't a drop anywhere! He turned it again.

The needle jumped to half-register. Fuel! He twisted the selector again. Dead. A final turn. Again, half-full. Two tanks had gas in them, numbers one and four, out on opposite wingtips. How much did they hold? Enough to create a diversion? Maybe. He flipped the BATT switch off again.

Once more, the crickets clicked and chirped as the relays closed. Shig quietly joined him by his side. "What was that all about?"

"I have an idea. But it doesn't make much sense."

Shig put the ax aside. "I'm listening."

Bridger arrived at Shintaro's room at exactly eight o'clock. "Mr. Ishii?" He knocked three times on the heavy door. "Are you ready?"

"Just a minute."

The door opened. The air was heavy with perfume. Bridger's eyes bounced from Mikki to Yoshi to Shintaro, and back. Mikki was still in bed. The green-eyed hostess the young Ishii seemed to find amusing had the covers pulled up tight to her neck. Probably naked, thought Bridger. Yoshi looked his dour, disapproving self. Even a jacket and tie didn't brighten him. Shintaro was dressed in a dark suit, a camel-colored overcoat slung over his arm.

"She's not coming, is she?" asked Bridger.

"No." Shintaro leaned over and kissed Mikki on the lips, stroking her cheek as he did. She reached up, and the down comforter slipped enough to show the swell of her breast. Bridger had been right.

Ishii beamed. "Now I am ready. Where's Kazuo?"

"He's probably at the hangar by now."

"Then I suppose we should join him."

Together, the three men left. The black Chrysler was parked outside the lobby of the Hay Adams. In a few moments, it was moving fast and silent on the highway, the rising sun at its back, toward Dulles.

The 7X7 began its long descent for Chicago O'Hare from four hundred miles out. Once below ten thousand feet, there would be no talking on the flight deck except as the checklists required. The so-called sterile cockpit. Too many jets had gone in with their crews discussing the best places to eat or the merits of one mutual fund over another.

"This will be your landing," said the captain, who was rigorous in splitting them fifty-fifty with the first officer. It made him very popular with copilots.

"The Octopus says it's landing number one thousand. We should have a celebration, shouldn't we?"

"I celebrate every landing you don't screw up."

The first officer grasped the controls. They felt good. "Don't worry. The Octopus won't let me ding anything."

The captain eyed the center stand between the two seats. Even though he knew better, he still thought of it as the brain case of the 7X7's elaborate computer system. "I wouldn't be so sure," he said as he hit the FASTEN SEAT BELT sign switch. "Who the hell knows what that damned thing is thinking about?"

"What do you mean he isn't there?" Case demanded. He stood in a phone booth next to the Dulles service road. "He was supposed to meet me."

"Agent Freeman is not available, sir," said the voice on the other end of the line. "He's involved with an ongoing investigation. What is this in reference to?"

"An ongoing investigation." Case turned, cradling the phone to his ear. The day was turning bright and sunny. "If he calls in, tell him I'm writing him out of my will. Tell him . . ." Case stopped when he saw a long, black limo appear.

"Sir?"

The car swept by him. He couldn't see into the back to tell who might be arriving. Japanese executives? Boeing bigwigs? J. William Regano from Treasury? Take your pick.

"Sir?"

"Tell Aaron he's too damned late."

Shig crawled back out of the bombardier's seat. "Can you really do this, Mr. MacHenry?"

"We'll find out."

"What about Mr. Dole?" asked Ishii as they drove along the Dulles perimeter road.

"I believe chances are excellent." Bridger pulled his sleeve to expose his watch. "It's a real opportunity for the Republicans to show they can forge new linkages with labor, with industry. At home and abroad." Bridger was feeling the rhythm of the words, he could sense the impact they would make on tonight's news, on tomorrow's poll numbers, on next week's election analysis. Plus, plus, and plus again. How could they not show? And who could they thank for it?

Arthur Dean Bridger. Who could deliver the next president to the Japanese? Arthur Dean Bridger. Who had cleared the way so thoroughly, so professionally? He turned to the young Ishii. He could see why Ibuki chose him. "Ready for the big morning?"

"As ready as I will ever be, Mr. Bridger."

The long, black car came to a security gate and stopped. The driver entered a code, and the gate began to open.

Oka met them at the rear door to the hangar. Wow Wow stood back as she handed the wallet to Kazuo Ibuki and bowed deeply.

"What is this?" he asked her.

She didn't look up or break the bow. Ibuki was higher ranked by far. He must acknowledge her, bow, then rise first. "It belonged to a federal policeman. FBI."

"Police?" That got Ibuki's attention. "Please. Stand up. Your foot looks like it must give you pain." He flipped the wallet open. His bottom teeth immediately went to his upper lip. He sucked in a short breath. He handed the wallet to Wow Wow as though the leather burned his fingers.

"Bridger's men killed him. It's unlikely that he was working alone."

Another hiss. "Why was he here? What was he doing? Apes!" he shouted. "They will ruin everything! Where are they?"

"One is attending to the body. The other is in the main room cleaning the floor."

"Of all the days for this to happen! We cannot permit this to affect our plans. The ceremony, the announcement. They must take place. Afterward, we will deal with those two." Ibuki turned to Wow Wow. "We will make it look as it needs to look. Understood?"

"*Hai!*"

A car pulled up outside. Ibuki angrily motioned for Wow Wow to go see who it was. A federal policeman! The FBI! And Bridger's two idiots killed him! Trust a gaijin to blunder! To destroy with one swipe of his hairy paw the careful mechanism Ibuki had so cleverly fashioned. They were impossible!

Sturgis picked this moment to appear. He'd changed into a clean shirt and pants. He carried a navy blazer over his arm.

"You!" said Ibuki. "What have you done?"

"Perhaps it would be best if you finished securing the hangar," she told Sturgis. "Check the airplane from nose to tail. We cannot afford any more surprises."

"Sure," he said, and left.

"What if something happens?" asked Wow Wow. "Something bad?"

Ibuki scowled as he watched Sturgis leave. He heard Bridger's hearty greeting outside, then turned. "This is what we must do," he whispered.

"You're sure, Shig?"

Shig took two chips from MacHenry and stuffed them into the pocket of his baseball jacket. "I am sure."

MacHenry put the three other back into their cloth sack and pocketed them. "If anything goes wrong, take those straight to the NTSB. The Technical Analysis section. Or to Roger Case. He'll know what to do."

"I will." Shig paused at the floor hatch as MacHenry positioned the control levers to draw fuel from the tanks that had gasoline in them. "Mr. MacHenry?"

"Yes?"

"I want you to know it has been a great honor to work with you." Shig looked so serious. "The things that people say about Americans are not all true."

"Thanks. Wait. You mean *some* of them are?"

Shig grinned. *"Gamman!"* He eased down into the hatch and was gone.

Sturgis ambled along the body of the old bomber. He closed the open door at the tail turret. The damned thing was spooked. Shooting a fed! That was major league. He realized that it was a problem Ramón just might not find his way clear of. And what about me? If the ship was headed for the bottom, he wasn't volunteering to ride it down. No, sir.

Something was up. He could see it in the old Jap's eyes. Not that you could tell much. It was like trying to guess what a lizard was thinking. But there was a stiffness, an electricity that he picked up on like a hound dog smelling a blood trail. No, he just might have to . . .

A motion where there was not supposed to be any caught his eye. Legs? He stopped. Had Ramón . . . No! Dangling from the belly of the bomber way up near the nose. The cockpit ladder. Legs? Shit! There *had* been someone in there! He almost shouted, but he wasn't impulsive. He wasn't like Ramón, all balls and brains like a twenty-cent taco. He was far more sensible. A trooper. Disciplined.

Sturgis watched as the legs elongated into the body of a man. He remained silent, took cover behind one of the red workstands wheeled up to the *Enola Gay,* then reached behind him and drew the Walther TPH. It was a miserable weapon for anything beyond close range. It couldn't hit reliably over fifteen yards. Range to target? Thirty plus. Sturgis waited until the man who'd dropped from the ladder turned away from him. Hurrying on the balls of his feet, Sturgis dodged forward to the next piece of cover. Twenty yards. Better.

There was a scrape, then a *thock* as wooden chocks were tossed away from the bomber's nose. He peered around the workstand. What was that son of a bitch up to? He was bent down over something. Sturgis silently crept closer. Fifteen yards out. The TPH came up, the iron sights nicely centered on the intruder's backbone. Front blade nestled between the double squares at the back. A killing trio, that. Left thumb on the safety. Trigger slack taken up. Breath out. The small autopistol now in a steady, two-handed grip.

Squeeze.

TWENTY-ONE

Shig toggled the switch and the heavy motors began to whine. The gearing strained to take up the slack, then with a sudden jerk the first door began to open. A crack of brilliant sun appeared at the widening joint between the doors. An icy breeze swept inside. That's one, he thought.

As he bent over to turn on the other one, something slammed him hard from behind, throwing him against the opening doors. He heard the shot an instant later.

The expanding bullet entered low on his back, split into razor-sharp splines, then ricocheted up a long, ragged tunnel before exiting near his left shoulder blade. He gasped and propped himself up, reaching behind to feel for the wound, and a second round spanged against the steel doors not an inch from his head, mushrooming into a bright metal crater rayed with hot white sparks.

"Freeze!" yelled Sturgis as he advanced, running from cover to cover in case Shig had a weapon. It was good small-arms tactics, but it gave Shig the chance he needed. He felt all hope rise from him like a heavy weight. All thoughts of the future dissipated like a faint fog under a powerful sun. He'd been shot. He would die. Now, he could only choose the circumstances associated with his death.

The motors were at full speed now. The doors were open a good two feet. His eyes were fighting to focus, a slash of agony burned his back where the little Stinger round had gouged him like a ragged nail. He fell through the opening to the outside, rolled, got to his feet. A big corporate jet was parked nearby. He would die. He thought of his father, how sad he would be. With one glance over his shoulder at the nose of the *Enola Gay,* he ran.

★   ★   ★

Bridger, Shintaro, and Yoshi were just coming in from the parking area when Yoshi shouted and threw his arm around the young Ishii, dragging him down to the ground. Bridger stood back as though the bodyguard had gone mad. But Oka knew he had not.

She spun and looked back in the direction of the *Enola Gay*. The muffled pop of Sturgis' .22 was unmistakable. "Stay here!" she told them, then took off back inside, passing a frightened-looking Kazuo Ibuki. Wow Wow, like Yoshi, had thrown his charge to the ground and was now sitting on the struggling old lawyer. He pointed into the main hangar space as Oka ran by. A wooden pole with a small metal hook on the end was propped against the wall by the door. She went for it by pure instinct.

In her hands it wasn't merely a pole meant for adjusting the operation of ceiling fans. It was a *naginata,* a bamboo rod with a deadly blade afixed to the end. The traditional weapon of Japanese women left behind by their samurai men to tend and protect the home. In her hands it was the equal to a kendo stave, a katana blade. A pistol.

When she emerged from the closed room at the back of the hangar and into the main space, the rolling doors were nearly wide open. A cold wind set the rows of flags set up in front of the bomber's wings shifting uneasily.

She stopped when she saw Sturgis out on the tarmac. He was running, a pistol in his hand. A white puff. A tiny pop. He was shooting. She took off after him, her injured foot forgotten. In one hand the *naginata*. The other held the black stiletto. Long range and short. One to stun, the other to kill.

Up high inside the cockpit, MacHenry had a front-row seat. One shot fired. Two. He saw Sturgis run through the widening gap between the doors after Shig. Had he missed? He could only hope so. Now it was all up to him.

Two seats. Two wheels. Rudder pedals. An airplane, he told himself. He yanked the parking brake on while pressing the rudder pedals down with his boots. An airplane. You used to fly them for your living. He turned and went straight to the flight engineer's station.

The *Enola Gay* was a big, complex bird with a crew of eight. It was no computerized jet, ready to do the work, and the thinking, for its pilots. It took a precise set of acts to bring it to life, and even if MacHenry could have recalled what they were, there was no time to do it by the long-forgotten book.

He'd set the fuel-control levers already. Now he toggled the switch marked BATT to the ON position, slapped the four mixture controls to AUTO RICH, and cracked all four throttles open. His hands were shaking when they found the engine primers.

When had he last done this? As a flight engineer on a Constellation, even before he moved up to the right seat with Joe DelVecchio at his side. A very, very long time ago. This was against everything he had ever learned as a professional pilot. He was hurrying, blundering into an unknown land. It might start the engines. It might as easily get him killed.

He hit the primer button on the number-one engine and was rewarded with a greasy odor of high-octane gas. Thank God there was fuel in this behemoth! His hands flew over the old engineer's panel. There was no time for finesse. No time to worry about doing it right. He knew he risked blowing the engines with hydro lock. Not just any engines, either. Museum pieces. So be it. His hand went to the START switch and pushed the number-one engine toggle to ACCELERATE.

A loud whine and a heavy vibration began at once as the big paddle blades out on the far-left engine began to turn up faster, faster. He twisted the magneto switch to BOTH, and with a clatter of ancient pistons rising, falling, rising, falling, the big Wright was summoned back from a half-century hibernation in a dense blue cloud of oil smoke.

He jockeyed the throttle until the engine submitted to running. He did the same thing on the number-two engine. Number three. Finally, far out on the right wing, the number four. All four Wrights were turning up now, their voices a ragged chorus of mechanical discord, even surprise. Summoned from the grave of time. No one could have been more surprised than MacHenry.

He left the engineer's panel and returned to the front left seat. The pilot's place. He made sure the floor hatch was closed as he jumped over it on his way.

The hangar was fogged in oil smoke and vapor. His left hand

reached out and grasped all four throttle levers. They were vibrating so badly it looked as if his hand was palsied. He ignored it and pushed.

The radial engines popped, roared, and backfired in protest. They were still cold, the oil sluggish in their arteries. MacHenry was asking too much, too soon! He reached over onto the center aisle stand and rotated the turbo boost all the way to full military power, then yanked the emergency brake off and fed in more throttle. The old pistons gathered themselves into a full thundering gallop.

Nothing happened. Wheel chocks! Shig must have forgotten to pull the chocks! There must be . . . a loud bang made him turn his head. Another. Someone was trying to batter through the floor hatch! The heavy metal panel shook under each blow.

With a hard shove, he spun the turbo boost to the stops, then rammed all four throttles forward. The engines shuddered, then caught, surging, roaring fire and smoke.

The *Enola Gay* jumped her wheel chocks and started to roll for freedom. Her wings took down the row of flags set up in front, mowing down four wildly flapping Rising Suns and chewing the fabric to shreds with her whirling steel teeth. Four Stars and Stripes went down as the other wing sliced them like a scythe through standing wheat. The cockpit emerged from the hangar into the sun. There, finally, MacHenry saw Shig.

Sturgis had the intruder cornered, or at least trapped, behind one of the landing-gear legs on the Hibakusha Foundation jet. The tall Japanese was wounded. A stream of blood led right under the Gulfstream's wing. But the thunder coming from behind was loud in his ears and growing louder by the second. He risked a quick look back and saw the silver snout of the old B-29 emerge. When he turned, Shig was running.

"Freeze, motherfuck!" Sturgis tracked Shig's fleeing back and squeezed off another shot, only to find the Walther pointed at empty space. Yellow sparks came from the concrete as the bullet whined away into the distance. Shit! He couldn't sit here and plink at him all morning. And he couldn't run after the little fuck all the way to the runway. And look at him! Even wounded, the Jap could dodge and weave! He took after Shig, vowing to end this right here, right now. He would not reload the Walther. He would not need to. One bullet. One bullet.

Shig ran two steps, lurched left, then right, doing his best to keep the terrible pain from coming back, keeping the little droplets of death that stung the air around him from finding their mark in his body. He caught sight of the *Enola Gay* as it rolled clear of the hangar. It was trailing dense white smoke, coughing and belching fire from its stacks. But it was moving! *Gambare,* MacHenry! Be brave!

He dodged beneath the wing of the corporate jet. Twenty feet beyond was the open grassy verge that separated the ramp from the runway. A bullet struck the ground and whined up in a wicked bounce, striking the underside of the Gulfstream's wing. Immediately, a shower of cold kerosene fuel sprayed over him.

Now what's he doing? Sturgis skidded to a stop and brought the weapon up again. The target was headed for open ground, the killing zone between the Hibakusha jet and the hangar. He shut out the rest of the world as he brought the pistol up in a rock-steady, two-handed grip. The target was running straight and true. Easy. Easy. He made a bridge of bone that welded the hot, smoking Walther to his hand; the hand became rigid with the wrist, the arm, the muscles steel cables holding that weight, tracking, tracking. Leading the target. Distance? Twenty yards. Fifteen. Still running straight! Making it damned easy. The front sight blade swept the air in front of Shig's body. Chest shot. Centered, now raised a hair to take in the drop, the slight wind. Nothing existed outside the weapon and the target. He breathed out and took up the trigger slack.

MacHenry slammed on the left brake. The big bomber squealed, screeched, then pivoted on locked wheels. He rammed the right engine throttles full forward again, and the B-29 swept its wing through a hard left turn, her propeller blades turning at two thousand revolutions per minute. Thirty times each second, a metal blade taller than a man swept an invisible path. Four blades to an engine, the shimmering disc might as well be made of solid steel.

Sturgis knew he should move, that he should do something. That something was nagging him, some alarm bell was ringing. He even knew the name for what he felt: target fixation. His rifle instructors at Ft. Benning had told him as much so long ago. Not that it mattered now. Only the perfection of the shot made any difference. But he kept the TPH on target. He squeezed off the round just as the roaring propeller bore down on him from behind. The prop sucked back the puff of white gunsmoke. Lifted his jacket off his back. Snatched at the blond stubble of his nape. He half-rose to run, twisting to face his new attacker, and met a descending blade face on.

A faint shudder coursed through the bomber. Had he run him down? What had . . . a spray of red mist swept up and over the right wing. A crimson cocoon of blood. It told MacHenry all he needed to know. He straightened out the *Enola Gay* and ruddered her down the taxiway. Where was Shig? The B-29's left wing nearly brushed the Hibakusha jet. His eye caught the glimmer of a spreading pool of fuel under one of its wings. A loud thump from behind told him he had other worries.

Someone was right below the cockpit, hanging on to the ladder, banging for entry. Not Shig. His worry had a very different face. It was a blonde with eyes of glittering, anthracite black. Without deciding, without a conscious act of any kind at all, MacHenry was headed for the taxiway that led out onto the runway. There was escape for a pilot. There was freedom. Surrounded by clever predators, here he was an awkward beast, slow, ungainly, vulnerable. But there, there he was in his own element. His own sphere of expertise. Let them try to follow.

He gripped the throttles and nudged them ahead, taxiing fast to the end of Runway 19 Right. He couldn't announce himself on a radio. He couldn't find a radio to save his life. He only hoped the controllers in the tower cab were alert. He hit the left brake again and brought the two right engines up to a shuddering shout. The bomber turned out onto the runway. Ahead, the long black ribbon stretched two miles flat and true. "Shig," he said out loud as he evened up the throttles, toggled the props to full increase, and listened to the roar of his engines shout, "this is for you."

★　　★　　★

The wind blew the sound of the bomber's engines away. Roger Case didn't hear them at all. He waited by the gate, waited for Mac-Henry and his newfound partner to return. Waited for Aaron Freeman to arrive. It was well past the appointed hour, and Freeman was a pain in the ass, but Case had never known him to be late.

He was about to go call from the phone booth again when a long, black limousine, the third of the morning, slowly purred up to the security gate. Who was it this time? He was about to walk over to peer in when a new sound made him stop. A roar. A thunder. The voice of ghosts fifty years dead, returned from the grave of history.

He turned and looked into the sky.

"Jesus," he said as sun glinted from bright metal. He watched it. "MacHenry," he said out loud. It had to be.

The back door of the limo popped open. Eight thousand galloping horses made the air tremble. A tall, silver-haired man unfolded himself and stood, shielding his eyes from the bright sun as he watched the *Enola Gay* climb strong and fast, the wind under its wings. The wheels were still down, and something swung, trapezelike, from under its nose.

Case squinted, matching face to a name. "Amory Tasker?" he said, moving closer so that his words could be heard above the thunder cascading down from the sky.

The Boeing CEO looked at the old man in his tweeds and cane. "Yes," he said cautiously.

"I'm Roger Case. Case, Rudge, McDivitt."

Tasker's eyes narrowed. "I've heard of you, Mr. Case."

"Doesn't surprise me in the least. After all, as of this morning, we're filing a civil suit in the District on your behalf."

"What are you talking about?"

"Wrongful death. Sabotage of a commercial aircraft. There will be a class-action suit I'm sure, and the insurance companies will be out for Boeing's blood. You need some help, Mr. Tasker. And you need it fast. I can provide it."

"You're mad."

"I'm mad as hell. You will be, too. We'll cooperate with the criminal investigation, of course, but it won't shield Boeing from claims of negligence and restitution. After all, it *was* one of your employees who allowed Nippon Aerospace to put a virus on your new plane. We'll fight to put the blame where it belongs. Don't you worry. And our fees are very reasonable."

Tasker stared. "Mr. Case, I'm sorry, but I have no idea what you're talking about." He turned to leave.

"Wait!" Case hobbled up to the limo's open back door. "If you'll give me a lift, I believe I can explain it to your satisfaction." He surveyed the nest of antennas sprouting from the rear window. "There's only one condition. If you buy the evidence we've developed, I expect you to ground every Boeing 777 in the fleet as of this morning. No hemming and hawing. No calls back to Legal Affairs. Just action. Deal?"

"What evidence?"

Case nodded for Tasker to get into the limo as though he were offering the CEO of Boeing a ride, not the other way around. "Now you're asking smart questions."

TWENTY-TWO

MacHenry wedged the control yoke between his knees and managed to fasten his lap belt. The *Enola Gay* rumbled through the cold morning air, its four engines stiff with age, catching, missing, belching flames and smoke but running all the same. He left the gear down. Who knew whether the wheels would actually come up and, more important, go back down again?

He banked the half-circle control yoke to turn the bomber away from the active runway at Dulles. He didn't know how far the fuel he had in those two tanks might take him. But he couldn't stay here. Why were midair collisions so common around airports? Because that was where all the airplanes were.

He set the trim slightly nose up and let the ship find its own climb. He eyed the altimeter on the instrument stand in front of him. They were through one thousand feet—seven hundred feet above the brown earth—eastbound, climbing at over six hundred feet per minute. He could see the Washington Monument poke out of the morning haze. He used it as a steering point and aimed the *Enola Gay* for it.

He glanced at the unfamiliar rows of flight instruments and engine gauges, trying to make sense of them. Four throttles sprouted from his left, along the sidewall; the props were governed by toggle switches on the center aisle panel. The mixture settings were unreachable way back at the flight engineer's station. It reminded him that flying this plane was a job made for three good men. Here he was on his first, and possibly last, flight in a B-29. Solo. A frail little collection of flesh and blood and bone, wrapped in seventy-five thousand pounds of antique aluminum, sloshing with high-octane fuel.

MacHenry focused on the three killers. Altitude. Airspeed. Needle and ball for coordination. Altitude was no problem. He was fat with it. The Virginia countryside rose behind him to the west, but it was pancake flat from here all the way to the gray line of the Atlantic. The airspeed needle was jumping all over the place as the plane shook. But the wild swings seemed to average at the 140-mile-per-hour mark. He hoped that was enough. The ball was way off in the corner of its glass tube. MacHenry stomped rudder and centered it. Something was still banging underneath the cockpit floor.

She was there, all right. She was hanging on in a hurricane of slipstream wind, hanging on to that ladder! Was all that pounding her desperate movements to get free? To break through the cabin floor, to come at him with that knife he could still see all too clearly?

He turned around in his seat to be sure the floor hatch was still locked. He could only too well imagine her rising through it, blade in hand.

He could end it, he knew. One quick flip of the landing-gear toggle and the big nosewheel strut would tuck up and crush her. It would end it right here. The floor hatch bucked under another powerful impact. He reached for the gear switch on the center stand. It was just a simple silver toggle, not the elaborate, wheel-shaped device he was accustomed to. Should I? Should I? His hand trembled. He'd killed that man with the gun back at Dulles. He was already once a murderer. And Shig. What were his chances down on the ground? Some plan. It was too late now for recriminations.

MacHenry swallowed as a bead of sweat dripped off his nose. He touched the landing-gear toggle. It shook with the vibration of the engines, alive. A tremendous bang made him jump against his belt. It was louder than the others. A dry-bone snap. End it! Now!

He threw the switch and held it against the stops. With a loud rumble the wheels began to fold. The banging on the floor hatch became frantic, faster, faster. The mechanism hit something solid and stopped, the motors whining in protest. It squeezed up tighter, smaller. There was a slight shudder, a crunch, then a pause in the awful sounds from underneath him. Thank God, he thought, it's over. He turned.

A wooden pole was wedged under the edge of the floor hatch, levering it, higher, higher. Then, with a gunshot crack, it broke.

With a final shove, the floor hatch burst free of its hinges. A head appeared. Blond hair. Black eyes. An arm. A hand bearing a broken pole. The pole clattered to the deck. Another hand. A black stiletto.

★   ★   ★

It wasn't the first time in his long career that a mynah bird's memory had come in handy. Case sat back into the plush seat of the limo after laying out the particulars of MacHenry's case, detail for detail, name by name.

The CEO of Boeing looked skeptical and worried in equal measures. "You say you've already worked this out with our flight-test department? They concur?"

Case nodded. "I wouldn't want Joe to get into trouble . . ."

Joe, thought Amory Tasker. He knows Joe DelVecchio. "And our chief programmer. You've spoken with him?"

"Mr. Tasker, as I suspect you know, Tom Kelly is dead."

Tasker kept a plain face. Case might be an irascible old lawyer. He might be a bottom-feeding litigator who would like nothing so much as to nail a billion-dollar donkey tail onto Boeing. But here he was, offering to *protect* the company. He looked over at Case. "What about these chips? You have them where we can examine them?"

Case smiled, paused, then spoke. "We have them. Yes. Absolutely." It wasn't the first time in his long career that a little lie had come in handy, either. "Now. What about that grounding order?"

The weary crew from Hawaii filed off the parked 777.

"Bit gusty on final," said the captain. He knew the copilot wasn't pleased with the landing he'd made.

"Yeah."

The two pilots had just enough time to get out, take a walk, drink some coffee, and come back. By then, the refueling would be complete, and it would be time for pretakeoff checks to begin. So much for employee ownership.

Julia looked up as the PA system came on. "On behalf of all our crew today, we'd like to welcome you aboard the continuation of Flight 11, service to Washington, D.C."

The plane shuddered to a stop and sat there, its two engines turning up to a roar. With a surge of power, the 777 pivoted away from the terminal and began its taxi.

She sat back. Takeoffs always made her nervous. All that mass moving so fast so close to the ground. She closed her eyes. Maybe it came from spending time with MacHenry. After all, he made a career out of the dark side of airplanes.

She didn't relax until the 7X7 leveled off after a steep banking departure, its nose pointed to the east.

"United 11, Chicago. Climb on your present heading, cleared to three seven zero, expect higher at Giper. Contact Departure now on one two five point zero."

"Out of eighteen thousand for three seven zero and over to Departure." The captain looked to his right. "What was that frequency?" He was tired, and his brain was not firing as fast as it should.

"Twenty-five nothing."

The routing was already programmed into the Octopus. The computer throttled up both engines and the lightly laden ship began to climb.

The pilot hit the transmit button. "Departure, United 11 is with you in the climb to three seven zero."

"Radar contact for United 11. What will be your final altitude request?"

"Ah . . ." What was it? Oh. "Four one zero, United 11."

"Roger. United 11 is cleared to four one zero."

"Feeling okay?" asked the copilot as the big jet entered into another climb to its cruising altitude. Maybe what they said was right, after all. A captain was nothing more than a first officer who'd been hired first.

The altimeter display rose through twenty thousand. Twenty-five. Thirty.

"Like a homesick angel."

Thirty. Thirty-eight. The forty-thousand-foot marker was near. The climb was strong and sure.

"United 11, Chicago Center."

The pilot glanced to his right. "Was that for us?"

Thirty-nine thousand feet.

"United 11, Chicago Center. How do you read?"

"Ah, United 11, go ahead."

As the controller spoke, his voice fast and plainly worried, the altitude display continued to rise. A tiny line of light separated the rising needle from the forty-thousand-foot mark.

"Christ!" The pilot took the yoke and stopped the ascent. He grasped both throttles and pulled them out of climb mode, back, back, all the way to flight idle. He banked them steeply around, north, then west. Lake Michigan was a cold blue line off to their right. The stubble of Chicago's skyline poked above a haze layer. O'Hare was dead ahead.

"What's it all about?" asked the copilot.

The pilot shook his head. "You heard the man. They've grounded us."

A dense cloud of oil smoke slowly cleared from the open hangar. The flags of Japan and the United States lay shredded on the floor. The pilots of the Hibakusha Foundation jet were peeking out from the cabin door now, their eyes white as they looked at the body on the ramp. In the distance, a siren was wailing.

Shintaro Ishii coughed oil vapors as he watched the *Enola Gay* merge with the fire of the rising sun. It had thundered overhead, its motions unsure, like a poorly shot bird, before turning east. A body was out on the ramp. A body surrounded by a pool of red, and another object, small and rounded. "Where is Bridger?" he asked his bodyguard.

"Still inside," said Yoshi. Of course, he added to himself. Where else for a coward to be when shots are fired? He looked at the body. He could tell it was one of Bridger's guards. And the cannonball near it, resting at an angle that showed half a sphere of blond hair, half a sphere of black gore, that was the fool's head. It was none of Yoshi's business. "I think that you should consider withdrawing," he told Shintaro. "Let the gaijin fight it out with one another, and let them make the explanations to the police." He listened to the siren draw nearer.

"We should go find Ibuki first."

"No need. I am right here."

They both turned as the old lawyer emerged from the hangar with Wow Wow right beside him.

Ibuki stared at the tiny silver speck of the fleeing B-29. The bomber's rumble began to grow faint as the silver of its wings blended with the horizon. He'd heard the siren, too. This was not Japan. Explanations would be demanded. The situation could become complex. Difficult. He glanced at Yoshi and Shintaro. "Shintaro, events are moving out of our hands. Our reputations must be protected. We must reconsider from a place of safety. And we must act quickly and resolutely. America is a dangerous place with too many guns. We were frightened by the events, and so we left. That is what we shall say. Are you ready to listen and to obey?"

"Yes, Uncle."

The old lawyer looked first to Yoshi. "The body must be put out of sight before the police arrive. They will find it, but they must not find it too soon. Am I understood?"

Yoshi looked at Shintaro. He didn't like taking orders from Ibuki. And he didn't like dirtying himself with another man's death.

"He understands, Uncle," said Ishii. "Perhaps you could tell us—"

"While he is doing that," Ibuki interrupted, "you will tell Bridger we cannot be here for the ceremony this morning. Offer our regrets. We will contact him after he smooths everything out once more. That's what we pay him for." Ibuki motioned for Wow Wow to follow him out onto the ramp. He made straight for the Gulfstream jet, walking gingerly around the wreckage, both mechanical and human, that the bomber had left in its wake.

Yoshi shot another questioning look to Shintaro.

"Do as he says. He knows best. I'll find Bridger."

Yoshi looked skeptical, but he said *"Hai!"* and made off to do as his lord had ordered.

Ibuki took the airstairs up into the cabin of the plush corporate jet. The two pilots clung to the side of the oval doorway as though gunfire might erupt at any moment. "What are you two staring at?" he demanded angrily. "Get to work!"

"Work?" asked one of them.

"Quickly! We are leaving."

Wow Wow pulled the hatch closed and locked it.

The captain watched. "Where are we going?"

Ibuki slammed the flat of his hand down to the polished cherrywood table. "Japan!"

*   *   *

Oka got to her feet and landed lightly on the tilting flight deck. Her dark blouse was slick with grease and hydraulic oil, and her sweat pants were torn. But she didn't look helpless. Not one bit. The blade in her hand sought a metal surface to touch, a high-voltage line aching to discharge against the nearest conductor.

He gave the wheel a savage yank that sent her falling against the flight engineer's seat. He threw the great bomber into an opposite turn, keeping her off-balance. She drove her blade up into the cockpit padding and used it to anchor herself through MacHenry's gyrations. As they came level, she lurched forward. Once more he tilted the wings. Once more she pinned herself in place with that long black blade. Another lurch forward. Fifteen feet. Ten. Five. She let go and sprang for MacHenry, this time meaning to anchor herself by driving the stiletto into his back, sinking it until the hilt came up hard against his jacket, steel against bone.

He braced for the blow. A banshee shriek filled his ears, then a terrible, piercing scream. There was a thump. He turned and saw not just the woman in black, but another figure covered with blood. They were locked in combat on the floor, twisting, turning over and over, the knife rising, falling, a scorpion's sting seeking its target, legs scrambling for purchase against the sides of the cockpit.

MacHenry's mouth dropped open. It was Shig.

The first airport police car responded to the Smithsonian/Hibakusha hangar, screeching to a stop next to Ibuki's parked limousine. The officers got out warily. The tower crew had seen everything, seen the hangar doors open, the bomber suddenly and most unexpectedly emerge. They'd seen the two men perform a silent, deadly ballet of hunter and prey, and finally, saw one of them fall under the glittering arc of the *Enola Gay*'s number-four engine. The first cop approached the hangar's rear door and tried it. It was locked. He pounded on the metal. "Better stand to one side," said his partner.

The first cop scooted over immediately. "Police!" he yelled as he drew his weapon.

Bridger heard them and stepped back from the door. "What do you mean, leaving?" Bridger said angrily. "What about the signing ceremony? Amory Tasker from Boeing. Regano from CFIUS. Maybe even the next president of the United States! You can't just leave. It will destroy everything we planned."

"You heard them!" said Shintaro. "The police are already here! Your men killed a federal agent."

"That's an absurd allegation." But Bridger looked worried.

"Police!" The back door pounded, metal against metal.

Bridger turned, then swung back to Shintaro. "Where's Ibuki?" he demanded. He pushed by Shintaro and ran right into Yoshi. The guard's clothes were bloodied. "Get out of my way." He pushed Yoshi, but he might as well push a boulder.

Yoshi crossed his arms over his chest and glared.

"I'm sorry, Mr. Bridger. But we will . . ." Shintaro stopped and swung his head to face the open hangar doors. A faint scream of turbine engines was building out there into a roar.

Bridger sneered as he saw what was happening. "Well, isn't that something. It looks like you've been elected to hold the bag. You know what? It's your lucky day. You'll get my vote, too."

The back door rocked. "Open up this door!"

Bridger shrugged. "I never should have agreed to work with people like you. You just don't understand how the real world operates. Japan is one thing, but here, well, you're just going to have to pay for your ignorance, I'm afraid. It's a hard lesson. Expensive, too. And I certainly am not going to remain around to pick up the tab."

"Pay?"

The second engine on the Gulfstream began to roar.

"A Japanese executive with ties to organized crime brings undisciplined hired guns over to America." Bridger eyed Yoshi, amused. "And when someone tries to steal their pretty little prize, they go crazy and start shooting. That's the story, my young friend. And I promise you, it will be believed."

"But that's not what happened!"

"I think that between us, the police will find my version of events a lot more understandable." As Bridger turned to open the back door, Yoshi reached out and grabbed him by the collar. He pulled him off the ground like a puppet. He squeezed the American's windpipe.

Bridger clawed at the hands around his neck, then suddenly changed his mind. He reached into his suit jacket and hauled out a silver automatic pistol. Without taking aim, he squeezed off a cracking shot that smacked into the rear wall, sending the two policemen outside scrambling for cover. He twisted to point the little weapon at Yoshi. But the guard's hands were closed around Bridger's neck like iron bands. Bridger squeezed the trigger again, more by panic and reflex than by anything more. This time he was luckier.

Yoshi took the round in the pit of his stomach. It entered high and tunneled deep. He could feel a hot probing finger against his backbone. It was a bad one. He could tell. But it was no time for worrying over mere pain. He had a job to do. It bled, but he felt nothing. His grip only got tighter around Bridger's neck. Bridger's face went red, then black. His tongue lolled out obscenely, flapping as though the American were screaming his lungs out. There was only the faintest gurgling noise.

Yoshi stood firm as a statue until Bridger's eyes rolled up into his head. Then, wearily, he dropped the limp body to the floor. From the mouth of the corpse, a whistle escaped and slowly, eerily, fell away to silence.

Shintaro stood there, stunned. He was about to speak when Yoshi turned and bowed deeply.

"It would be best if you waited here. Give me a moment, then let the police in."

"Wait? But . . ."

"I will take responsibility. Tell them as much. You should suffer no consequences. This is all of Ibuki's making. He has raised his blade against you. I will raise mine against him."

"You . . . why would you do that?"

Yoshi gave Shintaro a fierce look that silenced him. "I serve the Ishiis," he said, then hurried away toward the screaming jets of the Gulfstream.

Shintaro picked up the silver pistol. He would hand the evil thing to the police. It was still warm. The final act of a dead man. The door pounded again. He calmly walked over and unlocked it.

The first cop took in Bridger's body. The second saw Shintaro. "Gun!"

Shintaro was about to agree, to explain, when the cop's big Smith & Wesson boomed.

Yoshi made his way to the corporate jet. He noticed how much larger the pool of fuel had become under the punctured wing. The cold kerosene was still flowing vigorously. He ran to the wheel chocks and placed them securely around the landing gear once more, then stepped back and looked up.

Ibuki's face was pressed to the Plexiglas porthole, his mouth open, shouting some order that Yoshi knew would never be executed in time. The engines throttled up. The jet rocked against the wheel chocks, trapped. The engines throttled up again, louder. Still no good. He saw the main hatch begin to open. He felt some regret for Wow Wow. But that was the nature of war and warriors. He turned and ducked beneath the damaged wing.

Yoshi breathed in the oily stink of jet fuel, imagining instead the perfume from a garland of flowers placed around him in his honor. Raw kerosene splashed across his shoes. A man lives by honor, by duty, he thought as he pulled out a cigarette lighter. Old Susumu himself had given it to him as a present long ago.

He got the little flame lit, adjusting it until it was a hard blue cone of fire. He stepped directly under the showering kerosene, his head back, mouth open. It streamed down across his face. There was a muffled whump, and then he could no longer hear the throb of the jet engines. Everyone dies. But to die for something, that was paradise.

MacHenry looked over his shoulder at the tangled mass of limbs and bodies. He saw her arm rise with its blade and yanked hard on the control yoke, nearly standing the bomber on its tail. Oka and Shig slid back down the deck, hitting the aft bulkhead with a muffled thump and a curse.

Oka clawed at Shig's back, grabbing the bloody edge of his wound and pulling it. Shig screamed, still holding on.

One of his feet rested on the metal, but the other one pushed through the open bomb-bay hatch at the base of the bulkhead. The one he'd crawled through on his way up from the tail. His back was on fire. He was off-balance. Propped up on a bent leg, one foot dangling back into the black bomb bay.

Oka rolled away from him and got to her feet, swaying like a cobra ready to strike. He saw her lead with her broken foot for a full swivel kick at his head and correctly assumed it was a feint. Even she could not kick with broken toes. He moved into the blow as she spun in midair like a top, kicking empty space with her good leg.

She slashed the air in front of his eyes with the blade. He felt the wind of its passing, then realized as the blood welled from the bridge of his nose that she'd not quite missed. She struck again, this time connecting with her good foot, driving Shig farther into the hatchway. His leg was nearly folded double at the knee, half his body wedged into the hole, his arms waving wildly, trying to fend off the next attack. First the kick. Then the blade. He knew what would be next.

When it came, slower, more stealthily than he expected, he was ready. She's tired. She feels the pain. Good. He threw up the flat of his hand into its path. The black blade pricked his palm, then slid in with an eerie lack of resistance. It was very, very sharp. He saw surprise register in Oka's odd eyes. The surprise changed to sudden under-standing, too late, when he closed his pierced hand around the stiletto's handle and yanked her off her feet.

Together, they tumbled back into the thundering, uninsulated bomb bay, all the way down to the doors. A streak of light leaked in at their seam. When they struck the doors, the gap widened, but the door pins held. They rolled, seeking each other's vitals. She yanked her blade out of his bloody grip.

As Shig evaded a wild slashing strike of her knife arm, a sudden realization burst inside his brain. The walk. The moves. The fighting skill. This woman was no gaijin she-demon. Some foreigner he could never hope to conquer or even understand. Blonde or no blonde. She was Japanese! The realization flooded him with new power, new confidence. He was fighting something very familiar. Something he knew. Something he could defeat if he could only endure.

He jumped to his feet, his good hand closing over the steel bomb shackle hanging from the overhead structure. As she rose to meet him, he sent it careening into her. It connected. The knife dropped with a clatter of steel on steel. She tried to find it. Shig could see the wicked point outlined against the light coming in from between the doors. He jumped down from the catwalk. The gap of light widened under both their weights. He kicked the stiletto, sending it spinning, spinning, until it lined up with the opening in the doors.

"Ihihe!" she screamed again as it fell through and disappeared. She *was* Japanese!

He turned. "MacHenry!"

The capital lay like a model at MacHenry's feet as the bomber thundered over the Potomac, still eastbound. The spire of the Washington Monument was right off the nose, no more than a few miles away. Beyond the monument, the Mall, and a bit farther, at the end of the strip of greenish brown, the dome of the Capitol building.

"MacHenry!"

MacHenry swung when he heard his name. All he saw was the flapping pressure hatch leading down into the bomb bay, the place where he had discovered the cache of computer chips. It swung open, then shut, as the *Enola Gay* shuddered.

"MacHenry!" Shig screamed. "Open the doors!"

Oka sprang at Shig's knees. They fell back to the bottom of the bomb bay again, struggling. Shig felt an icy wind chill the wetness streaming from his back. He turned his head. The gap between the doors was wide enough to see the earth go by thousands of feet below. "Open the doors!" he screamed again.

The bomb doors! MacHenry hunted for a control. But there was none in sight. This plane was meant to be operated by too many men! The bomb-door switch would be under the command of the bombardier. Who knew where such a thing might be?

Oka delivered a staggering kick to Shig's chest. Her aim was off, but it sent him sprawling. He slowly, painfully, got to his feet. It was coming to an end. He could no longer raise his arms to fend her off. He was at the far front of the bay. She at the back. The doors lay before them both.

She was perched on the edge, not moving, her eyes glowing, reflecting. Breath came hard for her, too. She panted, resting, coiling her energies for one final, killing blow. Her blouse was torn to shreds. She ripped it off to clear her arms for the final action. Her powerful shoulders glistened with sweat and blood, both her own and Shig's. She wore no bra, and her breasts were flat, more like two well-developed muscles. She got to her feet, hopping lightly down to the doors, legs splayed wide for steadying. Oka came at him again one step at a time. Her legs trembled.

"MacHenry!"

Think! There must be some emergency means of dumping the bombs! There must be! There must be! His hand swept over the center stand panel. Nothing! He looked at the copilot's set of controls. Nothing! He looked to his left.

A tangle of radio leads, wires, and tubes ran along the cockpit wall. Behind the four throttle levers were three T-handles. The first was a cabin-pressure dump. The next was marked LDG GEAR REL. The last was simply marked EMERG BOMBS. He gripped the handle and yanked.

It was like pulling on a trick rope. The handle came out easily, more and more and more of it. He threw the handle away and grabbed the steel cable, yanking another foot of it out. It wasn't connected to anything!

Oka came for Shig one last time. She began to move faster as she neared him, both her hands now formed into hard, killing wedges held in a classic full attack pose. Shig was no longer able to defend. She could see it in his eyes. She sucked in a deep breath and let loose a paralyzing, curdling scream of victory. There was a click. She took one more step before the steel cable yanked the safety pins from the bomb-door lock. With a terrifying gust of wind, they snapped wide.

With a look of puzzlement, then terror, Oka fell, twisting, turning in the autumn air, the Washington Monument spearing first the ground, then the sky, the world a flash of browns and blues, tumbling, tumbling. She spread her arms as the ground continued to rise, faster, faster. First a color. Then texture. Finally a smell of damp earth. Oka. Cherry blossom. A petal falling from a branch at the height of its beauty, its power. But she was not ready! This was not her time! She let out a final scream of rage as the hard ground rose to strike her.

★   ★   ★

The first engine to suck its lines dry was the number one, far out on the left wing. He punched the prop-feathering button and the prop began slowly to wind down. The number-four engine stumbled, belched, backfired, and quit. He feathered that one, too. The big ship angled down. She was headed for a landing someplace. But where?

Out ahead, the crisscross of white concrete runways loomed out of the morning haze. Not BWI. He was too far south. Then he saw a huge jet parked far away from any other structure. A Boeing 747. Air Force One? The airport ahead was Andrews Air Force Base! He swung the yoke and put the descending bomber into a bank. The silver wings glittered in the sun. He made out the tower. A surprisingly bright light was flashing at him. It was green. A welcome.

MacHenry gave a silent prayer, then hit the silver toggle that would drop the wheels. A whine, a rumble, and three green lights from the panel. He pulled all four throttles back and ran his flaps out to landing configuration.

The runway rose to meet the old bomber. In 1945 she'd flown only one combat mission, and in doing so, she'd ended a war. As he pulled back to flare, the big wheels reaching for the ground, reaching, reaching, MacHenry wondered, had she just done it again?

EPILOGUE

They'd intended to arrive early for Shig's flight home, but a dusting of early snow over ice had slowed the drive out to Dulles. In deference to the wheelchair, Roger Case had rented a van. MacHenry drove. The trip was silent and slow. Nobody wanted Shig to miss his plane, and nobody wanted to see him leave, either. By the time they parked and maneuvered Shig to the ground, they were already announcing his flight over the terminal PA system.

MacHenry hurried the wheelchair through the busy corridor, dodging as he went. Julia ran interference on the left; Roger Case used his cane to prod open a path on the right. Shig had a small wrapped box on his lap. Outside, through the soaring windows of Saarinen's elegant terminal, they all could see the quiet gray hangar, empty and abandoned-looking across a field whitened with last night's flurry.

"JAL Flight 7, service to Tokyo, is now ready to board at Gate Eleven. All passengers should . . ."

Julia put her hand on Shig's shoulder. He wore a brand-new baseball jacket with the Baltimore Orioles insignia on it. His old Yomiuri Giants jacket was ripped beyond redemption. His hand was swaddled in white bandages. "You'll be okay back home?" she asked.

Shig nodded. "I hope so."

"You could stay with us, you know."

"No. I must return to work. Section Chief Ozawa will not be pleased at my holiday."

"Holiday? You solved the case for him," said Case.

"Even worse." Shig knew enough not to try to explain these things. There was already too much Japan bashing going on in the wake of the failed takeover of Boeing by organized criminals. "I must also see to my father's things." Shig said the words, but not with his heart. "And what of your own friend, Mr. Case?"

Aaron Freeman. "The FBI can be very good about catching people when it wants to," said Case. "And it wants to."

"Passengers needing assistance in boarding should now . . ."

"That's you," said MacHenry as they rounded a corner. The Japan Air Lines gate was at the end. A neat line had already formed. "We can get you settled in before—"

Shig put his good hand onto the rubber wheels and brought them to a stop. "No, Mr. MacHenry. I'd rather spend more time with my friends."

They joined the end of the long line. MacHenry pulled out a sheet of paper as they moved up one space. He showed it to Shig.

```
7FAA:  000F  83E960000      CMP  WORD PTR  [0096],0000
7FAA:  0014  7C22           JL   0037
7FAA:  0016  7508           JNE  0020
7FAA:  0018  813E9400E803   CMP  WORD PTR  [0094],03E8
7FAA:  001E  7218           JB   0037
7FAA:  0020  833EAE0600     CMP  WORD PTR  [06AE],0000
7FAA:  0025  7C11           JL   0037
7FAA:  0027  7508           JNE  0031
7FAA:  0029  813EAC06409C   CMP  WORD PTR  [06AC],9C40
7FAA:  002F  7207           JB   0037
7FAA:  0031  33D2           XOR  DX,DX
7FAA:  0033  B86400         MOV  AX,0064
7FAA:  0036  CB             RETF
7FAA:  0037  8B16AA06       MOV  DX,[06AA]
7FAA:  003B  A1A806         MOV  AX,[06A8]
7FAA:  003E  CB             RETF
```

Shig looked up. "What is it?"

"The virus," said MacHenry. "It was embedded in every one of those five chips we found inside the *Enola Gay*."

"What does it do?"

"It has three parts," MacHenry explained as he pushed the chair up another space. "First, it keeps tabs on the number of takeoffs. After one thousand departures, the virus erases the safety limits and then breaks down the interlocks on the thrust reversers. Then, if the ship climbs above forty thousand feet, it commands the engines to throttle up and overthrust. Joe DelVecchio ran it through the simulator at Boeing. The ship does a high-speed cartwheel that flings the engines off, but by then it's too late. After primary wing structure gets damaged, no pilot can save it."

"And nobody else at Boeing knew?" asked Shig.

"That will be our contention in court," said Case. "Tom Kelly sold his knowledge to the Ja—" Case stopped. "To the *criminals,*" he corrected himself. "We will say he acted alone."

"Ah. Of course. Yes. And the companies that belong to Nippon Aerospace?"

"I think it's safe to say the corporate entity will no longer exist after the punitive settlements," said Case. "But the individual firms, if they are proven innocent, should have nothing to worry about."

Shig remembered the hollow headquarters of Nippon Aerospace. The empty room with its one secretary. "What if the assets will not cover the damages?"

Case smiled. "I've already discussed that with Boeing. I assigned Abrams at Legal Affairs to draw up an asset sheet on each company in the Consortium. It will probably boil down to a trade."

Shig cocked his head. "What kind of trade?"

"I imagine that more than a few aerospace companies in your part of the world will become Boeing subsidiaries."

Shig bowed his head. It was masterful. To fend off the attack, and to use the enemy's own motion against him. Japan seeks to steal Boeing. Boeing winds up owning more of Japan. It was devilish. "That is a very Japanese conclusion, Mr. Case, I think you'd do very well in Tokyo."

"What is that supposed to mean?"

"That perhaps we are more alike than we like to think. Though MacHenry says you are not a typical barbarian."

Case gruffed, but with a sparkle in his eye. "Now he's insulting us. What about you? You aren't exactly stereotypical either."

"That," said Shig, "is a bit of a problem."

MacHenry pushed the wheelchair forward. "The programmers looked at every Thrust Management Computer in the entire 7X7 fleet," he said. They were just one space away from the agent now. "They found eight more ships with infected computers." He looked at Julia. The plane she'd flown in from Hawaii had been one of them. "They retrofitted clean units and held on to all the virus chips as evidence."

Shig turned. "How did you convince Boeing to ground all those airplanes, Mr. Case?"

"I ran into Amory Tasker at the gate outside the *Enola Gay*'s hangar. I let the evidence do my talking."

"But you did not have the evidence," said Shig. "They were with us when we took off in the bomber."

"Details," said Case.

"My boss was right about one thing," said Shig. "Americans are very sneaky."

"Only when we have to be, my boy," said Case. "Only when we have to be."

MacHenry pushed Shig to the door of the gate. He handed the agent his ticket.

"What will happen when you get back home?" asked Julia as the ticket got ripped, refolded, then stapled.

"Home?" said Shig with a wistful look. "I will try to find my place again. It will not be easy. I disobeyed orders. I embarrassed many people. Many powerful people. Stepping out of line is a big problem in Japan. When you try to step back in, sometimes there is no place left."

"You could stay, you know," said MacHenry. "There's a place for you here."

"Hell," said Case. "What's one more accountant?"

The corridor to the people mover was empty now. A line of impatient passengers waited behind Shig. It was time to go. Shig bowed his head slightly. "*Domo arrigato gozaimasu.* Thank you, but I don't think so. There are many things I like about America. But Japan is one thing no other country could ever be."

"Oh, yeah?" said Case. "What?"

"It is my home. Please," Shig said to MacHenry, "take this." Shig took the small case on his lap and handed it to MacHenry. Shig took hold of his wheels and spun them. The chair rolled out into the corridor. It ramped down to the people mover. In a moment, he was gone.

MacHenry unwrapped the gift. He opened the lid of a little jewelry box.

"What did he give you?" asked Case.

MacHenry held it out for them to see.

A white Japanese Army knife lay nestled in red velvet.

Case stared at it. He plucked it out and opened one of the blades. "It's broken. I don't get it. What good is a busted knife?"

"You'd be surprised." He stuffed the little knife into his pocket and looked at Julia. "He also told me something else. Giving up is easy. Anyone can do it. But enduring, that's a lot harder. And," he said to her, "a lot better."

"I like this Shig Onishi more and more," she answered.

"Let's go see if the car's where I left it."

They made their way upstream against the flow of passengers.

"Nippon Aerospace was underwriting the costs of shipping the *Enola Gay* to Japan," said MacHenry. "After you're done with them, Mr. Case, we'll have to foot the bill for our own history. She'll probably stay right here in Washington."

"I've been accused of worse things."

They left the high overhanging eave and stepped out over a light dusting of new snow. A flurry was in the air, sparkling in the light like diamonds against a pale sky. The real storm had come through overnight, and the few leftover clouds drifted by overhead like cattle anxious to rejoin the herd.

MacHenry stayed close to the elderly lawyer, ready to offer a steadying arm in case he slipped on the ice. They were close to the short-term lot before he looked up and saw the tow truck. It was right where he'd left the Wagoneer.

"Brian?" asked Julia. "Isn't that your car?" The tow hook was descending; a man in insulated coveralls and a heavy ski mask shoved it under the front bumper.

"Stay here!" MacHenry sprinted ahead, slipping on the ice for his trouble. He landed flat on his back right in the middle of a pool of sheet ice. He slid again when he tried to get up. Completely humbled, he crawled on his hands and knees to the edge of the ice before trying to stand.

The hook operator signaled, then he hopped up into the warm cab as the hook began to reel in. The Wagoneer jerked as the slack drew up tight.

"Hey! That's my car!" MacHenry got to his knees.

The Wagoneer tilted up onto its rear wheels.

"Looks like he's going to need a good lawyer in a minute or so," observed Case as he stood with Julia watching.

A flash of white light, a column of dirty orange fire roiled upward. The concussion slapped at their coats as it blasted by. Shredded metal flew up, twisting, rising, slowing, then falling like great black flakes of dirty snow. A dozen car alarms began to honk and shriek like frightened geese.

"Brian!" She twisted away to run, but Case caught her first.

"Jesus!" Case shielded Julia with his body as a rain of tiny ball bearings fell, a steel hailstorm.

"No!" She pulled away and ran straight for the eager fire that was eating away the hulk that had once been the old Wagoneer.

The pall of filthy smoke cleared enough to reveal the burning car, still on the tow truck's hook. Its roof was blasted wide open, the steel corner pillars bowed out from the explosion. The glass was gone, of course. The hook man cowered behind the open door of his truck as a siren began to wail.

She saw him, flat to the ground. "Brian!" She ran, not slowing for the ice, not slowing for anything. When she got there, he was already back on his knees. She reached down and hugged him when she saw he was all right. "Oh, God, I thought—"

"It's okay," he said, wondering whether it was true. Could there still be someone out there who wanted him dead? "You know something," he said to her as she helped him stand, "maybe a little vacation wouldn't be so bad after all."

Case came up warily, his cane slipping. "I suppose you're going to submit a bill for this," he said gruffly when he saw MacHenry was all right. A police car skidded around the corner and accelerated fast toward them, lights flashing.

"Christ," said Case. "They'll probably try to pin it on some Arab."

MacHenry arched an eyebrow. "Or some Japanese."

"Don't push, MacHenry. I was half-right, wasn't I?"

"Sure. Just remember that the other half of the case was solved by a guy named Onishi."

Case growled his answer.

Finally, the tow-truck operator tottered up, unsteady on his feet, shaking his head as though he had plugs of water in his ears. "That your car?"

MacHenry nodded, his ears still ringing.

"I don't know, mister," said the hook man. "I been working this job for five years. I ain't *never* seen a car alarm like *that*."

The roar of a departing jet drowned out the cacophony of car alarms, the crackle of fire. They all looked up as the JAL 747 climbed strong in the cold air, the sun glinting off its wings as it rose.

"He's okay," said Case. "For one of them, anyway."

MacHenry reached into his pocket and pulled out the white pocketknife. He flipped open the broken blade, then folded it back together. He stared up at the departing jet. *"Gamman,"* he whispered.

"What's that?"

"It's Japanese," said MacHenry. "It means, endure."